The Voice of Wild Places

Noah Hawthorne

NESHAMA PUBLISHING

The Voice of Wild Places cover art illustrated by Thistle Arts.

The Simplest Words by Narcissist Cookbook, lyrics used with permission by the musician.

No portion of this book may be reproduced in any form without written permission from the publisher or author, except as permitted by U.S. copyright law. No portion of this book may be used for generative artificial intelligence. All rights reserved.

Copyright © 2025 The Voice of Wild Places by Noah Hawthorne.

Contents

Preface

The Voice of Wild Places is a work of historical fiction, the interpretations of the people and places referenced therein are fictional. For more information on the historical aspects of the story, see the note in the back of this book.

This book contains elements of transphobia, homophobia, discussion of a transgender person being outed in the past, alcoholism, racism, colonization, discussion of the Canadian Indigenous Peoples residential schools, ableism, serious injury, drowning and resuscitation, medical experimentation on animals, snakes and snake bites, post traumatic stress, depression, wartime flashbacks, swearing, and smoking. There is also reference to a parental death, and grief.

Dedication

'This body is built on the ruins of
All the people I have ever been
Wise men build their houses on rocks
While the rest of us settle for skeletons'

THE SIMPLEST WORDS – THE NARCISSIST COOKBOOK

to those still building

March

Something Wild

Philadelphia, Pennsylvania
March 1st, 1930

Watt's heart seized at the possibility he entered an alternate reality a mere three steps past the threshold. Tobacco clouded the atmosphere, tinged with spilled wine and an overwhelming amount of cologne. The combination reminded him of the estate. He turned away from the thought, offering his fedora to the hat-check, a friendly woman in a well-tailored pantsuit.

All the patrons were exceptionally dressed, but the staff even more so. The small place could almost pass for a fine gentlemen's club. Watt fought the urge to take in his own comparatively dressed down state, there was nothing for it now.

He had no worries before when he stood outside, basking in the warm light of a gas lamp as he studied the dingy brickwork of the unassuming place squatting on South Carmac. The floor above the speakeasy was a restaurant, and he'd heard rumors of the scene the place played host to during the night. When he began this search, he had the delusion that if he wandered long enough he'd simply come across Annie, for surely fate had a vested interest in reuniting lost ... what?

Acquaintances? Friends? Strangers?

Regardless, doubt shadowed the late night hour. Narrowing down which speakeasy Annie frequented in a city rumored to have thousands of them had proved to be a monumental task, one that stretched into a week long affair. Time was of the essence, considering that he'd be leaving Philly in four—no, three days. If Annie's mother had elaborated more than 'somewhere on Carmac,' he certainly would've found her by now. It didn't help that he'd only sought out the speakeasies back home once, and as such had very little experience in navigating them, let alone in a city he didn't know.

Sheer desperation and the need to set things right propelled him deeper into the belly of Maxine's. A guilty conscience was not an easily assuaged thing, but it wasn't forgiveness he sought. Forgiveness from others was nothing if you couldn't forgive yourself, and this he most certainly could not do. This was more about things unsaid, and the desire to let it be known that he still gave a damn, that he always had.

Watt casually searched the room while making his way to the bar. The crowd was thick, and he became temporarily distracted by a piano tucked into the corner of the place, and the Italian pianist perched behind it. Nearly as pretty as the music brought to life by his elegant fingertips, his lips were stained pink and a smooth throat was exposed from beneath a thin shirt. He belonged in a theater, not exactly the sort you'd expect to find on a street that played host to street fights and raids on a nightly basis, if the local gossip was anything to go by. Watt had seen no evidence to support the claims, having only witnessed one arrest in this part of the city so far, and the night was nearly over now.

Watt claimed an empty stool at the bar without incident and ordered a gin. Silently, the bartender slid a glass across the clean if not battered counter towards Watt, his stare hard and evaluating.

"Much obliged," Watt ventured, not quite shouting.

The bartender crossed his thick arms over his chest. "Ain't seen you before."

"Ain't been here before."

The man studied Watt for a moment longer, then the tension in his shoulders broke a fraction. "Let me know if you need anything else."

Watt started to ask the same question he'd asked every other bartender he encountered in the last week, but a gentleman down the way flagged the bartender's attention before Watt could get the words out. He sipped on his drink instead, and his gut immediately twisted on the invasive substance. Despite this, his mind settled a bit, and warmth smoothed over his frayed nerves. The classical music tapered off into tepid silence, and cheerful applause erupted from the patrons. The pianist stood and bowed dramatically, eliciting a few whip-whistles. An encore was called for, but the pianist cited the need for another drink and cleared the stage. A band took his place, a singer, pianist, and a few woodwind players, together they birthed a tune jaunty enough to swing to. Nice enough, but Watt preferred the slower, more drawn out music.

A group of bright young people kept the new musicians company. They sang boisterously, unrestrained and carefree, their arms linked around each other's shoulders and drinks held high in the air. The sense of camaraderie there was palpable, something Watt hadn't felt since the trenches. The emptiness where his heart should be churned, not with joy as it should, but ugly jealousy. Emotion, no matter how hideous, was humanity, and he clung to the idea.

Something about the man in the middle caught Watt's attention, whether it was his unabashed and terrible singing, or the way his eyes creased with unchecked laughter, he wasn't sure. He was shorter than Watt, thick around the waist and blessed with some bulk in his broad shoulders. The suspenders he wore over his button up were loose and kept drifting down his shoulders, and the rolled up sleeves kept sliding down his arms. His hair was cut into the modern fashion, a more trim and neat version of Watt's own hair, and much darker. His glasses kept sliding down his nose, which was unimpaired by previous fractures. In all, he was unremarkable. Aggressively average.

Watt found it hard to stop staring at him, but the man only had eyes for the crowd, his friends, and his drink. After the chorus finished, he desperately threw back his drink and slammed the cup down on the piano. "Une autre!"

Watt flinched at the violence inflicted upon the instrument, and he belatedly recognized the Parisian call for another. His trance broke when the pianist perched on the stool beside him. "Charles!" The man called, raking a hand through dark hair that curled around his ears. He glanced sideways at Watt and winked quicker than a flash. "Hey, angel. Thirsty?"

"I—" Watt blinked at the man, unsure if he heard him correctly. Angel? Him?

The man's smile spilled like liquid gold, slow and beautiful. "Oh, you are adorable. Let me buy you a drink."

"One and done for me, thank you." Watt nodded to his empty glass as he pushed it away from himself. Truth be told, he didn't imbibe often and the alcohol was already getting to his head.

Charles returned, sliding something deadly in front of the pianist. "Done for the night?"

"Oh, even stars need to rest." The man murmured, then gingerly sipped at his drink.

Watt's gaze stuttered on his painted lips settling on the rim of his glass. He forced himself to shift his attention, sweeping the room from this new vantage point. It was small enough that he could see clearly across the place, but the crowd was like fog, constantly moving and revealing the far reaches of the room only in fragments. He should leave, call it a night and give up on this futile endeavor. There was a reason Annie never returned any of his letters. He didn't know how it all went so wrong, and what did he have to apologize for exactly? Doing what he was told?

Then again, blindly following orders had proven to be an ineffective way to live thus far.

Watt decided to play the only card offered to him tonight. "Do you play every night?" He asked the pianist.

The pianist gave him another sly grin. "Did you like it?"

"Yes," he said, completely genuine.

"Only on Saturdays, so it's your lucky day." The pianist winked again, then took another sip of his drink. In the precious seconds before the liquid met his lips, the corners of his eyes hardened and his jaw tensed, a preview of the man without the mask.

Something about him was unsettling, disorienting, but Watt couldn't put his finger on why. He couldn't accuse him of being too kind, although that was the only thing he could think of to blame it on. Regardless, exhaustion and desperation paired together to negate Watt's need to err on the side of caution.

"Would you be able to tell me if someone was a regular here?" Watt asked, tracing a finger over the rim of his glass.

He hummed, and caution fell like a curtain over his dark eyes. "Looking for someone?"

"A friend of mine, but I'm not sure if she'd come here."

He chuckled softly. "Ah, yes. It is quite the gentlemen's club, but we don't mind sharing with the ladies too. Over there." He nodded to a corner of the room partially obstructed by those on the dance floor, and Watt caught glimpses of women through the haze of cigarettes and reckless abandon.

It was then that he finally noticed.

The intimacy the women shared with each other, bodies pressed close and smiles full of desire. Men leading men on the dance floor, hands wandering and noses brushing, eyes bright with pleasure. Endless skin, endless shades of black, brown, and white.

Watt looked over at the pianist. The Italian's rosy lips curved into a smaller, knowing smile. Watt cleared his throat, pushing away from the bar. "I don't think she's here. Thank you."

"Good night, angel." The pianist called after him, fingers waving loftily through the air.

Watt kept his eyes down as he retreated, not at a walk so much as a barely restrained run, the room too small and the smoky atmosphere too thick. Prickling heat flashed over his neck and down his spine, causing the edges of his vision to darken in time to his throbbing pulse. The sensation was so arresting, and Watt's panic so rampant, that he made the ultimate mistake. He walked straight into another patron.

Liquid courage and glass crashed to the floor, followed by a cry of outrage at the loss. Kept upright by those around him, the offended person whirled around with a fist raised. Upon seeing Watt, the man faltered.

Something like recognition and fear widened his bloodshot eyes, and his lips parted in a way that reminded Watt of childhood. But what tipped Watt over the edge and into impossibility was a mole beneath the man's left ear. Dark and round, the size of a pencil eraser. Watt's fingers twitched at his sides. He could not restrain his tongue, or his inevitable curiosity. It's what nearly ruined him time and time again, after all. Asking what *if*.

And today was no different. He whispered, "Annie?"

The patron laughed, and it was so damn glacial that Watt's blood froze.

"Nah," he said, and punched Watt in the face.

Watt's nose suffered for his mistake, fracturing beneath the impressive force behind the other man's knuckles. First blood spurred fights between those who had nothing to do with the matter and those who did, giving those itching for release the excuse to do so.

The man's aggression didn't wane, and neither did his attempts to land another blow. He was paced and methodical, but his favored left leg betrayed his weakness. Watt clung to defense, but it was a struggle to stay out of the man's reach. Despite the man's size he was quick on his feet, and he nearly landed several blows.

Hot blood trickled down the back of Watt's throat, and the white hot pain in his nose was a brilliant reminder that his heart wasn't as dead as he once thought.

"Enough!" Watt shouted.

His opponent said nothing, only growing more furious with each missed opportunity. If there was one thing Watt was exceptionally good at, it was avoiding bloodshed. Unfortunately, avoiding violence required a knowledge of how to inflict it in the first place, and God knew he'd done enough of that.

"Hey! I'm sorry!" Watt tried again.

Again, the man said nothing. He came at Watt like his life depended on it, his eyes like knives glinting beneath the bar's dim lights. His hair had been slicked back, but now it hung over his forehead in sweaty impressions of curls. Perhaps if it were longer, the curls would be more pronounced.

There was something wild about the way he moved, his limbs cut through the air with a deftness that threatened to distract Watt. Unable to deflect a particularly vicious wallop aimed for his kidney, Watt shouted and the man growled in response like a feral animal. Watt spun around, prepared to block again, but his opponent had forfeit. He slipped through the chaos and further into the bar, curses rolling off his tongue in French and English.

Watt staggered forward, hands opening at his sides. He paused, then shook his head and opted for escape. He fled in the opposite direction his enemy had gone, and within moments he stumbled out onto the street, which was twice as loud as when he had left it last. Blood oozed from his nose onto the wooden pavers, the leakage at a slower pace than before. A siren wailed at the opposite end of the narrow street, followed by shouting.

Fear was a belated guest, riding on the heels of the realization about the type of place he'd been, the consequences of his presence there. Not only a speakeasy, but one with an eccentric crowd that could be arrested for simply existing, let alone drinking.

"And you're not one of those filthy fairies, are you?"

Watt limped back the way he came, doing his best to bury his father's voice and avoid confrontation with others wandering home and elsewhere. He did his best to keep the hotel in his mind's eye, but it was a difficult task considering that a massive fucking headache, a bruised kidney, and whirlwind thoughts dogged his every step. Nonetheless, he prevailed in this venture, at the very least. The late hour ensured Watt made it through the hotel's lobby without incident, and a generous tip kept the concierge from asking questions regarding his battered face.

He encountered no one else, the narrow halls were dim and the overwhelming silence broken only by his keys jingling as they slid home. He glanced over his shoulder at the door directly across from his, then shook his head. She didn't need to be woken up at this hour with his personal problems. Watt entered the cool darkness, and shut the door behind him.

For a moment, only worrying silence welcomed him. Then the bed frame groaned, and a long yawn followed. He sighed with relief and proceeded to cross the room, settling down on the edge of the bed. He peeled his shoes off, eyes adjusting to the dark. Maggie rubbed against Watt's side, inhaling the places he'd been from his clothes and skin. She huffed against his neck where she discovered the night's events and licked his cheek, then sneezed her dismissal when he flinched away in pain. Maggie returned to her very important job of warming up the bed, and Watt's lips quirked at her nonchalance. Oh, to be a dog. She was a typical German Shepherd, with more black fur than brown. White and grey peppered her thick coat, and a plethora of minute scars decorated her snout. Her eyes, a soulful brown, spoke of many years.

After slowly undressing, Watt dragged himself into the bathroom and turned on the light. His face was an ugly mess of blood, and his nasal bones were wrenched out of place. Luckily, it appeared to be an easy fix. Watt reset the rebellious bones, not for the first time, and groaned in response to the nauseating pain that exploded through his face, nearly worse than the break itself. He gripped the edges of the sink, steadying himself against waves of agony and nausea. After a few moments, he shakily washed his face the best that he could. Blood lingered in the stubble along his jaw, and stubborn bits dried in the hair at his temples.

He closed his eyes.

Recognition. Fear. Anger, oh, was there anger.

Watt shut off the bathroom light and crawled into bed beside his companion, naked as the day he was born. Maggie laid atop the blankets, which Watt pulled up around his neck. He rested his hand between her ears, gently stroking her fur. He stared into the dark and finally allowed himself to examine, and accept, several hard truths.

He found Annie, who most certainly did not want to be found, least of all by him.

The prospect of dying in the jungle without speaking his piece was a hard truth to swallow, but he had no choice.

And perhaps this was the world's way of telling him he never deserved to be forgiven in the first place.

It was not the first time Cornelius' roommate nursed him back to health, but it was the first time he'd done so in such silence. Giovanni was disappointed in him, which cut deeper than his anger would have. He flushed blood and grime out of the scrapes over his knuckles, and proceeded to wrap his hands. After withdrawing from his fight with Watt, Cornelius had sought out others. He'd been winning until Giovanni found him, and the distraction had landed him with a black eye.

Cornelius summoned all his willpower in order to do the only helpful thing he could. Stay still, and not throw up on Giovanni's shoes. It was a difficult feat, and it had nothing to do with the drink. If Cornelius had one positive trait, it was that he could handle himself after even the most ambitious of nights. But his pain was beyond belief, both in his leg and heart.

Cornelius stared down at his own loafers, scuffed brown toes inches away from the polished black leather of Giovanni's. Irritation coursed through him with vicious intent, preventing the night's events from passing in a pleasant blur like they typically did. He couldn't help but twist himself into knots over the whole ordeal, and closed his eyes in an attempt to shut it all out. Like that ever helped.

Never in his wildest dreams did he imagine that Watt Johnson would waltz back into his life, interjecting himself into the one corner of the world Cornelius had carved out for himself and deemed safe. His, and his alone. Cornelius' family knew where he lived, but they hardly intruded upon his life in person.

Cornelius couldn't fathom why he was there, or how Watt had recognized him. It wouldn't surprise Cornelius if his ever meddlesome Mama told Watt where he was, but why? Watt had closed the door between them years ago, and Mama and Papa had practically locked it shut behind him. It'd been fifteen years, and the idea that parts of who Cornelius used to be lingered in the person he was now was unsettling, to say the least. The sound of his old name on Watt's lips danced on the fringes of his brain over and over again, and his skin crawled with every rendition of it. He'd imagined their reunion, long ago of course, and despite his clear disgust over Cornelius' new identity, he never imagined Watt using his old name.

He hadn't heard it in years, and forgotten how much it made him want to scream.

"There," Giovanni said, tapping Cornelius' forearm once before leaning back. His chair creaked, and Giovanni sighed with great effort.

Cornelius opened his eyes, clearing rawness from his throat. "Thank you."

Giovanni lit a cigarette and took a few drags before offering it to Cornelius, patiently waiting for an explanation. It wasn't uncommon for Cornelius to get into fights, in fact he was rather good at it, but tonight was different and they both knew it. Giovanni hardly said anything while dragging Cornelius home from the bar, which spoke volumes on its own. Normally he'd give him shit, rib on his lack of a solid win.

It shouldn't be so hard to say, '*I loved him. I loved him, and he abandoned me. He left me, and I didn't ever want to see him again.*'

Giovanni would understand, so why couldn't Cornelius *say* it?

Cornelius took the cigarette and puffed while searching the room for something to say, for an excuse or honest truth he couldn't decide. Their apartment was warm, softly lit by the candles resting on the sturdy table between them and throughout the kitchen. Giovanni preferred to use as little electricity as possible, something Cornelius doesn't mind in the least. The phonograph, of course, was an exception. It was always on if Giovanni was home, and the habit rubbed off on Cornelius long ago. Ma Rainey filled the apartment, her voice a strong rasp that made the wind blow all the while. The audacity. The courage. Would she have done what Cornelius did?

'*Last night, had a big bad fight, everything seemed to go wrong,*' she admitted.

Cornelius offered a lame smile and gave the cigarette back, then pushed away from the table. "I've class in the morning."

Giovanni frowned. "In a few hours, you mean."

"Ah, yes. Thank you for reminding me." Cornelius winced, relying on his cane far more tonight than he had in a long time. He leaned down, kissing the top of Giovanni's head. He inhaled that clean, reliable fragrance that clung to Giovanni like a warm blanket, unbothered by the soft hair which tickled his nose. "Sleep well," Cornelius whispered, and walked away.

Giovanni hummed, watching him go. In true, dramatic Giovanni fashion, he waited until Cornelius opened his bedroom door before making his thoughts finally known. Cautiously, he said, "You can talk to me, Neil. We're still friends, aren't we?"

"Yes, of course." Cornelius ran a hand through his

mussed hair and lifted a shoulder. "I'm fine. Honestly."

"Are you?"

"Yes."

Giovanni allowed a moment of disbelieving silence to pass, then bowed his head and said, "Good night, love."

"Good night, Giovanni."

Cornelius stepped into the modest room shrouded by night, quietly shutting the door behind him. He exhaled, mentally preparing for the ritual ahead. Guided by moonlight, he extricated the needed supplies from a small box on his dresser, then methodically rolled up some reefer. Tobacco was fine and all, but tonight called for more desperate measures. The routine and mundane were usually sure fire ways to eliminate all thought, but a dusty old box stored in the farthest reaches of his mind groaned from the growing pressure of the explosive contents within, threatening to blow apart rotten wood and sharp, rusted hinges.

Thin paper slid against his dry fingers, and dried to hell weed spilled out the ends of the loosely rolled tube.

He cracked open the window, and lit up.

He inhaled greedily and stared out into the darkness, listening in vain for signs of life from the rest of Rittenhouse.

Sometimes, on a good night, the park was so full of life that you didn't have to try that hard to hear it. But most nights, like tonight, the natural world was overrun by man.

Cornelius smoked the joint down to nothing, then

butted it out on the sill before tossing the thing out the window. His mind grew heavy, and his muscles relaxed. He lingered for a moment longer, listening for the call of a nighthawk or perhaps a screech owl, for he tended to hear those even on the worst of days. He left Rittenhouse Square's silent, impenetrable depths behind and shut the window for good measure.

Blood stained and damp, articles of clothing unceremoniously fell to the floor one after another. He tugged the bandeau off and his ribcage expanded, lungs greedily sucking in air. He frowned at the elastic and cotton in his hands, which had deteriorated after nine years of use. He had others, but none as good as the Boyshform in his hands. Sara had accompanied him to the presentation held in Philly and convinced him to buy one. Now flat chests were no longer in fashion, and finding a quality replacement was near impossible.

Gaze focused on the bed and nothing else, he dressed in thick trousers and a long nightshirt, fingertips skimming over the pendulous flesh on his chest and the thick, dark hair on his calves. He fell into bed and the old mattress welcomed his tired body, springs and all. He thrashed this way and that until finally curling up into a ball like an armadillo, layers of quilts tight around his neck. The room spun around him, and he groaned.

Cornelius closed his eyes. Only once in complete and total darkness did he withdraw the key for his heart and unlock it, examining the contents before they escaped on their own time.

Birthdays spent alone.

Years of whispers and backhanded compliments, blatant insults and grotesque assumptions.

Stacks of letters filled with unidentifiable words, indecipherable meanings. The cruel tease of a foreign friend or lover perhaps, Cher Ami.

A heart doomed to never mend, poisoned and twisted by rejection after rejection.

Broken promises.

The promises.

They meant something, didn't they?

Didn't they?

Man Hunting

March 3rd, 1930

A stranger sat in Cornelius' classroom.

Perched in the back, spine rigid and eyes curious, she was a whole world above the semester worn students around her. Cornelius did his best to ignore the woman, but it proved difficult. She was likely an auditor of some sort, they had a penchant for surprises. It was almost the end of term, though. Hell, the academic year, at that. Why check up on his work now?

Something about the older, fair woman reminded him of Sara, which made it hard to dull the itch wracking hell in his brain. He turned his back to the classroom, focusing his attention on streaking chalk across the blackboard while dictating the semester's final assignments. This was his favorite class, the reason why he was here, and the only one of his that didn't cater to naive kids who thought archaeology was one step away from wild adventure.

Cornelius managed to occupy his curiosity until the end of class. As the third year students trudged out of the cavernous lecture hall, glancing at his bruised face and damaged knuckles, Cornelius' heart rate kicked up a notch in anticipation. The woman stood, waiting for the groggy crowd to clear before she approached. She didn't hide her interest, and when their eyes met a wry smile curled her lips. Mischievous, all-knowing, and perhaps a *tad* judgmental.

He'd never been audited before. His student's scores had been top notch since shortly after he was hired, and there'd been no problems. He'd only had three transfers since he began, nothing to do with him and all to do with their expectations, and the ones that graduated under his eye thus far went on to esteemed research programs. Cornelius was well aware he didn't have the best social reputation, but he was as professional and hardworking as one could be. Bizarre, yes, but effective. Intelligent. *Competent*.

What if ... what if news broke out of last night's scuffle?

What if word got out where he'd been?

The woman finally stood before him, chin raised and lip quirked. She wore a pretty navy blue dress that hung at her knees, and a smart handbag dangled from the crook of her arm. A dark jacket hung over her arm as well, finely made but by no means new. Deep lines creased her eyes and mouth, and her skin was weathered by time and the sun. Cornelius got the sense that the woman spent most of her time outside, but wasn't sure why. She seemed to straddle the line between middle and upper class, but Cornelius knew better than most that clothes were simply an illusion.

Swallowing panic, Cornelius bowed his head and extended his hand. "Good morning, miss ...?"

With a kind smile, she reached for him. He clasped her palm which was gloved in soft leather, and his gentle but firm pressure drew a smile from the woman. With an accent that was more British than American, she said, "Fawcett, if you please. I must say, Dr. Sawyer, your perspective on astronomy and its application in regards to archaeology is a refreshing take, one I'd love to discuss with you further."

Absolutely stunned, Cornelius fought the urge to bow fully, because in the back of his mind he knew it'd be an awkward thing to do. But this was Nina Fawcett, not only wife to one of the most famous explorers of his time, but an accomplished person in her own right. To Cornelius, that made her as good as royalty.

Gathering his thoughts best he could, Cornelius said, "Mrs. Fawcett, it's an honor to meet you. I—of course. Are you free now, or ...?"

"In fact, I am." Nina Fawcett smiled, glancing down at their still joined hands with a raised brow.

Cornelius' cheeks flushed and he released her hand. He took hold of his cane leaning against the podium, then gestured towards the door. "Please, this way, I've some coffee in my office, it's just a few halls over."

Mrs. Fawcett nodded, following as he led the way. "That would be splendid. I hope you don't mind, but

I'm accompanied by a like-minded colleague of mine. He's an avid follower of your work, actually."

If the room became any hotter, Cornelius might evaporate. "Oh, not at all. Who—"

They stepped into the hall and veered to the right, revealing Watt Johnson standing at parade rest. He stared at a photo on the wall, and the right side of his face was shrouded in furious red, purple, and blue. His nose was clearly shattered, but Cornelius knew for a fact that it wasn't the first time that strong bridge had been fractured. He looked all the better for it, of course. He looked painfully familiar, aged but still recognizable as the boy Cornelius had once obsessed over. There were more wrinkles, bulk, and last night Cornelius had noticed the top part of his left pinky finger was missing. Today, he noticed the various scars on the backs of his hands. But he was still handsome.

Still Watt Johnson.

He'd always had the casually rugged and handsome look down pat, and the worst part was he never had to try. Unlike Cornelius, who picked every article of clothing with great care. Watt wore a gray three-piece suit done in herringbone tweed, collared by a strange dirt brown bow tie, and fancy capped oxfords. The outfit was exquisite, but Watt's bed tousled hair and two day old beard contrasted the beauty of it. Cornelius owned one formal suit, and he hardly wore it. Today was no exception, and he'd never felt more under dressed. Slacks too tight around the high waist, the pinstripes on his vest too odd and the muslin of his white long sleeve too heavy.

He told himself the discomfort was due to Nina's presence, not Watt's.

Upon seeing the pair exit the lecture hall Watt turned to face them, disrupting Cornelius' brief observations. Watt joined Nina's side and, like nothing had ever happened between them, extended his hand to Cornelius. He met Cornelius' eye, but just barely. Accent softer than his words, he said, "Watt Johnson. It's a pleasure to meet you, Dr. Sawyer. I hope we're not imposing on your schedule."

Violence was a near, seductive thing. Cornelius had to beat down the part of himself that wanted to run, to fight, to scream. How dare he. How *dare* he.

Why—was last night—*why*?

Pressured by Mrs. Fawcett's presence, Cornelius took Watt's hand, channeling all his strength into the shake. "Dr. Johnson, not at all. Please, right this way."

Watt flinched, but whether it was from the venom in Cornelius' voice or his grip, it was unclear. Cornelius led the way to his office, thankfully he'd brought his cane with him today and it was a short walk. No one in the halls paid any mind to him, per usual. He passed Esther's office, but the door was closed. Not that she could do anything to save him from the impending train wreck. Mason was milling about outside his office, and he heralded Cornelius a warm greeting.

"Sawyer, good to see you," J. Alden Mason said,

pumping Cornelius' hand vigorously. He preferred J to John, and Cornelius never had a problem with respecting preferences. He was a thin and hardened man, with excellent hair and a thick nose. His eyes flicked to Cornelius' black eye, then his cane. He usually needed it a few days a week, so it wasn't uncommon. Perhaps paired with the black eye, it told a story of a greater pain. "Alright there, son?"

Cornelius smiled, despite his nerves. "Morning sir, I'm fine, thank you."

"Good, good." J nodded, crinkled eyes bright, and his mustache twitched as his gaze drifted to Nina and Watt. Recognition upturned his features, and he shook Watt's hand with the same energy he had Cornelius'. "Dr. Johnson! What a pleasant surprise. Don't tell me you made the mistake of debating with Sawyer here." J gestured between Watt and Cornelius' faces.

Watt transformed in that moment, confident with a blinding cocksure smile. His Transatlantic accent became proud and smooth as he said, "It's good to see you again Chief, it's been too long. And no, I haven't had the opportunity." He glanced at Cornelius with that stupid fake smile, then back to J. "Frank sends his best, by the way. Speck too."

"That it has, oh do tell them hello for me, will you? And Mrs. Fawcett, is it? What a pleasure to meet you." He was far more delicate when shaking Nina's hand, and if Cornelius wasn't mistaken, there was a slight flush to his cheeks. Which was understandable, for

Nina was likely around the same age as him and quite handsome. And widowed.

Nina said, "Oh, the pleasure is mine. I hear you are a talented curator of this fine establishment."

"Indeed, but one of many I assure you. I oversee the American section."

Nina smiled, and there was something conspiratorial about it. "And is it true that some of these curators are women?"

Mason returned her smile. "Of course, of course." His gaze flicked to Cornelius briefly, then back to Nina and Watt. "I'm not sure what business you have, but if you would like I could arrange for you to meet with our newly appointed Egyptian Curator, Ms. Mazur. I think you especially would enjoy those exhibits, Dr. Johnson."

"If it pleases Mrs. Fawcett, then I would be happy to oblige," Watt said, bowing his head slightly.

Nina laughed. "That would be splendid. Will you be available in say ... an hour or so? We can work out the details then."

Cornelius' throat burned as he listened to the conversation spin out of control. There were too many coinciding tangents, the social circles of Watt's life and Cornelius' colliding with such violent force that it made his head ache. Mason, a well known anthropological titan of America, was well acquainted with Boas, Watt's mentor and America's other great mind of anthropology. As such, Cornelius had heard quite a bit about Boas' prodigy, archaeologist turned anthropologist Watt Johnson, all without having to search for him. All without *wanting* to hear a damn word about him.

Cornelius had managed to put on a good face back then, and he did so now. He liked Mason, was grateful that the man allowed him onto the tail end of his Colombian expedition after Cornelius had fled Ur, even if their trip together ended in a snake bite that changed the trajectory of his life. It wasn't Mason's fault, even if the man still looked at Cornelius with pity in his eyes, like he'd wronged Cornelius greatly.

As the others spoke, he hastily tried to make connections between Watt's visit last night, and today. Was he scouting Cornelius out? And for what? To talk about archaeology? The *stars*?

That didn't sit right, and Cornelius tried another angle. Perhaps Watt truly had no idea that Dr. Cornelius Sawyer and his precious Annie were one and the same, and last night was an accident. A pure coincidence. He'd never told Watt his new last name, after all, only revealed his first name to him. Watt had come to Philadelphia for a meeting with Cornelius Sawyer, prematurely met him, and recognized him as a former friend.

No, he'd seen too much to believe in nonsense like coincidences.

They said farewell to Mason, who watched them go with a gleam in his eye that suggested he knew far more about their 'business' than he let on.

When they entered Cornelius' office, he cringed. He cleared a stack of papers from one of the guest chairs, carefully depositing them in the dusty nook behind his side of the desk. He said, "I apologize for the mess, I don't have many visitors, and I've been working on a project. As you can imagine, the papers tend to take over. Please, take a seat."

"What a pleasant space you have, Dr. Sawyer." Nina remarked, and Cornelius smiled a little. It was narrow and overstuffed, decorated with leaf litter from unruly plants who spilled dirt here and there. He wasn't half the gardener that Mason was, but the man kept insisting on giving him plants. For his birthday, for Christmas. Just because.

A great window occupied the wall behind the desk, and the deep sill played host to a carafe and coffee paraphernalia, among other things. The view was nice, blessed with grass and trees, albeit managed and manicured. Cornelius' office was his lunch room, break room, study, and haven. As such, it was well organized chaos. Bookshelves covered both sides of the room, and while there were certainly enough books to consider the office a library, old tools and random bits and bobs were on the shelves too.

A small and simple shelf hung above the upper ledge of the big window, a little crooked, where Cornelius' most prized possessions kept watch over everything.

Three books that had seen better days were sandwiched between a new set of binoculars, and an old

Kodak Brownie. Neither the new nor the old had been used in many years, and it was only in times of great melancholy did Cornelius venture to choose one of those three particular books depending on his mood, and read it from start to finish in one sitting. And only then would the despair clear, and he could take on the world once more.

Back turned to his guests and hands flitting over coffee mugs, Cornelius said, "I hold a great deal of respect for you and your husband's work, but I was not aware you held an interest in mine." He poured coffee into the first cup, then the second. "And Dr. Johnson, I understand that you are an anthropologist now, correct?"

"No. I—yes, I mean. I am," Watt said, his prim accent now rife with anxiety. The utter opposite of how he spoke to Mason. "I was an archaeologist, but only for a short time before switching."

Cornelius bit the inside of his cheek and arranged a makeshift tray. The mugs were mismatched, and the sugar container was a discarded jar from the lab (cleaned thoroughly) accompanied by a tiny silver spoon. Oh, the fucking spoon. Watt had given it to his Mama the second summer they knew each other, and Cornelius had somehow ended up with it. He'd never gotten around to getting rid of it. It was nothing special, but it was just so damn perfect for sugar though. It was fine, Watt wouldn't even remember.

Nina cleared her throat, deftly moving on from

Watt's awkwardness. "I appreciate the flattery, but I shall be blunt with you, Dr. Sawyer. I'm not really here to speak with you about the stars, although I do find your theories regarding the convergence of archaeology and astronomy to be truly fascinating. It's a wonder it hasn't been explored sooner."

"Oh." Cornelius' heart sank, and heavy disappointment intermingled with prickling, self directed irritation. He should've known. Should've realized he was being deceived. But why?

He turned away from the window and set down the tray on his desk, closer to Nina and Watt's side of things. Cornelius took up residence in his own chair, a second hand thing supported by four legs and a prayer. Having tucked his irritation deep within himself, Cornelius folded his hands and looked at Nina, who had already taken the mug closest to her.

"I'm afraid I don't have any milk," he said.

Nina took a sip, then nodded once. "It's perfect the way it is."

Watt, on the other hand, proceeded to dump approximately five spoonfuls of sugar into his coffee. He was entranced by the tiny yet mighty spoon moving through the black liquid, forcing sugar and coffee to become a cohesive entity. Cornelius cursed internally.

Nina glanced at Watt while he fixed his cup and shook her head, then set her own mug down. She studied Cornelius, her spine straight and wrinkled eyes keen. "You've led an impressive life so far, Dr. Sawyer, and have many merits to your name—"

"Oh, I'm not sure about that, ma'am," Cornelius interjected. Nina flashed him a scolding look that reminded him of Mama, then continued on like he'd said nothing at all.

"You attended university in France and graduated with your doctorate in America at a significantly young age, and you specialize in ... niche research, let's say. I'm told that you're an exceptional teacher, and an enigmatic man. You've attended digs with the likes of Woolley and Mason, no less. A Mr. Shotridge as well, if I hear correctly."

"Whoever you spoke to was far too kind." Cornelius cut in, feeling like the rug had been pulled out from beneath him.

"Sara always was, wasn't she?" Nina said, and the last bit she added with a touch of fondness, which paired with the sound of Sara's name made Cornelius' heart clench. It'd been eight years, and grief had yet to fade. Sara Yorke Stevenson was his mentor, his advocate, his friend in a strange world. Now, she was six feet beneath the ground in Laurel Hill. Cornelius supposed it shouldn't be a surprise that Nina and Sarah knew each other, besides the fact that one was American and the other was not, they were in similar fields and seemed to have similar personalities. But when had they talked about him? And why?

Cornelius swallowed treacherous hot emotion and cleared his throat. Slowly, he said, "And here I was under the impression you weren't familiar with me. I—I don't understand, Mrs. Fawcett. What do you want from me?" Cornelius briefly glanced at Watt who startled at the eye contact, like he'd been staring and was caught in the act.

Cornelius bit his tongue on, '*and why are you here?*'

He convinced himself that it didn't matter. Watt was extraneous.

For the first time, Cornelius had taken Nina off guard. It was subtle, her face was smooth and devoid of anything but nonchalance. But she took another sip of her coffee, and the mug trembled before meeting the desk once again. No, not off guard. She was nervous.

Nina Fawcett said, "An archaeologist named Joaquim da Silva has discovered ruins near Cuiabá, between the rivers Teles Pires and Xingu, in the same area where an Enchanted City is rumored to be. The site keeps expanding, and so is the workload. Columbia is assisting," Nina gestured to Watt, "along with several other universities. However, they are in need of another archaeologist. Someone with your experience, and frankly, your wits. I've been assured the University Museum is more than happy to lend a hand. Yours, particularly. In exchange for glory and the like, of course."

A cluster of mangled nerves in Cornelius' left calf flared up, and he inhaled sharply through his nose. Overwhelming heat, pain, and—and—

He took a sip of coffee to drown out the pain, the uncalled for panic. He carefully set his mug down on the desk, then turned it so the handle was facing the right way. "Unofficially?"

Nina leaned ahead, and Cornelius found himself doing the same. Determination set between her brows, and her eyes burned anew. "Unofficially, I am asking you to find my husband, and bring him home. You see, the area they are studying is where Percy meant to go, the *true* area. Penn will provide for your basic expenses, and Colombia's donors will compensate you for your efforts. I will be honest with you, it's not an extravagant sum."

Cornelius stared at her, unable to comprehend what she was saying.

But there'd been a nagging whisper since her arrival, hadn't there? Something that sounded a lot like far fetched hope?

"Mrs. Fawcett, I—I thought it was determined that he was dead?"

Nina's hand swept through the air dismissively. "I am not inclined to believe Dyott's findings, as hard won as they were. He was more concerned with a good story than the truth, if you ask me. '*Man Hunting In The Jungle,*'" she scoffed, shaking her head. "You know the story, then?"

Cornelius nodded. Instead of admitting he had a binder that looked suspiciously like one a stalker would use regarding Fawcett's last trip, he said, "The Kalapolo told Dyott's party that Percy and the boys disappeared into the forest, and after five days their fires could no longer be seen, that they were possibly killed by the Nafaqua. Except the Nafaqua say that it was the Kalapolo who committed the murder, not them."

Nina nodded, looking every minute of her sixty years. "And three years ago Sergeant Couturon claimed he saw Percy while hunting alligators," Nina said softly. She glanced at Watt, who smiled gently in return. There was so much warmth between them that Cornelius felt compelled to look away, but didn't.

With much less vigor than before, she quietly added, "Every year there is a new fantastical tale, a new child of Jack's or bones of Percy's. But the rescue missions thus far have been conducted in entirely the wrong area. I've received letters from the local rancher Percy stayed with, Hermenegildo Galvão, that can attest to this, and I've my own evidence that Percy is elsewhere as well."

"Oh?"

Nina rubbed at her temple, looking away from Cornelius. Her eyes glazed over with thought, and Cornelius found it hard to stop watching her.

Watt cleared his throat and proceeded to pick up where she left off, his voice low. "Our main objective is to assist in the dig and do what we can there. It's in an area that the Colonel took great interest in, and isn't far at all from his true coordinates. I think it would be best if we retraced his steps exactly, from Bacairy Post to Dead Horse Camp and beyond. I'm not personally familiar with the area, or South America for that fact, but ..." Watt parsed out his next words carefully. "I understand that you spent a good deal of time there a few years ago."

Cornelius frowned. "In Colombia, and some in Peru, but not Brazil. I've never been there, all of South America is not all the same." Cornelius looked away, afraid that he might give himself away. His leg screamed at the thought of trekking through the wild, a stark contrast to his whooping heart. The *Wild*.

How long had it been since his skies were clear, and the stars ever so bright?

How long had it been since he heard the creeping howls of snakes, and felt the sting of their bite?

"While that may be true, it does not change the fact that your skill set would be a great asset to the expedition." Watt nudged the conversation. "I need a trustworthy guide, and you are greatly familiar with the Colonel's work, as you said. The terrain varies throughout South America, true, but there is much that is the same, yes?"

"Yes ..." Cornelius allowed, too confused to say much more.

He didn't understand.

He was not special.

Adventurers were a dime a dozen these days, and most of them were much more fit for a journey like this than he was. More ambitious, too. He was more fortunate than most to have a roof over his head and money to his name in these desperate times. He could've used the money and fame, sure, but he didn't need it, not like others did.

Then again, the adventurers who *had* gone looking for Fawcett hadn't all made it back.

There wasn't much rhyme or reason to surviving the jungle. You could throw the most seasoned explorers in with a bunch of greenhorns, shake them about, and each time get a different result. The only reason Cornelius escaped with his life was the same reason others did. Wicked luck.

Cornelius shifted his attention to Nina and caught a glimpse of hope in her eyes, the slackening of tension in anticipation of a yes.

It nearly changed his mind. Nearly.

"Mrs. Fawcett, I cannot deny that I've had my own suspicions regarding Dyott's findings, and your proposal is intriguing, but I'm no longer the man I once was. I would be a burden on an expedition like this. I must refuse, but I can recommend some reputable men who would be up for the task."

"But I do not want other reputable men, Dr. Sawyer. I want you," Nina said, like she'd already told him a hundred times before. She bent down and reached into the bag at her feet.

"I understand that, ma'am," Cornelius said, although he truly didn't. "But I—"

Nina withdrew a hefty journal from her bag, and all air ceased to exist. Without a word having to be uttered, Cornelius knew what it was. Knowledge and adventure seeped from the rough pages hidden between those leather coverings. Nina laid the journal in her lap and smiled down at it, running a finger over its face.

"Did you know I was the one who found Raposo's document?"

Cornelius swallowed. "Yes, ma'am."

Without looking up she said, "I asked to go, you know. All my life I stayed behind while he went on adventures, and on the trip before his last one I all but demanded it of him. But the jungle was no place for a woman, he said. He was awfully backwards that way, insisting that the Indians are our equals while still calling them savages. Accepting my help and education, while firmly believing a woman's purpose was only to run the household."

Nina Fawcett exhaled, and placed the journal on the desk between them.

That damned curiosity of his sparked Cornelius' nerves, forced his muscles into motion. He reached for weathered pages and worn leather, then paused upon remembering his manners. He looked to his guest for permission and Nina smiled, tired and quivering. She said, "Brian, bless him, compiled all his father's journals. We thought we could find answers within its pages, we've found enough questions, certainly. Brian attached some of his letters, and Jack's too, along with a few from Raleigh. The only people to have seen this are my family, Mr. Johnson, and now you. I—we are not ready to publish it yet, but you may read it. If I cannot convince you to join this adventure, perhaps my husband can."

Nina stood, and Watt did the same. She smoothed her hands over her dress and nodded, as if everything was settled. "I will send Mr. Johnson for it, and your final answer, on Wednesday morning by eight o'clock sharp. I do hope you change your mind, for my husband's sake just as much as your own."

Nina Fawcett cast her gaze over the room, and him, one last time. Chidingly, she said, "You're meant for adventure, Cornelius." She and her companion turned away, leaving him behind.

Cornelius stood abruptly. "Wait, Mrs. Fawcett!"

Nina glanced over her shoulder, brow raising at his exclamation. "Yes?"

"You—" Ever so slowly, Cornelius rested his palm on the journal entrusted to him. "You've no idea who I am, not really. How could you trust someone like me, a stranger, with your husband's work?"

Nina hummed, allowing a hint of that mischievous smile to return. "Because he told me I could."

And then she left, taking Watt with her. He turned to shut the door behind him, and his eyes met Cornelius'. Watt's lips parted, then he ducked his head and closed the door. The silence left behind was deafening.

Cornelius filed away his disappointment, and anger, for later. The treasure beneath his fingers wouldn't allow him to linger on anything else but satisfying that itch called curiosity. He meticulously prepared another cup of coffee, having finished his first one without memory of doing so. He sat down at his desk and took a sip of the warm, bitter brew. Bracing himself, he opened the journal to the first page. He wasn't sure what he expected it to contain, but a romantic dedication to '*Cheeky*' in microscopic handwriting was not it.

Sweet praise for his wife's support of his adventures filled the first page, along with his sincere declaration of love. Cornelius never knew Fawcett personally, but in that moment he could feel the man in the room, whispering words of gratitude that read like goodbye, all to a woman who was here only moments before. Breathing, living.

Left behind.

Cornelius took a breath, and turned the page.

A Shame

March 4th, 1930

Common sense dictated it was rather stupid to engage with someone who recently shattered your nose, but Watt had never been one for things like common sense. He couldn't help but obsess over the next day's impending meeting. He wished for so many things, including the ability to redo the entire last week, but knowing what he knew now. He didn't know whether to hope for Cornelius's agreement, or further refusal.

The person he'd known would have dug their heels into the ground out of sheer spite, but Watt didn't know Cornelius Sawyer. He knew Annie Tremblay. And while he expected adulthood and all its traumatic facets to change her—*him*, he hadn't expected such a drastic change. Watt had so many questions that he dared not inspect any of them too closely, for they gave way to other curiosities that he shoved deep within himself long ago.

But he wasn't Callum. He wasn't an unkind man, and he wasn't so naive as to not be familiar with the concept of gender versus sex. He held no ill will towards Cornelius, and wanted to do his best to respect him, regardless of the man's decision to participate in the expedition or not.

He and Nina toured the University that morning, meeting with J. Mason and the aforementioned Esther Mazur. She was a remarkably clever woman of middling age, and it was clear that she had great potential. She was friendly, but when she spoke directly to Watt there'd been a distinct caution in her tone. Subtle, but there. But that's how it was with most who held an affinity for morals, and had an idea of what he'd been part of in Egypt. It only made him respect her more. Archaeologists and their cousins were a mixed bunch, many didn't see the harm in what Watt's team had done in Luxor. To be fair, Watt had not been part of the distribution of artifacts, simply part of the team who had found the tomb.

Mason introduced them to Louis Shotridge, Assistant Curator of the Museum. They hadn't met before, but he knew of Shotridge due to his work with Sapir and Boas on their research of the Tlingit people in Southwestern Alaska. He was a Chilkat Indian, who were part of the Tlingit, and had a strong jaw and dark hair cut in the same modern style as Cornelius'. Short on the sides, with a thick length on top swept back fashionably. He was a sturdy and quiet man who reminded Watt much of himself. He was kind, and happy to see Watt again. Like Mason, he gave Watt kind words to pass along to his Columbia colleagues.

Shotridge gave them a tour of the Pacific Northwest exhibit, which he was the curator of. Watt admired the Klukwan Village model, which was Shotridge's own village and crafted by his own hand. It was fantastic, with houses and trees, everything to scale. There were artifacts such as clan emblems, a wolf helmet and a wolf baton. There was the ceremonial regalia that Shotridge used to wear in his early days, back when he taught programs for children, and what seemed to be an infinite number of hats. Grizzly bear helmets and painted basketry hats, and a knife with a wolf head as the handle. The exhibit was a well tended labor of love, and it temporarily made Watt forget about his aching heart. It was marvelous, archaeology as it should be.

Next was the Egyptian exhibit, which brought Watt back to the present, a ridiculous notion since it should've brought him back to the past. But all it made him think of was the Valley of the Kings. Of greed in men's eyes, and decadence beyond belief. And it was here, too. It was in the way these exhibits were larger, imposing and overfull with artifacts. There had to be an Upper and Lower Hall, six rooms in all. There were great slabs of stone with inscriptions upon them, plucked from the sands of Giza or Meydûm or elsewhere. Pottery, unpainted and otherwise. Arrowheads, hairpins, an ivory wand with an animal's head. It went on, and on, and on. Despite his mood, Watt made sure he showed appreciation and asked questions. He didn't want to slight Ms. Mazur, and was indeed fascinated. He would always be curious about new, or rather old, things. Archaeology could be good, if done right.

They also visited the Americas exhibit next. This was Mason's domain, and he had an impressive amount of artifacts. Less than Egypt, but more than the Pacific. He had been to Mexico, Puerto Rico, Colombia, and all the little places in between. The man was happiest in the field, and he kept hinting at his next expedition to Guatemala, that there was plenty of room for extra hands. Watt answered in the same fashion each time, citing that he had plans this year, but perhaps the next.

After the tour they reconvened in Mason's office, a beautiful space filled with plants. The others became deeply involved in a conversation that Watt had long lost the meaning of. He didn't mean to, but sometimes his mind just ... wandered. Something about Horace, the Director. He smoothly excused himself to use the facilities, and his departure was barely noticed.

He managed to find his way easily enough, and his heart raced as he stood on the other side of Cornelius' office door. He needed to clear the air, broach the personal subject Watt had originally sought him out for. He needed to remove the weight from his shoulders. God, he hurt. He wished Maggie were here, to let him know it was all okay. He'd be okay.

Fingers shaking, he knocked on the door.

Nothing.

He glanced at the posted office hours and, seeing how

he was supposed to be in, tried again and quietly called, "Dr. Sawyer?"

Nothing. He tried the door handle, and it was locked.

Watt sighed. It was clear that Cornelius wanted nothing to do with him, in fact he'd done a better job at pretending there was nothing between them than Watt had. And really, *had* there been anything between them?

All the unanswered letters and unaccepted apologies spoke volumes, if one read into the silence. And what were three summers in comparison to the lifetime they'd lived apart?

Watt joined Nina for dinner in a small Italian restaurant down the street from their hotel. Despite their simple meal, she wore a fine but simple dress and a pretty head scarf. This was how she preferred to dress, and Watt had found it endearing she insisted on dressing up to visit a bunch of professors. Then again, he'd tried to dress up a little too, hadn't he? Yesterday, anyway. He'd been looking forward to the meeting, before.

Cornelius Sawyer was known as a dedicated and outspoken archaeologist, and he traveled in many of the same circles that Watt did, but out of sync. He was associated with great figures like Mason, Gordon, Woolley, and Louis Shotridge, for God's sake. He was everywhere, hopping from one dig to another, but never at the same time as Watt. He'd never given it much thought, but now he wondered if that was the point. The idea that Cornelius actively avoided him was as upsetting as it was pleasing. At least Cornelius had been thinking of Watt, even if it was to steer clear of him.

Before ... everything, Watt had wanted to ask about his astronomical studies, what it was like to study in Ur with Woolley, and if all the Colonel's stories about Peru were true or greatly exaggerated. He wanted to know what to expect from the jungle and its rivers, to ask someone who had a true idea. Someone his age, at least. Because honestly, Watt was nervous about the whole affair. He owed the Colonel a favor though, and he'd be damned if he didn't repay it.

Nina had been quiet since the meeting yesterday, and so had he for that matter, but for different reasons. Watt had always admired the Colonel and spoke with him during his family's social events, but that didn't compare to a partner's despair, not at all. Nina was one of the strongest women Watt knew, but everyone had moments of weakness.

"Why didn't you tell me that you were previously acquainted with Dr. Sawyer?" Nina asked, pulling him back down to earth.

Watt dabbed at his mouth with a napkin, buying himself precious seconds. Of course she had picked up on his awkward flailing, the kind that took place when meeting someone you used to know. He couldn't tell her the truth, not all of it. Not that Watt believed she would think badly of Cornelius, but it simply wasn't his truth to share.

"I ... did not think it was relevant."

She raised a questioning brow.

Watt swallowed. "We were friends as children, but had a small ... falling out. It was so long ago, and I didn't think he would remember me. I didn't want to make things awkward."

Nina hummed, because that was *exactly* what Watt had done. "Will it pose a problem for you if he chooses to come?"

'Most likely.'

Watt ran a hand through his hair. "No, no. It will be fine."

"If you say so," Nina said, appraising him. "In my experience, you want men you can trust by your side in the wilderness, but what do I know?"

"I do trust him," Watt said, and was momentarily startled by how much he meant it. Regardless of what happened between them, Cornelius wouldn't leave him to die in the jungle. He wasn't that kind of person.

Nina dipped her chin. "And I trust your judgment. But I do have to pry now, dear Walter. What happened between you?"

He stared down at his lasagna, stomach churning on what he'd devoured thus far. It was excellent on the way down, but now lay bitter in his stomach.

After a long moment, Nina gently added, "Well, I

won't bother you—"

"My family vacationed near where he lived, and we were friends. Best friends. It wasn't for long, but ... well." Watt smiled grimly and shrugged. "Childhood friendships are just different, you know?"

Nina smiled. "I do."

Watt sighed. "We made promises to—" And here Watt realized he couldn't say the truth, because as *men* it wouldn't be right—"We had plans for the future. But during our last summer my father forbade me from seeing Cornelius. He never said why, only that he was a disgrace to his family. And I—I believed him. I didn't question him. I did as I was told, and we never went back."

Watt trailed off, thoughts crashing into another like tidal waves upon the rocks. Was that the summer Annie became Cornelius?

Did his father know the entire time?

Is that why they never visited Harbor Springs again?

Was Cornelius alone during all of this?

What did his parents think?

Cornelius' mother never corrected Watt when he asked for Annie's whereabouts, and Watt wasn't sure whether that was for Cornelius' safety, or a failure to recognize Cornelius as the man he was.

"How lonely." Nina remarked quietly, breaking Watt out of his spiral. "For both of you. What a shame."

Watt bowed his head. "What a shame, indeed."

They ate in companionable silence after that. He paid

the bill and he helped her slip into her coat before putting on his own, and they took to the street. Late winter in Philadelphia was temperamental, and the evening's mood was cold but hopeful, with none of the bitterness that New York possessed. Watt offered his arm to Nina, and she took it. It was that weird time beyond twilight, and yet still not fully night. There was no moon, but the street lamps were lit and headlights of passing cars streaked across the buildings.

After walking for some time, Nina asked, "Do you think he'll say yes?"

"I don't know." Watt answered honestly. "I hope so."

Nina sighed, patting his arm.

"What do you think?" Watt asked, looking down at her.

Nina hummed, staring upwards. Not at him, but further. Watt followed her gaze, but there was nothing to see that they hadn't already. Street lamps, enormous brick and steel buildings, vehicles huffing exhaust into the night. The upper atmosphere was framed by buildings of all shapes, sizes, and age. Trees lingered here and there, but lonely and restrained. There were no stars, the sky was nothing but endless bruised black clouds.

"I don't think Pugsy would've sent me all this way for a no," Nina whispered, never having sounded so old as she did right then.

Watt smiled faintly, not having the heart to rebuke her. The Fawcetts had a strong interest in the infallible and took superstitions to heart. They dealt in prophecies, astrology, and more of the like. He couldn't count how many times he'd heard the Colonel's ghost stories, or been pulled into seances by Nina.

He liked to believe he had a fairly open mind, and had experienced his share of the unexplainable, but he found it hard to believe that Colonel Fawcett sent his wife a telepathic message to organize an expedition with specific people, including people he'd never met, to delve into Brazil and find him.

Then again, why else did she seek out Cornelius? The man wasn't wrong, there were hundreds of men who would jump at the chance to search for the legendary Fawcett, and were likely better suited for it. But none of them were Cornelius.

And by the time they reached the hotel, Watt decided he wouldn't want anyone else.

———◈———

Dear Annie,
 March 18, 1918
 It has been some time since we last saw each other. I hope you and your family have been doing well in Harbor Point.
 I'm not a particularly good writer, but I wanted to send you a letter before I went overseas. I'm going to France, you see. If only your French lessons included more than your favorite curses, but then

again they may come in handy.

I'm part of the 307th, and let me tell you the men here are like nothing I've ever seen before, from every nook and cranny in New York. We'll be going to a training camp next week, and then to Halifax before making the final voyage to France.

It's all a bit overwhelming, to be honest. Father doesn't want me to go, but it's done. I've been drafted, and I won't fight it like he did.

I'm not sure he'll be seeing me off, but what can you do? I'm not better than any other man, and it's my duty to go. This is too big a decision for him to make for me. Again.

I wanted to say that I wish we could've said goodbye, before. So I want to say goodbye now, in case I don't make it back. The others are so full of confidence and grit that it's hard to believe otherwise, but you know me. Prepare for the worst, and hope for the best.

And this is too big of a thing to leave undone, you and me. Take care of yourself for me, yeah?

Thank you for being my friend, Annie, a real and true one.

I'll never forget you.

Yours, Watt Johnson

"Neil?"

Cornelius flailed backwards, shouting unintelligible nonsense. After gaining his immediate bearings (on his bedroom floor curled up with Fawcett's journal) he blinked at Esther kneeling beside him. Unbound black ringlets framed her stubborn jaw, and her hand hovered over his shoulder. He looked between her, the darkness outside his window, and his bedroom.

Fawcett's journal was spread bare, revealing the birds and insects of Bolivia that Fawcett was most enamored by. Butterflies. Ah, yes. Cornelius had fallen asleep to Fawcett waxing poetic about the butterflies. There had been a method to Cornelius' madness, simultaneously reading and jotting down all pertinent details on a blank sheet of paper, until setting it aside and starting another one. And another one.

And *another* one.

Cornelius couldn't help but think everything was important, even the butterflies on a trip that took place seven years prior to his disappearance. But now the formerly neat piles had toppled this way and that, creating a swath of papers arcing out around him, threatening to merge. Cornelius scrubbed at his eyes, then shook off the dustings of sleep and began to straighten up his mess. Most of the work was rewritten and edited by Brian Fawcett's hand, but some of the pages were original maps or journal entries. He found the dozen year old letter from Watt and discreetly shoved it out of sight.

"What time is it?" He asked, throat raw. Oh God, had he been snoring? He inconspicuously checked the papers for drool, thankfully finding none. It wasn't the first time he'd fallen asleep while working, but usually it was in a much more comfortable position. Even in sleep he had been careful of the journal, not daring to roll onto it or wrinkle a single page.

Esther sighed heavily. "Midnight. What're you doing down here?"

"What're *you* doing here?"

Esther's dark eyes narrowed, and her tone flared in that way it did when she thought a person was being condescending. "Giovanni called earlier, he's worried about you. I wasn't able to sleep, so I figured I'd come and see what you're up to."

His friend looked around his bedroom with a bare-ly veiled grimace. His bed was unmade, the blankets tucked around his back like a makeshift shawl. Cig-arette and reefer ashes had long since overfilled the tray on the dresser, and several cups of cold tea sat untouched on the small table beside his bed. Every hour he'd spent here since Mrs. Fawcett's visit was plainly obvious, the air rank with sweat and old smoke. A sudden desperation to open the window yawned in his gut. The blinders had been removed from his eyes, and he saw his state from Esther's point of view. From Giovanni's, too.

Giovanni, who Cornelius had hardly given more than a handful of words to. Giovanni, who had been leaving meals for Cornelius, who in turn hadn't thanked him or bothered to take care of his dishes, which were stacked haphazardly here and there.

Guilt squeezed Cornelius' heart and he straightened out the wrinkles on the front of his nightshirt, deciding how much to say. Talking to Esther was like talking to mountains. There was something endless about her soul, and her heart was one of the most steadfast Cornelius had ever known. She wasn't Sara, no one ever could be, but Esther had patched together the hole that the loss of Cornelius' mentor had left behind.

Besides his family, those at Ur during the Incident, and Giovanni, she was the only person that knew Cornelius was a self-made man. But there was one thing that Esther knew that the rest of his confidantes didn't. At least, none of his local confidantes. Dimitri and Gabriel knew about Watt, but they weren't here.

Once upon a time, Cornelius had drank too much and revealed a secret to Esther. That he'd been madly in love with a boy, a boy who had been his best friend, his everything. A boy that turned his back on him. And even though the boy shunned him for being who he was, Cornelius still *cared*. Cornelius hated himself for it more than he hated Watt, really.

Cornelius told her everything, from the confrontation at the bar to the mysterious meeting and all it entailed. When Cornelius mentioned Watt's appearance at the bar and how he'd greeted Cornelius with an old name, Esther frowned in understanding and anger.

But she said nothing, always letting Cornelius finish instead of interrupting the crashing stream of words that always escaped when he was stressed. Her eyes widened when Cornelius told her about the meeting with Watt and Nina, but again she remained quiet.

After ensuring he was finished, Esther haltingly asked, "So ... he recognized you, but didn't know that it was *you*? Or he did know, and didn't care?"

"I don't know," Cornelius said, rubbing at the headache blooming in his temple. He dislodged his glasses, which had been smudged during sleep.

"I mean ... that's why you two stopped talking, right?"

Cornelius went still, fingertips pressed hard against his skin. Cornelius always assumed that Watt knew, that he remembered their discussion. But if he didn't, surely Watt's father would have told him. After all, Cornelius' new name, his new existence, was the reason Watt stopped talking to him in the first place.

His father had certainly made it clear to Papa that was the case, that he and his family wouldn't tolerate an abomination like Cornelius. False rain doused Cornelius. He shivered against the memory of thunder, against the rage in Callum Johnson's eyes, against the creak and slip of bones beneath an angry man's hand. Callum had found Cornelius, dressed in men's clothes for the first time and hair freshly cut, laying in bed beside his convalescing son, telling him stories and truth in an intimate matter. Watt had been awake, but unable to do anything to stop his father from throwing Cornelius out into the rain, dislocating his shoulder for good measure. Oh, Papa had been so angry. Jimmy, too.

Cornelius' oldest brother had been friends with Watt, and in addition to feeling betrayed he'd been furious with Callum for hurting Cornelius. But instead of wallowing in anger and grief, Jimmy had comforted Cornelius. Most importantly, he'd taught Cornelius how to be a man. At least, in all the small and juvenile ways that someone like Papa didn't get. How to spit and curse, walk with swagger and keep his chin up when faced with danger. But only a few short months after Watt left, Jimmy crossed the border and volunteered in Canada for the war effort and left too.

That was it for Cornelius, who left soon after to study in France and stay with relatives. He'd told his parents it was to start over, make a new life for himself, and while that was true it wasn't the whole reason he left home. He'd left because home felt like the God damned loneliest place on earth.

The rest of his siblings had stayed in Harbor Springs with their parents, except for him and Jimmy. Jimmy became an air force pilot, and after the war he married a nurse he met overseas. Rebecca Goldman, a nice girl whose family lived in the Catskills, and so she and Jimmy did too. Jimmy was now a pilot at the new airport in Albany, while she worked at the local hospital. Cornelius liked Rebecca, even if the most time he'd spent with her was at their wedding. It was a beautiful Jewish affair, with so many people that it made Cornelius' head spin. Their entire life was beautiful, to be fair. The progressive American dream.

Esther cleared her throat and Cornelius startled, pulling out of childhood memories.

"I ... don't know," Cornelius whispered, and began to tremble as if he were twelve years old all over again.

Esther sighed and pinched the sweeping beautiful curve of her nose, then carefully cleared some papers from beside Cornelius and sat down properly, pulling the blankets around both of them. "I met him today. Him and Mrs. Fawcett came to take a tour of the University."

Cornelius groaned. "I'd heard they were going to do that. How did it go?"

Esther shrugged. "Fine. He was polite, quieter than I expected. He was kind of ..." She hummed. "I don't know. Preoccupied."

Cornelius snorted. "I bet."

Esther studied him for a moment, her hazel eyes peeling him apart layer by layer. Finally, she asked, "Well. What are you going to do?"

Cornelius shook his head, angry at the question—no, at *himself*. Hell, how long had it been since he felt this pathetic?

Tone hot, he said, "I've been asked to find Percy Fawcett. That's what matters, isn't it? Watt is ... he's extraneous." Cornelius waved a hand, frustrated. "Dyott's findings have never made sense, and for some reason or another Mrs. Fawcett thinks I stand a chance where others haven't."

A playful smile teased the corner of Esther's lips. "Sounds like you've decided to go then?"

"No ... I don't know. I feel that at the very least I owe it to the family to read this in its entirety before I make a decision. But it's so ..." Cornelius waved a hand. "Edited. And the pages that are in Fawcett's hand are so difficult to read, his script is so tiny and he writes in what I think is code. I only have until Wednesday to get through it, and then ... well, it'll be out of my hands. I'll be fine, go home and get some rest."

"But why take notes if you're not going?" Esther bumped her shoulder against his, and Cornelius rolled his eyes. She smiled. "It'll go quicker with the two of us. We'll stay in tomorrow, get up early, and have breakfast while looking for clues. Breakfast that you'll make, and serve to dear Giovanni in bed before the poor man has a heart attack."

"You make it sound like an adventure," Cornelius said, chuckling. He looked at her, feeling oddly light. "Thank you."

"Anything for you, Neil. And call Chief in the morning, will you? Damn man kept sniffing around all day, wondering if I'd heard from you."

Cornelius laughed, genuine and whole. "What, does everyone know now?"

Esther lifted a shoulder. "I haven't heard anyone talking about your meeting except for Mason, but everyone else is chattering up a storm about your Watt Johnson. If you ask me, he's the one that told Watt where you were."

Cornelius stilled. Mason wasn't part of the team at Ur, but he knew that Cornelius had fled for 'personal reasons.' He'd never asked Cornelius about it, and Cornelius assumed the man didn't care for gossip. But maybe he didn't ask what happened, because he already knew. He knew who Cornelius had been, and had told Watt. Watt, who'd been looking for Annie.

No, that was reaching. That was paranoia talking. Right?

Perfectly Reasonable

March 5th, 1930

Watt knocked on Cornelius' office door at exactly eight o'clock Wednesday morning. Cornelius gathered himself on the other side, allowing a moment to pass before he opened it. Watt stood at parade rest. He was alone, and wearing the same suit as before. No brown bow tie this time, but a few strands of what appeared to be animal hair stuck to his wrinkled trousers in places, and Cornelius fixated on them for a moment.

"Good morning, Dr. Sawyer. May I come in?" Watt asked in a pleasant quiet tone, not unsure like before but confident and at ease.

"Of course. Please." Cornelius gestured for him to enter, and Watt looked at him strangely before doing so. Cornelius closed the door behind him, reminding himself to breathe through the thick, awkward tension that had developed. They stood together, alone, in the middle of his slightly tidied up office. This felt like the true reunion, and his anxiety was a difficult thing to quell. He'd been fine all morning, but now he was face to face with his past. Cornelius did his best to remain civil, professional. "Has Mrs. Fawcett departed, then?"

Watt nodded. "Yes, her train left early this morning."

"Ah."

Watt studied Cornelius, not his body but his soul, maintaining a sort of eye contact that was impossible to break away from. Watt's own eyes were an unforgettable hazel, and they beheld a spark that was lacking before. Perhaps it was the way sunlight streamed through the window, lighting up the gold that danced around brown and green. Today, it was Cornelius who broke the staring contest first.

Spotting Fawcett's journal on his desk beside an envelope, Cornelius made a dash for the desk and nearly tripped over a guest seat in the process. He grumbled at the damn thing, then picked up the journal and carefully handed it over to Watt. Despite having read it front to back several times, and nearly writing an entire book of his own filled with notes and conspiracies, Cornelius felt a keen sense of loss upon relinquishing Fawcett's work.

"Ah, thank you," Watt whispered. He tucked the journal under his arm, fingers digging into the leather. Cornelius noted the faded criss-crossing scars on the backs of his hands. Watt cleared his throat, raising his voice. "And did you ... that is, have you given any thought to—ah." He rubbed the back of his neck with his free hand. "Did the Colonel change your mind? Will you come?"

Truly, Cornelius hadn't made a final decision 'till now. He'd spent days exploring Bolivia, Peru, and Brazil with Fawcett. Countless hours reading between the lines in attempts to decipher the man's journey, and the biggest mystery of all was the dual sets of coordinates. The route he planned to set off from was different from what was publicly discussed, or even what Brian listed in his manuscript. The only clue to Fawcett's true route was buried in an original journal entry. Cornelius could still picture the faint words in the margins, and the corresponding coordinates to a new, true location. '*DEAD HORSE CAMP*'

Fawcett shrouded his notes with mystery, and frequently used words like quest and scheme. The journal was censored, this fact was made clear by vague references in margins, like there was an entirely different conversation occurring between Fawcett and true desire. Fawcett was searching for something, and it wasn't just an enchanted city. Cornelius had written it all down in a journal of his own, every detail that intrigued or confused him. Even the damn butterflies.

But what piqued Cornelius' interest most were the letters sent home to Fawcett's remaining family. Jack was so full of vigor and enthusiasm, growing stronger each day they spent on the adventure. For Percy, the expedition was just another day in the woods. He was confident in his son, and their return home. Then there was Raleigh. It was almost certain that Raleigh died from infection, brought on by a tick of all things. The bugs, as incessant as they were, would be the least of their worries even though they killed just as easily as anything else.

"Cornelius?" Watt asked softly, and by God. If hearing Cornelius' old name in Watt's mouth was heartbreak, the sound of it now was pure ecstasy. Warm, like laying on the beach with the early summer sun beating down upon your face and a whole lifetime ahead of you.

Cornelius cleared his throat, doing his best not to fidget with his suspender clips. He said, "I have conditions."

Watt's eyes practically lit up and he straightened to his full height. He opened his mouth, then checked himself and assumed a less eager disposition. The move was painfully familiar, even over a decade later. Watt, much taller than the average man even at a young age, always felt the need to make himself smaller. Less intimidating.

"Of course. Should I—" Watt glanced at Cornelius' desk, which was for once devoid of scraps of paper and chaos. "Should I write them down?"

"No, there's not many. First, I must insist that we maintain a professional working relationship, nothing more. Second, any decisions made will be a joint effort."

Watt blinked. "That's—that's perfectly reasonable."

Cornelius raised a brow, he wasn't finished. "And lastly, if I shall fall behind or become ill, you will heed my wishes even if that means going on without me. If we are separated, do not come looking for me."

Watt's lips pressed thin and his eyes narrowed. Slowly, he said, "I do not think I can promise that."

Cornelius wanted to look away from the sudden intensity of Watt's gaze, but this was too important. "Then no deal."

Watt's chest rose and fell with great effort as he considered Cornelius. Watt didn't ask why, but Cornelius supposed it was obvious. Cornelius wasn't a fit man, and his leg would most certainly have him be the less apt of the two. While Watt had never been in South America, Cornelius knew he could understand the concept of survival from his time as a military man. You did what you had to do, and Cornelius didn't want to come in the way of someone else's survival. Better off to give permission now.

In the end, Watt relented with a nod.

"Good. When do we leave?"

Watt winced. "Ah, only a few weeks."

Cornelius bowed his head in assent, finding it hard to meet Watt's eyes now that the deal was done. "Fine. I need to wrap up my affairs here, then I shall meet up with you. We'll be departing from your city, I assume?"

"Yes, but I—"

"Perfect, then—"

"I can wait for you." Watt blurted out. "And we could travel together, if you'd like. Extra time to go over the plan, and—"

"No." Cornelius stiffened, overcome with a surge of fierce anger. "Thank you. Now if you don't mind, I have some work to do, much preparation." Cornelius partially turned away from him, bracing himself on his desk with a sweaty hand. He stared down at the neat, beautiful writing across the front of the torn envelope on his desk.

"Right. Okay. Well. Thank you." Watt stiffly turned towards the door, then stopped. He looked back at Cornelius, and didn't move until the man glanced over his shoulder at him. "Thank you."

"It's not for you," Cornelius said, unable to help himself.

Watt flinched. "I know."

He left, and Cornelius turned his attention back down to the envelope. He had no idea how Watt would feel about a letter from Germany being in Cornelius' possession. The war had been over for nearly a decade, but Cornelius knew some men found it hard to bury their resentment towards the Germans. Cornelius hadn't fought in the war, but he had visited Berlin for a short time when he'd first struck out on his own. It was the first of many steps that changed his life.

It didn't matter what Watt thought of Cornelius' affairs, anyways.

Cornelius took a seat behind his desk, reading the letter once more before putting it away. Just once more. It was postmarked from a little over a week ago, having made its long journey from Tiergarten, Berlin, and written in French.

Dearest Cornelius,

February 24th, 1930

You sound terribly bored, stuck in the depths of winter and monotony. I have shared your love with everyone, and we miss you fiercely. Although, I'm sure the weather is much better in your part of the world than it is ours. And the atmosphere too, hopefully. People are on edge here, tense or zealous in equal measure.

There have been these terrifying torch lit parades at night through Berlin, and flyers and newspapers everywhere that announce an uncertain future. They speak of the restoration of German Glory, warning against anyone who does not fit the image of such. As you can imagine, the population within the Institute's walls is not their idea of glory.

We are going home, although it breaks my heart to say so. We have been spoiled in the confines of this place, complacent in this new landscape that is so fraught with tension. We are not the only ones thinking of fleeing, but Dr. Hirschfield will not. In fact, he is preparing for dear Lili's operation which shall still take place on March 5th. We will stay long enough to see her make it through, and then go home. You can direct any future letters to Dimitri's mother, whose address I've attached below. We look forward to hearing from you, your words shall serve as a homecoming gift.

Stay safe and strong, Gabriel and Dimitri

Cornelius put his head in his hands. Oh, the relief he'd felt upon receiving their letter. But now that relief was nearly eclipsed by worry and sheer longing. He missed his friends, his people. It was nothing like Berlin here, or Paris. It was lonely, and he had few confidantes that understood him so completely. His eyes stung and his lip trembled, but he did not cry. He wouldn't.

Cornelius recomposed himself through the help of several cups of coffee and nearly a mile's worth of pacing. He straightened up his desk, his clothes, and his hair, then made the short walk to Esther's office. He knocked on her door, and moments later she called, "Come in."

Esther sat at her desk, back straight and loose curls hanging around her face. On the surface she appeared none the worse for wear, but the effects of their late night endeavors lingered in the puffiness beneath her dark eyes. "How'd it go?"

Cornelius took a seat in one of the chairs opposite his friend, putting his feet up on the spare. Esther's office was prim and proper, everything in its place. It had to be, for it was terribly small and poorly lit. Certainly not a proper place for someone in a position such as hers. Esther filled the role that Sara left behind after she left, and the extra duties of the great number of staff who left with her. Sara wasn't the sort to take injustice quietly, and neither was Esther. But Esther wasn't ready to leave or back down, not yet.

She raised a brow at Cornelius' loafers, and he set them back down on the floor with a great sigh. He spent another moment trying to get comfortable, clearly procrastinating. Esther tapped her desk with a finger, beholden with all the patience in the world. Cornelius settled for an ankle over a knee, folding his hands together in his lap. He finally gave Esther a small smile, which was answer enough.

Esther grinned, lightly slapping the table. "You bastard, I knew there was no way in hell you'd say no."

Cornelius' smile widened despite his misgivings. He couldn't deny he was elated, temporarily overcome with a type of joy only those at the beginning of their journey feel. Before they realized what a terrible mistake they'd made.

He gave a little shrug and said, "Yes, well. What can I say, I'm a glutton for punishment. As long as you're still willing to take on my course load next semester, or two."

"Yes, yes." Esther leaned forward. "What did he think of your conditions?"

Cornelius scratched at his temple. "He agreed to them."

Esther frowned. "All of them?"

"Yes," Cornelius said, trying not to scowl at her. "It's only fair."

"Hmm." Esther considered Cornelius for a moment, then extended her hand across the desk to him. He took it, waiting for her to try and change his mind. Esther shook her head and said, "I sincerely hope that you find what you're looking for, and that you come home. And if you don't ... well, it'll be nice to have a bigger office."

Cornelius laughed, but his mind caught on her words. What else could Cornelius be looking for besides Fawcett?

⎯⎯ ◈ ⎯⎯

Horace H.F. Jayne wasn't much older than Cornelius, but infinitely more accomplished. Cornelius couldn't help but remind himself of that fact as he sat across from the Director of the University Museum of Archaeology and Anthropology. The man frowned as he read through Cornelius' inelegant tornado of a proposal, having already listened to the verbal portion. He'd only been Director for a year, but Cornelius had known him since '22. He was the man who coordinated Penn's team on the Ur dig, and introduced Cornelius to Woolley.

He was one of the few men who knew Cornelius' secret, all thanks to that shithead Andrea Carmine.

Thankfully, Horace was a decent man and hadn't told a soul. Or if he had, it'd been one who was equally quiet on the matter.

Cornelius had gathered that Horace facilitated Nina's visit and sang his praises. So he couldn't understand why the man appeared so ... disappointed? Irritated? His mustache twitched while he slowly leafed through pages upon pages of Cornelius' notes, the final draft much better than his initial attempts but still tainted by mania and a lack of sleep.

Cornelius shifted his attention away from the minute changes in Horace's expression, and took to admiring his waistcoat. All of his clothing, for that matter. The man always dressed fantastically, the picture of a gentleman. He made it look even easier than Watt did, albeit less handsomely.

After staring at the man for what felt like much too long, Cornelius' gaze traveled to the confines of Horace's office. Beautiful Japanese paintings framed by elaborate golden frames hung on the walls, along with a few tapestries. Not only was Horace the Director of the University Museum, but he was Chief of the Division of Far Eastern Art as well, and he loved it all with a passion.

Cornelius never had the honor of doing work out there, but he always wished to. First it was Alaska, his very first work for the Penn Museum with Shotridge, then Ur at the behest of Dr. Gordon, the Director of the Museum at the time. Then he was in Peru with Mateo, and Colombia with Mason. Peru especially stole his heart, but it was far more dangerous than anywhere else he'd been. Greedy white men had long violated the natural treasures of the south and continued to do so, but there was a cruelty to the rubber gangs that Cornelius never experienced before.

If it wasn't rubber and quinine in Peru, it was silver and tin in Bolivia, or coffee and cocoa from Brazil. And those were only the big players, not to mention the abundance of other resources South America had to offer.

Until now Cornelius hadn't realized just how badly he wanted to return to the depths of South America, see for himself how the southern regions compared to the north. If Fawcett's journals were anything to go by, they were two sides of the same coin, albeit lending more love to Brazil and her people than Bolivia or elsewhere.

Cornelius opened his mouth to say something, *anything*, when Horace straightened out the stack of papers with a singular *clack*, then set them aside. He folded his hands in front of him on the desk and leveled Cornelius with a concerned expression. "I must say, Dr. Sawyer. I'm surprised you took Mrs. Fawcett up on her offer. Are you sure you're up for this?" He gave Cornelius a very pointed once over.

While Cornelius' faults were obvious, he didn't care to be so plainly wanting. Cornelius nodded curtly. "I am familiar with the risks, and have accepted them. This is too important an endeavor to let pass by, as was made clear to me by Mrs. Fawcett."

Horace's lip twitched, and his eyes hardened in the way schoolgirls did before they slit you from carotid to femoral with nothing more than clever, sharp words. "Well, you don't truly believe Fawcett is alive, do you?"

"I do," Cornelius said, unsure whether he truly did or not. He added, "And Mrs. Fawcett was under the impression you did as well."

Horace smiled, and in it lay the cruel truth. "I'm afraid I didn't have the heart to tell a grieving widow otherwise, and I thought if anyone here could set her straight, it would be you."

Cornelius was stunned. "You expected me to say no."

Horace spread his hands. "Indeed, and you can see the predicament you've put me in now that you've said otherwise."

"Or you could say yes, and be in no predicament at all." Cornelius grasped at another angle. "There's hardly anything to lose, but everything to be gained. If I find Fawcett, or his lost city, and do so on the University's behalf? The boons would be astronomical."

"Nothing to lose but money we don't have, and who will finish your classes for the semester?" Horace countered, but the sternness had fled his brow. He sighed and said, "You are not as easily replaceable as you might think, Dr. Sawyer. And if you *are* feeling up to the field again, might you return to Ur as has been requested? Or with Mason, even."

Cornelius grit his teeth, sidestepping *that* discussion. "If I may, Miss Mazur is more than an adequate substitute in my place. She is familiar with the coursework, and willing. She's assured me it will not interfere with her duties."

Horace pulled a face, and Cornelius moved in for the final blow before the man could get another word in. "I understand your reservations, but I truly believe this expedition will yield good results, even if we don't find Fawcett. The site they've established in Mato Grosso is substantial, and so are the finds there. If Brazil is offering us a way in, we should take it before they cut us out entirely. And say we do find Fawcett. Well, you wouldn't want to be the man that passed on that opportunity, would you?"

Horace sighed, sliding the papers across his desk. He stood and offered Cornelius his hand. "Not like I've got much choice, do I?"

Cornelius stood and shook the man's hand. "You've made the right one."

———◦◉◦———

Giovanni was waiting for him when he returned home.

The phonograph was on, playing the blues. Giovanni put out his cigarette and rose from his place on the couch, dressed in his tailor's version of himself. Grey straight-legged trousers and an evening blue jacket over a cream sweater that Cornelius knew to be soft. His hair was slicked back, longer and darker than Cornelius' own. Hells, he was handsome. During the week, Giovanni worked with his family crafting quality Italian pieces for men and women alike, their business a lucky one for it resonated with the upper class who weren't hit as hard as the lower classes had been by the economy. His passion for clothes was nearly as strong as his passion for music, a fact that they had bonded over.

Truly, they had been good together. Better than he and Andrea had ever been, or any of his previous partners. They lived together without issue, and the biggest complaint Cornelius had was that Giovanni cooked too well. So of course Cornelius had sabotaged their relationship, like everything else good in his life. He wasn't on the lease to Giovanni's beautiful, if not small, apartment. The only thing that kept him there was Giovanni's good will and pity, because he was that kind of a guy. Despite his fuck up, Giovanni insisted they remain friends. If times had been better, Cornelius would've packed up his pride and his things and found somewhere else to live.

Giovanni smiled at Cornelius standing just inside the door, briefcase in one hand and cane in the other. He said, "Hello."

"Hi," Cornelius said, breaking out of his fugue. He crossed to the dining room table, depositing his brief-case upon it. It was heavier than usual, but not unbear-able. Cornelius grimaced at the slight amount of time he had to get fit. Three weeks was nothing, especially when much of it would be travel time for him.

"How was your day?" Giovanni asked, joining his side. He smiled, but the tightness at the corners of his eyes betrayed him. He was worried.

The moment struck Cornelius, the fact he had some-one to come home to that cared about him and wanted to know how his day went. Someone who truly knew him, and that Cornelius could be himself with. Someone who worried about him. He steeled himself. There was no use in prolonging the inevitable. He said, "Horace said yes. He agreed to Esther taking over my classes, and gave me his blessing. He's not pleased about it, but he said yes."

Giovanni's dark brows rose. "Really? That's wonderful news." He reached for Cornelius' hands, allowing him to close the distance. Cornelius slipped his fingers between Giovanni's, gripping tight. He didn't step closer yet, though.

Cornelius blinked. "Really?"

Giovanni chuckled. "Were you hoping I'd say otherwise?"

Cornelius shrugged. He'd thought for sure that the steadfast and logical Giovanni would've convinced him to stay. He might've welcomed the effort. "No, not all. I'm just ... I don't know. Need to hear your honest thoughts. Am I doing the right thing?"

Giovanni's eyes softened. "I won't lie, I'm terrified for you. And if I thought I stood half a chance, I'd ask you to reconsider. But I've seen how you warred with this decision and the toll it took on you, and it's plain that you've given it some serious thought."

"I have." Cornelius allowed, stepping closer.

"And I think," Giovanni lowered his voice conspiratorially, "that if anyone can do this, it's you. I really do."

"You do?" Cornelius asked in a surprised whisper. He considered Giovanni's word to be ironclad, and while he didn't believe in the sentiment a hundred percent, it edged him closer to fully accepting that he might actually find out what happened to Fawcett. That at the very least, there was a chance.

"Yes, I do." Giovanni tugged Cornelius into a hug. He rested his chin on Cornelius' head and just held him for the longest time. It was grounding and wonderful, even if they were both sniffing a little afterwards. Giovanni patted his back once before pulling away. "Now, let's eat, dinner's getting cold."

Cornelius smiled to himself. He enjoyed a night full of food and music with Giovanni, packing the memory into his heart for later.

Too Late

New York City
March 8th, 1930

Watt was quite sure if Cornelius knew who the main benefactor to this expedition was, he would refuse to go. And he was also sure that if Callum knew he was paying for Cornelius' passage, and who he was, he'd refuse to do so.

As a young man, Watt had never received an answer from his parents in regards to the questions that plagued him for years upon years. Why did they abandon their vacation spot at Harbor Point, and why did his father forbid him from speaking to the Tremblays?

He knew in his heart the questions were connected, and that something had happened while he was submerged in the fever delirium of measles. He remembered Cornelius sitting at his bedside, nursing him back to health with photographs and stories of the town. Always talking, always there. Having already survived measles, Cornelius was the only other person Watt saw during that time, besides the medical staff and his parents. Well, he didn't really remember seeing them, but surely they checked in on him. That time was one of several gaping holes where his memories should've been.

He'd survived, and lost his best friend for reasons unknown. The moment he was able to be moved, the family fled Harbor Point and never returned.

Watt needed answers, but by God he did not want to ask questions.

Watt sat in the dining room of his parent's townhouse, a beautiful manor on a sprawling estate in Midtown. Besides the three summers Watt spent in Harbor Point, this is where he grew up. His father and mother sat at opposite ends of a Victorian era dining table, and Watt filled the space between them. His father wore an old fashioned tuxedo, while Watt wore a double breasted evening suit. His mother shone in a rose colored dress that came to rest around her ankles, and her signature pearls hugged her throat. This evening was dedicated to Watt's upcoming journey, or more importantly, what could be gleaned from it. He'd been told it was a celebration, but it was only them. The Johnsons attended many social events and were held in high regard, but they had little in the way of what Watt considered to be true friends.

Watt's accomplishments were not his own, they belonged to the Johnson family. Not only his success, but his failures as well. Or what his Father viewed as failure. Leaving archaeology for anthropology had been a disappointment, but paired with Watt's abrupt departure of Carter's team before their ultimate discovery, the move was a personal blow to his Father's reputation, especially during the height of mummy fever. He made this clear to Watt on a regular basis, and any new projects that Watt took on would always be cast in the shadow of what could have been. That would explain why tonight's affair was mild. They ate in affable silence, as important conversation could not be held until after dinner had been consumed. After the staff cleared the dinner service, Callum Johnson affixed Watt with his full attention. He said, "Now, Walter. Tell us how your man hunt played out."

Watt tried not to flinch. "Very well, sir. Dr. Sawyer has agreed to join us."

His old man scoffed. "Well of course he has, what fool would say no?"

People often told Watt that he looked just like Callum, and Watt tried to find himself in the deep frown lines surrounding his father's mouth. He could allow the broad forehead and stubborn jaw, expected and even welcomed the thick head of silver and bronze, but he hoped to God he never developed such a permanent expression of distaste.

"Sawyer ... I dare say it rings a bell, but I cannot place the man. What's his first name?" Callum asked, dark eyes contemplative.

'*Anyone with a lick of sense would've said no,*' Watt thought. He had to go about this next bit carefully, and he tried not to let his apprehension show. He said, "He worked under Woolley, sir. I believe that was his first dig before doing some survey work in Peru and Colombia. Dr. Cornelius Sawyer."

"Cornelius Sawyer ..." Callum studied Watt's face for a long moment, then shrugged. "Must not be noteworthy, but if it is he who Mrs. Fawcett desires to accompany you, then accompany you he shall."

"Yes, sir." Watt nodded, nearly sagging with relief. If Callum decided to withdraw his funding, it would've put a real damper on things.

"Come now, Watt. Tell us something about him," Alice said. She had a particular look in her eye that Watt knew all too well. She had something to say, but wouldn't in Callum's presence. "I'd like to know what type of man will be gallivanting in the jungle with my son."

Callum frowned. "They'll hardly be gallivanting, Alice."

"All the more reason," she replied, keeping her cool gaze on Watt. She was father's opposite, pale with dark hair, willowy and petite. Her health had always suffered in the city, which is why they vacationed for most of the year in the country. Before attaining the manor upstate, they'd spent that time in Harbor Point, the scenic tourist section of Harbor Springs.

He didn't have a friend in his mother, per say. She treated him the same way she treated her husband. Distant, and aloof. As he understood it their marriage was a love match, but if there had been any sentiment between them it'd fled by Watt's early childhood. And so Watt found it odd, her sudden interest in his life.

Carefully, he said, "It is in my opinion that you cannot find the true measure of a man in such a short visit, Mother, but from what I can tell he seems to be honest and knowledgeable." He stared into her sharp green and yellow eyes. "Someone I can rely on."

Alice Johnson evaluated him for a long moment. Finally, she said, "Good."

March 14th, 1930

Central Park was freezing, but Watt hadn't missed Frederick's birthday in over ten years and didn't plan to now.

He stepped off East 72nd Street and into Central Park, utilizing the same path he walked every month for the last decade. There'd been times that he wasn't in the City and missed his visits, but he always made up for it. It was damned cold and the sky was a miserable grey, but no snow or rain fell. Watt focused on his breath propelling into the air in great thick clouds, doing his best not to think about anything in particular at all. He'd been doing so much thinking over the past few days that his nerves were raw.

After five minutes of brooding, Watt came upon

The Grove. A paved walkway demarcated a large area that held eighteen oak trees. White concrete pedestals were beside fourteen of them, and a boulder sat in the center of them all. The trees were taller than Watt, much taller than they'd been when he and his comrades planted them a decade ago. It was not a cemetery, but it felt like one.

Watt's hands flexed at his sides, and his feet were temporarily glued to the walkway. He stood there, staring. The plaques full of names were hidden by snow, but he knew by heart they were affixed to the boulder and the pedestals. He wished Maggie were here, but he didn't like taking her out for so long when it was this cold out.

He sighed, and stepped into the snow. His polished shoes disappeared beneath the powdery stuff, but that didn't stop Watt from approaching the tree in the very back, the one dedicated to Company G. His heart thrashed against his rib cage, swollen with exercise and longing.

Watt brushed the snow off the white concrete pedestal situated upon its own little hill, revealing the shield shaped plaque. The names were small and the font filled with ice in places, but he knew them. Knew them all. The air in his lungs crystallized, and he coughed. He'd been smoking again, and his lungs were already sensitive from the damage wrought by measles and gas.

He knelt in the snow, shrouded by Company G's tree.

Quietly, he said, "Happy Birthday, Frederick. I—" Watt dashed a hand at the burning in his eyes. "I'm going to be leaving soon, so I won't be visiting for a while. Not sure if I'll be coming back, actually. I guess what I'm trying to say is, I think this might be goodbye, for good this time. It's a real dangerous route we have, and if the land doesn't kill me my companion just might."

Watt coughed again, then wiped furiously at his eyes which wouldn't stop leaking. He searched desperately for something grand to say, but found he had nothing. In fact there was a great nothing growing inside of him, yawning and stretching its claws, ready to tear him apart. He stood, knees cracking, and whispered, "Goodbye."

Before he left, Watt cleaned off the rest of the plaques, saying goodbye to the rest of his comrades that he'd loved and fought alongside. Men that he should've been in the ground with. But for some damn reason he was above dirt, filling his shoes with snow and planning hopeless adventures into South America with a man who couldn't stand him.

Last but not least, Watt stood before the boulder which was relatively new compared to the trees, having joined them only four or five years ago. An enormous tablet covered the back, filled with names, while an inscription covered the face of it.

Beneath the snow, the inscription read:

'To the Dead of the 307th Infantry A.E.F
509 Officers and Men
1917-1919

——◈——

A package was waiting for Watt when he returned to his apartment.

Watt did not receive much in the way of packages at his residence. Letters and such of the like, yes. But never packages. He did all of his own shopping right in the city, having never felt the need to order from any kind of catalog. The package had no return address, and the relatively small box was light enough to hold in one hand. The concierge said it'd been delivered by a non-descript messenger with instructions to directly hand it off to Watt.

After securely locking himself in his apartment, shucking his frozen outwear, and greeting Maggie, he set the box down on his bed. He sat down on the mattress, and stared at it. Maggie stared at it too, her ears perked. Surely a mysterious package with such an ominous arrival shouldn't be opened. Right?

He opened the package.

Meticulously.

He unfolded the cardboard flaps one at a time, chiding himself all the while for treating a simple box like a bomb. The scent of paper and old smoke wafted out of the box, and the hairs on Watt's arms stood on end. He peered into the depths of the box, and found a stack of papers.

Curiosity outweighed everything else and Watt reached inside the box, gingerly bringing the loosely arranged papers into the light. He shifted, unsure what he was looking at. Two sheets of paper. Folded in three places, like they'd been tucked into an envelope, but if there had been one it was missing. Scorch marks had eaten away most of the pages, leaving what remained a hardly legible smudge of French and ash.

Watt spoke French better than he could read it, having been introduced to the language by Cornelius, then reacquainted with it during war time. But on the first page, clear as day, was his name. Not Walter, but Watt.

He painstakingly put as many words as he could together, and what was revealed broke his heart in two.

My Dearest Watt,
August 30th, 1914
I hope this letter finds you well, there has been no news of your death in the papers so I have to assume that you've beaten the measles, not that I ever doubted you. I write this apology in French so its contents will be kept secret, at least from your family. My last letter to you went unanswered, but I cannot be sure you ever received it, so I write to you again in hopes that you do not think less of me, and under a name no one but you and my family knows.

I am not sorry for speaking my truth, for you will

always have it from me. I am sorry for the pain it has caused you. I should have waited, should have told you in the privacy of our place. But I thought you ... I thought it was the only chance I had, and how was I to know your father was there, listening on the other side of the door?

I knew he was an unkind man, but I never expected him to discard me so easily, and without thinking my father wouldn't retaliate for my broken heart and broken bones. I do not blame you for what your father has done to Papa's employment prospects, as I hope you do not blame him for breaking your Father's nose.

If you cannot bear to be friends with me any longer, I cannot say that I understand because I promised not to lie to you. But I will accept it, as long as you tell me so yourself. Your father says you want nothing to do with me, but I cannot believe it. I cannot believe that you would throw away everything we had because I have grown into a man. I always thought a part of you knew and loved me for it anyway, but maybe I am wrong.

But if you do wish to stay friends, know that you have a lifelong one in me, no matter the distance. I look forward to hearing from you, whether your words are full of goodbye or hello, I will be waiting for them.

Yours,

Cornelius Tremblay

Watt,

January 18, 1915

I told myself that I would not write another letter and that I would take your silence as an answer, or at the very least an ill omen. But even after all this time I find it impossible to move on, and I do not know why.

We have spent far more time apart than we ever did together, and my life is approaching a direction that promises adventure and new friends. You were but a brief interruption in the grand scheme of my life.

But I find myself stuck on that beach, with the ghost of you beside me.

Am I really that reprehensible? Is my existence that difficult to fathom?

Or did I ever matter that much to begin with?

I don't know why I'm sending you this letter, other than the fact that I will be leaving Harbor Springs soon, and all of our memories behind. I've decided to change my last name as a birthday gift to myself, and so you will no longer be able to find me as I am now. Papa understands, and I do not think he hates me much for it, but Mama is not so easily swayed. But it is a necessary action, to keep me and them safe. I'll be staying with family overseas, where I can grow into myself.

Not everyone is as understanding of my situation

as I once hoped you were. I thought I'd have more anger or disappointment to put to words, but I fear once I start dressing you down I will not be able to stop. So I will say this.

I sincerely hope that you have a beautiful and wonderful life, Watt Johnson.

Goodbye.

C

Watt had never been in such a rage all of his life. Was it any wonder that Cornelius never responded to Watt's letters, when he was only returning the apparent silence he'd received from Watt? Not that it was Watt's fault these letters were stolen, and had never reached the intended recipient. How could anyone fathom that their own family would interfere in such a violating and cruel manner?

Someone had clearly tried to destroy the letters. And Cornelius' confession, and the resulting confrontation that took place during Watt's gap of forgotten memories, for no one had told him. Watt desperately tried to remember Cornelius at his bedside, admitting his innermost truth, but he could not. Watt had been so sick that the entire time was nothing but slippery fog. He felt monstrous for having lost such a sacred memory, and that his father had invaded it. Stole it and twisted it and hid it.

All this time, Cornelius thought Watt had known. He thought Watt had known, and cut ties. Would Cornelius believe him if he said he'd only just now come into possession of these letters, and that he had no memories of what happened before? No, he didn't think Cornelius would. It all seemed too convenient, and besides. It was too little, too late.

Watt's hands flexed, tightening dangerously around the papers. He immediately stopped himself, staring down at the burned words. Who had saved the letters, and why?

If Father had read through these letters, he would've recognized the name at dinner and thrown a fit. Watt thought about his Mother, her inquisitive and knowing stare at dinner. But why only burn them partially and keep the remains?

Watt desperately tried to recall the first letter he sent to Cornelius, wondering how tone deaf it must've sounded. How disrespectful. No wonder the man had been so hostile. The once-upon-a friend who had shunned and abandoned him was now asking for his help, and not with something like furniture. It was a wonder he said yes at all.

Watt vowed to try and make things right, even if he had no clue how.

March 23rd, 1930

The first time Watt called Cornelius, he fully expected to be hung up on.

"This is Cornelius Sawyer."

Watt breathed. He said, "Hello, Dr. Sawyer. This is Watt Johnson, I was wondering if you had a moment of time to spare."

Cornelius did not respond for a long second. It had been two weeks since Cornelius agreed to participate in this trip, and Watt had restrained himself from calling half a dozen times already. He had questions, and eventually decided that it was completely normal of him to call and simply ask.

Watt was capable, he'd been in hostile environments before. But this was different, and he wanted to prepare as best he could. Most of his colleagues from before the war had been to Egypt like him, or in Europe. Those he met after were much younger than him and had done very little fieldwork. The perils of switching disciplines later in life, he supposed.

"I do." Cornelius allowed, using that same polite and cold tone from their last meeting. "What do you need?"

Watt sorely wished he could say that he didn't need anything, that he was calling just to say hello. "I was curious if there was anything in particular I should obtain for this trip beforehand. There will be opportunity to resupply in São Paulo and Cuiabá, so what do I need from here? I was also thinking it might be useful if we compared and pooled our resources, so we each carry as little gear as possible. But if you are opposed to sharing, I understand."

Cornelius huffed against the phone's receiver, and the faint sound scratched at Watt's eardrum. "You're calling me for help with packing."

"...Yes."

"I see. Do you have a paper and pen, then? Or would you rather I sent you a list?"

Watt already had a pad of paper and pencil at the ready. "What is best for you?"

Cornelius proceeded to list his belongings in a roll call fashion that was nearly too fast to keep up with. He explained what was best to buy there, and what would be hard to find. They decided who would be responsible for what, and hashed out some other details like where they would meet in the city and when. As more words passed between them, the tension in Watt's shoulders eased. But soon there was nothing else left to say.

"Okay, thank you, I truly appreciate it," Watt said.

Cornelius hummed. "Was there anything else?"

'I'm sorry I didn't answer your letters. I didn't have them. I didn't know.'

"Ah, no. Thank you for your time."

"And yours," Cornelius said briskly, then hung up.

Watt returned the receiver to its place, then put his head in his hands. He could see the disaster blooming out of this mess from miles away, and yet was still running towards the fallout.

Pier 95

March 28th, 1930

Watt despised New York City.

It wasn't the chaos and noise, it wasn't the perpetual smoke and impossible buildings.

It was home.

There was a certain way that familiar places crawled through your skin, twisting you from the inside out. Despite standing on the absolute fringes of the city, he could feel the weight of his father's expectations from miles away.

The North River crashed against Pier 95, doing its best to distract him from the blunt farewell that consisted of his father's doubt and his mother's hollow apathy. He wasn't sure why he thought today might have warranted something different from either of his parents, but alas. He felt incredibly defeated, which was a terrible way to begin an adventure. Not only defeated, but anxious.

Cornelius had given many reassurances that he would be here on time and not a minute sooner, and *no* he didn't want Watt to pick him up from the hotel. They communicated by telegram several times, but Watt didn't dare call again, and Cornelius didn't either. Any details regarding the trip were ironed out through paper and wires. It didn't bode well that Cornelius refused to spend a minute longer with Watt than he had to, and Watt truly didn't know what to do about it.

He wanted to talk, to *learn*, but he felt like he'd only crush eggshells in the process. He'd never met anyone like Cornelius, but he knew he wasn't a novel concept. Not in comparison to the hundreds of people throughout history who considered themselves a different gender from what they had been born, but this was different. This was someone he *knew*.

But did he?

And, circling back to his previous thought, how could he be so sure that he *hadn't* met someone like Cornelius? God, if only he had a word. There were terms, he knew this, but transvestite didn't seem right to him. Even he could see that Cornelius' choice wasn't a simple matter of cross dressing. He was a *man*.

And how ... well. His mind wandered back to his last encounter with Cornelius, how the other man's chest puffed with pride and defense. Mountainous shoulders sloped down to a chest that was as relatively smooth as his own. Were his breasts ... bound? Was it uncomfortable?

His thoughts stuttered as one question gave way to another, compounding in their inappropriateness.

Maggie huffed at his feet, ears perked. Watt followed her line of sight back to the main dock, and his heart jumped in his throat at the sight of Cornelius and the pianist from the bar. Watt had no idea he was coming, and he wondered at how they knew each other. They hadn't seen him yet, Cornelius was nervously staring up at the Eastern Prince. The impressive ship was nearly five hundred feet long, its hull painted red.

The pianist elbowed him, mouth moving until Cornelius smiled bright enough to dispel the light fog surrounding the harbor. He used his cane, but wasn't leaning on it as heavily as he had been last time they met. Unbidden, Watt's gaze descended over Cornelius' figure. The man looked raffish, but Watt couldn't put his finger on why. Cornelius' dark hair was slicked back neatly, and he wore a long sleeve shirt tucked into earthy tweeds. The trousers rested high on his waist, where they cinched his slightly bulging stomach. He wore no waistcoat, only suspenders. The white fabric was tight around his wide shoulders and pectorals, leaving little room for imagination. If he had breasts, they were well hidden.

Watt sucked in a deep breath, wiping his mind of all thoughts and steeling himself for the encounter ahead.

The pier was small compared to its brethren at a stocky seven hundred feet. It was filled with passengers mounting the gangplank, a scenario that was claustrophobic to say the least. He technically should've already been in line, but he didn't want to do so without Cornelius.

Watt opted to wait right where he was, standing on the precipice between wood and water. It would've been so easy to take a step and fall into the depths of the harbor. Tug boats approached, huffing thick gray smoke into the air which were insignificant in comparison to the cruise liner's columns of black wafting into the cloudy sky. This was it. No turning back.

The dock hummed beneath the force of the engines waiting to be fully unleashed, beneath the tension of families, friends, and lovers saying goodbye. Once again, Watt was struck with an ache for something that did not exist. Someone who cared enough to send him off. Perhaps if he had siblings, there would've been a chance. But no, there was only him.

Cornelius and his companion caught up to Watt. Cornelius shook his hand, breathless as he said, "Sorry for making you wait, the traffic was chaos." His vowels were long, allowing for some of his childhood accent to come through like it had when he was drunk. Watt had assumed the French-Canadian accent had been buried, but perhaps Cornelius merely hid it well beneath his carefully spoken tone.

Cornelius gestured to the pianist, who offered his hand to Watt with a dashing smile. "This is Giovanni Toliver, a good friend of mine."

Watt took Giovanni's hand, shaking it firmly. "Good afternoon, it's good to see you again."

"Hello, angel." Giovanni smiled, giving Watt a wink.

Cornelius raised a brow and opened his mouth, but the SS Eastern Prince bellowed. The cacophonous noise rattled Watt's skull, and he couldn't help the flinch that overcame him. Maggie pressed tight against his leg, alert and quiet in the face of danger. Cornelius, unbothered by the horn that in truth sounded more like an exponentially amplified dying bull than anything else, side-eyed Maggie.

After the racket ended, Cornelius pointedly asked, "Are dogs allowed in first class?"

Fighting the tremble in his voice, Watt said, "This one is."

Cornelius nodded, then looked over at Giovanni and gave him a quivering smile. "That's it, then."

"Come here." Giovanni pulled Cornelius into a fierce hug. They whispered and patted each other on the back, for all intents and purposes it appeared like two good friends saying goodbye. But Watt had to duck his head, half turning away from them. It felt profoundly more intimate than that. Once again, he remembered the sort of place he'd first met Giovanni, and Cornelius.

After a moment Giovanni called, "Angel."

Watt looked up, cheeks flushing. Giovanni and Cornelius were separated now, and Giovanni's hand was extended to him once more. Watt took it, slightly confused until Giovanni pulled him closer, into a hug. It was awkward and took Watt far longer than it should have to reciprocate, simply because it'd been years since he'd done this with anyone, and he didn't know Giovanni.

In a quiet demand, Giovanni said, "Take care of him, yeah?"

"I will." Watt answered in kind, compelled to assure the man.

After saying farewell to Giovanni, Cornelius and Watt approached the ship. Their luggage had been transported early this morning, and all that remained was to climb the gangplank. Watt and Maggie lead the way upwards, with Cornelius following close behind. It wasn't as nearly of a crowded experience now, but the officer on deck who checked them in raised a brow at their late arrival. He parsed through Watt's documents a moment longer than necessary, glancing at Maggie. Watt could see the math formulating in the man's head, and the moment it gave way to an obvious answer. Service dogs for veterans weren't a common aid, but they weren't unheard of either. Especially for a man with a medal of honor.

The officer said, "Welcome aboard, Mr. Johnson. Your valet will be along shortly." He bowed his head and added, "Thank you for your service."

The process was smoother for Cornelius, who received none of the officer's previous apprehension regarding their lateness. Watt led the way to a section of railing that was clear, and Cornelius followed closely behind. They were able to see Giovanni from here, and when the man caught sight of them he waved. Cornelius waved back, and Watt did as well but with half as much heart as his companion. Watt scanned the dock, but there was no one else there he knew. He swallowed and looked away, only to find Cornelius watching him. Cornelius didn't ask where Watt's parents were, and he didn't offer an explanation for their absence.

A minute or two passed and they spent it in silence, elbows jostling every now and then as people moved around them, but otherwise they stood decidedly apart. The inches between them could've been a chasm, and Maggie neatly occupied it. The ship's horn called one last time, and the proud black and red chimneys released smoke anew. Watt didn't flinch this time, but he did stiffen beneath the overwhelming vibration of the ship's twin diesel engines working overtime. For a tenuous moment it was as if the dock itself was pulling away, not the ship. Disoriented, Watt clenched his hands into fists and fought the rolling of his stomach, then gripped the railing. Cornelius was soon after, one hand clenching the railing so hard his knuckles turned white, while the other gripped his cane. Neither man let go until the dock was but a distant memory.

Their valet arrived, and Watt gratefully accepted the young man's offer to show them to their room. He wore a suit, one much more formal than Watt's. Cornelius appeared to belong in second class, or third if either was an option on this particular ship. Perhaps that's what made Cornelius look so roguish, his lack of regard for society and its expectations.

They descended into the belly of the ship, passing

down long alleys and brushing past other guests. The stairways were broad, the walls alternating between painted or paneled. There was a cross breeze, even in the closed hallways, no doubt from the highly boasted ventilation system.

In a British accent, the valet said, "If there is anything you gentlemen require, please don't hesitate to ask. And I'm more than happy to assist with …?" He glanced at Maggie, who was still close by Watt's side. Cornelius watched the exchange, bringing up the rear of the group.

Watt said, "Maggie, and I will take care of her myself. I understand there's an area below decks?"

The valet nodded, leading them down yet another corridor flanked by doors. "Yes, sir. I can take you there, if you like."

"I'd appreciate that. After we're settled though, if it's not too much trouble. Mr …?"

"Not at all," the man said, smiling a little. "And it's Jones, if you please."

In short order they were shown to their quarters, and Mr. Jones left with promises to return in an hour's time. Their sponsors had found one ordinary stateroom sufficient enough for their needs, and while the quarters were large it was clearly intended for a pair of people at most. The room was warm and homey, with wooden furniture and large square windows that provided an excellent view of the harbor. It was a cozy setting with upholstered easy chairs and a bookshelf to pass the time, and ceiling fans kept the room free of stuffiness. In addition to the enormous bedstead, there was a bow fronted bureau and fitted wardrobe along with a dressing mirror. A bedside cabinet beheld a shaded reading lamp, and Watt suddenly had the urge to crawl beneath the bedclothes and read a book.

Cornelius and Watt stood awkwardly in the sitting area, then Cornelius wordlessly took off to inspect his luggage placed on the floor at the foot of the bed. Watt did the same, doing his best to ignore Cornelius as the man was so obviously doing to him. He opened his suitcase, surveying for any potential damage. None that he could see.

Maggie stretched, back arching as she yawned. Watt raised a brow, then reached down and stroked a hand down her back. He breathed as he did so, doing his best to shed his nervousness.

When Watt stood again, he found Cornelius watching him. Cornelius turned away, focusing on his own luggage. Always watching but never talking, it would seem. Watt said, "She won't be a hindrance."

Cornelius stiffened, half turning his head. He opened his mouth, shut it, then tried again. "And if she doesn't make it?"

It wasn't an impractical question, but the bluntness of it had Watt stiffening beneath the pressure. There weren't many things he was firm on, but Maggie was one of them. "I don't go anywhere without her, and she doesn't go anywhere without me."

"That's what I'm afraid of."

Watt said nothing, opting to close his luggage case.

"The Amazon is no place for feelings, Dr. Johnson. If something—"

"With all due respect, Dr. Sawyer, she is my responsibility. Dogs are an asset in the jungle, Fawcett himself used them. I am well aware of the dangers, and what I must do in the worst case scenario."

If Watt had been looking, he would've seen the flash of surprise that overtook Cornelius before he bowed his head. "Very well."

Case in hand, Watt said, "You can have the bed, I'll sleep out here." He nodded to the sitting area. Cornelius opened his mouth to protest, but Watt continued on, turning away. "I'll be back shortly."

He left before Cornelius could get a word in, Maggie hot on his heels.

Cornelius had spent the entire train ride to New York, and nearly every day before that, anticipating how his next reunion with Watt would go. All of that time had been for nothing, because none of the scenarios he dreaded came to fruition. He expected the man to be emboldened by their time apart, ready to push Cornelius' boundaries and ask questions. Try and get personal.

But the man had performed exactly the way Cornelius told him to. Civil, professional. Distant. He hadn't even been outright rude in response to Cornelius' intrusive questions, simply matter of fact. So why was Cornelius so damn frustrated?

Cornelius sighed, snapping his journal shut. He pressed it to his forehead and stopped pacing, shoes protesting against the polished floors. He glanced at the door to their suite, wondering if Watt would return soon. Their valet had come to collect Watt ages ago, and was only mildly surprised that he'd taken off without guidance. It was nearly dinner time now, and Watt still hadn't returned from presumably taking his dog below decks for relief.

At least with Watt around, Cornelius was able to distract himself from his other worries. He hadn't heard back from Dimitri or Gabriel before leaving, unable to confirm they made it home safely or that Lili's surgery went well. He'd thought that Dimitri and Gabriel would stay in Berlin and work at the Institute for the rest of their lives, but how quickly things changed.

And the surgery. Cornelius rested a hand over his heart. Of course Lili's surgery was different from the radical mastectomies he'd researched and shied away from, but all surgeries beheld risks. Especially novel ones. It would be the first of many to change Lili's body from man to woman, and Cornelius hoped that she got the results she wanted. That she came out on the other side, happy. He'd only met Lili and Gerda a few times at Dimitri and Gabriel's parties filled with artistic folk, before the boys had made the move to Berlin. But that was enough for Cornelius to like her, to find kinship in her like he did with nearly everyone else he met in Dimitri's artistic circles, and at the Institute. Longing struck his heart like a match, demanding the air from his lungs.

Cornelius palmed the flask tucked into his jacket, heart pounding. He'd poured a glass shortly after Watt had left, and that first drink felt dangerously like another, and another. They were decidedly at sea now, and the reality of his situation was sinking in further now that Cornelius was alone with himself.

Cornelius wasn't a drunk. He didn't need to drink every day, during all hours of the day. He could wait until appropriate night hours, when in the privacy of a speakeasy or at home. He could last from weekend to weekend, and pull himself together the next day without a problem.

The problem lay in stopping, in dragging himself out of the sweet, obliterating relief before he became too lost in it. And he couldn't lose himself here, no matter how much he wanted to. He made a vow to himself that he wouldn't overindulge on this trip. Cornelius spent the remnants of his free time in the same fashion. Pacing, worrying. Taking his flask out, and putting it away. At one point he dug out a worn paper bulletin from his suitcase titled, '*The Pennsylvania Museum Bulletin. Number 70. February, 1922.*'

He ran his fingers over the words. '*Mrs. Cornelius*

Stevenson. In memoriam.' The ink was starting to
fade from rough handling and overuse. He brought the
bulletin with him on every trip since she passed, and
soon he'd have to leave it behind, or face a blank page.
He read the passage he loved most several times, eyes
flicking back and forth, back and forth.

'*To us there will always rise, at the mention of Mrs.
Stevenson's name, the dignified little figure with
the black bag out of which she brought, like the
unexpected mother in the Swiss Family Robinson,
precisely the thing needed at the moment. For wise
counsel, for tolerance, for understanding sympa-
thy, we all of us came to her and never were refused. Her counsel was based on an experience of
the world which included half a century of real intimacy with brilliant and wise people who sought
her as a companion; it was poignant with interludes
of the Mexican capital, Parisian days and Egyptian excavations. It was invariably moral and direct,
but tempered with a worldliness that was never the
counsel of the fear of consequences.*'

Eventually he put himself together again, piece by
piece. He put away the bulletin. Smoked a cigarette,
then hid in the bedroom and changed into the suit
Giovanni had gifted him. He did his best to focus on
the fabric as it passed through his fingers. Stiff yet soft,
well made and quality materials. He loved the winged
collar of the draping black jacket, and the roominess
of the trousers. Using his fingers and a comb, he did

his best to rearrange his hair into the style he'd fixed this morning. Worry and the wind had tousled it into a sorry state, but there was no time to wash it now.

He stared at himself in the mirror, feeling at once large and small. His suit, despite its impeccable fit, felt like his father's. Too big and impossible to grow into.

The door to the suite opened, and Watt's following footsteps were so quiet that if he hadn't been straining to hear, Cornelius would've missed them. His breath caught in his throat, despite being fully dressed. He hadn't mentally rearranged himself yet. Not fully.

Watt stood on the other side of the door separating the bedroom from the rest of the suite and cleared his throat. "I was wondering if you'd like to accompany me to dinner."

"No," Cornelius said, and after a pregnant pause he added, "Go on without me, I'm not ready yet."

Watt said something, but Cornelius didn't catch it and didn't ask the man to repeat himself. A moment later Watt's footsteps retreated, trailing through the space for a few minutes before leaving the suite entirely. Cornelius exhaled a sigh of relief. He braced himself on the dresser, seriously debating staying behind. Except he *was* hungry, and he didn't want to seem like the coward he was. And it was the first of many meals they would be sharing together. Would he avoid all those too?

Cornelius passed Maggie on the way out, she lay on the chair Watt had claimed and watched him with a shrewd look as he collected his cane. After leaving the room, Cornelius shook off the judgmental energy she had been radiating.

The Eastern Prince was ritzy as hell, perhaps one of the finest ships Cornelius had been aboard. One of four, Cornelius couldn't help but wonder if she was identical to her sister ships, or different in ways that were obvious or perhaps more subtle. The last time he visited Colombia, it was in steerage on a similar ship, a fact he didn't mind. The company was far less snottier than those in first class, and ten-fold more entertaining. He wasn't used to all the valets flitting around, with their curated British accents and eagerness to please.

The craftsmanship of the upper decks themselves were undeniable as well. Most of the furniture was finely crafted and warm, giving the ship a wholesome but rich feel. It wasn't all that different from the places back home that were designed for the tourists, not the people who actually lived there. While he walked, Cornelius corresponded what he saw with what the brochure in his hand promised. He was keenly interested in the dark room, but it eluded him.

He wasn't the last one to enter the societal hall, but there weren't many other stragglers either. The space currently played host to dining amenities, but could be swiftly transformed into a ballroom by sweeping all the neatly placed tables off to the side of the grand room. The thought of dancing upon the waves made Cornelius slightly seasick, a new discovery. Sea travel had never bothered him before.

He quickly found himself overwhelmed, unsure where to sit. He'd gotten used to playing the part of someone more socially apt than he actually was, able to play the right games, wear the correct mask and say the right things. Engaging with the upper class was simply a performance, but did the spectacle change when at sea? He felt like a dancer thrown onto stage without having practiced the choreography.

Mr. Jones appeared at his side in that bizarre way good wait staff did, appearing when needed most and without a word. "Right this way, Mr. Sawyer."

"Thank you," Cornelius said, bowing his chin.

He followed the man to one of the tables at the head of the room, near the stage area where Cornelius assumed the captain would soon be. Watt was already seated beside an older couple, hands waving through the air and an animated story tumbling off his lips. The woman laughed, a hand to her chest. Her companion seemed more delighted by her joy than Watt's story, but he paid the storyteller respectful attention nonetheless.

The steward bravely led Cornelius through the crowd, not quite all hundred or some odd first class passengers. Cornelius was no stranger to stiff crowds like this, but at least he usually knew the lot. Aristocrats who loved to invest in the latest trend; philanthropy. Assign some moral value to the act in order to make themselves feel better about flaunting their wealth, and it was a pissing contest for the ages. Also a necessary evil for people like Cornelius, having to prance beneath chandelier lights like a damned show pony in order to secure funding for the University.

But this was different. These people were complete strangers, with motives that could not so easily be assumed. Cornelius couldn't help but feel *seen*, like everyone could see beneath his clothes, peel away his skin and see the truth of his heart. His clothes itched, and the layers were all wrong. How long had it been since he felt so exposed?

Cornelius wanted to turn back, to hide in the suite for the rest of the trip, away from all of these people. This wasn't home. These weren't his people. He could feel every finger ready to raise and point, to declare, *'He is Other.'* Cornelius swallowed against the ever tightening knot at his throat, fighting the urge to loosen his tie. He opened his mouth to tell the steward he'd changed his mind, but it was too late. They were already there.

Watt stood to greet them, looking reliably rough. Wind swept bronze hair, the same nice gray suit he wore to the museum, and freshly shaven cheeks. He'd abandoned the bow tie, and his trademark nervous stare. They traded civil greetings, then took their seats and promptly offered their selections to the wait staff. Mr. Jones offered to take Cornelius' cane, but he politely declined and propped it between his feet, allowing the pommel to rest against his thigh. Afterwards, Watt introduced Cornelius to those seated at the table.

The elderly couple's names went right out the window, but Cornelius latched onto the why of their trip. A honeymoon in Rio de Janeiro, for they never had one after eloping to America. They were mirrored by a young and freshly married couple who did not elope, and were celebrating their nuptials. A widow sat between the couples, pleased as a peach as she spoke of returning to Brazil in order to visit her son attending university in São Paulo.

Conversation moved around Cornelius, and he took a long drink of ginger soda. It didn't parch the thirst building in his gut, and he did his best to ignore the urge. He'd just begun to drift into darker thoughts when the widow asked him a question, the first to do so. "So tell me, Dr. Sawyer. Are you an anthropologist as well?"

Cornelius set his glass down and glanced at Watt, then back towards the woman. "Ah, no, ma'am. Archaeologist."

"Oh, dear. Is there much difference?"

"*Yes*," Watt and Cornelius said at the same time, then blinked at each other. The table erupted into lighthearted amusement.

"Well, then," the elderly man said, gesturing to Cornelius. "Please, enlighten us."

In his finest lecture tone, Cornelius did just that. "It is true that both fields study the past. However, archaeology focuses more on physical facts, like what is left behind by older cultures or where they lived, whereas anthropology focuses more on biology and the social aspects of those peoples. It is a common misconception."

The newlywed husband leaned forward, an eager gleam to his eyes. "Do you work together often, then? Archaeologists and anthropologists, I mean."

"Yes, and no," Cornelius said, tilting his hand back and forth.

"Not as often as we should," Watt said, and Cornelius looked over at him. Watt slowly added, "Ego tends to be an obstacle to such things, but there is some change in the community. We all share a common goal, furthering our knowledge of the past. While our methods are different, we're all putting together the same picture. My teacher, Dr. Boas, is making great strides in this area, and I intend to follow in his footsteps."

Cornelius blinked at Watt, surprised by not only the amount of words unfurled at once, but their meaning as well. Cornelius cleared his throat, dipping his head in assent. "You're not wrong."

"Oh," the newlywed wife said, looking between Cornelius and Watt with an excitement sure to come from reading far too many adventure novels. "*Oh*, are you off to secure some mysterious artifacts?"

Watt chuckled softly. "I'm afraid not."

The wife looked hopefully at Cornelius, who merely smiled.

The chattering of the dining hall was brought to

a soft murmur when the captain arrived, coming to stand not far from where Cornelius and the others sat. He addressed the room at large, warm and welcoming, thanking everyone for choosing the Furness Prince Line for their voyage. His speech was followed with polite applause which Cornelius participated in.

Despair and panic threatened to poison Cornelius once again. Cornelius told himself over and over that he had the strength to stand before the weight of ten days spent in polite society. Then it'd be two more weeks of traveling via train and steamer, meeting all sorts of people. And then it would be just Watt to deal with, for an indeterminable amount of time. Weeks, or months. A year, even.

It didn't matter. He could do it.

He could.

Too Personal

March 28th, 1930

The thing about being a man was that there were certain experiences you could not skip. Not if you wished to uphold the illusion.

On a day he was feeling more solid, more secure in himself and his place in the world, Cornelius wouldn't have followed the men in their suits. But now he was among them, a cigarette in one hand and a glass of whiskey soda in the other. The beautiful thing about cruise liners was that once they were six miles off the coast, Prohibition was nothing but a distant memory.

Men drank their poisons of choice, and no one batted an eye at the affair. His heart pumped liquid gold throughout his body, and his mind finally felt clear. Shame prowled in the distant recesses of it, along with disappointment in that he so quickly broke his vow to himself. Not that he had done so yet, technically. He could have one drink. One drink, and turn in for the night. He would not lose himself, not tonight.

But damn, he felt better than he had in days. Weeks,

even. When he felt desperate like this it was as if he were a vampire, having to leech off the masculine energy of men surrounding him, doing the same as what other men did. Which was the same as the women, to be frank.

They talked.

Cornelius sat in a high back chair, knees spread in a wide, careless posture that signaled he belonged there. This was *his* space. He listened to the men talk of what they left behind and what was ahead, watched cards pass hands and alcohol of all kinds fill glasses. The smoke room was of a Piccadilly style, vaguely familiar in the way all uppercrust bars in Great Britain were. It was disconcerting to be surrounded by this false veneer of British aesthetic, considering they'd just been in America.

Watt trailed into the room long after the first cigarettes and cigars had been sparked. He directly approached Cornelius, who gestured for Watt to take the empty seat beside him. Watt eyed the chair warily, then Cornelius' glass of what appeared to be ginger soda, likely noting the darkened color to it. After a hesitant moment he sat down, looking to all the world like a rabbit ready to bolt. Cornelius offered him a cigarette, not expecting the man to take it, but feeling charitable nonetheless.

Watt did, and quietly said, "Thank you."

Cornelius watched him light the end with a match, transfixed by the cherry glow. Watt took a long, hard pull off the gasper, eyes shuttering in relief. He exhaled through his nostrils, and opened his eyes.

Cornelius quickly looked away and lit his own cigarette. They listened to the men talk around them, their shared air tense. Cornelius longed for it to stay like this forever, this stiff coexistence cushioned between them. But it only took two glasses for the alcohol to traitorously loosen his tongue. He quietly asked, "Feeling better?"

Watt's brows pinched in confusion.

Cornelius gestured vaguely to his own face. "You didn't look so well, earlier."

"Oh," Watt said. He took another drag before continuing. "I'm fine, thank you. I—I do not do well on boats."

Cornelius laughed, startling Watt. "What a trip this is going to be for you."

"I'll manage," Watt said, not quite snapping but without a doubt on the defensive. Cornelius thought, *the pup has some bite after all.*

"I know." Cornelius exhaled into a cloud of smoke. He watched Watt examine his words, searching for the hidden meaning within them, except there was none. "I think it'll take much more than a sensitive stomach to bring you down, Johnson," Cornelius added, clarifying that he was sincere.

The corner of Watt's lip twitched upwards. "Thank you," he said, but it came out almost like a question.

Cornelius nodded. There. Olive branch extended.

"I was wondering if we could talk," Watt said, and the branch trembled.

"Hmm?"

"About the route. Perhaps over breakfast tomorrow?"

"Perhaps," Cornelius echoed, butting his fourth cigarette of the night out. He tossed back his drink, then fixed Watt with a faux solemn stare. "Or perhaps we could talk now."

"Oh. Alright," Watt said and shifted in preparation to stand up, but waited for Cornelius to make the final move.

Cornelius stood and exited the saloon without looking back to see if Watt was following him. Only once he stepped up to the railing on the upper deck did Cornelius allow himself to glance over. Watt stood close beside him, hands in his pockets and shoulders tense. When their gazes met, it was Watt who looked away first. Cornelius would be damned if he spoke first, so he listened.

He listened to the ship's relentless droning as it carved through the ocean. He listened to water struggling against metal, against the ingenuity of man. The inevitable. It was late, but not so much that they were the only ones awake. Cornelius tried to remember the last time he was somewhere that held none of the noise pollution that humans brought. Even here, in the middle of the ocean, it was inescapable.

"I need rules, Cornelius." Watt admitted.

Cornelius' gaze cut sideways to Watt, who watched him intently. Watt didn't look away this time when their eyes met, in fact he seemed empowered by Cornelius' attention.

Cornelius scoffed, but was unsure why. "I told you. Treat me like a colleague."

"I don't like my colleagues."

Cornelius laughed.

Watt didn't.

"Oh, come on. Everyone likes a fella like you." He motioned to Watt's entire being.

"That's not what I said." Watt bit out, crossing his arms.

Cornelius withheld another laugh, but just barely. Everything was soft from the whiskey, and Watt was acting like a petulant child. It was adorable. "Alright, you don't like them." Cornelius allowed. He turned and leaned back against the railing, crossing his arms as he faced Watt. "But I'm willing to bet you give every single one of them a smile and your best manners, eh?"

Watt wrinkled his nose, then winced in response to the pain that must've been lingering there. Watt turned his gaze to the ocean, which was just as well. Cornelius didn't have room for anything like guilt. If anything he'd done Watt a favor, adding some character to that statuesque nose. One thought collided with another, and soon Cornelius was in dangerous territory. Staring at Watt, cataloging every decades-aged feature of his face.

Quietly, and without looking at him, Watt asked, "Does that mean you want me to smile at you, then?"

Cornelius said nothing. His pride wouldn't allow him to answer honestly, and he didn't have the strength to lie. Methodically, Cornelius pulled out his cigarette case and retrieved one of the sticks inside. He lit up, and Watt stared at him as he took a full drag. Cornelius lifted a brow and offered him the cherried cigarette, and was shocked when the man took it again. Cornelius lit up another, and the men smoked in relative silence. Watt coughed every now and then, but he didn't put out the cigarette until it was fully burnt out.

Cornelius wanted to assault Watt with every question he'd been withholding for the last seventeen years. He wasn't angry anymore—no, that was a lie. He was angry, and probably always would be. But he was tired, too.

Tired of wondering. Of wandering.

Of asking himself, what did I do wrong?

Later, long after the men had turned in and darkness had settled in the suite, Cornelius answered Watt.

Cornelius whispered deep into the pillow, where only he could hear the truth. "Please. Please, smile at me."

March 29th, 1930

Watt roused for the day earlier than he normally

did, and found it was impossible to return to sleep. He cleaned up and dressed quietly, then took Maggie for a walk. By the time he returned from taking Maggie below decks to relieve herself, Cornelius was awake.

He sat in one of the easy chairs, wrapped in a dressing gown and hair mussed from sleep. His cane was propped against his chair, and an unlit cigarette was pinched between his lips. There was something different about him this morning, but Watt couldn't say what.

Cornelius quietly said, "Good morning," which further marked the encounter as suspicious.

"Good morning," Watt said. He'd already dressed for the day, but felt wrong-footed all the same. He hesitated for only a moment before taking a seat beside Cornelius. With last night's conversation in mind, he gave Cornelius a small, practiced smile and asked, "How're you feeling?"

Cornelius groaned, rubbing his temple. "I've certainly been better. I don't think the sea has ever treated me so unkindly before."

Watt did not suggest that perhaps it had been the combination of alcohol *and* the sea. "Is there anything I can do to help?"

"No, thank you," Cornelius replied absently, watching Maggie circle a few times before settling on the floor beside her master's feet. Cornelius rubbed at his eyes, highlighting his lack of glasses. Hesitantly, he said, "If I remember correctly, you said last night that you wanted to discuss things?"

Watt inclined his head. "I did, but if you don't mind, after coffee."

Cornelius' shoulders loosened. "Oh. Yes, that would be good."

Watt stood, and in turn Maggie did as well. Watt caught Cornelius watching her and encouragingly said, "She's friendly, you know."

Cornelius cleared his throat. "I don't want to distract her."

Watt smiled and said, "it's fine," which really meant, *'I'm fine.'*

Cornelius looked up at Watt, a brow raised at his casual tone. The moment stretched, and Watt thought perhaps the ice would break between them. But in the end Cornelius said nothing, nor did he reach out to Maggie. He excused himself in order to get dressed for the day, and Watt set about securing coffee.

He spoke with the valet, Jones, who agreed to deliver coffee and breakfast to their room. Watt didn't feel like dining in the societal hall, and he doubted that Cornelius did either. On the rare occasions Watt endured a hangover, he found a heavy breakfast and solitude was the best aid. He further busied himself by gathering the necessary paraphernalia from his suitcase and meticulously laid it all out on the sitting room table, mentally repeating the names of everything like a chant.

Journal.

Pencil.

Up to date maps of the area.

Protractor.

Ruler.

When there was nothing left to do, Watt took a seat and glanced at the closed door to the bathroom. He listened, surprised to hear the distinct tap of a razor. After another minute, he retrieved his sketchbook from his pocket and began to doodle in it. Cornelius rejoined him, cane in hand and smartly dressed. He wore an outfit not dissimilar to the one he boarded the ship in yesterday. Casual trousers, long sleeve shirt, and suspenders. His face had a certain freshly tended to glow about it.

Watt smoothly closed his book and set it off to the side, tucking the extra pencil beside it. "I requested for breakfast to be delivered." He braced himself for Cornelius' potential annoyance.

The other man simply nodded, surveying the materials spread out on the table. Cornelius had a journal, a pile of papers, and a folded map of his own tucked close to his chest. He set them down into a haphazard stack and reached for Watt's hand drawn map of Mato Grosso. He'd traced over the original, which he preferred to keep for safekeeping. Better to run his copy ragged instead of the original. He'd done the same for his map of Brazil and the surrounding states. Just before touching it, Cornelius paused and looked up to him for permission. "May I?"

"Of course."

Cornelius picked up the map and unfolded it, laying it out on the table over everything else. Watt shifted in his seat at this, but said nothing. Cornelius' eyes narrowed as he studied the paper, and his wire-rimmed glasses were perched back upon his nose. Cornelius donned a wrist watch, which glinted as his fingers traced over several key points in their upcoming journey.

Dead Horse Camp.

The archaeological site.

Fawcett's public route.

The one his journals actually depicted him to follow.

"I don't see anything amiss," Cornelius said finally, not taking his eyes off the map. "Things may change once we enter the area proper, there's always the chance we'll have to take detours if we encounter obstacles. I have a few more points marked on my own map, landmarks to guide us by and indigenous villages. You can copy them over, if you'd like."

Watt nodded, secretly pleased. They ended up on the floor, comparing coordinates and planning alternate routes at various points in the journey. Cornelius marked the places that Fawcett had been sighted, noting the date for each. He frowned every time Watt said, "Our route should be easier than his," but Watt couldn't help it. Despite this, Cornelius was relaxed, the natural teacher. Faced with Watt's lack of political knowledge regarding the area, Cornelius heaved into a long and surprisingly patient lecture.

"Well, we're stepping into quite the hornet's nest, you see. It's always been a coffee and milk sort of arrangement with the presidency in Brazil, each term the candidate hails from either São Paulo or Minas Gerais, alternating each time in order to keep things fair. Mind you, São Paulo and Minas Gerais aren't the only states in Brazil, simply the most powerful."

"Wait, what does that mean? Coffee and milk?"

"Oh, São Paulo is largely dominated by the coffee industry, while Minas Gerais leads in dairy. Brazil *is* well known for its café com leite," Cornelius said, an edge of sarcasm in his voice which could have been teasing or reproach.

"I knew about the coffee," Watt said weakly.

Cornelius gave him a tiny smile. "Right. Well, in this last election that took place a few weeks ago, the governor of São Paulo, Júlio Prestes, won and has been declared Washington Luís' successor. But that's a problem, because Luís is also from São Paulo. There's been great push back from the governor of Minas Gerais, who'd previously promised not to lay a claim to the presidency in favor of a third party, Getúlio Vargas, governor of Rio Grande do Sul."

Watt rubbed at his forehead. "So ... now what? Are they going to move forward? Will there be ..." Watt trailed off, but Cornelius caught the lost thread.

Slowly, he said, "I don't think there will be a war, it wasn't that long ago that Brazil was fighting among itself and I don't think anyone wants to do that again.

But there has been talk that Minas Gerais, Rio Grande do Sul, and Paraíba want to form an alliance, with Vargas as its leader. It's all very messy, quite the time to visit."

Watt shook his head. "I had no idea, shouldn't we have been told this?" He glanced at Cornelius, curiosity sparking. "How do you know all this?"

Cornelius lifted a shoulder, adjusting his glasses. "I have correspondents in Peru and Colombia, and a few in Brazil. And there is such a thing as the news, you know."

A small, self-deprecating grin curled Watt's lips. "Ah. Tell me, do you know anything about a General Rondon? According to Senhor Antunes, he nearly didn't allow us to come."

Cornelius gaped. Watt stared at him.

"What?"

"Don't you?"

Watt flushed. "I'm afraid not."

Cornelius recovered, but only slightly. He pushed his glasses up his nose. "I'm sorry, that was rude, but I assumed that at the very least since you were close to Fawcett, you would've known."

Watt bristled, waiting.

"Well, they were ... on unfriendly terms, of a sort."

Watt blinked. "What kind of man would be on unfriendly terms with someone like Fawcett?"

"A man who was in Fawcett's opinion, part savage. You heard Mrs. Fawcett, what she said about him. And even she herself used the term Indian, which is wholly inaccurate," Cornelius said, visibly uncomfortable. Quietly, he added, "Or in the case of Dr. Rice, a well privileged man. They didn't get on either."

An awkward silence descended upon them. During this time, Watt searched his brain for any discussion of General Rondon at social gatherings, but came up empty. Fawcett had been a friend of Callum's, but Watt only had a few encounters with the man himself, seances aside. They'd all been pleasant social encounters, but he'd seen Fawcett's diary, noting the superior way he compared himself to the people who lived in the places he explored. He thought of what Nina had said in Cornelius' office, the duality of Fawcett and his beliefs. Then Watt thought of himself, and winced internally when he realized he'd been guilty of the same fault as Nina on more than one occasion.

"Fawcett was a great explorer," Cornelius said hesitantly. "But not a great man, I think. At the very least, there was room to improve in many ways."

Watt didn't know what to say to that, too afraid to speak ill of the dead and too cowardly to speak ill of himself. Instead, he asked, "What happened?"

Cornelius swelled with knowledge, and began. "Well, Cândido Rondon helped to overthrow Pedro The II, you know. Ended the empire at an age younger than we are now, and came from a small Bororo village. He's incredibly smart, and can live off the land like no one else. He's a Positivist, and similar to Fawcett he would rather die than kill. But Fawcett saw the Indigenous peoples as savages, not people. Human, but less than. Same for people of color, too. Well, he said that Rondon had ambitions 'above his station.' Rondon of course was furious. He's spent his entire life dedicated to Brazil, and science, only for the so-called superior white men of the east to declare they know best. I think for the most part he lets his work speak for itself, like the line. He did call Fawcett and the other RGS fellas poseurs, though. Serves them right. He's currently on a border-inspection expedition, otherwise we might've been able to meet him."

Watt laughed. "You're enamored."

Cornelius blushed, an unexpected development. "I find his work fascinating, and you would too if you knew the half of it. Not only is he an intellectual in several fields, and the largest contributor of specimens to Rio's museum thus far, but he also organized the construction of a fourteen hundred mile telegraph line, most of it through swampland. It took a little more than six years, and he worked *with* the native peoples, there it would be the Bororo, instead of against them. In doing so, he proved that the local people could be collaborators in the 'Brazilian National Project,' open to progress and expansion if they weren't being crushed by violence. They called him the Chief of Chiefs." Cornelius sighed, or perhaps swooned. "I'll be honest, his astronomical work is what I find most illuminating."

A knock sounded on the door. They rose from the

floor and Watt let Jones in. He delivered their breakfast and coffee with a swift yet courteous good morning, and after they assured him they needed nothing else, he departed with a hefty tip from Watt. They sat at the table, pleasantly silent as they ate a great feast. Once their plates were clear, Watt took a long sip of coffee. Cornelius watched him, and after a second Watt realized he was staring at his hand, or rather his pinky finger curled around the mug.

Watt didn't want to talk about it. He said, "I'd like for you to teach me."

Cornelius blinked, successfully thrown off. "Teach you?"

Watt inclined his head. "Yes. There's so much I don't know, especially with all the politics. And I've been doing my best to study the local flora and fauna, but I find that first hand accounts are the most helpful with such things. I know that there are snakes, and jaguars. And piranhas as well."

"It's not really my job to teach you," Cornelius muttered, then asked, "Have you read the journal?"

Watt frowned, watching Cornelius lift the mug of coffee to his lips. "Yes, many times. But butterflies will not kill me."

Cornelius nearly choked on his coffee, coughing harshly. Watt sat upright with alarm, but his companion held up a hand. Cornelius carefully set the mug down and recomposed himself. He said, "Indeed they *can*. The Blue Morpho can cause intense hemorrhage, and that's just one."

Watt leaned forward, truly intrigued.

Cornelius reached for his collar as if he might adjust it, then his hand fell back to his lap. "And the Giant Silkworm Moth can cause systematic bleeding. It's the enzymes, you see."

And then Cornelius was off, spouting more words in the next half hour than he had in all their conversations thus far. Most of what he threatened Watt with, the man already knew. Snakes, bugs, plants. It all wanted to kill you, and in the most exquisite and creative of ways. But what he spoke most of were the snakes, and in great detail.

When Cornelius stopped to take a breath and a sip of long since turned cold coffee, Watt asked, "Do you like snakes?"

Cornelius set his coffee down and leaned back in his seat. He turned his attention to the large square window, contemplating for a moment. There was nothing but a shining ocean out there, no birds or clouds. Finally he shook his head and said, "I used to." He glanced back at Watt and sharply added, "You know that."

Watt shrugged. He did. He had incredibly fond memories of Cornelius bringing him gifts in the form of docile garter and rat snakes. But he promised to play this game of acquaintances with Cornelius, and wouldn't break the rules just because Cornelius was.

Cornelius scoffed, shaking his head. He turned his

attention to the water once again. "I'm a bit more skittish now than I used to be, I'll admit. I was bitten by a fer-de-lance during my time in Colombia."

Watt watched him. "And you lived to tell the tale?"

Cornelius smiled tightly, his attention elsewhere. "I was lucky. Lucky that we were close to aid, and that the indigenous tribes were generous enough to provide it. There's antivenin for fer-de-lances now, but not for every type of snake that's out there. And it doesn't always work, depending on conditions. The best defense is knowing what you're going up against, and how to avoid them if at all possible. The people at Vital Brazil—er, Butantan, will be able to explain it all much better than me."

"Does it bother you?" Watt asked. Cornelius turned his head, and Watt nodded to his leg. "There were probably lasting effects, yeah?"

Cornelius stared pointedly at his cane.

Watt's face heated. Of course there had been. Why the hell had he asked that? That was too personal. Too rude. And hadn't he been trying to deflect an incoming personal question only minutes ago?

"I'm sorry, that was a terrible question."

"It was."

Watt nodded to Cornelius' cane, unable to stop himself. "Will that hold in the jungle, do you think?"

"Oh yes."

Cornelius laid the length of wood across his lap and began to unscrew the silver top, which was a knob-like shape. Watt leaned ahead in his seat, curiosity piqued. Cornelius set the top aside, then removed a screw from the middle of the cane before moving onto the tip, which he also unscrewed. After doing so, the stick opened into two halves, revealing a treasure trove of instruments inside. Watt spied a pen, pen knife, and handheld telescope before Cornelius withdrew a cylindrical piece that appeared to be a stake, and held it up.

"If the ground is particularly wet or muddy, I use this. And the wood is oak, so it'll last forever."

"That's incredible, did your father make it?"

Cornelius' lips twitched, but he did not allow the smile to break through. "He did, actually."

"It's beautiful."

"Thank you," Cornelius said, and he proceeded to close the cane back up.

A heavy silence descended upon them, and Watt cursed himself. Too personal, once again. He said, "You'd said something about the crew, do you want to go over that?"

Cornelius' shoulders sagged a little. "Yes, please."

That 'please' tripped Watt up, and he cleared his throat before beginning to list the names and professions of those at the site.

Joaquim de Silva; director of the expedition and crew chief.

Severino Antunes; translator and liaison.

Thomas Anderson; archaeologist.

Charles Rowland; botanist.

Francesca Carmine; geologist.

Andrea Carmine; anthropologist.

At first, Cornelius nodded along with no recognition until saying, "Oh, I've worked with him," about Anderson. When he heard the names of the Carmine siblings, he went dead still. Watt internally sighed, knowing full well who the problem child was.

"You're serious?" Cornelius asked. "Andrea—Dr. Carmine—I mean, he's there?"

"Yes, he's with the rest of the NYU folks." Watt tried very hard not to sound chastising as he said, "I believe you have a copy of the list? It was in the first batch of letters I sent to you."

"I don't remember seeing it, but that doesn't mean it wasn't there. Rest of the NYU folks ..." Cornelius removed his glasses and rubbed his temple, then glanced at Watt with narrowed eyes. "Were you offered an opportunity to work the site as well? Before?"

"Yes, but I wasn't available at the time," Watt said, and found he couldn't say much more. He wasn't obliged to tell Cornelius anything personal, that much had been made perfectly clear. As long as he could keep his own damn questions to himself.

Cornelius studied him for a moment, lips parted on a question.

Watt decided to strike preemptively. "Did you two work together?" He asked, although he'd already deduced the answer. After returning home from Philadelphia, he'd spent days comparing the timelines of their life, who had been where and when. Now that he had the proper name to search, it was remarkably easy. Even still, all he had were academic papers and newspaper articles.

Cornelius shot him an accusatory look. "We did. In Ur, before I left and he jumped ship to join your team. Anderson was there too, but he's far better company than Carmine."

"That was Carter's team, not mine." Watt clarified. "I was hardly more than a graduate at the time."

Cornelius studied him. "Why'd you leave?"

"What?" Watt asked, taken aback.

"The team, why did you leave when you did? You missed out on all the glory."

Watt felt like he'd been dunked in cold water. "Glory isn't why I got into this life."

"No, your father's what got you into this life. Well, your days as an archaeologist, anyways."

Watt stood. "You know, for someone who doesn't want to get personal, you seem to be asking a lot of questions."

He didn't say, '*and it's unfair that you know more about me during our time apart than I do about you. There's gaps in the timeline. I want to know it all.*'

Cornelius stared up at him, eyes wide. A moment passed, then he shook his head and looked away. "You're right. I—I'm sorry."

Watt thought maybe Cornelius was genuine, and he couldn't take it.

"It's fine. I'm going to take Maggie for a walk."

He needed air.

When he returned from below decks, Watt found he could not open the door to their suite. He stood there, heart racing and Maggie waiting patiently beside him. He felt like a fool after having cooled off. Cornelius had not asked anything outrageous, nothing he hadn't been asked before. But he hated talking about Egypt, hated that everyone found him interesting because of it. That they approved of what he'd done. For years he wanted someone, just *one* person, to tell him he was a grave robbing sack of shit.

But he did not want that one person to be Cornelius. Watt actually gave a damn what the man thought about him. Always had. Watt's head was starting to turn inside out again, and he breathed hard against the wave of thoughts.

The door opened, revealing Cornelius on the other side. Cornelius' fingers tightened around his cane, and after a pause he gave Watt a grim smile. He said, "Coming in, or going out?"

"What are you doing?"

"Going for a walk. It's ... stuffy, in there."

"Can I join you?"

"Yes."

And so began the first of many morning promenades

around the ship. They said nothing for a while. Simply walking and listening to the people move around them. Watt's tension bled out of him with each step, and when the sun hit him it drew out a little smile. After some time, they ended up at the same spot they had occupied last night. Wordless understanding passed between them as Cornelius withdrew his cigarette case. Watt supplied the match, lighting Cornelius' cigarette before his own.

The men stood there, watching the ocean as the ship broke through its vastness, smoking in silence. Watt thought he could stay like this forever, in this liminal space between continents, between phases of his life.

Cornelius said, "I'm sorry—"

Watt shook his head. "No, I shouldn't have—"

"You were *right*." Cornelius firmly took hold of the conversation, exhaling a heavy stream of smoke. "I think we can both agree this is hard for both of us. Peculiar for both of us. Let's just pretend that this morning never happened."

Watt took a drag, then let it out slowly. "Yes. Alright."

Cornelius adjusted his glasses. "Alright."

April

Rash Decisions

April 3rd, 1930

The rest of the trip passed in a relatively fruitful and pleasant, if not boring, blur. While ten days on a luxury ship was nothing compared to months in a hostile environment, it was long enough for certain habits to manifest. Cornelius rose later than Watt, but not by much. Watt was much quieter than him, and it made Cornelius hyper aware of how much he moved, how much noise he made and how much space he took up. He felt chaotic compared to his well organized and meticulous companion.

They spent their time in either silence or deep conversation, nothing in between. Watt smiled and bade Cornelius the minimum social niceties required, like he said he would. They didn't speak again on personal matters, not since that morning where it all went so right, and wrong. Cornelius felt rather like he was looking at his own cold persona in a mirror, except Watt smiled more than he did.

Cornelius could imagine the man going about his

day, smiling through it all until going home and allowing the mask to fall. It led him to wonder, what was home like for Watt? He had no siblings that Cornelius was aware of, and his parents were clearly not the loving sort. Cornelius couldn't imagine it. He grew up surrounded by his kin, and loved by them. His Papa was firm but loving, and his Mama ensured they all were well educated, not only in schooling but in life. Cornelius' brothers learned how to be fathers and brothers and community members, not just working men. Whereas his sisters learned to be more than mothers and sisters, and to aspire for independence.

On the last night of their trip, tucked into the safety of the warmly lit sitting room in their suite, Cornelius asked, "Will you be missed?"

Watt raised a brow, glancing over the top of his book. He was slumped back in the big chair, an ankle crossed over a knee. "Planning on throwing me overboard?"

Cornelius laughed quietly, shaking his head. "No, I was—"

Watt's face twitched between surprise and a true smile. Cornelius stumbled over his words before clearing his throat, closing the book he'd been reading. "Friends. You must have friends, or a sweetheart back at home that'll miss you."

Watt shifted in the chair, closing his own book. "There are some I will miss. Whether they will miss me, I cannot say. And you?"

Cornelius shrugged. "A colleague of mine back at the

University might."

"And Giovanni?"

"Ah. Yes, I suppose he will."

"He seems like a good man. Good music, too."

"He is." Cornelius admitted quietly. He blinked in surprise. "How—oh, yes. He did say that you two had met—" Cornelius cleared his throat. "Earlier in the night. That night." The moment ballooned with tension at the vague reminder of that evening, pressurized with secrets. Cornelius felt Watt knew many things Cornelius himself did not tell him. It made him sick.

Watt stood, nodding politely to Cornelius. "I think I'll turn in." They'd decided to take turns with the bed after the second night, Cornelius had felt too much like a pauper making Watt sleep on the couch for the entirety of their trip. He crossed the room, and Cornelius swallowed, unable to bid him goodnight.

Not without first asking, "How did you know?"

Watt stiffened at the precipice between rooms, then tilted his head in Cornelius' direction. The movement revealed the faint scar on his cheek, where he'd been nipped by a dog when he was young. Cornelius fixated on the mark, unsure why as he'd seen it for days upon days now. Like reading the same page over and over again, skimming over the same line until it finally jumped out.

"Honestly?"

"Yes."

"That mole by your ear."

Cornelius exhaled. "Oh."

Cornelius stood too, although he had nowhere to go. "Get some sleep, we have a long day ahead of us tomorrow."

"Are you angry with me?"

"No," Cornelius said, because he wasn't angry with Watt. He was with himself, with the impossible task of—

"It was your smile, too. And the terrible way you sang. I don't think—" Watt ran a hand through his hair. "I don't think your core's changed, just what surrounds it. You've always been Cornelius. You've always been curious and mischievous and lonely." Watt's mouth snapped shut after the last word, and his eyes widened.

Cornelius chuckled. He suddenly felt scooped out, hollow and exhausted.

"Cornelius, I—"

Cornelius shivered, turning his gaze away which effectively ended the conversation. For good measure, he quietly said, "It's fine. Good night, Watt."

Watt gave him a solemn nod, and went to bed. Eventually Cornelius turned in as well, but he didn't fall asleep for a long, long time.

———◈———

April 4th, 1930

The next day Cornelius was awake, washed up,

shaved, and dressed before Watt. He spent his last precious moments of solitude turning Watt's words from last night over and over in his head.

He was right, of course he was. Cornelius had been shoving parts of himself deemed too *much* into the dungeons of his soul all his life, when perhaps he should've been embracing them. Instead of severing bits and pieces of himself in order to make himself more palatable, he could've been stitching.

He was hyper aware of Maggie watching him. The dog lay outside the bedroom door, which was unusual for she normally slept right beside Watt. Cornelius felt as if the dog could read his mind and was judging him. *'Surely you have bigger things to worry about.'*

And he did. Rio was on the horizon, and their days of leisure and study would come to an end. First was to complete their necessary duties at the embassy, and then meet their guide and translator, one Senhor Antunes, at the hotel.

The day after tomorrow they'd board the train to São Paulo, riding it for a week until reaching the place where the Paraná melted into Paraguay, at Corumba. Once there, connect with Dr. Afranio do Amaral at the Butantan Institute. Cornelius shuddered at the thought, but obtaining antivenin and the most up to date education was paramount.

And then leave São Paulo on a steamer, via Paraguay to Cuiabá and onto the São Lourenço beyond that, which would take another eight days.

It would be weeks before they reached the point where only their own feet could propel them further, into the depths of the jungle proper.

And only then Cornelius could say that their trip had truly begun in earnest.

⬤

Rio de Janeiro, Brazil
April 6th, 1930

Watt was quite sure he'd never seen anything like Rio de Janeiro, and he never would again. It wasn't due to its beauty, although plenty of that lay in the sweeping granite mountains which cradled the sparkling bay and the raucous colors saturating vegetation and animals alike.

For all its rising tourism and bulging population, Rio appeared impossibly tame. The port was situated in the Old City, and they passed the promenade of Rua do Ouvidor, full of quality shops and docile social gatherings in the outside seating of pretty cafes. People lay stretched out on the beach under striped parasols, and they walked down the street without a care in the world. No one rushed here, and they acknowledged each other in passing.

Concrete and stone reigned, from the streets to the buildings. The more modern architecture all looked the same to Watt, enormous square towers with too many windows to count, but the older buildings bore a French aesthetic. The motorcars shone beneath the sun, free from slush and mud and just as orderly as the people who drove them.

The car they rode in was as clean on the inside as it was the outside, and Watt was distinctly aware of the driver eyeing Maggie's lost hairs clinging to the back seat. When they arrived at their hotel, Watt tipped the driver a few extra mil reis in addition to their fare, which pleased the man far greater than Watt expected it would.

The hotel was neither grand nor in shambles, and situated a bit more inland than the more ostentatious hotels like the Copacabana dwelling closer to the shoreline, which was fine by Watt. He paid for their room and board, and they were shown to their room efficiently but no less courteously. They deposited their suitcases in the room, which had two single beds and the barest of furniture. A mirror, a couple of chairs and a few stands, along with two large dressers. They chatted amicably about the pleasant weather, of all things, before taking turns in the public washroom.

Watt hadn't been sure how he felt all morning. But now, standing by the window and gazing outside while Cornelius busied himself, his emotions crashed down upon him. There was excitement dampened by a heavy fog, which was further overshadowed by anxiety and exhaustion. He'd spoken with Severino Antunes several times, but he'd never met the man and was apprehensive about inviting a stranger into this strange and awkward partnership he had with Cornelius. He'd be meeting with them soon, prepared to herd them to the next tedious thing.

He couldn't shake the keen sense he'd forgotten something upon the ship. He knew he ought to look through his suitcase like Cornelius was, but couldn't bring himself to leave the sights outside their window. A busy city, similar in some ways to the one he left behind, but still unknown and different. Maggie sat at his feet instead of claiming the bed, and he wondered if the numbness spreading throughout his brain was the formations of an attack that would descend upon him later, when not in the relative safety of an enclosed and quiet room.

How did he ever think he could do this?

There was a distinct click behind him, one that had become familiar in the past week and a half. Watt looked over his shoulder, spying Cornelius looking a tad sheepish behind his camera. Three times now Cornelius had taken his photo, having asked before the first time if he had Watt's permission to take candid shots.

Watt rather thought that him brooding in a hotel room was a waste of film, and was surprised to find himself saying so.

Cornelius chuckled. "Every explorer needs a good before and after photo, you know, before they're beaten to hell by their perils."

"Then what were the photographs on the ship for?"

"Practice," Cornelius said. There was an easy air about him this morning, which Watt was grateful for. He wasn't sure if he could handle prickly Cornelius today.

Watt straightened from the wall, extending a hand towards Cornelius. "Then you should have a before photo as well, yeah?"

Cornelius cleared his throat. "Oh. I suppose so."

He carefully handed off his camera to Watt, who inhaled upon gripping the cool metal and leather, and the subsequent brush of Cornelius' warm fingers. "It's already set for the light at the window," Cornelius said, pointing out the viewfinder and lever for the shutter. It wasn't an enormous box like the camera his family had, this one fit nicely in the hand, probably even more so when folded up. Now the red bellows were unfolded, supporting an extended lens.

Watt held the camera close to his abdomen and looked down to study the ridiculously tiny viewfinder. "Could you come forward? Into the rays of light there."

Cornelius shot him a look, but did as he was asked. Watt looked down into the viewfinder again, and caught the moment Cornelius' scowl transformed into secretive pleased amusement. He was skewed into an upside down perspective, but it was brilliant all the same.

Watt took the shot, and by the time the shutter clicked the expression was gone, replaced by his usual casual indifference. Cornelius took the camera, and his hands lingered for longer than seemed necessary to Watt, but he wasn't so quick to pull away either. Cornelius looked up at him, eyes full of something ... familiar, Watt thought.

It was only a few seconds in the grand scheme of things, nonetheless it was a moment suspended in time, one that Watt would turn over and over again in the weeks to come.

The camera slipped from beneath Watt's fingers, and Cornelius turned away. He tucked it away with the rest of his things and said, "We better get going. Senhor Antunes is probably waiting for us. And I'm starving, aren't you?"

"Yes," Watt said, and found he could say nothing else.

Senhor Severino Antunes was far more charming in person than on the telephone, and he and Cornelius got on like a brush fire. He was about the same height as Watt, barrel chested and dressed in a smart and well tailored suit that had Watt feeling worse for wear. He had a dark complexion with close cut inky hair, and thick eyebrows slanted over eyes warmer than amber stones. He appeared to be of a similar age as themselves, but when he spoke it was measured and thoughtful, the words of a man who'd seen plenty and learned even more. His handshake was firm, palms calloused, and his smile reached his eyes.

They ate dinner in the hotel's dining area, an expansive room that was well furnished but not extravagant. It didn't take long for Cornelius to start peppering the man with questions, ones he would already know the answers to if he'd properly read any of Watt's correspondence.

"So what exactly do you do, Senhor Antunes?" Cornelius asked after drinks had been served.

"Oh, the question should be what don't I do." Antunes chuckled heartily, then took a sip of his caipirinha. Watt and Cornelius had ordered the same by Antunes' recommendation, and Watt found the drink painfully sweet. He drank it anyway. "Until now I have been Joaquim's right hand and translator for the team, but with your arrival I am a guide now as well. Not that I mind, of course. Gives me a chance to visit home."

"And where is home for you now, senhor? You are from Portugal, yes?" Cornelius asked, absently spinning his glass on the table. It was full, and threatened to spill over onto Cornelius' fingers.

Antunes seemed pleased by this question. "Please, call me Severino."

Cornelius' accent thickened when he said, "Severino," and the sound of his voice was enough to kill a man. The way it rolled off his tongue, as if he were born and bred here. His eyes had darkened, reminding Watt of the glint of steel beneath a full moon.

Was ... no, surely Cornelius couldn't be. He had no idea who Antunes was, or if he was ... inverted? Was that the word? Was there a sign that Watt had missed? But Antunes did not seem to notice the lilt in Cornelius' tone and the hunger in his eyes. Watt wondered if perhaps his mind was putting a spin on things that did not exist, and he took a long pull from his drink.

Antunes said, "I met my wife at Coimbra, and followed her here. She has family whereas I do not, and I have come to love Brazil with the same passion she does. We have lived in Rio for a good number of years now."

"How romantic," Cornelius said wistfully. He tilted his head back and took a long drink, leaving mostly lime and ice behind.

"Do you not miss them?" Watt asked sharply, then blinked in surprise at his tone. He cleared his throat. "I apologize, that was too forward."

Antunes evaluated Watt for a moment before speaking, and when he did it was solemn. "I miss them with such ferocity it hurts, Senhor Johnson. But let me ask you this. Did your dear Colonel Fawcett not miss his family? Or our own Marshal Rondon? Or any of the other great explorers of our time, for that matter."

"I believe they did," Watt allowed.

Antunes sighed. "And yet we press forward, leaving those we love behind in order to achieve our own ambitions, for better or worse."

"And what is your ambition, Antunes?"

Antunes studied Watt for another long moment. When he spoke, it was with careful and genuine intent. "I wish for the world to see Brazil as I do. To see her as beautiful and full of life as I do, rich not only in history, but in people as well. People think of Brazil and her neighbors as a land lost to time, but this is not the case. We are on the cusp of a new era, one full of revelations and discovery, and I want to be at the forefront of it."

Watt couldn't help but think of Nina. Of all the women left behind to tend to the family while their husbands sought glory. "And what is your wife's ambition?"

He'd thought this question would've disarmed Antunes, but it made the other man smile, quick as a shot. "Are you under the impression wives and mothers cannot have ambitions? Tell me, have you heard of the Brazilian Federation for Women's Progress?"

Watt swallowed, trying very hard not to look at Cornelius. He'd already felt a fool for not studying more of the country's current issues, and here was more proof of it. "No, I have not."

"Ah," Antunes said. "Well I can assure you, it keeps Isabela plenty busy, and personally satisfied. She has no need for a man like me, all we do is get in the way. My children ..." Severino sighed, and he met Watt's eye. "I do regret the time I have not spent with them."

Watt begrudgingly awarded the man a point. He wondered if all Brazilians were so honest.

Cornelius abruptly asked, "And what do you think of the place?" Both men looked over at him. Cornelius cleared his throat. "The site, I mean."

Antunes grinned. "Are you asking what I think of

it, or if I believe it is the cidade?" He uttered this last word in a mere whisper, as if saying it any louder might tempt fate.

Cornelius lifted a shoulder. "Both?"

"The area is ... compelling, yes. There was most definitely a settlement there, but there is also ..." Severino hummed, tapping his clean shaven chin. "I cannot describe it. You have to see for yourself, yes?"

"Compelling in what way?" Watt asked.

Antunes fixed him with a contemplative look. He asked, "Have you ever stood in a place where you could *feel* history, Senhor Johnson?"

Watt nodded, throat dry.

"It feels like that."

Cornelius felt as though he'd been here before, and he couldn't put his finger on why. Rio was not Lima, or Bogotá, but its own inherently beautiful corner of the world. He stood at the window, leaning heavily against the wall as he smoked. Watt sat in his bed, reading with Maggie at his feet. He'd been largely quiet all night, save for his interrogation into Severino's motives during dinner. That was fine by Cornelius, who was marinating in the peace and quiet.

Rio had appeared domestic at first glance, but now that night had settled over her there was music and warm light in the streets. Cornelius fiercely wished they had come in time for his birthday during Carnival, but nevertheless was grateful for being able to set eyes upon the coastal city at all. The night felt endless and fleeting all at once, like sand slipping between the fingers.

"I have to admit something," Watt said.

"Hm?" Cornelius looked over his shoulder. Watt was tracing his finger over the book's edges.

Watt didn't look up when he said, "I'm nervous."

Cornelius finished his joint, contemplating what to say. He stubbed it in the ashtray and took a seat on the bed beside Watt's feet, leaving his good leg dangling over the edge. He'd only had the one drink at dinner, but was full of drunken emboldenment nonetheless. "You'd be a fool not to be."

Watt shyly glanced up at him, then back down to his book.

Cornelius waited for him to continue, but he didn't. "What're you afraid of?"

Watt said nothing, and Cornelius wasn't sure whether to keep pressing the issue. Watt had brought it up, after all. Maggie watched them from the other side of Watt's feet, ears pricked. Cornelius slowly reached over Watt, fingers wiggling in her direction. Maggie was still for only a second before bumping her nose against his fingers. Cornelius couldn't help but smile, feeling childish for not petting her sooner, and stupidly proud. She huffed against his knuckles, then scrubbed her forehead against his palm. He obliged her, gently petting with the grain of her fur. It was dense, and softer than he imagined. There were also far more grey hairs than he'd previously given her credit for. For the first time, he wondered how old she was.

"Do you know about the 77th Division?" Watt whispered.

Cornelius stilled. He wanted to say, *'of course I do.'*

Of course Cornelius had known that Watt was part of the Lost Battalion. That much he'd been able to glean from the man's letters, and not for the first time he felt a pang of guilt at having not answered them. To have survived such vicious bloodshed and come out on the other side with some semblance of self. It was a miracle. Especially considering many soldiers still fought, if only in the battlefield of their minds. And like Watt's commanding officer, many of them lost those battles. His death was simply more sensationalized, due to the drama of the 77th's ordeal, and the way he chose to go. Cornelius had previously wondered if Watt fought battles in his mind, too. Now he was quite sure the man did.

Instead Cornelius started to pet Maggie again and quietly said, "Yes."

Watt sighed, but it was more like a shudder. He was quiet for some time again before starting his tale in an even quieter whisper. "It was only four days, but Cornelius, it felt like four *years*. Hundreds of men died, deep in the woods and surrounded by the enemy. It was cold and miserable, nothing but bullets and explosions, mud and blood. Towards the end they even had flames and gas. That *damn* gas."

Watt cursed, shaking his head. "Laying there, slowly burning alive from the inside out, all I could think was why couldn't it have been a bullet? Something quick and personal, not—" Watt broke off abruptly and sniffed. Breath sawed in and out of his lungs. Cornelius was very careful not to look his way, unsure what to do other than listen. Men were fussy about tears, and Cornelius didn't want to interrupt Watt's truth.

"I'm sorry, I didn't mean to—the point is—I don't want to ...." He trailed off, sighing. "I don't know what I'm trying to say."

Cornelius understood, though. "If anything happens, I won't let you suffer."

Watt flinched beneath Cornelius' arm. When had he rested it across Watt's legs?

Cornelius looked up at him then. His eyes were wide and glassy, and Cornelius had a sudden urge to take his hand. He waited for Watt to speak again, but when it became clear he wouldn't, Cornelius said, "Don't worry. I'll make damn sure you're headed that way before making any rash decisions. And for what it's worth, I'm glad you made it home."

Watt stared at him, eyes searching. Always searching with such intent. Then he smiled, and a few tears escaped from his eyes in the process. He laughed a little and whispered, "Okay. Thanks."

For a moment Cornelius could see that young man

laying on the sands of Harbor Point, before life had its way with him. Hopeful and tentative. Ready for adventure, a promise freshly rolled off his tongue.

Cornelius nodded curtly. "Then it's settled. You'll leave me behind if needed, and I'll put you out of your misery if needed. Now, if you don't mind, we have a long day tomorrow and I'd like to turn in. What sweet dreams we'll have."

Watt's smile grew. "Alright, boss."

Cornelius looked at him incredulously. "I don't think so."

Watt shrugged. Cornelius got up to shut the lights off, and when he returned to his own bed Watt had already laid on his back and folded his hands over his stomach. The way he usually slept. His eyes shone in the moonlight, head turned as he watched Cornelius settle into a similar position.

"Good night, Cornelius," Watt murmured.

Unbidden, Cornelius' muscles began to relax, one by one and with great relief. "Good night, Watt," he whispered.

Watt's chest rose and fell with great effort, and not another word was said between them. There didn't need to be. Not when there was even and slow breathes, the rustle of fabric, and the call of the world outside their window.

C'mere Girl

"Do you think you could deal with me for the rest of our lives?"

Watt turned his head, blinking those calm eyes of his. Sand clung to his cheek, and the setting sun beat down upon a face caught between boy and man, transforming every dark eyelash into threads of gold. His hair used to shine, too. But his father forced him to cut the bronze treasure down to nothing a few days ago, transforming Watt into a civilized man in time for his birthday.

The day had gone well enough, but the relief that had come over Watt when Cornelius suggested they ditch the last few hours of Watt's own birthday party was strangely satisfying. There was a version of the boy that only Cornelius saw, and was only ever fully revealed at their spot on the point, right on the lake. And while on the outside Cornelius appeared to all the world a growing woman, he had started to learn he was no such thing. He was thinking of telling Watt, and nearly did right then. But he didn't have enough words, not for that, not just yet.

Distant and thin wheatgrass whispered beneath the wind's influence. Birds called from the open sky whilst their younglings cried from meticulous nests in trees that tossed and turned in the wind. The constraints of polite society were weightless in this place, and practically invisible when the friends were here, together. Sometimes Cornelius' siblings came and the other boys would swim or canoe, or simply lay on the sand and tell stories. On special occasions they'd have picnics, or eat what was left of their ice creams from Juilleret's. For now they were utterly, and blissfully, alone.

"Say what you mean, yeah?" Watt said, but not unkindly.

Cornelius' fingers dragged through the sand at his sides, and he struggled to keep his breathing cool. "They fought again last night, and ... Papa said he'd consider it. Sending me away."

Watt's nostrils flared, a magnificent show of surprise on his part. "He won't. He won't throw away your potential like that. I'm sure it was only to soothe her, he's said it before."

Cornelius chewed on the inside of his cheek before admitting a partial truth. "Something's different," he said, but really he wanted to say, to scream, that he was different. His body was changing, and with that exponential change was panic, which expressed itself in rebellion. As such, he had no one to blame but himself for this predicament. His Mama would only take so much, and this time she'd been pushed too far.

Cornelius carefully added, "He found out she was on the phone with Linden yesterday, and I thought—I thought he was going to give in. Allow Mama to arrange my future while I'm helpless to fight back, ship me off to that dreaded school so I can become a proper lady, an educated housewife. But they both love you, and I ..." He cleared his throat, delicately stepping over a sentiment they both knew existed

Watt's skin was tanned by the sun, but the flush in his cheeks was still evident from all the words Cornelius didn't say, and their gazes skittered away before hesitantly meeting once again. They had loved each other from the very first time they met. Cared for another. But as time went on, Cornelius knew the way he loved Watt wasn't the same way he loved his meddling Mama or indulgent Papa, or his siblings that were so unlike Cornelius it was as if they were born on different planets.

Watt stared at him, expression hopeful and eyes ever so fond, and in that moment Cornelius knew he felt the same way. The back of Watt's hand brushed against his knuckles, soft enough to be mistaken for sand but infinitely warmer. His strong, persistent attention gave Cornelius the strength he needed to ask him the biggest favor of their lives.

"I—we—could be free if we married," Cornelius

whispered. "Think of all the discoveries we could make together, and the places we could go. Nothing would have to change, it could just be you and me, like it's always been. It doesn't have to be—it can be an arrangement, Watt. You can do what you like ... be with who you like. Then there'll be no reason for me to go away, and I ... I just can't be what she wants me to be."

Watt inhaled sharply through his nose, turning his attention to the sky. Hot emotion built in Cornelius' throat in response to Watt's silence, and he closed his eyes in an attempt to keep stubborn, heated tears at bay.

It was a ridiculous thought. Watt was three years older, and had a lifetime of opportunities ahead of him. The reality of it was they lived in two different worlds, and only this transitive space and time that was summer in Michigan allowed them to co-exist. Besides, Watt's father would never allow his only son to marry someone so infamous as a laborer's child.

"Where would we go?" Watt whispered, entertaining the idea of them against the world, if only for a moment.

Cornelius couldn't help but smile, eyes closing and wind upon his cheeks. "Where wouldn't we?"

April 7th, 1930

When the men stepped out into the growing rays of sunlight, the world was remarkably quiet. Breakfast had been satisfying, and Watt hadn't slept so well in ... well, a long time. He felt better than he had last night, his melancholy temporarily swept away by curiosity. And he was not the only one in a good mood.

Antunes met them at the hotel first thing in the morning in order to fit in a full day of sightseeing. They were in what was called the Old City, and there was a great promenade along the water just nearby. They walked, passing by gallons of milk and loaves of bread on doorsteps, unbothered by thieves and whole. The sight was picturesque to Watt in a simple way, and he became entranced by the world as they moved through it. The extravagant reform in the last few decades was clearly visible, and he could see why it was called the 'city of decent people.' Watt had to agree with this sentiment, at least in the area they frequented.

According to Antunes, who gave a running commentary on the city and her limbs, the growing favelas that overlooked the coastal part of the city were full of decent people, too. They were simply lower working class, and 1930 had treated them as harshly here as it did in New York City, or anywhere else. They made do with what they had, cobbling sheets of metal and planks of wood into homes. The affair wasn't unlike the tenements in the City, but here they did not compete with snow for space.

He found it hard to look at them, given the distance and his heartache. They reminded him of France, but he had no idea why. There was no physical similarity between these cobbled together neighborhoods and the aftermath of desecrated villages. And while there were the typical sounds of a waking city, motor cars roaring to life and pleasant 'good mornings' bid in their direction, it was remarkably quiet. Nothing like screaming, shouting. No bullet fire, or—

"Watt?"

Watt blinked, then looked down at Cornelius's hand on his shoulder. His thick fingers gently dug into his muscles, and it forced Watt to focus. He glanced around, having lost track of himself for a moment. They were upon the beach now, Antunes had ventured a little ways ahead of them where the mosaic sidewalk gave way to sand. The ocean was right there, beautiful beneath the rising sun. There were a few people on the shore, but not many at this early hour. This beach wasn't as popular as their later destinations. There was nothing but sand, palms, road, globular street lamps, and buildings for a good distance in either direction. Birds stirred in the air overhead, making their way in from the fringes of nature surrounding the bay.

Cornelius' hand fell away from Watt's shoulder.

"Would you like to go back? You look terrible."

"I always look terrible. But no, I'm fine. Thank you."

Cornelius gave him a wry look. "You are far from terrible looking, Watt Johnson, and you know it." He tapped the ground with his cane dismissively, then turned away in a flourish and joined Antunes.

Watt's heart skipped a beat. He stroked a hand between Maggie's ears and recomposed himself before joining Cornelius and Antunes where the tide lapped against the sand. They had no parasol or blanket, but Watt didn't mind. He sat down a little ways back from the water's edge and heaved a great sigh, wrapping an arm around Maggie as she sat beside him. Cornelius and Antunes deposited their shoes and other personal belongings beside Watt, then rolled up their pant legs. Cornelius had dark hair on his legs, and Antunes did too. But it was starker on Cornelius, whose skin was much paler than Antunes' dark complexion.

"Could you hold onto these for me?" Cornelius asked, offering his cane, wallet, and camera directly to Watt.

Watt shook his head in mild disbelief, then nodded. "Yes." The camera was secured in its leather case, and he draped the strap around his neck. He took Cornelius' cane and laid it across his lap, drawing his knees up to his chest. Watt and Maggie sat together while the others stepped into the water. He didn't want to get wet right now, but he could see that Maggie did. He just wanted to sit. To be in one place for a moment. And he did feel better now, enough that he could be alone.

If only for a little while. Watt disentangled from her comfort. He raised his voice and said, "Cornelius, call her over."

Cornelius straightened from where he had been dipping his hands into the edges of the Southern Atlantic. He didn't hesitate before whistling and calling out, "Maggie, c'mere girl."

Maggie's eyes went wide, and her body tensed. She looked at Watt. He tilted his head towards the water and said, "Go get him."

Maggie took off like a shot. Ears tucked back against her head, she galloped until reaching the water's edge, then jumped clear over it. She landed between Cornelius and Antunes with a great splash, dousing the men who'd previously only been wet up to their knees. Watt laughed, and his companions did too. Maggie chased the water as it ebbed and flowed, then proved her worth as a swimmer. She chased after Severino, and Cornelius cheered her on.

Watt took out his book, and began to sketch.

He warmed up in the waves, the surrounding bay and rising sun. His sketches were loose yet detailed, and they grew in depth and subject as time went on. Pages filled with palms lining the beach and mosaic sidewalks, designs on nearly every block. Eventually he returned to the view directly before him, forming a more serious type of drawing.

A curved bay with sand stretching for over a mile in either direction. A good amount of time had passed, and parasols had been erected in the peripheral areas. The focus was two men silhouetted by the distant embrace of mountains and the mid-morning sun, playing in the water with the most loyal of canines.

He bit back a smile, reveling in the diminishing lead and growing picture. He became lost in his work, and was startled when Severino dropped on the sand beside him. His legs were wet and water splattered his shirt, but he wasn't too soaked.

"I must know her story," Severino said, grinning as he watched Cornelius and Maggie come out of the water. "She has a certain fire, no?"

Watt liked the sound of that. He rested a hand over the page he'd been working on. "I've always thought so. She's a stray. We sort of found each other one day and I ..." Watt shrugged. He didn't want to talk about this. "I couldn't leave her."

Antunes glanced sideways at him with an easy smile. "That's wonderful." He stared at Watt, and it seemed like there was something more he wanted to say. But Cornelius walked up to them with a sopping wet Maggie in tow, and the conversation broke.

He looked so happy, he and Maggie both. Her tongue hung out the side of her mouth, and her eyes were bright with a pup's spirit. She hadn't much of a chance to be a pup, like Watt she had been put to work at a young age. Also like Watt, she'd defied expectations and ran away from her masters. Watt wished he could heal as quickly as she did, but then again maybe she still thought about those days. Prior to Maggie he'd thought an animal was an animal, but the way she looked at him sometimes or helped him when he needed it most ... there was some humanity in that.

"I didn't expect to get so wet," Cornelius said, grinning. His delight brought Watt back to the present. On a beach in Brazil, with his colleagues and his best friend. Right now, it didn't matter how rough their start had been. Right now, everything was okay.

"You? Take a look at me," Antunes said, feigning despair.

Watt chuckled. "Joy finds us when we are least expecting it, wet or dry."

"Who said that?" Antunes asked.

Watt lifted a shoulder, closing his book in order to hide the blush plaguing his cheeks. "Me, I suppose."

"How true," Cornelius said.

Watt glanced up. Cornelius was smiling. That earnest smile made Watt's stomach lurch, which made no sense. He'd seen Cornelius smile plenty of times now. There was nothing new or different about it. But then Watt remembered he hadn't eaten yet today. That was the likely suspect.

He was hungry, that was all.

Before they left the beach, Watt slipped off his shoes and socks. He rolled his pant legs up and stepped into the water. It was cold, but not drastically so. He got far enough that the water licked at his calves, and stood there. Maggie joined his side, and she did not leave it.

Together, they enjoyed the water.

After dropping Maggie off at the hotel and excavating sand from their clothes, they called for a share taxi and rode past the two and a half mile stretch encompassing Copacabana Bay. The sand was filled with more people and parasols than the beach they'd visited before, bodies of all colors bared to the sun. They passed the magnificent and relatively new Copacabana Hotel, a glorious and decadent piece of architecture. Cornelius was glad they weren't staying there, it was far too ritzy and unfamiliar, but he was also wistful.

Like many buildings in Rio, there was a distinct French influence to it. It made him think of Dimitri and Gabriel, and his heart ached. He'd given everyone the address of the hotel in São Paulo, and he planned to send his letters then. The thought of Jimmy's sure to be scathing letter waiting for him was nerve wracking. He hadn't the courage to tell Jimmy on the phone that he was taking a surprise trip to South America with Watt Johnson. As they rode and Cornelius stared out the window, he imagined Jimmy's disbelief, and the resulting conversation.

'Yes Jimmy, I'm going to South America to search for a dead man with the same Watt whose father dislocated my shoulder and destroyed Papa's livelihood. No, I don't think he'll fuck me over. Why not?

Well I gave him permission to leave me behind. I probably won't make it back home, love you!'

Mama had been unsurprised when he'd called to let them know, considering she had been the one to direct Watt to Cornelius, and even less so that Cornelius had decided to go. Mama had spoken to Watt in February, he'd called on Cornelius' birthday of all days, Watt had asked for his old name and seemed to not know about Cornelius. She had left the 'conversation' and truth up to Cornelius himself, which is why she hadn't corrected Watt.

From the safety of his apartment, Cornelius had asked her, "Why did you tell him where I live?"

"I didn't tell him where you lived, I told him where he could find you."

"Did it not cross your mind he might've wanted to hurt me, Ma? Or that his family wanted to ruin our lives some more?"

"Honestly, dear. It's like you don't even know the boy. And you decided to go, didn't you?"

Papa had been ... quiet. He'd said, "Be careful, Cornelius. You still have your cane? Do you need another?"

"No, I'm good Papa. I'll be fine, thank you."

"Are you sure you need to go?"

Cornelius had breathed, and stared at the ceiling of Giovanni's living room. He'd said, "I feel like it's important."

Papa clicked his tongue. "Best get to it then, son."

"I will. Love you, Papa."

"We love you too. Be careful."

Cornelius sniffed. Maybe he'd send a batch before leaving Rio, write them up tonight. To Esther, Giovanni, Dimitri and Gabriel and so on. For as much as he struggled with people, he enjoyed being around them. Well, the genuine and authentic sort of people, at the very least. Cornelius glanced over at his companions beside him in the taxi. He thought Watt was asking Severino about architecture, but hadn't been paying attention to the details. It really didn't matter, get him talking about anything he liked and the man opened up like a morning glory, bashfulness aside. Cornelius felt Severino could be that sort of authentic person, and maybe Watt still was too. Hesitant optimism bloomed in Cornelius' gut, and he thought he just might let it grow. Perhaps this journey wouldn't be so bad after all.

They arrived at the foot of Corcovado Mountain. Cornelius' knee and calf cramped viciously when they departed the motorcar, and he fought the pain with gritted teeth. Together, they explored the Botanical Garden. Severino gave a quiet but informative tour as they walked, first down Barbosa Rodrigues Alley, an avenue flanked by over a hundred trees that had all sprouted from one ancestor. They were enormous and overwhelming, their mid-day shadows inescapable. Cornelius shivered when passing beneath the flitting columns of darkness.

Severino said, "The Gardens were first opened to the public in the early 1800s, it was originally designed by the royalty to acclimate and grow plants from overseas. But over time its purpose changed, and now we have this park full of Brazil's own wonderful flora and fauna, for all sorts of people to access."

Eventually they reached an intersection of sorts which beheld a beautiful, and enormous, cast iron fountain. It was more of a sculpture though, depicting the Greek muses of poetry, music, science, and art. There were multiple levels to it, and stone carved to look like rocks formed the base. Watt seemed to have an eye for all things art, but especially sculptures. Cornelius stood beside him and rested his hands on the railing, which surrounded the fountain.

"This is the Fountain of Muses, yes?" Watt asked.

"Chafariz das Musas, yes." Severino nodded, his smile approving. "Are you familiar with it?"

"A bit. It was brought to the Gardens in 95', crafted in England I believe."

"Impressive," Severino said, and went on despite the blush in Watt's cheeks. Perhaps he was oblivious, but Cornelius wasn't sure how he could be. "It was sculpted by Herbert W. Hogg, very beautiful work, but it lived in the gardens of a villa before coming here."

Watt nodded, but Cornelius strongly suspected that Watt had already known that.

After a little bit more admiration they began walking again, and Cornelius sidled up to Watt. "How did you know that? About the fountain?"

Watt hesitated. He said, "My mother collects artwork, she has a piece he did for the Walker Gallery. It was before my time, but growing up I always thought it was ... I don't know, I just liked it. So I keep up with some artists I like now and then." This last bit Watt said a bit defensively, and Cornelius elbowed him.

"Don't say that in the park too loud, might give a man a wrong idea," Cornelius teased, then immediately went red with regret, all the way to the tips of his ears.

Watt blinked in that slow way he did when he was processing. "Say what?"

Cornelius thanked the heavens Watt was clueless. He coughed and said, "Nothing. We better—uh—catch up with Severino. Come on."

Severino wasn't all that much ahead of them, but Watt didn't push the subject. Toucans flew between the trees and birds that reminded Cornelius of some type of quail ran through the brush. Marmosets with white tufted fur and black capuchins cried and barked, seeming to laugh at the humans as they walked past. There were ruins of an old gunpowder factory and sugar mill, and Cornelius desperately wanted to search them. But that wasn't in the plan.

And neither was visiting Christ the Redeemer. They could barely see the distant statue perched atop Corcovado's peak, shrouded in scaffolding and fog, it's back to them. "Do you know much about it?" Watt asked Severino, nodding to the statue.

Severino grinned. He seemed to know everything and anything, and loved to talk. He said, "In 1888, Princess

Isabel signed the Golden Law into effect while acting as regent while her father was traveling, effectively abolishing all forms of slavery in Brazil. They called her the Redemptress, and there was discussion of building a statue in her honor. Princess Isabel suggested an image of the Sacred Heart of Jesus instead, as he was the true redeemer, but the republic ended. Church and state were separated, so the idea was dropped. But In 1920, The Catholic Circle of Rio made another proposal for a great symbol to be constructed atop Corcovado, but something to bring Godliness back to Brazil. Through fundraising and donations, they got together the means to commission the statute. Construction started in 22', they plan to have it finished later this year, actually."

"And who did they commission?" Watt asked, staring up at the mountain. "What's it made from?"

"Concrete and soapstone. Heitor da Silva Costa designed the statue, and Paul Landowski sculpted the majority of it. Georghe Leonida crafted the last piece, the face. It's all made of pieces, you see. The head, the hands, and the torso. It's over 90 feet tall, not including the over 20 foot pedestal."

"The largest art deco statue in the world. Beautiful," Watt breathed. Cornelius found it hard to look at anything but Watt's face turned up in wonder.

O Progresso

April 9th, 1930

There wasn't much time between departing the hotel and boarding the train, and Cornelius was glad for it. His mind swam, and his heart was heavy. It was easier not to think if you were busy. Perhaps all the travel was catching up with him. The past few days, weeks even, had been enjoyable if mildly stressful. The other day at the beach was especially nice. Last night he and Watt had gone to bed early, both had spent the evening writing letters. Cornelius had gotten a decent amount of sleep, but Watt had dark circles beneath his eyes. He didn't seem worse for wear though, smiling when Cornelius gave him attention and making small talk without being prompted.

Severino met them outside the Estação Central do Brasil right on time, having spent yesterday and early this morning with his family. The station was generously sized with three lofty levels and dressed in the same stone architecture much of Rio offered, with many great arches across its face. There was a figure cast in bronze high above, standing astride a clock. A nude man with all the important bits covered by a draping of sorts, and in his right hand he held a shield across his chest, which depicted a locomotive. His left hand was raised, clutching ...

"Electricity," Severino murmured, smoking a cigarette beside Cornelius.

"Oh, I see now," Cornelius said, able to interpret the jagged, wiry construction in the man's hand as lightning bolts. His heart clenched with thoughts of Dimitri, who had always reminded Cornelius of lightning. He was passionate and confident, defiant and radiant just like the sculpture. Gabriel's opposite, to be sure. Gabriel was a quiet intellectual with a fondness for art, and the artist. Dimitri dabbled in watercolors and oils, men and women and everything in between. The pair had an interesting arrangement that involved partners coming and going into their relationship in different ways, although the core remained the same. They had taught Cornelius a great deal, and it had been an electrifying time.

"O Progresso," Watt said, a solid presence at Cornelius' other side. "Almeida Reis' work, yeah?" He asked Severino with a slight quirk of the mouth that said he already knew, and Cornelius shook his head fondly. He found Watt's lingering animosity amusing since Severino was the epitome of pleasantness, while Cornelius was the complete opposite and Watt tolerated him just fine.

Severino nodded, exhaling a plume of paper and tobacco. "Indeed, commissioned by his long time friend and director of the station at the time."

"Your family isn't seeing you off?" Watt asked, an abrupt change of subject.

"Oh no, we said our goodbyes already. I will not subject Isabela to the terror of children at the train station," Severino said, chuckling.

The smell of Severino's cigarette had Cornelius craving another. But Watt had stopped asking Cornelius for them, resorting to habitually smoking his pipe once a day, usually after dinner. So Cornelius had tried to limit his smoking to only a few times a day, for Watt's lungs sake. It hadn't been going so well. "Should we get going?" Cornelius said, prompting them to get a move on.

There was a mild hangup at the station regarding Maggie, but after some words from Severino the dog was allowed at Watt's side instead of holed up in the luggage car. Their luggage was attended to and they boarded the train in short order, despite how crowded the station was. They had a cabin to themselves, fit with two upholstered benches. The space was snug with three men and a dog, but not uncomfortable. The air coming in through the window was thick with smoke, heat, and chatter. When the train pulled away from the station, dust entered the equation as well.

Maggie did not like the train. As a result, she sat on the seat beside Watt, leaving Cornelius to sit beside

Severino. Cornelius liked the man well enough, but he didn't know him as well as he knew Watt. Regardless, they made conversation easily enough, having to talk somewhat loudly in order to be heard.

The ride to São Paulo was as boring as it was beautiful. They climbed the steep cliffs separating Rio de Janeiro from the rest of Brazil, and Severino pointed out where the construction on a new road was taking place, the Petropolis Road, which was predicted to be a far more efficient mode of travel than the train. Cornelius couldn't imagine cars having an easier time carving these mountainsides than trains, but figured the engineers knew best.

By the third day, Cornelius was starting to feel restricted. At least on the Eastern Prince there were places to retreat to, to hide and reset. But there was nowhere to go on the train, which was beautiful but too industrial for days on end. He tried to focus on the positives instead of the cabin walls shrinking with each passing day.

The food was good, and the company was pleasant. He and Watt had finally found their stride, able to behave as true colleagues with little awkwardness between them. Severino was a good addition, even if Watt hadn't fully warmed up to him yet. He wasn't rude to Severino, but withdrawn in a way that he wasn't with Cornelius, not anymore. He tried not to feel too smug about that.

The landscape was ever changing. Thick jungle

and curving tributaries, scrub country and marshland. They passed through tunnels that seemed to never end, and bridges that were impossibly tall. At one point Cornelius remarked on the astounding ingenuity of Brazilians, and Severino beamed with pleasure. There was a great patriotism that South Americans had, one that Cornelius had read about but never experienced. He'd never felt attached to his own country, a fact that he'd never admitted to anyone. Or to any other country he'd visited. It felt strangely selfish, and wrong. But there it was.

On the fifth day of their trip, there was an uncomfortable conversation.

"We are fairly certain the area was occupied by a Toltec era civilization, but there are some discrepancies that we are still investigating. I have a feeling we will be here for some years. It is a pity that you cannot stay," Severino said.

He'd been patient, Cornelius had to give him that much.

"I'm looking forward to seeing it," Watt said.

Cornelius met Severino's inquisitive gaze. "What do you know of our intentions, Severino?"

Severino flicked a glance at Watt, then to Cornelius. He said, "I know what Joaquim tells me. I know you are retracing Colonel Fawcett's steps, and searching for him. And if not him, the Enchanted City, where the lights never go out."

"You think it's a fool's errand," Cornelius said, shifting on the bench to get a better look at Severino beside him. "Does Joaquim feel the same?"

"Yes." Severino nodded. "I have told Watt this." He gestured to Watt, who watched them with great intent. When Cornelius caught the other man's eye, Watt dipped his chin. Not quite a nod, but affirmation enough. Cornelius wondered when they would've talked about it. While making arrangements, he supposed. Back when Cornelius was barely talking to Watt and making an ass out of himself. Still, he felt cut out somehow.

"And yet, Joaquim granted us permission. You're taking us there. Why?"

"I do not know what Joaquim is thinking, he did not tell me why he agreed to this deception. But I am telling you it is pointless to go any farther than the site, because that is where Fawcett disappeared. To go where he went is to disappear."

The word 'deception' stoked the fire inside Cornelius. He knew what they were doing was a lie, but he didn't like to be called out on it, not by a man he'd come to like. Severino didn't seem angry or to think less of them though, just ... confused, or pitying?

He darted a look at Watt. "Did you know about this?"

Watt shook his head, looking at Severino strangely. "You did not tell me that. How do you know?"

"I do not know for certain, but I believe it to be true. All these landmarks," he gestured to Watt, or presumably the map that Watt had been showing him that morning, "the stone tower, the waterfall. They are there, just to the north of the site. He was there, I'm sure of it."

"I made a promise, Severino," Watt said, and he sounded very tired. "I have to look for him, I can't say 'well that's far enough' based on a good feeling. I at least have to find something of his, something genuine, to bring back to his wife. I can't go back empty handed."

Severino lifted his hat and ran a hand through his hair, then replaced it. He said, "Do what you must, and I will do what I can to help. But this plan you have, with retracing the steps. Are you sure it is necessary?"

Cornelius frowned. "His path doesn't diverge from the one you have planned, does it?"

Severino hesitated. "No, except for the detour to the Galvão estancia, before the Post. I do not think that is necessary, do you?"

"Yes," Watt said. He did not elaborate, and the following silence was thicker than hell. Severino wrung his hands. Watt added, "Is that a problem?"

"We shall see," Severino muttered, and lit up a cigarette.

By the last day of their train ride, Cornelius felt distinctly unmoored. Melancholy saturated his senses and emotions like a fog, and he couldn't pinpoint why. It came upon him the same as it always had, no matter where he was or what he was doing. He'd spent so many years trying to outrun or ignore it, but all his efforts made no difference. He tried many times to understand where the sudden sadness intermingled with anger came from or why, to dig up his roots and search every inch for the black veins that pumped his being with foulness. If he could find where it originated, then he could cut it all out.

When all else failed, Cornelius usually turned to drinking. He'd been doing so well keeping his intake to a minimum, only partaking at dinner with Severino that first night in Rio. He'd been fine, more than fine even. Sure he was thirsty, but the itch beneath his skin was manageable, easy to suffocate with smoke (his attempts to limit his intake had failed) and conversation with his companions.

Tonight they'd be turning in fairly early, they didn't have time to sight see in São Paulo like they did in Rio. Tomorrow they'd visit the Butantan Institute, and the day after was for sending letters and picking up supplies. Besides Cuiabá, it would be the last major point to get anything they needed. Cornelius wanted to develop film and obtain more, and he was pretty sure Watt had his own errands to run. Severino had some business to conduct for Joaquim, and while Cornelius was disappointed they wouldn't be visiting the university here, he was glad for time to decompress.

Cornelius decided he would stay at the hotel instead

of going out for dinner tonight, eat in and enjoy a couple hours of solitude and drink by himself. It sounded depressing on the outside, and it probably was, but he wouldn't get carried away if he was by himself. He simply needed to recalibrate, and it'd be the last safe opportunity before he couldn't.

Cornelius felt giddy at the idea of a plan setting into place, but the relief was immediately eclipsed by shame. Normal people didn't act like this. Normal people ... talked to people when they weren't feeling well, right? They didn't schedule time for drinking alone in order to cope with a vague and choking sadness. Then again, Cornelius tried to think of anyone he knew willingly confessing vulnerability. Not many came up. Except for Watt, like when he'd spoken about his time overseas. Cornelius thought Watt would tell him anything, if he asked. He was an anomaly though, too open for his own good.

But was Cornelius being too harsh on himself?

He didn't know.

———◈———

April 9th, 1930

Cornelius wanted to be alone.

Truthfully, Watt wanted to be alone as well. He wanted to eat, and sleep. Everything was painfully quiet since departing the train, and his ears rang with the absence of chaos. The hotel was about ten minutes from the station via taxi, and was much nicer than the one they'd stayed at in Rio. While Severino secured their rooms, Cornelius smiled weakly at Watt in the lobby before announcing his plans to turn in early. Each man had his own room and bathroom, Watt's was situated between Cornelius and Antunes.

The thing was, Watt had been hoping to be alone *with* Cornelius.

A few hours after they settled into their rooms, Watt left Maggie dozing on the bed and quietly knocked on Cornelius' door. It was long after supper and Watt had changed into sleeping clothes, he didn't think much of his attire until Cornelius opened the door. He was still dressed in his traveling clothes, the top few buttons of his shirt were undone and suspenders hung loose off his shoulders. His hair was a mess, sticking up in all directions. His face was flush, and his eyes were surprisingly hard. Despite his cold expression, Cornelius hoarsely asked, "What's wrong?"

Watt's heart stuttered. "Nothing, nothing's wrong. I—" He cleared his throat. "Could I come in?"

Cornelius lifted a brow, and for a moment Watt thought he'd be denied. Had he done something wrong?

Cornelius motioned for Watt to come in, and when he took a step back the movement was jerky and stiff. "It's a bit smoky in here, just to warn you."

And so it was. Smoke veiled the ceiling in layers,

a bluish black haze that swirled as they disturbed it. There were two ashtrays full of ash and cigarette butts, one on the coffee table and one on the dresser. Rings decorated the furniture, and Watt traced their origins to a half full glass of whiskey. A bottle sat on the coffee table, also half full. More disturbing than the drink or smoke were the papers. On the floor, on the tables and chairs. Some were crumpled into piles, some were trampled on and caught in the crossfire of what looked to be an intense pacing session. Others were simply laying about, half filled with words. It looked like something from a mystery novel. Watt stood in the entryway and stared, unsure what to do.

"Fuck. Donnez-moi un moment." Cornelius snapped, and abruptly began snatching up sheets of paper like they were nothing. It was like watching a thundercloud move through the room, and Watt couldn't stand it. He started forward, taking Cornelius by the wrist. No thought entered the movement, and when his mind caught up to his body he immediately let go. Cornelius glowered at him, brows set in a hard line and lips pressed thin. He lowered the arm once caught in Watt's grasp, balling his hands into fists.

"You're ruining it," Watt whispered.

Cornelius reared back, stricken. His hands opened spasmodically, and papers fluttered to the ground. His lip trembled, and his bloodshot eyes filled with something like rage. They were so blue, the water building in them magnified the pigment tenfold. Watt braced for the incoming hit by closing his eyes. He thought, *'Go on, I can take it.'*

It wasn't a hit so much as a body slam.

Cornelius' arms slid around his middle, cinching tight around his rib cage. His face scrubbed against Watt's sternum, throwing his glasses to the floor. Watt caught them before they hit the ground, and reflexively hugged Cornelius back. The fierceness of Cornelius' embrace was at once familiar and all encompassing. Watt's arms encircled Cornelius' shoulders, and he held the man with all the strength he had, doing his best to ground him to the earth. He held Cornelius for the longest time, basking in his warmth.

"Do you want to talk about it?"

Cornelius shook his head, rubbing his nose back and forth against Watt's chest. His sleep shirt was thin, and wet with Cornelius' tears.

Watt swallowed, trying for courage. "Listen. Could I stay here for a little while? We don't need to talk, and you don't need to stop what you're doing. I just needed some quiet company, and ... maybe you do too?"

Cornelius stiffened for a tenuous second, then relaxed and nodded. He pulled away and wiped roughly at his eyes with his sleeve, and Watt pretended not to pay attention. Cornelius glanced up at him, face flushed. "Okay," he said, and whiskey perfumed the air between them.

The bed was the only place not covered in papers, so Watt sat on the edge of the mattress. Cornelius offered him a drink, and Watt took it. Cornelius did not sit on the bed, still rigid and restless. He stood beside Watt and lit up a joint, frowning at the mess he'd created. Watt took a sip of the whiskey which was warm and frankly, terrible. He lifted a hand towards the stick and Cornelius lifted an eyebrow. "It's not tobacco, you know."

"I can smell that."

Cornelius passed it over without further argument. Watt inhaled the thick smoke derived from earth and paper, it was drier than hell and burned going down. He coughed and handed it back over. "Have you had that since New York?"

Cornelius took a hit, lifting his shoulder as he did so. On the exhale he said, "Philly actually, but yes."

Watt shook his head. "Nothing if not prepared."

Cornelius said nothing. He offered the joint back to Watt, and they shared it in silence. A syrupy warmth spread throughout Watt's body, and his mind slowed. The thing was it didn't feel slow, but more like what he supposed normal to feel like. He was able to examine each thought before it fled away, and his anxieties were slippery, unable to take firm hold. He simply existed within himself, content to do so.

Cornelius butted the joint and slid onto the floor, his back propped against the bed. If Watt moved his leg a little he could bump against the man's side. Cornelius said, "It helps."

"With your leg?"

"That too."

"Me too. I think." Watt nodded. He took a sip of his whiskey, then decided to give up on it. It was making his stomach sick, and he felt pleasant enough already. Cornelius was playing with his glass, slowly turning it in place on the floor. He said, "I'm a drunk, you know."

Watt rolled the words over in his mind, thinking about their time together. Cornelius didn't seem like a drunk. He'd hardly consumed any alcohol in their time together. Three times that Watt could remember, and it'd been over a month now. He didn't know what to say.

Cornelius went on, quieter than before. "I'd been arguing with myself all day whether to settle in and drink alone, or go with you and Severino. By the time I got to my room I had myself all worked up, proud as a peacock. I decided to eat dinner with you, instead of being alone."

Cornelius deliberately tipped his glass and spilled his drink onto the floor. They both watched the amber liquid spread across the wood. Whiskey met paper, soaking into the fibers and intermingling with the ink. "But I had a feeling I needed to check the mail first. It couldn't wait." Cornelius sighed, drawing the air from deep within. "And in the stack of letters waiting for me was one from Mama."

"Is she—?" Watt began to ask in a whisper, but Cornelius threw his glass at the wall. Watt startled at the deafening impact, half rising from the bed to brace himself.

"Papa's dead," Cornelius hissed, then buried his head in his hands and tore at his hair. His shoulders heaved, and he began to weep. Enormous, brutal sobs that tore Watt's heart right out of his chest. Watt slunk onto the floor beside Cornelius and embraced him for the second time that night, holding the man while he grieved.

He'd never seen Cornelius cry before. Not as children or otherwise. The man always seemed so unshakable, too stubborn for anything like tears. When they were younger Cornelius had idolized his father, followed him around everywhere, which in turn meant that Watt did too. Watt had always been envious of their relationship. In truth, he'd never known that fathers were supposed to treat their children with anything other than indifference at best and brutal punishment at worst.

Cornelius' father hugged his children. He spoke to them, kind and stoic and gentle. He asked his wife and children about their day, and Watt's too. He'd taken Watt under his wing, taught him how to shoot a gun and paddle on the lake. Most importantly, he taught him what a father could be. Ought to be.

Watt sniffed, and Cornelius lifted his eyes to Watt's. "Are you alright?"

Watt shook his head. "Yes, sorry. I just ... he was a good man."

Surprisingly, Cornelius smiled a little. "He always did like you."

"I don't think there's anyone he didn't like."

Cornelius was quiet for a minute. Then he said, "He

did break your father's nose, you know."

Watt swallowed, arms flexing around Cornelius who had tensed up again. Oh, he was still holding him. Was he supposed to let go now?

"Could you ... I understand if you don't want to, but could you ... tell me?"

Cornelius had already started shaking his head when Watt began to speak. "No. Forget I said anything."

"Cornelius, I—"

Cornelius pushed away from him, staggering to his feet. "No. I don't want to talk about this right now," he whispered, bracing himself against the wall. He held a hand to his forehead, decidedly not looking at Watt.

Watt stared at him, feeling bereft, cold, and idiotic. Why the hell had he thought now was a good time to talk about this? Cornelius had brought it up, but it was clear the man was not in a good state of mind. Belatedly, he got to his feet. "I'm sorry, I shouldn't have—"

Cornelius' hand fell from his forehead to cover the rest of his face. "Just please go, Watt. I want to be alone now. Actually alone."

Watt's hands flexed at his sides, and his left one cramped and spasmed painfully for a fleeting moment. He shook off the feeling, then started towards the door. He paused at the entry and said, "If you need me, don't be afraid to knock."

Cornelius' hand fell away from his face and he nodded. "Thanks."

Watt closed the door between them.

He returned to his room, and only when night began to twist into morning did he fall into a fitful sleep. He willed his mind to dream of memories he'd long forgotten, but all was darkness.

As Intended

April 10th, 1930

Watt listened to Cornelius and Antunes talk, their conversation shifting from Brazil and her decades long transformation, to the Institute. They chatted about snakes and the exponential growth of antivenin research, and everything in between. There had been so much damn talking from the moment they met up for breakfast, that Watt had barely gotten a word in with Cornelius, to check in with him or otherwise. He looked tired as hell, but otherwise acted like his usual self. One would never know the type of night he'd had.

"And what about you?"

Watt tore his attention from the passing landscape out the window and blinked at Antunes. "What?"

"Are you familiar with snakes?" Antunes asked. He smiled and his dark eyes were warm, but it all had the opposite intended effect.

Watt shifted in his seat, doing his best to dislodge his irritation. "Ah, yes. Cobras and horned vipers mostly."

"A snake is a snake, the only difference is how they

like to take their prey," Antunes said.

Cornelius opened his mouth, but then the car turned onto the drive and the Institute was in view. The building was enormous, all white with tall rectangular windows and intricate stone carvings along the rooftop. The words *'INSTITUO BUTANTAN'* were carved across the front of the building, and as they approached it became clear just how large the building was. It seemed to loom over them, even taller than the decorative palm trees standing vigil outside. The lawn was meticulously cared for and several ferns decorated the place along with some short hedges and other nicely trimmed vegetation.

'Sterile for a lawn,' Watt thought.

They were deposited onto a stone and dirt drive. Cornelius wielded his cane and walked at a leisurely pace, taking in their surroundings. Watt kept close to his side, hands in his pockets as he studied the establishment. Antunes did not seem to be in an exceptional hurry, but he did eventually lead them into the facility. It had a punctual air about it, very clean and filled with people dressed in white jackets who kindly bid them good morning. They met with the director, an older man who only spoke Portuguese. The ensuing conversation, relayed and translated by Antunes, regarding what type of snakes they may encounter had Watt feeling a bit queasy. Cornelius on the other hand appeared unbothered, which made Watt suspect that he was actually very bothered indeed.

"Would you like to see how the antivenin is made?" Antunes asked, glancing between Watt and Cornelius. "It is not required, but they have offered."

Cornelius stiffened at the question, then glanced over at Watt. His eyes were wide, and his lips set in a bloodless line. Watt felt it would be rude to say no, and education was gold. He inclined his head to Cornelius in an 'up to you' sort of way.

Cornelius nodded curtly. He shifted his attention to the others and said, "That would be fine."

Watt followed behind everyone else as they were led outside to where the majority of the snakes were kept, feeling like he'd done something wrong. Again. He could brood on it later, for now he tried his best to pay attention. There were palms everywhere, along with a variety of prim and proper plants. A tall stone wall with short metal fencing atop it surrounded a large area, which was further sectioned off into small pens with waist height stone walls. The grass in the pens was neatly manicured, furnished with stone mounds that had small arches for snakes to pass through, the surfaces of which were covered in growing grass. Pathways connected each mound, as if snakes cared for such things, and little saplings further decorated the area. Big fancy white signs accompanied the area, and Watt couldn't read much of it besides the *'serpentario'* bit. He figured that it had something to do with snakes.

He asked Cornelius about it, and after a moment of squinting at the sign Cornelius whispered, "Don't throw any objects into the serpentarium."

Close enough.

One of the scientists used a long pole that had a hook on the end to ferret a snake out of one of the mounds, then pressed the curve of the hook to the base of the snake's head before scooping it up with practiced ease, fingers secured where the hook once had been. The snake curled and writhed immediately, thrashing its body this way and that.

It was downright pissed off, and for good reason. The scientist wasn't harsh, but he wasn't kind either. Yes, it was a snake, but still. Watt shifted in place, and noticed that Cornelius had taken a step behind him. He could still see the snake, but had room to hide if necessary.

Watt made a mental note to keep an eye on Cornelius for the rest of this endeavor. The man was too stubborn to say enough was enough.

Cornelius was sickly fascinated by the drops of venom as they rained down like tears from a perfect set of extended fangs. Only a few drops of the stuff had been enough to completely change the course of his life, and nearly end it. It seemed impossible that something which appeared so much like water could be so deadly. His fingers ached from where they curled around his cane, but he couldn't relax his grip no matter how hard he tried. His leg had been in a flare up due to all the traveling, and the stress didn't help.

After the venom was milked, it had to be processed. They were shown vials of previously processed venom, then the scientists brought them outside for another demonstration. There was a sort of makeshift stall outside, square in shape and accompanied by horse shit. A thin horse with a dull coat was brought out from the nearby stables, and it balked upon reaching the stall. It refused to go in, clearly familiar with whatever came next. It threw its head, and the whites of its eyes showed as it chuffed and complained.

Two men forced it into compliance. The one leading the horse stood on the opposite end of the stall and pulled on the rope while the other swung a crop, skimming the horse's gaunt flank but not making hard contact. It took a couple of minutes and ultimately the use of a twitch to get the horse into position, and by then Cornelius' teeth were set firmly on edge. He leaned hard against his cane, folding one hand over the other.

"Doesn't that hurt the horse?" Watt asked Severino, nodding to the twitch snugged around the horse's upper lip. Watt was tense too, standing close enough to Cornelius that his presence was palpable.

"No, not on the lip. If it were the ear, yes. But the pressure provides a sort of calming effect. See?" Severino pointed to the horse, its head had drooped into the arms of the man holding its lead. The scientists were preparing the great muscles of its neck with iodine, and it reminded Cornelius of days caring for his own wounds.

"It all seems—" Watt flinched, watching as a metal catheter was promptly jammed into the appropriate place on the horse's neck. It shuddered, but otherwise did not move as the humans injected it with venom. It stood there as they poisoned it, and they stood by and watched. Cornelius' guts turned, his hangover unrelenting in the face of such ... medicine.

The scientists began talking and Severino translated, which was just as well because Cornelius' brain felt slow as he watched the process, his own translating skills useless. They explained that the horse would be monitored for a few days, and if there were positive results its blood would be withdrawn and processed, separated into its basest components where the prized antibodies were hiding. This is what the antivenin would be made from.

Cornelius glanced at Watt, wondering why he kept brushing against his arm. Then Cornelius realized that it was the other around, that he was swaying a little. But Watt did not try to steady him or ask if he was alright, at least not aloud. He looked down at Cornelius, face drawn and a question in his eyes.

All morning he'd been staring at Cornelius, quietly concerned. Cornelius had felt too embarrassed to try and set things right, and apparently Watt wasn't going to let last night slip by undiscussed. Rationally, Cornelius knew a conversation was due between them. For now, Cornelius gave him a short nod and a grim smile, then turned his attention back to the scene at hand.

The needle had been removed from the horse's neck, and all that remained was a bubble of fluid beneath the skin. In English, Cornelius asked why they used horses. Severino relayed the question to the scientist, who gave a long reply in Portuguese that Cornelius only caught half of.

Severino said, "They handle the venom remarkably well, and have a better metabolism than cows. The short term effects to the animal are fairly minor."

"And the long term effects?" Watt asked, watching the horse as it was led away to a nearby area with a hose. The scientist explained that a chronic inflammatory response could develop, or renal failure. If he or Severino could tell Cornelius or Watt were discomforted, it did not show on their faces.

The men began to wash the animal down and groom it, which made Cornelius feel a little better. His stomach was still knotted though, and he felt like he'd taken that needle in his own neck. Thankfully they would not be witnessing the exsanguination process, and were led back inside.

Next was a room full of microscopes and women dressed in smart uniforms. There was so much white, and so much glass. Cornelius was keenly aware of his own body, and tried very hard not to touch anything. The scientist gave them a small lecture, and Severino once again translated. "Their job is to process the blood taken from the envemonated animal, and create an immunobiological solution to counteract and neutralize the effects. This solution, the antivenin, is then tested. We will go there now."

It was time to witness the testing of the bothrops antivenin.

In another room, a pigeon was secured within a birdcage. Cornelius stood close to Watt as the pigeon was injected with venom, trying not to remember stepping in the wrong place at the wrong time. The haunting howl that had preceded the fiery bite, processed by Cornelius seconds too late.

The scientists began the clock, waiting for the venom to take hold/Mason killed the snake and discarded it quickly, then began first aid and called for a runner to send for help.

After about a quarter of an hour, the pigeon began to stumble and thrash, fighting the venom running through its veins/Cornelius shook with adrenaline, but soon the shaking became violent as his body fought the invader with everything it had.

Cornelius flinched when it fell against the side of the cage, then got back up and tried to fly/Mason and the others carried Cornelius back to camp where people had gathered to help but then it all faded into pain and fire and howling darkness.

Watt squeezed Cornelius' hand. It was quick and hard and discreet, more than enough to draw Cornelius from his past. Cornelius inhaled deeply through his nose, keeping his eyes on the fumbling pigeon as the scientists quickly administered the antivenin, needle sneaking between the bars.

They watched, each minute agonizingly slow, as the pigeon began to calm down. The scientists worked, diligently checking and documenting and moving too fast for Cornelius to comprehend. They announced that the antivenin was working as intended thus far, and the animal would be watched closely for the next few days. Cornelius swayed in place again, and this time when his arm brushed against Watt's he pushed against it, against *him.*

Watt pushed back, steadying Cornelius. The moment didn't last longer than the blink of an eye. And yet it felt like hours were contained within that precious second of reassurance.

The visit took up the rest of their day, but they secured several ampules of antivenin for themselves in addition to a small batch to deliver to the site. When they left, Cornelius stopped to take a photo. He stood on the drive, searching the beautiful architecture and pretty landscaping for a good shot. He decided on the building and was fidgeting with the settings for the camera when Watt asked, "Could I take your photo?"

Cornelius looked up, surprised. "What?"

Watt lifted a shoulder, glancing between him and the Institute. Quietly, he said, "It's kind of a fuck you to the universe, isn't it? Being here, I mean. Like standing on top of a mountain that's tried to crush you the entire way up."

Cornelius laughed, the sound harsh and braying. He slapped a hand over his mouth, eyes wide. He lowered his hand and whispered, "Watt Johnson, did you really just curse?"

Watt's eyes lit with amusement, and he grinned. He looked so damn handsome just then, and Cornelius was helpless to do anything but give him the camera. He adjusted his hat and stood with his back to the Institute, one hand in his pocket and the other curled around the top of his cane.

Cornelius tried not to smile as he looked into the camera, and wasn't entirely sure he succeeded.

———◆———

My Dear,

What an adventure you're having, and it's hardly even begun! I'm nearly jealous, but I've had an adventure of my own since you left. I met someone at Grand Central, one thing led to another and we both realized we didn't have any pressing engagements, so we took a train. Where to, you may ask?

Well, everywhere. We rode for days, hopping from one route to another without a care in the world. It was the most exhilarating and spontaneous thing I've ever done, and I'm sure I can hear your distress now. But truly Cornelius, it ... it woke me up. I've never been happier.

We're back in Philly now, and I think we'll stay here for awhile. He loves the place, and me, I think. Oh, Cornelius. I do not say this to hurt you, but I never thought I'd love another. It's quite the feeling, loving again, and I hope you feel it again one day too. Maybe there's a chance of it where you are now, even.

There's a few letters here for you, I'll be sending them along with my own. One's from your family, and the other two are from your usual correspondents. We are looking forward to hearing about your next adventure, please write soon.

G

Cornelius smoothed out Giovanni's undated letter, frowning at the damage it had incurred in last night's tantrum. He couldn't even remember how his letters and papers had gotten into such a state. He'd returned from picking up his mail from the concierge, a stack that had initially elated him. He'd told everyone where he was going to be, but he didn't expect so many people to write. He'd opened Giovanni's first, and then Mama's. Everything afterwards was ... hazy. Including the phone call back home.

What an idiot he'd been, a foolish drunk. But really, what else did an alcoholic do after hearing their Papa died?

They sat and drank, trying to figure out what the last words had been between them.

They sat and drank, wondering where they'd buried him.

They sat and drank, writing ten different letters of resignation from this whole endeavor.

Before Watt came, Cornelius had fully worked himself into the idea of going home. Being with Mama, his family. He hadn't been home since he left for France, and how frail was Mama now? Cornelius had always envisioned Papa the way he was when he left, but he knew that couldn't be the case.

But then Watt had came to his door and asked for company. And just like that, the spell had broke. Cornelius couldn't go home. Not now. He'd go after this was all done. He'd call Mama again tonight, and as often as he could before phones were no longer an option. She would be pleased to hear he decided to stay; she hadn't been happy when he'd floated the idea of abandoning his responsibilities.

Cornelius sighed, and began to write. To Gabriel and Dimitri, to Mateo, to his siblings and to Giovanni. He acutely felt these were his last words, which was ridiculous. He'd be able to send another fleet of letters in Cuiabá, and perhaps even more from Bacairy Post. But this was the last time he'd be able to write freely, taking his time to get everything that he wanted down onto paper.

He stayed up well into the night, beginning each letter with similar content. How his voyage had been, what the weather and region was like. The food, the beach, and Watt. That his partnership was going well, that *everything* was going well. He set aside certain photos that he'd developed and wanted those at home to have.

He told Giovanni that he was happy for him, and to take a train and visit Mama for him, if he had the time.

He told Gabriel and Dimitri that he was envious of their new residence, a little cottage tucked into the woods like a damn fairy tale, and to give the recovering Lili his best.

He thanked his Peruvian friend, Mateo, for all his hard work these past few months, all the research and letters full of information he sent to acquaint Cornelius with South America's current affairs, particularly those of Brazil.

He told Mama that he loved her, and that he was sorry he couldn't be there to bury Papa. He asked her to pass on his love to the others, and ended the letter promising to write again as soon as he could.

There was one sibling who did not live at home, and Jimmy was the one Cornelius needed to speak with the most. He should've called him before, tried to meet up with him in the City or something, and regret curdled his gut. Especially when reading the letter he'd sent in response to Cornelius'. It was full of concern, of confusion and demands that Cornelius explain himself. Was he safe? Was Watt dangerous? Had he tried to blackmail Cornelius? Honestly, becoming a father had turned his worrying streak into something fierce.

Cornelius hoped the news of his patching things up with Watt would comfort Jimmy the way he'd comforted Cornelius all the time ago. To know that Watt hadn't meant to leave them behind, and that he turned out okay. That he was in fact, a good man. Cornelius had enclosed pictures in most of the letters, but he sent his most personal ones to Jimmy with a request to keep them safe, and a soft warning that he'd be sending along more.

And when it was all said and done, he didn't tell anyone that his heart had broken tonight.

That he would give anything to see Papa one last time.

To tell *him* goodbye.

How Typical

April 18th, 1930

Watt was not having the time of his life.

Cornelius, on the other hand, hadn't felt so alive in days.

Yes, the steamer was crowded and dirty. Yes, the ship exhumed an ungodly amount of smoke. Yes, crocodiles lazily swam below and birds chattered endlessly above.

But there were crocodiles and birds. Screaming monkeys and carnivorous fish. There was such fierce *life* all around them, and Cornelius was at once exhilarated and overwhelmed. He didn't realize how much he'd missed this, how bored he'd been back in Philly. And all the ceaseless noise did wonders for his grief stricken thoughts and dehydrated cravings.

Cornelius gripped the edge of the boat, imagining that he was in a separate place from the too-close people that were so loud, like they were part of a background and he was on a different layer. There were no secrets with all the shouting, half of which were complaints. He mentally counted playas, categorizing them based on whether they held people, animals, or nothing at all. He marked down in his personal note-book every species of animal he recognized. He also noted the landscape at each dawn and dusk with a quick sketch of words. Anything to keep him busy. Engaged. Part of the world outside the boat.

Watt was nervous, not that he'd said so. He'd uttered hardly more than two words since departing Corumba (or since *that* night) and was stiff as a pole, alternating between standing at ease when the current was calm, and gripping anything permanent fixed to the boat for dear life when it wasn't. The three of them stood at the railing together, watching the river and all it entailed.

Maggie was not a fan of the people, but she didn't mind the boat. Everyone wanted to pet her, and she tolerated it like a martyr. Now she was engaged in what Cornelius had come to think of as her 'working' mode. There wasn't much to it, on the surface. Maggie sat at Watt's left, and Cornelius stood at his right. Air coursed in and out of Watt's broad chest in short and shallow bursts, and while he was standing at ease he looked anything but easy. He'd been wound up tighter than a spring since arriving in Brazil, and Cornelius didn't know how to help. It was like the man was convinced they were marching to their certain death, which to be fair Watt might be right. But he also might be wrong.

It didn't help the situation that until now Cornelius had been just as tense. Back in São Paulo they'd done their errands, mailed letters and obtained supplies. They ate meals together, but otherwise the trio recuperated socially, so to speak. Corumba had been just another stop in the trip for them, a short rail ride away from São Paulo and just as quiet. They'd kept to themselves, and even Severino was more subdued than he had been in the beginning of their journey. Cornelius thought maybe he was missing home already. Cornelius had developed film and bought more, sent most of his photos with his letters. He kept the photos of Watt for himself, though. Along with a few others.

Watt. Damn, what was Cornelius going to do about him?

Nothing had been said between them about that night, not about Papa dying or Cornelius' ridiculous and drunken behavior. It was that awkward and pleasant fake professionalism between them again, and he hated it. Had he really craved it only a couple of months ago?

An odd feeling crept over Cornelius, a sense of timelessness. How long had they been traveling together now? At first he thought it was only a couple of weeks, but no. Two months?

No. No, it'd only been a few twenty days or so, give or take.

It felt like nothing at all, and like they'd should've arrived at their destination a decade ago.

Cornelius found it difficult to balance, and he told himself that was the reason he leaned against Watt's right side. Watt returned the pressure without preamble, in fact he seemed comforted by it. His ribs flared against Cornelius' side as the other man sucked in air long and slow, and his breath evened out after a few more deep inhalations.

Cornelius, for his part, found it a bit more difficult to breathe. Watt's body was warm beneath fabric damp with sweat, and Cornelius' left hand twitched. He thought about putting his hand on the small of Watt's back, or perhaps his shoulder. The boat was packed enough that no one would think anything of it. Just two colleagues using the other to stay upright.

Cornelius slid his hand across the span of Watt's shoulders and rested a hand on the space between neck and shoulder. Eyes on the river, Cornelius lightly asked, "Do you remember that time we borrowed the canoe from Juillerets?"

A silence ensued. Watt didn't look over at him, but his body moved beneath Cornelius' hand. Closer. He said, "I think the word you're looking for is stole, but yes."

Cornelius chuckled. "We brought it back."

"We did." Watt allowed, humor warming his voice. He glanced at Cornelius then, who returned the attention. "Are they still open?"

"As far as I know." Cornelius thought about the little store, the candy he traded with his siblings and Watt, and the ice cream cones they let melt for too long. He could distinctly remember the chocolate ice cream smeared across Watt's face on that day, his grin so widespread that it had brought out Cornelius' own smile.

They'd carried the canoe out to the beach together, and weren't caught until hours later when they brought it back to Juillerets, where Papa was waiting. They'd flipped once or twice, and as a result were soaking wet. Papa handled their trouble the same way he always did. With a stern lecture ensuring that we righted whoever we wronged, and that we apologized. Cornelius had been in trouble with Mama later, for swimming unsupervised with a boy. It was the first summer Cornelius had been allowed to swim at all.

Papa wasn't a brute, but by the way Watt flinched in his presence you would've thought so. The lecture Cornelius had earned that day was well worth it. Large bits of his childhood and even teenage memories were blurry on the edges, and there were even chunks of time he'd forgotten all together. But that smile Watt had given Cornelius, with the lake and sun behind him, the canoe's rope in hand and chocolate on his face.

That might've been the moment Cornelius fell in love with him, even if he'd no idea what that meant at the time.

The question was, did he still?

Cornelius shook his head minutely, feeling like he'd been slapped. What the hell did that matter? What was he *thinking*?

"Are you trying to say we'll make it back to shore?"

Watt asked.

Cornelius smiled. "Yes. We'll make it back to shore."

That was all he was trying to say.

Watt had to concede that the voyage had its perks. The food was infinitely better than the decadence of the Eastern Prince, and endless despite the three dozen or so people aboard the ship. There was goiabada, a sweet and pasty guava conserve that Watt could only eat small amounts of at a time, and meals were usually a mixture of rice, beans, and chicken with macaroni mixed in sometimes as well. There was always bread and cheese, and black coffee. The stuff was potent enough to punch Watt in the gut with every sip, and despite how much he loved the strong brew he found he could drink very little.

He'd fought his stomach the entire trip, but the first day on that steamer had been the worst. Of course Cornelius and Severino appeared unbothered, although Cornelius did seem to be smoking more tobacco cigarettes than usual. But Watt didn't think that had anything to do with the churning São Lourenço, and everything to do with the trip that lay ahead and the news of his father. Cornelius spoke in his excited professor tone more than usual, and at such speed that it made Watt's head spin. He wondered if he should slow the man down before he had a fit or something.

Cornelius told Watt about everything.

He ranted about the crocodiles, giving a lecture about the difference between them and alligators. On the third day, a few of the passengers had taken shots at the reptiles, but they all missed. Watt was pleased by this, and Cornelius wore a smug little grin too. Watt would shoot one if he was in danger, but the idea of shooting such an ancient creature from the relative safety of a boat seemed so absurd, and entirely human.

Cornelius delighted in the macaws, always quick to point out the blue and yellow streaks across the sky. The birds were always there, the river boasted everything from kingfishers to finches, cormorants and ducks, toucans, woodpeckers and cardinals. Watt had a hard time keeping track of them all, but he did keep an eye out for a harpy eagle. He'd read about them once and as a young man who was fascinated by Greek myths, he found them intriguing. So far, they eluded him.

Watt was thankful for the distractions, even if he couldn't talk about things a little more important than the passing world. How was Cornelius doing? How was his mother, his family? Was he homesick? Did he want another hug?

Did he want to go home?

The days were long and boring, cramped and loud. They passed endless marshes and grazing land, which was occasionally interrupted by scrubby forests and banks which descended into sandy playas. Some of them were covered in tiny rocks, but most were sandy and often occupied by Indigenous people. In this region they were the Bororo people, according to Severino. There was wildlife too, but overall the view was by and large mostly the same the entire way throughout.

He'd taken to playing cards with Severino in the morning, and the time was used for Portuguese lessons as well. He'd been studying for over a month now, but it hadn't been sticking very well. However, learning from a person rather than a book helped his situation immensely. Severino focused on conversational speaking, rather than all the formalities Watt had previously been trying to learn.

According to Severino, if you could carry on a good conversation, or give it your best shot at the very least, you'd get far with most Brazilians. If you could tell a joke, then you'd really be set. Watt had begun to like Severino, or at the very least he didn't mind his company anymore. The man was humble and knowledgeable, and the only thing he'd done wrong so far was give Cornelius too much attention. Even Watt could begrudgingly admit he'd been ridiculous about it.

Cornelius frequently took shots from the edge of the boat, but of the photographic variety. He focused on people, always incorporating them into the surrounding landscape. On the last day of the trip, he'd taken a photograph of Watt and Severino standing together at the front of the boat, hats on and inches between them.

Watt felt wrong standing there without Cornelius in

the picture, and after Cornelius took the shot he called a fellow passenger over to assist with the problem. Cornelius' face reddened, but he offered the fellow his camera and quickly explained how to use it. He joined them and stood between Watt and Severino, adjusting his hat before tucking his hands into his pockets. He nodded to Severino, then shot Watt a withering look.

"How typical for the photographer not to like having his photo taken," Watt murmured, fighting a grin.

"It's just a very valuable piece of equipment," Cornelius shot back, quiet and whip-quick. Despite his tone, his lip curled upwards. They stared at each other for a moment, then Cornelius winked and turned his attention forward. Watt looked at the camera too, unable to stop smiling.

Watt had never been so happy to see dry land.

They left the wretched ship behind, hauling their luggage to one of the nearby hotels by foot. The air was thick with wet heat and tiny black flies. Sweat dampened Watt's forehead and he wiped at it with the back of his free hand. The ground was muddy, and although the wet season was technically over the mire had not given way to dust yet. Not all the roads were paved, and the well trodden ground was a mess to say the least. Watt chanced a look at Cornelius. He seemed to be managing well enough with his cane, walking beside Severino while Watt and Maggie took up the rear.

Cuiabá was far more modern than he expected, and he wondered how the Colonel could ever think of this place as a ghost town. They passed a cinema and other venues for entertainment, along with some decent looking stores. Watt made a mental note of them, wanting to stock up on a few things before leaving. The people they passed were mostly of the working class variety, hardened by the land and her troubles, but there were finely dressed gentlemen and ragged drifters present too.

True it wasn't the peak of modernity, but it was from the backwards place that Fawcett had described. Perhaps a handful of years had done the place wonders. Perhaps Fawcett had been looking at it wrong. Walking through the town, he thought of something Severino had said on the ship, quoting Mato Grosso's former Governor Peixoto in order to describe Cuiabá to them.

'At the end of the world there exists a river; at the end of this river there rises a hill; behind the hill stands Cuiabá.'

It did feel like they were lingering on the precipice at the end of the world, but it wasn't an ominous feeling. More like they were at the end, and a new beginning was in sight, lingering in the distant and surrounding scrub country.

The hotel Severino brought them to was the one he usually stayed at while in town. It was clean and steadfast in its construction and furnishings, lots of deep reds and nicely lit spaces. The room and board was a bit steep, and non-negotiable. Watt and Cornelius allowed Severino to make the arrangements and when he returned, it was with a slight frown. His dark hair was mussed, and his eyes were ringed with exhaustion.

"They only have one room available, but it does have two beds," he said, his tone grim yet hopeful.

Watt's brain short circuited at the obvious math. Someone would have to sleep on the floor, or share a bed with someone else. He opened his mouth to volunteer for the floor, but Cornelius processed faster than he did. He said, "Looks like we're not the only ones wanting to take advantage of the dry season. Watt and I can share." He gently elbowed Watt in the stomach. "Like we're schoolboys again, eh?"

It wasn't the whole truth, and they both knew it. They hadn't been schoolboys together when they shared a bed, and Watt didn't even remember—but he did, didn't he?

The words slapped Watt across the face, branding him with a memory. Cornelius in Watt's bed, curled up beside him as he told a feverish Watt a story about the ancient Egyptians.

Watt swallowed. Things weren't the same anymore, and they both knew that, too. And yet he embraced the terrible idea, because it was clear Cornelius would rather share a bed with Watt than Severino, or have the floor become a factor for anyone. "That's fine," he lied, trying very hard not to blush.

Severino was too relieved to notice Watt's plight. His shoulders lowered and he said, "Good, good."

They settled into their room and resolved to begin their errands manhã, a concept that Watt had hoped to avoid thus far. According to Fawcett, everything in Brazil was done manhã, which led to days, or even weeks long, delays. But today Watt was happy to embrace the prospect. It was mid-afternoon, and yet it felt like seven at night.

The room was larger than Watt expected, but there was no bathroom. That was in the hall, a large communal one shared with the other guests. The beds were large enough for two people, but two people of Watt and Cornelius' size were a different story, though.

"Window," Cornelius said, dropping his luggage onto the bed by the window. It faced the street rather than the bush, but Cornelius opened it and stuck his head outside anyway.

Watt flashed an apologetic smile at Severino, who just chuckled and set his bag on his own bed. "I shall see about a shower. It is early enough, there may not be such a wait."

Watt set his luggage beside Cornelius' on their bed. *The* bed. Cornelius pulled his head out of the window and grinned at him, hair tousled and glasses askew. "What?" Watt asked.

Cornelius shook his head, but was unable to shake away his smile. "Look," he said, but only moved away from the window a fraction.

Watt stared at him for a moment, then knelt on the bed beside him, careful not to knock their things onto the floor. Maggie jumped onto the mattress, sneaking in beside him. She knocked Watt into Cornelius, who momentarily stiffened. Watt glanced sideways at him and said, "Sorry."

Cornelius merely smiled, and nodded to the window.

Watt looked out the window. At first he only saw the street, buildings, and people. The types were varied, from stiff Englishmen to Turkish shopkeepers, Brazilian locals and otherwise. They walked the streets, outpaced by cars and carriage and fully immersed in their lives. In a way, it was a city like any other. A congested area full of people whose lives bounced off others in the most mundane of ways, like shopping for food or crossing the street.

But beyond the city, was the bush.

It was hard to discern, but it seemed to be what they were promised. Grassland and sparse trees, potential marshland and swamp. Really, it should not have been as exciting as it was.

But oh, it was.

Watt pulled back and looked at Cornelius, returning his smile.

⸺◈⸺

"Watt, you awake?" Cornelius whispered into the vague

space between midnight and dawn. Severino's soft snores filled the room, and the wall was cold beneath Cornelius' fingertips.

Watt's foot jerked, heel scraping against Cornelius' calf. He made a low noise of affirmation, one that barely escaped his chest. A pang of guilt went through Cornelius, and something far warmer.

"Nevermind—it can wait," he whispered, his palm flush against the wall. After all this time, he'd chosen the middle of the night to have this conversation. *'Brilliant thinking, Cornelius.'*

"S' alright, what's keeping you?" Watt murmured, and his spine seemed to vibrate against his own, which was absurd. Cornelius liked it when Watt talked like that. Long words, filled with thought and a hint of Scottish. He couldn't tell the man that it was *his* presence keeping him awake, the man had hardly moved all night. Watt wouldn't—*couldn't*—understand that Cornelius was electrified by the man's body pressed against his, and the idea that after all this time only a few layers of fabric separated them. Cornelius was pretty sure Watt was hugging the edge of the bed, but they were still squished together. How could Watt stand it?

'Because he doesn't like you like that. You're lucky he likes you at all,' an ugly part of his brain said.

And yet, Cornelius had no choice but to speak exactly what was on his mind. It was his nature. In a low whisper, he asked, "What is a aventiage?"

Watt tensed for a split second before rolling over, careful and quiet yet effortless. Cornelius did the same, but with much less grace. They were face to face now, sharing air and mildly confused looks. It was dark, but there was enough moonlight to reflect in Watt's eyes.

"A what?"

Cornelius took a deep breath, and he did his best to speak slowly and quietly. "In the last couple of letters you sent me, you kept referring to me as ... your aventiage. To be honest I really couldn't understand much. They were hard to read. Jumbled. I'm not ... I understand why you might've been confused writing them. But I remember that came up a few times."

Watt blinked, long and slow. His fingers twitched in the space between them, brushing against the sheet. They'd be so easy to take, and nothing Cornelius hadn't done before. But that was before. This was after.

Voice thick, Watt said, "I don't know if it makes me feel better or worse that you received them after all. I never knew, but I'd always hoped that you didn't. Before, anyways. I'd thought maybe that was why ..."

'Why you didn't write me back, a soldier heading off to a war and unsure of return.' He didn't say it, but it hung between them all the same.

"I kept all the letters you sent me. I—" Cornelius shut his eyes, unable to say what he needed to with Watt staring at him like that. "I was so angry with you. I thought why should I answer your letters if you never answered mine? But I wish, now, that I had written you back. How cruel of a person am I not to have done so?"

"I understand, I—"

Cornelius opened his eyes, despite the burn in them. "No. Please don't forgive me for something I haven't forgiven myself for yet."

"I never received yours, you know. I didn't know they existed until last month." Watt blurted out, then bit his lip.

Cornelius blinked. "What?"

Watt grimly explained his situation with the mysterious package and the state the letters were in. He said, "I know it sounds absurd, but I swear that's the truth."

"But who kept them from you?" Cornelius asked. His voice shuddered, and his heart raced.

"I don't know. I thought maybe my father, but he would've let them burn."

Cornelius felt like he couldn't breathe. Oh, he'd been such an asshole. All this time, all these years. Cornelius whispered, "You never knew. They never told you, and you don't ..." He shook his head a little. "But we had a whole conversation, you and me. I thought at least you would've remembered that."

Watt shivered, and his beard scratched against the pillow. "I'm sorry Cornelius, I don't remember things well, especially from that time. All I know is that I was forbidden to see or talk to you again, or any of your family, and we never visited Harbor Point after that year. I fought for you, I really did. But it wasn't enough. I should've tried harder to find out what happened, to reach you and tell you that I missed you. But Father was so ..." Watt sighed. "I'm truly sorry."

Cornelius closed his eyes, fighting tears. A tentative hand rested on his jaw, and a thumb wiped at his tears. Cornelius inhaled and opened his eyes, surprised. Watt startled and began to pull his hand away. Cornelius reached up, laying his hand over Watt's and securing them both in place on his cheek.

Watt swallowed. Stammering a little, he said, "I—I believe what I was trying to say was my—my aventurier. I'm not the best at writing in French, and it w—was ... disorienting, over there."

Oh, hell. Cornelius' heart was on the verge of collapse.

He wasn't sure how it began, but their joined hands drifted from his jaw to the space between their chests. Watt stared at him with such intent, Cornelius thought he was about to be kissed. But no, Watt didn't feel like that about him. They were simply feeling familiar, vulnerable.

That was all.

Cornelius smiled. "Oh."

Watt's fingers tightened around Cornelius. "For what it's worth, I think we would've been friends back then."

Barely audible, Cornelius said, "Me too."

"Can I ask you something?"

"Can I ask you something else, first? About the letters."

"Yes."

"Who ..." Cornelius wasn't sure why it mattered, only that it did. He had to know. "Who is Cher Ami? What was she like?"

Watt blinked in surprise, then a smile crested his lips. "Oh. Cher Ami. I'd nearly forgotten about him, although I'm not sure how. He saved our lives, you know. God, those days were a mess. One miscommunication and inflated ego after another led us into such chaos that eventually we were being fired upon by our own troops. The artillery." Watt's smile faded, and he sighed. "There were eight others, but only Cher Ami made it back, with the message and in bad shape. He lost a leg, and suffered a chest wound that later turned fatal."

"Oh, I'm so sorry." Cornelius immediately regretted asking. There had been a letter from Watt after he'd made it out of there, pages upon pages of which were filled with mostly incoherent scribbles focusing on someone named Cher Ami. The emotion behind his words had been nearly enough to make Cornelius crack. He'd always assumed Cher Ami was a woman, but the French always were the more interesting sort. Once again, he wished that he'd buried his pride and written Watt back.

"He lived a good life, and did his duty. I visited him a few years back, actually. It's ... odd, seeing him on display like that. But at least others can learn about him, I suppose."

"Oh?" Cornelius asked, confused.

Watt frowned. "At the Smithsonian."

"I ... think something has been lost in translation here." Cornelius tried.

Understanding dawned on Watt's face, and he chuckled quietly. "Cher Ami was a messenger pigeon, not a human."

"*Oh.*" Cornelius' cheeks immediately flushed. "Oh. That—that makes much more sense."

Their soft laughter filled the room, and a giddy sort of feeling rose in Cornelius' chest. Watt playfully hushed him when Severino's snores changed tempo, and they smiled at each other. After a few moments, Watt said, "Do I get to ask my question now?"

Cornelius nodded. "Yes, of course."

"Why Sawyer?"

The atmosphere shifted from quiet joy to grief. Cornelius closed his eyes on reflex. He swallowed against his leaping heart, then said, "For Papa. Sawyer ... it pays homage to him and his work. I won't be carrying on the family name, but this is—it's a way for me to be close to him. To where I come from."

"Oh," Watt said. "Oh, Cornelius."

Watt moved closer. Cornelius, quite sure he was not reading the situation correctly, remained still. He was glad for his second intuition, for Watt merely brought their foreheads together. They could have kissed. It would have been so easy. Neither of them seemed to be breathing, but Cornelius knew he had to be because his heart was racing a million miles an hour.

But they only laid together. Quiet, hands entangled between them. Foreheads pressed together and noses aligned. There was nothing romantic about it, not really. And yet, Cornelius had never felt more intimately touched in his life. They lay there in the moonlight, Severino's snores and the distant sounds of a city at night lulling them into a sense of ease. Of comfort.

Cornelius had started to drift off to sleep when Watt murmured, "You know, I do remember you telling me stories. I wish I remembered the rest, I really do. But I'm convinced listening to you got me through it, you know. I always thought you'd become a writer some day, or an actor."

Cornelius chuckled. "No, it's as you say. I was born to be an aventurier. But a man can be good at many things."

"Thank you, Cornelius." Watt grinned, and Cornelius thought he could almost feel it.

"Don't thank me yet," Cornelius whispered.

May

Hen House

May 12th, 1930

They left Cuiabá after a month, and not a moment too soon. Not only were they behind schedule, but Cornelius thought if he had to sleep beside Watt and keep his hands to himself for one more night he might perish. He'd never gone so long without releasing his ... *frustration*, and sharing a room with someone else for three months made self relief impossible, let alone a bed.

Cornelius had a passion for all things that made him feel alive. Alcohol, cigarettes, danger, and a good fuck. Since all he had to cope with life now were cigarettes and danger, he was eager to dive into the latter.

He hadn't drank since that dreadful night in São Paulo, and while he had plenty of desire to drink more, his will for now was iron clad. His discussions with Watt helped immensely, in fact they helped so much that he was wanting things he could never have.

The time in Cuiabá had been well spent, albeit boring and tiresome. They secured seven mules and the feed and time needed to fatten them up for the journey ahead, playing a game of hurry up and wait while they did so.

Watt spent most of his time sketching and collecting little treasures, namely rocks. Cornelius spent most of his time writing, developing, and watching Watt as he worked. Severino was also an artist, his preferred tool a pen rather than a pencil like Watt. He wrote and sketched the most organized journal entries Cornelius had ever seen, and had quite literally taken notes on his style.

They all sent final letters, exercised daily, and sighted in their guns in the back country. Surprisingly, Cornelius was a better shot than Watt. Cornelius thought to tease him about it, but after seeing the way Watt's hands shook around the handle of his .44 revolver, he decided against it.

They walked nearly every day, stretching muscles that had gone lax during weeks of travel. Severino joined them as well, and the tension between him and Watt had practically dissipated by now. As had most of the animosity between Cornelius and Watt, although what now existed was an awkward sort of air that neither of them knew what to do with.

They sent back items they would no longer need such as suits, and resupplied as efficiently as possible. Cornelius had taken inventory of both his and Watt's packs more times than he cared to admit. They contained thus:

CORNELIUS

2 SMALL DIARY NOTEBOOKS

COMPASS

PENCILS

PROTRACTOR

RULER

MARBLE'S HUNTING KNIFE

WRIST WATCH

WATERPROOF BELT

2 TRAVELING OUTFITS

EXTRA PAIR OF BOOTS

MAP

KODAK EASTMAN

FILM

POWDERED DEVELOPER

TWO CASES OF CIGARETTES

FLASK

MOSQUITO NET

OILED PONCHO

FISH HOOKS AND 100 FT OF LINE

IODINE

ANTIVENIN AND FIRST AID KIT

4 LBS XARQUE

HAMMOCK

COFFEE

.38 PISTOL

BULLETS

MATCHES

Watt

SMALL DIARY NOTEBOOK

SKETCHBOOK

COMPASS

.44 REVOLVER

BULLETS

PENCILS

PIPE AND TOBACCO

CAMILLUS TL-29 POCKET KNIFE

POCKET WATCH

FLASHLIGHT

2 TRAVELING OUTFITS

EXTRA BOOTS

MAP

MACHETE AND SCABBARD

KEN-L RATIONS

SMALL TIN BOWL

2 LBS RICE

2 LBS BEANS

SWEETENED CONDENSED MILK

HAMMOCK

MOSQUITO NET

POT

TWO MUGS

OILED PONCHO

STRIKER AND FLINT

MATCHES

It felt like too much and not enough all at once. Severino seemed to approve, and Cornelius figured he would be the ultimate authority on the matter, given how many trips he'd made back and forth. He'd asked the man if he minded trekking in and out of the bush, and Severino had only smiled. "I'm the man Joaquim sends when things are needed," he'd said, and that was that.

They had their meeting with the Inspectoria de Protecção aos Indios on the second day there, providing the necessary paperwork to show they had permission to visit Bacairy Post and whatever potential people they may come across, Bororo, Paresí, or otherwise. It was not as easy to dive into the Amazon and meet her people as it used to be, but Cornelius was not complaining.

Brazil was understandably weary of foreign explorers claiming grand humanitarian and scientific purposes. Most often such explorers experienced great hardship which made for great headlines, and if they did come across any findings, most were not made public or if they were, it was in an adventure novel. Fawcett's recent disappearance and the rescue missions sent after him had created exactly the sort of publicity they did not want. Not to mention that Brazil had their own brilliant scientists and explorers.

Cornelius keenly felt like the fox in the hen house, and tried to not think about it too much. Harming the Indigenous peoples was not in their plan, and they *were* aiding the archaeological dig, if only for a short time.

It was their first real trek, about a month's worth of traveling without the aid of trains or ships, and Cornelius felt the tone would set the entire rest of the trip. His companions were in a good mood as they set off into the bush, and Cornelius smiled while listening to Watt talk with Severino and Antônio. It was as if by stepping into nature, Watt had stepped away from all his insecurities and anxiety, leaving them behind with civilization.

Antônio arrived on the second to last day, a Bacairy guide that Severino had called for when they first arrived and praised highly. He couldn't have been any more than eighteen, if that, and he neatly occupied the space between society and the fringes of it. His black hair was cut in a blunt bob in what Cornelius recognized as the usual Bororo style, but he wore trousers and boots, a workman's shirt and gaucho hat that had seen better days. He spoke Bacairí, and was fairly fluent in Portuguese as well. He was a serious fellow with an even more serious stare, and he listened more than he spoke. He reminded Cornelius of John, and his heart pulsed with dark fury. Not directed towards him, but home.

Home, and the dark, lonely summer when the world finally revealed its true cruel nature to Cornelius. He hadn't given much thought to what they would find at Bacairy Post, but of course there would be religion. Government depended on religion to tame and organize those who had been doing just fine without it. Society wielded religion and morals like a scythe, clearing 'wild' lands and peoples like it had a right. In fact, they'd been doing it for longer in South America than they had in the North. The Jesuits, the Catholics, even the damn Protestants. Back home it was, *'kill the Indian, save the man.'*

Here, with slavery abolished nearly twenty years later than America, the Positivists agreed that the Indigenous people had rights to their own land, and to defend it, but they still pushed for, *'order and progress.'* They stationed missionaries nearby friendly tribes, waiting patiently with a bible in one hand and tools of the trade in the other. After all, an educated and friendly 'Indian' was fit for work, wasn't he? All that time and erasure led to men like Antônio and John, Louis Shotridge too. Straddling the space between a washed away past, and an uncertain future full of people who wanted to step on you, use you. Make you palatable. Really, Cornelius should have connected with Antônio immediately.

However, it was Watt who formed a close connection to Antônio, talking the kid's ear off for hours at a time in his best, yet stilted, Portuguese. Antônio, for his part, mostly listened and provided one liner insights. Bacairy Post and its surrounding area were one of the few places Watt was familiar with, having studied Karl von den Steinen's work. The physician had paved the way for Brazilian ethnology, dabbling in anthropology and exploration alongside his medical work. Everything that Cornelius knew about the Bacairy, Watt had told him. Severino had filled in a little, providing the political background that had changed since Steinen's time.

Named the Bacairy by the Portuguese, although they called themselves Kurá, they had once been one people but were driven south and separated into three groups a little over a hundred years ago. Most of the Santana group fled the rubber plantations in 1847, moving east to merge with the Central group which had settled at the headwaters of the Teles Pires. The Territorio Kurá Bacairy was established, and by 1925 it seemed all the Bacairy, or what remained of them, had become one once again. Only time would tell how much remained of them after progress and order had their way.

Their group took it slow in order to preserve their mule's endurance, which was fine by Cornelius. He couldn't deny the terrain was treacherous in places, especially in the marshlands where water over saturated the grass and invited bugs in hordes. The insects were undoubtedly annoying and beautiful in equal measure. It was hard not to admire them as they tended to dive right for the eyes, settling for the face or neck if they had to, or any other bits of skin that were exposed. It made it hard to keep an eye out for whining bushmasters when the wasps were always demanding attention. Cornelius pestered Watt nearly as much as the bugs did, the man was terrible at proactively avoiding insects. In fact, he seemed to attract them. The choking wet heat was near unbearable, and Cornelius could see why Watt would want to roll up his sleeves or undo the buttons on his collar. It was a rookie mistake.

March was one of the wettest months in this area, and it wouldn't be until June before the ground fully soaked up the excess standing water. Cornelius tried to stay positive, appreciating the fact they were on relatively easy ground compared to the thick jungle they'd have to endure later. The first day was scrub country and grazing land, then they reached a plateau which eventually gave way to more grass. This new region was a transitional zone between the lush basin in the North, and the highlands in the South. What forest they did find was considered dry forest, the trees shorter and less full than their relatives to the North.

Antônio pointed out the cashew trees and other plants that could prove useful, like the shrub trees with yellow and white flowers called pau santo; the bark could be used as a substitute for cork and the leaves used for medicinal purposes. That was the thing Cornelius loved about nature itself, that everything had a purpose and use if only perceived the right way. He'd always wondered how something had been discovered for the first time. Who was the first person to take the leaves of a tree and say, this will cure malaria? Or sure, I'll smoke this. Why not? What a surprise trip that must've been. Obviously it had been the native peoples, but what made the very first one try it?

Severino knew some Bacairí, one of many Cariban

languages that were closely related and widespread, from Venezuela to Colombia, Brazil, and more. He'd been teaching Cornelius, but along the way Antônio taught him and Watt as well. The kid didn't drive words home or use them in different contexts like Severino did. He merely said what something was, and moved on. Water was páru, and fire was páto. He told them to keep an eye out for aká, or jaguars.

They put in seven miles the first day, and the second, a pace that was punishing despite their mounts. Cornelius couldn't imagine travelling with Fawcett, who'd been pushing ten miles a day by now. On the second night they camped near a stream, which beautifully reflected the enormous moon. It illuminated the bush better than any spotlight ever could, and it had Cornelius wandering a little. He jotted down the constellations he recognized, wondering what the ancient peoples in this region thought of them. Severino followed along and pointed out the ones Cornelius didn't know. Lobo, musca, toucan, and the ever so obvious Crux. A lifetime could be spent in the Amazon simply studying the world above it, let alone the world they stood on.

Later, after they'd gathered by a small fire, Cornelius broached the idea of visiting Hermenegildo Galvão once more. But once again, Severino met it with much resistance. He said, "There is nothing to be gained by visiting there."

"And is there anything to lose?" Cornelius countered.

Antônio made a noise of disapproval, but didn't say anything outright on the matter. Watt looked between him and Severino, then asked, "Is the man dangerous?"

Severino puffed on his tobacco pipe, quiet for some time. Finally, he sighed. "There is an archaeological site near his ranch. Or rather, was. He invited some people from São Paulo University to take a look at what he'd found, including a friend of mine, of Joaquim's. At first there wasn't much, but then they started digging, and well. You know how it goes. Fields of urns, petroglyphs on stones, and cemeteries.

"It was all theorized to be of the Toltec period, like our site, but the research there has been abandoned and now we'll never know for sure. The people there were harassed to no end, equipment broken and ..." Severino glanced between Watt and Cornelius, eyes full of meaning. "Traps. It was all made to look like the natives, but it wasn't. It was him, or rather, his bugeiros."

Antônio hummed, nodding along to Severino's tale.

Cornelius' breath caught in his throat. "How do you know?"

"Trust me, I know," Severino said, and he rubbed a hand over his face. For the first time during their journey, he looked tired down to his bones. "Roberto is no longer there, and neither are any more answers than you don't already have. I am telling you, it is a waste of time."

Cornelius blinked. They hadn't so blatantly spoken

of their objective thus far, and it was like a bubble had popped. A distinct line had been drawn between Severino and them. It had always existed, but now it was highlighted. They were merely using him and his archaeological site as a stepping stone before disappearing further into Brazil, searching for Fawcett or signs of him.

"When did the harassment start?" Watt asked, smoking from his own pipe. He grimaced and swat at a mosquito on his neck. "Where is the proof?"

Severino huffed out an angry laugh. "It is what you think, shortly after they started finding artifacts of value. Why else would he want the site to himself? Not for history's sake, that's for sure."

Watt contemplated this. "I've been specifically tasked with meeting him. We cannot avoid it, not for rumor and gossip. And if there's a chance it may be true and he's ... a problem, we will go in prepared."

"You are all the same." Severino cursed under his breath and shook his head. "Whatever you think is best, senhor."

They slept in hammocks, shrouded in bug nets that did nothing, and slept in shifts in order to keep an eye on the mules and each other. Antônio didn't seem concerned about hostile people in this area, but it was a good idea nevertheless. Watt's, of course. Cornelius wondered if this felt similar to trudging through France, but he quickly dismissed the thought. Two completely different experiences.

How bizarre it was though that they'd both been there at the same time, but out of reach and out of touch. While Cornelius was finding himself, Watt was fighting for himself and the lives of hundreds of other men, for his country. It wasn't like Cornelius had refused to fight, he was an American. However, he was legally a woman. He could've become a nurse or something else, but that wasn't him. He loved to fight, although he was technically unfit to do so for his country. Unfit to do many things, according to certain people.

———————⊛———————

May 16th, 1930

They were surrounded by the sounds of insects, tails swatting futilely at them, and birds screeching. As the days went on, the heat stifled most conversation and impromptu lessons, leaving them with the sounds of animals and vegetation protesting against their passing. It was just as well, since the air between Watt and his companions had grown tense. Watt agreed with Severino, although he couldn't admit it even if he wanted to. The search for Fawcett was their priority, and they would be careful. He told Nina he would visit Fawcett's rancher friend, and see what he knew. He couldn't go back on his word, only be prepared for the worst.

Their group was now in the rough land of the Pantanal, but they weren't isolated. They passed small estancias and talked to any moradors they came across, but otherwise kept to themselves. Watt felt distinctly on edge any time they came in contact with these men who lived on the trail, but so far they were kind beyond measure. Quite unlike the nomads prowling the city back home.

Watt thought of Fawcett's observation of the common belief the settlers here had, that they'd staked a claim in a never before discovered area while in all reality, they were surrounded by neighboring farms. While the States culled cattle and pigs by the thousands in an effort to raise prices for farmers struggling with surplus and land destroyed by dust, South America was picking up the slack.

Cornelius told a story about a rancher in Peru he'd met, a clever man from Texas that mastered raising cattle in high altitudes. One of many clever men who knew how to forge a living for themselves in this harsh environment. There was more to the Amazon than just coffee and rubber, and it was being harvested at an exponential rate. Castor oil, lemongrass, tropical fruit and of course quinine, along with hundreds of other medicinal plants. The opportunities were endless, and endlessly sought after.

On the third night of their venture they settled into chapada country, populated by enormous plateaus and cliffs that were once upon a time, a coastline. Whilst there, saube ants declared war on their bodies and equipment, eating through canvas and leather alike. It didn't take long for their morale to dive further, Cornelius especially was in a foul mood. A couple days later they found the river they'd been looking for, which uplifted spirits until a downright nightmare occurred that evening.

Garapata ticks swarmed, literally swarmed, all over the ground. Ticks weren't like any other bug, you couldn't just swat them away. You had to ensure the head and pincers were withdrawn properly from the skin, otherwise the damn things burrowed as deep as possible. Cornelius had to remove one from the base of Watt's neck, which led to an extremely awkward moment involving Cornelius' fingers on Watt's bare, sweaty skin. Cornelius said he hadn't been bitten, but he also wouldn't let anyone check him over. Watt had to pluck one from Maggie's belly, and it worried him that he hadn't found more than one. Surely there had to be more.

In short, the bugs were maddening, absolutely maddening.

The day after the tick incident, they found Colonel Hermenegildo Galvão's estancia without much trouble, which bode well since it was a close neighbor to the Post. Located at the headwaters of the Rio Novo, Hermenegildo Galvão had constructed his own world of sorts, settling directly on the river. Watt bet that during the wet season this area became an island. Isolated.

A large main house constructed of bright red bricks

and many smaller buildings were situated in the center of a grassy area, flanked by pastures and cattle. A towering coconut palm was planted near the front of the main house, casting a mid-afternoon shadow across the land. Watt stared up at it, the only tree in the clearing. It was rumored the property was roughly the size of Belgium, but given that Watt had never been to Belgium he couldn't say. But it was a substantial area indeed, at least from where they stood. Rows upon rows of houses for farm hands, a warehouse and church, even a school house for the children of the laboring families. Machinery neighbored what appeared to be a factory, and Watt was overwhelmed by the sheer amount of buildings, people, and cattle. It was a small empire contained within a pocket of Brazil, fit with a place for planes to land.

"A fazenda, more like," Severino muttered, and Watt hadn't the time to ask what that meant before they were greeted.

Hermenegildo Galvão was a large man with dusky weathered skin and an impressive mustache, he was well worn with wrinkled dark eyes that were full of energy. They were welcomed by the rancher with much hospitality, and true to Brazilian fashion all offers of repayment were refused. Senhor Galvão led them to a small house originally intended for laborers, but was empty and ready for use. The floors and walls were built of rough hewn lumber, the roof thatched with palms. There were no windows, and the house was split into a bathroom, bedroom, and living area. They dropped off their belongings and stabled the mules in a nearby fenced off area with an attached lean to.

They took turns bathing, the tub was too small for Watt and he didn't want to immediately dirty the water that he'd hauled in. Senhor Galvão said not to worry about using too much, but still. He dunked his head in the water, scrubbing his scalp with the rough but pleasantly fragrant soap. Lemongrass, perhaps. After rinsing his hair out he ran a washcloth over his body, dripping wet and laden with soap. He dunked the cloth, rinsing the soap from it, and ran it over his body again. Despite his best efforts, the water turned murky. He dried quickly, using a musty and scratchy towel from the cupboard. He felt immensely better afterwards, like he'd had layers of tension and worry built up within the dirt.

He drained the tub and brought in more for the next person, Cornelius, who adamantly said, "I can do that myself."

Watt said, "I know," and did it anyway.

Afterwards in the sitting area, Watt asked Severino, "How're you feeling?"

Severino was seated across from Watt and Antônio on an old chair at an even older table. He sighed, deft and clean fingers working to pack a tobacco pipe. "Does it matter?"

Guilt pinched at Watt and he said, "Yes, it does."

Severino said nothing. He puffed on his pipe, thickening the air with his smoke and tension.

Later that evening they broke bread together, speaking mostly in Portuguese with some English sprinkled in. Senhor Galvão was a powerful man, and he commanded attention easily. Severino had not been pleased with their decision, but it was too significant of a place not to visit. As such, he was unusually quiet over dinner that night. That also could have been due to the main topic at hand.

"So, what makes you think you can do what no one else has?" Senhor Galvão asked, flicking his critical gaze between Cornelius and Watt. He'd been treating them as the main attraction, hardly giving Severino or Antônio a second glance. It irked Watt, but given their discomfort he didn't want to turn the spotlight onto them. "I have watched men come and go searching for Colonel Fawcett. Or not go, in some cases. Always empty handed if they do make it out alive."

Cornelius' lip twitched upwards, his eyes steelier than ever. He'd been wound tight for days, and Watt could tell by the look in his eyes, the set of his jaw, that he was looking for a fight. Lightly, Cornelius said, "You and I both know everyone's going in the wrong direction. That has to count for something."

Senhor Galvão's eyebrow raised. "Does it?"

"We know that the others before us haven't been exactly ... open minded. But we are," Watt said, gently easing into the conversation.

Senhor Galvão scoffed. "Open minded? Try common

sense. I've heard this before, but it all ends the same. I cared for the Colonel, truly, but this is ..." He waved a hand through the air. "Insanity. The meaning is the same in English, is it not?"

Watt reached into his pocket and took out the letter he'd been tasked with delivering in person. The reason they had to come here. "Here, this will explain everything." He passed over the envelope addressed to Senhor Galvão in Nina's writing, and watched as the man opened it right there at the table. It had been too important, she said, to risk in the mail.

Senhor Galvão read the letter. And he read it again. Watt watched as the man's eyes flicked across the paper from top to bottom, then up again. Cornelius threw him a curious look, but said nothing. Watt had previously told Cornelius the letter was a personal matter he couldn't discuss, but that was a lie. And Watt knew he'd made a mistake in not telling him the truth when Senhor Galvão lifted his head and fixed his gaze on Cornelius.

But how could Watt have told him the truth, when he didn't believe it? He didn't believe that Cornelius was—

"You are the one he was hoping for, I think."

Cornelius' brow raised and he glanced at Watt, who had long since burst into flames. Cornelius turned his attention back to Senhor Galvão and said, "Excuse me?"

Senhor Galvão shook his head minutely and said, "The Colonel was a smart man, and a determined one.

He wanted to go and see that stone tower and the waterfall the day Roberto told him about it. The perfect location, he said. And now—"

"Mrs. Fawcett said it was important to him, this place. She said it was important for the quest," Watt said, emphasizing the second half of his sentiment. Cornelius looked at him askance, and Watt cursed internally. He'd hoped this wouldn't come up, but damn it. There was no point in skirting around it now, he'd just have to explain later. Severino watched the proceedings carefully, interest piqued.

Senhor Galvão nodded, and he stared at Cornelius anew. He said, "There is something different about you." He tapped the table with his finger, like he was marking the spot on a map. "I think you shall find the truth."

Cornelius' lip twitched, and Watt expected this was the moment he'd finally explode. He simply said, "Thank you."

Senhor Galvão considered Severino next, and their eyes locked for several moments before he spoke. "You work with Joaquim da Silva, yes?"

Severino nodded. "Yes, I do."

"What do you make of his latest project?" Senhor Galvão asked. "Do you think that could be the city the Colonel was looking for?"

Severino parsed his thoughts before answering in a slow and measured fashion. "There is much to be learned in the heart of Brazil, it is true many ancient peoples lived in this area. I can not say if it is the place Fawcett was looking for, but that does not make it any less significant." Severino picked up his drink, cachaca, a dark and sweet liquor reminiscent of rum which they all had been served. Watt noted that Cornelius hadn't touched his, though. To be more correct, he'd been playing with his glass, turning it and moving it around, but he hadn't taken a sip.

"And what are you doing, Senhor Antunes?" Senhor Galvão gestured between Watt and Cornelius, ignoring Antônio entirely. "Do you plan on going with them and abandoning your team?"

Severino stilled, but only for a second. He took a sip of his drink, then set it back down. He smiled and said, "I am merely a guide."

It wasn't really an answer, but Senhor Galvão smiled in response. An entire unsaid conversation occurred between them, and it didn't feel like a good one. Cornelius and Watt exchanged a look, but neither said anything. Watt glanced over at Antônio, who watched the proceedings with a mild frown of disinterest. Thankfully, the conversation moved on after that. They drank and smoked, discussing their trip and what they thought of the places they'd been so far. Cornelius asked about the ranch and its origins, and soon they were discussing the cattle industry in Mato Grosso. Which is when Cornelius stirred up trouble.

He said, "There's quite the smuggling problem in Mato Grosso, isn't there? Of cattle, I mean."

Senhor Galvão smiled, an echo of the same one he'd given Severino. Malignant and vague. He said, "You are a smart man, aren't you?"

"No. Too curious for my own good. One must be aware of the snakes residing in the pit before jumping in, after all. Besides, it's not like the ranchers have much choice, do they? Not even America deals in taxes and tariffs this outrageous." He scoffed and shook his head, like the situation truly pained him.

Senhor Galvão studied him before speaking. Amicably, he said, "Some do what they must to survive, but it gives the rest of us a bad name."

"I'm sure they do," Cornelius said.

When they turned in for the night, Watt felt like he'd been swimming in lead. They laid out their bedrolls on the floor of the main space, the bedroom had two rickety cots that no one wanted to claim. Watt laid between Cornelius and Severino, while Antônio slept on the other side of Severino. Cornelius and Antônio fell asleep quickly, but Severino did not. He hardly moved, his body tense and spine rigid.

Watt asked, "Are you alright, Severino?"

Severino rolled over and stared at Watt. He whispered, "I think we should leave at first light."

Watt chewed on the inside of his bottom lip, pondering his words and their evening. There had been something distinctly off about the whole affair. While Senhor Galvão was an older man, he seemed perfectly capable. Why hadn't he gone looking for Fawcett if they truly had been such good friends? He definitely seemed to know more than he was letting on, and there was that glint in his eye that Watt had seen too many times before.

Eventually Watt said, "I trust your judgment."

Severino sighed. "If only you did sooner."

Brave Enough

May 17th, 1930

Cornelius woke to the sounds of his companions packing. "What's going on?" He asked, bleary eyed and slow as he fumbled for his glasses.

"We're leaving," Watt said, offering them to him.

Cornelius quickly took them and slid them on, his fatigue clearing in a rush. "What? Why?"

Watt glanced at Severino, who said, "I think it's best we continue on our journey."

They both looked as if they hadn't slept a wink last night, and Cornelius felt the same even though he didn't remember waking at all. "But I—"

"Cornelius," Watt said softly. "Antônio is getting the mules ready."

"Okay." Cornelius sighed. "Okay, give me a moment."

Cornelius didn't bother changing his clothes, and it didn't appear the other men had either. He hadn't unpacked much last night, so it didn't take long for him to get ready to go. After relieving himself he stuffed his .38 in his belt, then slung his pack on his back. He groaned a little beneath its weight, unable to restrain the noise. Thankfully no one seemed to notice. He'd been looking forward to resting his leg for a few days, but he trusted in Watt and Severino. They were out the door within minutes. Dawn was merely a threat on the horizon, and the morning was remarkably quiet. The moon, reduced to its last quarter, was diminishing in the west. Even the birds only had the smallest bit to say, crying only every and now then. Enough to be heard, but not located.

They met Antônio at the lean to, where he had the mules all tacked up and ready to go. As Cornelius burdened his beast with gear, he ran the events of last night through his mind over and over. He winced, remembering his own part in things. He probably shouldn't have antagonized a man that was likely a smuggler, despite the man's protests otherwise. He was too sharp and ambitious, too well off in an area where people struggled if they didn't pay off the tax man. But maybe he truly wasn't, and Cornelius had offended him. Oh, and there was that whole damn business with Watt and Nina and the mysterious letter, and the bizarre way Galvão had looked at him after that.

"Zut alors," Cornelius swore under his breath, and mounted his mule.

Antônio led the way. Cornelius' walked between Severino and Watt, the same single file formation and order they usually took when coming across unfamiliar and unsteady ground. They slipped across the yard and away from the main house, towards the surrounding untamed bush in a north easterly direction. The ground was wet, but it was only grass and dirt. Nothing they couldn't handle.

"Leaving so soon, amigos?" Hermenegildo Galvão asked.

Cornelius turned abruptly in his seat and was subsequently met with a view of Watt's broad shoulders, and his horse's ass. Watt had an arm raised, his revolver in hand. Over his shoulder, Cornelius could see Senhor Galvão standing by the palm tree at the corner of the house, a rifle slung over his shoulder and his hand on the muzzle of the gun. He beheld a non threatening posture and a smile that seemed ... pitying, or condescending. Cornelius couldn't tell which.

In Portuguese, Senhor Galvão said, "You can put the gun down, soldier. I heard a racket and came to see what was what."

Cornelius glanced back at Severino, who was stiff as a board with a hand on his own gun. He hadn't unholstered it yet, though. Antônio frowned, watching the whole affair. Senhor Galvão slowly turned, showing his back to Watt as he rested his rifle against the tree trunk. Watt didn't relax, in fact when Senhor Galvão raised his hands in surrender, Watt stiffened further.

"I hope my hospitality has not offended you," Senhor Galvão said, his brows pinching in confusion.

"Watt," Severino said quietly. "Put down the gun."

A few seconds passed, then Watt did as he was asked.

He slowly holstered it, and Senhor Galvão smiled. Severino called, "We are eager to reach the Post, and are greatly rested. We did not want to impose on you any more than we already have."

"Nonsense, it is no trouble." Senhor Galvão approached, waving a hand. He closed the distance between them. "But I understand, the Amazon waits for no one. Tell me, will you visit on your way back through?" He directed this last bit at Cornelius and Watt.

Watt said nothing, so Cornelius said, "Of course."

Senhor Galvão extended a hand to Cornelius first, staring him square in the eye as they shook. He said, "I want to hear all about your adventure, and what you find. I shall live through you, so to speak."

Cornelius nodded, shaking with as much firm pressure as he'd received. "I look forward to it, senhor."

They said farewell and turned their back on Hermenegildo Galvão. Soon the estancia became nothing but a distant unsettling memory, but Cornelius still felt eyes on him. The feeling didn't go away, no matter how many miles they put behind them. No one spoke, not until Watt called for a break in the early afternoon. He dismounted and said, "I've got to stop."

Severino glanced back at the way they'd come, then nodded. "Okay."

Cornelius was grateful for the reprieve, but he didn't want to stop for long. His leg ached fiercely, and he had a feeling that it would hurt thrice as much after getting a taste of rest. He dismounted and stretched his leg out, then took a long drink of water from his canteen. He looked between Watt, Severino, and Antônio as they did the same. Tension was thick between them, and Cornelius couldn't take it any more.

To Watt, he said, "Are you going to tell me what the fuck that was all about?"

Severino's thick eyebrows flew up, and Antônio watched on with a mild expression of interest. Watt's cheeks flushed and he said, "Happy to, right after *you* explain why you thought goading a smuggler was a brilliant idea."

"I wasn't goading him, I—" Cornelius gestured vaguely. Honestly, he didn't know what the hell had gotten into him last night. He'd seen a fire, and wanted to pour gasoline on it. He couldn't even blame it on the alcohol, for he hadn't drank any. Maybe it'd been better if he had.

Watt sighed, running a hand through his hair. "Well, he certainly didn't like it." He shifted his attention to Severino and said, "I'm sorry. We should have listened to you. It—it wasn't worth it."

Cornelius folded his arms tight across his chest and cut in before Severino could respond. He said, "Kind of late to say that now. What was in the letter, Watt?"

Watt went to scratch at his neck, then thought better of it and dropped his hand. "I—" He shook his head, mouth opening and closing a few times. This was ridiculous, they were supposed to be a team, a team that was on the same page. Cornelius had a sudden urge to hit Watt, and it was so fierce that he had to turn away.

He said, "Forget it," and stalked off a short ways, lighting a cigarette as he went.

Damn Watt for keeping secrets. Damn Severino for being right, and damn Antônio for ... well. Cornelius didn't know what for, but fuck it all. He was tired and sore, and he wasn't too proud to realize he was being an asshole, had been for some time now. He allowed his anger to rage until the cigarette burnt out, then he stubbed the stick against his boot and jammed the butt into his pocket. He drew in a great breath, then made the short trip back to his companions. They were all taking a smoke break of their own, and Watt gently tapped out his pipe as Cornelius approached.

Watt frowned, and it looked as if words were on the tip of his tongue. But a couple of moments passed, and he said nothing.

Cornelius shifted his gaze to Severino and Antônio. In Portuguese, he asked, "Do you think he will follow us?"

Severino puffed on his pipe, then sighed and replied in kind. "I don't know. He has no claim to the land Joaquim is working, but ..."

Antônio said, "When has that stopped men?"

Cornelius removed his glasses and ran a hand over his face. After recomposing himself, he looked between Severino and Antônio and said, "I'm sorry that I didn't listen to you, and that I ..." Cornelius glanced at Watt.

"I antagonized him. I don't know what got into me. I just—" Cornelius waved a hand. "I don't know, there's something about him."

Severino smiled gently, and it reminded Cornelius of Papa after an '*I told you so*' moment. Not cruel or satisfied, but ... Cornelius didn't know, he couldn't think of the word for it. Compassionate? Understanding?

Antônio adjusted his hat and shrugged. "He will be looking for you, not me."

Watt chuckled. Antônio grinned, and then Cornelius and Severino were smiling too. Watt clapped Cornelius on the shoulder. "Ready to keep going?"

Cornelius nodded. "Yes."

They made camp in the abandoned Bacairy village that Fawcett had once stayed in, situated near the Paranatinga and less than a day's walk from the Post. Exhaustion and nerves was a common denominator within the group, even cool Antônio twitched at nearly every unexpected noise. There had been no followers, or at least none that they could hear or see.

Cornelius stayed up writing in his journal by the dwindling light of the campfire. They kept it lit, but not roaring. It was his shift, and the night was quiet. The moon was half full and twice as glorious for what it lacked. He was grateful that it was his turn to stay awake, he wouldn't have been able to sleep if he tried.

It was like every Big Thing that had been lingering in the back of his mind since agreeing to this venture had decided to shatter the bars of the cage containing them. His complicated feelings for Watt and their past, doubts regarding their mission and his own competence, and every insecurity that lingered involving his own manhood.

Watt slipped out of the old hut that once housed families and otherwise, but now only gave weary travelers temporary shelter. He was quiet and catlike despite his size, and Cornelius thought, *'He belongs out here.'*

Watt knelt beside Cornelius on the ground, offering a tired smile. Quietly, he said, "I can take over, if you'd like."

"Can't sleep?"

"No."

"To be honest, I don't think I'll be able to either."

Watt hesitated, then nodded. "Let me know if you want to switch." He began to straighten and Cornelius reached out, taking hold of his wrist. Watt stared down at Cornelius' hand, eyes reflecting the fire's light. Cornelius quickly let go, ducking his head. He closed his journal and said, "Can I ask you a question?"

"Of course," Watt said, and after only a moment's hesitation, sat beside Cornelius. He drew his knees up to his big chest, linking his arms around his legs. His body fit snugly against Cornelius', and it struck Cornelius then that they were alone.

"Where's Maggie?" He whispered.

Watt smiled. "Afraid we'll be caught out with a chaperone?"

Cornelius grinned despite his melancholy. "Careful, you might develop a sense of humor."

"Ah, and what a terrible thing that would be." Watt bumped his shoulder against Cornelius'.

Cornelius chuckled softly, then glanced over at the hut. "Are the others awake?"

Watt shook his head, but Cornelius still felt apprehensive. You could never be too careful. And yet Cornelius had to talk to someone about this, get out of his own head. He didn't want to wander far from camp, not after last night's events. What *had* he been thinking?

The fire cracked, a once whole piece of scavenged wood collapsed into cinders, and it wasn't unlike the epiphany that cracked Cornelius' upside the head. He'd been showing off. Posturing. Arrogant.

Cornelius ran a hand through his hair, the sides of which had grown long and unruly. He desperately needed a haircut. Watt watched him out of the corner of his eye, and waited.

"I've a lot on my mind," Cornelius started. He found it hard to say anything more, and went quiet. What an auspicious beginning.

"They don't have much storage space, do they? Minds, I mean." Watt murmured.

Cornelius' lip quirked. "No, they don't." He sighed, the night air far crisper than it was during the day. Cold, but not the kind that awaited one in Michigan.

Here it was sharp and sudden, so unlike the aching and endless cold that soaked one to the bone.

"I—I wonder if I am doing women a disservice."

Watt blinked, long and slow. "I don't understand," he said after a moment. "Can you explain?"

"I—do you remember when you came to my office with Mrs. Fawcett?"

Watt's confusion softened, and a smile touched his lips. "Yes."

"She wanted to go with him, to come here. But Percy said it wasn't her place, that she wasn't fit for it. And this is just one case of many, men telling women what they can or cannot achieve, that they are physically *less* capable. Too delicate. And yet, here I am. With a lame leg, to boot. It hurts like hell fire, but I'm here. Capable. But none of the credit will go to women, because I ..." Cornelius trailed off, frustrated. He desperately wanted another cigarette, or better yet a drink. But his lungs were heavy with all the tobacco he'd already smoked that day, and his throat was drier than sandpaper. He'd been the one to ensure no alcohol had come along with them, and now he was angry with himself for it.

Watt studied him, brows drawn together. Slight wrinkles creased his eyes and mouth, and Cornelius became strangely fixated on them. He wanted to trace them, feel how deep they went. It was too early to tell what they were carving into Watt's face, and the next few years of his life would determine whether they deepened into laugh or frown lines. Cornelius thought maybe they were leaning towards the latter, and he wanted to change that. But all Cornelius had done in his life was make people frown. Hell, Watt was doing it now.

Slightly baffled, Watt said, "But you aren't a woman, Cornelius. Why should ... 'the credit' go to them?"

Cornelius made a frustrated sound. He gripped his head with both hands. "I am *here*, but here?" His hands drifted downwards, grazing his throat, pausing meaningfully on his chest, then continuing until his hands came to rest in his lap. Voice rigid and angry, he said, "The physical proof they need is right *here*."

Cornelius felt as if he could tear himself open right then, and abruptly realized he had. He was set aflame, even if the fire was several feet away from them.

In that slow way of his, Watt said, "I hear what you're saying, but I think you're looking at this wrong."

Cornelius lifted his head to look at him. "Why?"

Watt scratched at the scruff along his jaw that had taken hold since Cuiabá, a much darker color than the hair atop his head which had grown, but lightened in color from bronze to gold. He said, "I don't know, because how can anyone know who someone *is* without being explicitly told, but you may be the first ... transvestite? I don't know the right word, I'm sorry if that's not right. But you may be the first American of that nature to go

.on an expedition into the Amazon of this magnitude. Isn't that something worth claiming the credit for?

And besides, there are women explorers. Hell, we'll be meeting up with one soon, and you know many. Women are more than capable of forming their own stories without us men doing it for them, you know."

Watt said this last bit playfully, as if Cornelius had been saying otherwise. Cornelius stared at him, at a loss for words. For a few moments they said nothing. Cornelius reluctantly turned his gaze to the sky when he realized he'd been staring open mouthed at Watt for longer than appropriate. Two thoughts hit him.

Watt was right. And Watt was playing with him. Comfortable enough to. He wasn't shocked by Cornelius' question, or put off. He even sounded interested, like he'd been waiting to be asked this very question. Or perhaps more simply, any question at all.

Cornelius lifted a shoulder. "That word never really fit me. It's … not about the clothes. Or not *just* about the clothes."

Watt nodded. "Is there one? A word?"

Cornelius shook his head. "I don't know. Man is fine enough for me."

"Alright." Watt rubbed at his beard again. "Can I … ask you something?"

"Yes."

"When did you know?"

Cornelius' fingers twitched, then relaxed. He glanced at the campfire, then to Watt. Their past temporarily superimposed on the now, of Cornelius telling Watt all those years ago how he felt, who he was inside.

He said, "I ... I was never a *girl*. Not in the way they were supposed to be. I was rough and played hard, asked too many questions and refused to be tamed. Mother said I'd grow out of it, that it was the hazards of growing up in the country. But I didn't. When I got older, after I'd ..."

Cornelius' face heated exponentially. "Once my body started changing, I knew something was wrong. Off. Everything fit wrong, including my own skin. I hated to be seen in dresses, or seen at all. I didn't know why, only that I was angry. I thought maybe it was the way women were treated, the expectations put upon them. But one day, when you were swimming in the lake with Jimmy ..."

Watt startled a little, surprised to hear of himself. When Cornelius didn't go on, Watt said, "What?"

Cornelius cleared his throat. There was no way around this. "During the last summer you visited, I—well. I thought it was a crush. I was just so fascinated by you, and in a way that was entirely unlike anything I'd felt before. And then that day at the lake came, and watching you swim I just thought ... I don't want him. I want to be him. Not *you* you, but ... I wanted your life. I wanted to be a man."

Okay, so he might have lied a little. But he couldn't make Watt uncomfortable, not now. Although, by the rising color in Watt's face Cornelius had already done that by tenfold.

"I remember that day," Watt whispered, and his eyes

glazed over with memories. "I almost didn't get in the water. It felt wrong somehow, that you and your sisters weren't allowed to swim. But you kept pestering me, telling me I wouldn't get another chance to dip my toe in Lake Michigan. So I did."

Cornelius grinned. "Me? A pest?"

Watt chuckled. "The most troublesome of them all."

"Oh, calm down." Cornelius bumped against Watt.

Watt bumped him back. They exchanged smiles again, then stared into the fire for awhile, digesting truth. Hesitantly, Watt asked, "And do you ... like men? Is that why you were there, at that place?"

Cornelius should not have felt as blown away by that question as he did. Nevertheless, he replied with a quick and deflecting, "Do you?"

Watt's throat clicked as he swallowed. He reached for the chain around his throat, running his thumb over the cool metal. The following silence was everything, and Cornelius shifted. Not away from Watt, just in place. The silence stretched on, and on, so Cornelius let it be. He felt sure of Watt's answer now, and he didn't want to pressure Watt into anything. Besides, he felt so hollowed out from doling out his own honesty that he was content to just exist side by side.

"There was a man in my regiment that I was fond of. It wasn't ... like that, but ... we'd the City left together, stayed together through training and everything. He was the only one who seemed to really understand me, and didn't mind that I didn't talk very much. He talked enough for both of us, anyways. He was a storyteller, but his tales were simple. Apple picking on the farm upstate, chasing after cows and persistent younger siblings. I hadn't heard someone speak with such vigor and life since ... a long time. Of course the stories were for everyone, not just me. But we had our own ... moments, I guess you could say. I'd always wondered about myself, and the way he looked at me sometimes I wondered about him too. And for the first time in my life there wasn't someone telling me—"

Watt paused abruptly, sucking in air. And then, so quiet that Cornelius could hardly hear him, Watt went on. "I've always known that I didn't like girls like *that*. Even when I was young. And my father knew, too. He tried to shame it out of me, beat it out of me. I still—I *haven't*, Cornelius, but when I was with him, I wanted to. I thought about it, dreamed about it. Wrestled with myself over what to do, because there was this shine in his eyes when he spoke to me you know? And was it because he felt the same way I did, or was it all in my head? But I wasn't brave enough, I couldn't—"

Watt broke off, mouth closing so hard his teeth clacked. Cornelius' heart ached for him, it really did. He was overcome with an intense desire to hug Watt, to hold him and tell him it was okay, that love had no bounds. But it sounded like maybe Watt was coming around to that truth on his own, and Cornelius didn't think his word would mean much to Watt. Instead, he slipped an arm around him, resting his hand on Watt's shoulder. He gave it a gentle squeeze, and Watt released a mighty sigh that might've been a little choked.

"What's his name?" Cornelius asked.

Watt closed his eyes. "Frederick." After a moment he opened them again, and tears spilled onto his cheeks. "His name was Frederick."

Was. Did Watt see him die? Or was he faced with a dead body, or perhaps worse yet, no body at all?

With his free hand, Cornelius reached into the space between their laps and curled his finger around Watt's. It was his pinky finger, the one missing the tip. A story Cornelius had not yet heard. Watt did not startle. He smiled, a small and tremulous thing. He leaned against Cornelius and held his hand in return, just by the one finger, and they sat there together for some time in silence. Watt drifted off to sleep and Cornelius took up watch again, allowing the man to rest in his arms. He stared up at the sky, realizing he'd spoken to Watt about damn near everything under the moon.

Everything but the contents of Nina Fawcett's letter.

He Knows

May 18th, 1930

Crossing the Paranatinga was a strenuous effort that demanded every ounce of thought and muscle that Watt had. He was glad for the distraction of simple labor, everyone was tired and quiet that morning which led to too much room for thinking.

They decided to ford the animals and supplies from one side of the river to the other, utilizing an area where the water was relatively low, but still high enough to reach their chests. Roots of scrub trees protruded from the reddish brown dirt of the steep river banks, exposing themselves in an effort to quench their thirst. The water ran quick enough to render it clear, and be a nuisance.

Guiding the mules on foot, Severino went first, followed by Cornelius, then Watt. Antônio remained, waiting for Severino and Watt to return for the pack mules. When Cornelius led his steed into the river, he nearly tumbled down the embankment and into the water. Thankfully the mule was steadfast and did not spook easily, providing Cornelius with a rigid source of support.

Of course he refused all offers of help, and Watt was helpless to do anything but watch the man struggle across the river. He'd thought it was because of the man's leg, but when Watt made his own crossing he found the river bed was the type of silt that sucked at you, doing its best to drag you down, and the current was surprisingly strong. Watt and Severino returned for the other mules, and Antônio, and by the time they all got across a break was needed.

Shielded by the mules and shrubbery, the men stripped down and changed into fresh sets of clothes and boots. Watt's cheeks were aflame the entire time, thus far they'd been able to change in relative privacy and isolation, but not like this. Needs must, however, when soaked to the bone. By the time he found a branch to hang his clothes on, Cornelius joined him fully dressed, his hair combed back and a lit cigarette pinched between his trembling lips. Watt hurried up and pulled a shirt on, but he could tell that Cornelius had already seen the ugly scar on his shoulder. His attention brought a burning phantom pain along with it, and Watt turned away to prop his wet boots upside down on a rock.

Cornelius did the same with his own boots, then hung his clothes beside Watt's. After hanging up his trousers, boxer shorts, socks, and a shirt, he glanced Watt's way and smiled crookedly around his cigarette.

"Your hair's long."

The tension eased in Watt's shoulders, and a smile escaped him as he withdrew his pipe. "You're one to talk."

Cornelius leaned heavily on his cane, shifting closer to Watt. A bit more serious, he quietly asked, "Did you sleep alright?"

Watt lifted a shoulder, cheeks flushing as he recalled how exactly he'd fallen asleep last night. Held by Cornelius. He'd awoken to the man staring down at him, gaze intent and a tiny smile cresting his lips, telling him to go to bed before the others woke. What a sight.

"I think so," Watt said, realizing he'd been staring at his companion for far too long without answering. "Thank you, for uh—" He coughed. "For talking to me. Did you? Get enough sleep?"

"Of course." Cornelius chuckled softly.

They smoked tobacco and drank their canteens dry, then refilled them with iodine treated water from the river. Cornelius took pictures of Antônio by the river and spoke quietly with the man in Portuguese. Watt wandered nearby, pleased when he found several unique looking stones that he tucked into his pocket for later. It was a running joke among the others at this point, that Watt was carrying more rocks than gear, but he really wasn't. He limited himself to a dozen, trading out the small rocks with more interesting ones as needed. His eyes wandered, too, glancing over at Cornelius every now and then, unable to stop thinking about their conversation last night. He'd revealed his greatest secret, and Cornelius had easily accepted it. Him. Watt wasn't sure why he'd thought Cornelius would do otherwise. Not because of his own nature, but because Cornelius had a heart. A good one.

It all had Watt rattled. Unsettled. He couldn't help but read his companion's every move and expression, certain that Severino and Antônio had overheard their conversation, or that Cornelius was looking at him differently. That last part may not have been all paranoia.

Cornelius had said he'd had a crush on Watt ... well, Watt from his youth, anyhow. Watt was not anywhere near the same person he was all that time ago, physically or otherwise. Too much had changed, broken. So Watt convinced himself that the look in Cornelius' eyes this morning was not interest. In fact, he convinced himself that there was no look at all. He was overthinking.

Watt joined Severino who was keeping the mules and Maggie company. She was eager to continue on their journey, she'd crossed the river twice without complaint and still had enough leftover stamina for days, but settled for attention instead. He wasn't sure how the old girl did it, and a pang of guilt hit him. She should be in retirement lazing about their apartment, not laboring through the wilderness.

"Traidor." Severino laughed when she managed to tug a stick out of his hands and dutifully delivered it to Watt when he approached.

Watt chuckled softly and tossed the stick into a patch of reddish brown dirt not far off. When he turned his attention back to Severino, he caught the man staring at his hand. Watt flexed his fingers and said, "Are we ready to go?"

Severino nodded, smoothly taking the hint. Man was too damn curious for his own good. "I am if you are. Or do you have more pebbles to fetch?"

Watt grumbled in response, unable to keep a smile from his lips.

———◈———

They traversed through sparse grasslands which gave way to thickening trees at a steady pace, talking little. Cornelius couldn't remember the last time he felt so exhausted. His body ached, and his mind was heavy. His mount seemed equally tired after the crossing, and Cornelius still felt bad for falling and clutching to her like he did. Embarrassed, too. His companions hadn't any trouble crossing, and if they suffered beneath the strain of their trip they didn't outwardly show it.

He did his best to keep his mind off his body, which worked out fine as he kept thinking about Watt's body instead. But not in the way he would've liked to be thinking about it. No, he was thinking about the bullet wound on either side of his right shoulder. He hadn't known that Watt had been shot. And then there were the scars on the backs of his hands. The missing tip of

his left pinky finger, an injury Cornelius assumed occurred during war time. What happened to him during
those days lost in the woods?

What he kept coming back to were the metal, circular tags hanging around his throat. He wanted to know
why Watt still wore them, were they his own or Frederick's? Was he still in love with a dead man? Cornelius
could believe it, Watt had a deep heart with enough love
to fill the ocean. He bet the man was a romantic. And
to lose someone so tragically, well. Nothing could beat
a love story like that.

They arrived at the Simões Lopes Post by mid afternoon, covered in sweat and assaulted by insects. This
part of the country was cerrado, dry prairie land. The
Post was well organized with government buildings
and the staff needed to run them, and fit with a local
for the missionaries from the South American Indian
Mission. They dismounted and met with the missionaries and the agent of the Indian Protective Services,
all were friendly and welcoming. The men of God made
Cornelius' skin crawl, but he did his best to be grateful and polite. Afterwards, they were brought to the
neighboring Bacairy Village itself.

Cornelius noticed a large building that seemed reminiscent of a warehouse. When he asked about it, the
IPS agent explained that it was indeed a warehouse.
All the posts serving Indigenous peoples were being
pushed to be self-sufficient, and as such they grew their
own rice, corn, cane, and other crops on reservation

land.

"And is any of it sold in the cities?" Watt asked, which surprised the agent.

The agent said, "Well, yes. It is a good way to support the post financially, especially when our residents are so hard working and bring in such yields that it is far beyond what we can consume here."

"I see," Watt said, and it sounded like he didn't see at all.

The agent picked up on this as well and quickly added, "It is our mission here to give the natives the isolation and privacy they desire, and any support they may need. This area is quickly becoming settled, as I'm sure you saw on your way in. And not just by the get rich quick sort of folk, but people who are here to stay. It is imperative that the people here have a way to ... bridge the gap, so to speak."

Cornelius opened his mouth, but Watt discreetly pinched the back of his arm. Cornelius nearly decked him. What the hell did Watt know about how *wrong* this was, and what gave him the right to shut Cornelius up?

Instead of hitting Watt, he scowled and rubbed at his arm.

They were confronted with a large, elevated dirt area surrounded by grass and fence. The soil was packed down between great square clay buildings thatched with palm leaves, and gallery forests waited in the distance beyond the fencing. A small cattle herd was also visible in the distance on the cerrado, another puzzle piece that did not fit. According to von den Steinen, the Xinguano Bacairy were fishermen that relied on the rivers, and grew their own food. Perhaps this was more of that self sufficiency the agent spoke of.

The Bacairy lived in four different villages on the reservation allocated to them, and this village beheld many people of the Xinguano sort, although there were some families from other villages as well. The Headman and many of the local families greeted them. They had dark brown skin and black hair that was cut in blunt styles. Most of them wore clothing of the khaki variety, and their houses looked entirely different than in the photographs he'd seen thus far. Doing his best not to glare at the men of organized religion, Cornelius noted more people were acculturated than he thought would be. Perhaps Antônio was not so much of an outlier as he'd originally thought.

Severino did most of the talking, acting as lead man of their group. He was well known and respected here, which made sense since he frequently stopped on his way to the site. All the children were taught Portuguese at the relatively new schoolhouse and some of the older people were familiar with it, but Severino mostly spoke to them in Bacairí, a fact that wrinkled the noses of the missionaries. Cornelius and Watt introduced themselves, using the limited Bacairí they knew thus far. Antônio stayed with their group as they were taken to a building known as the men's house, which would be their shelter for the next few days, and their mules were brought to a grazing area separate from the cattle. Cornelius hoped his steed would enjoy the reprieve. The mules hadn't lost much for weight, but they also hadn't gone far in the grand scheme of things.

The men's house would not be solely theirs, but shared among the men of the village. They piled their belongings in a corner, then sat with the agent, headman, missionaries, and other male members of the village at the center of the building. Cornelius sat between Watt and Severino, and he felt strangely pleased that Antônio sat on other side of Watt.

The Headman asked a question in Bacairí, and Severino relayed it to Watt and Cornelius. "What is your purpose for visiting?"

Watt looked at Cornelius, and after a pause Cornelius picked up the question. He said, "We are passing through, on our way to an archaeological site in the north. With Severino."

The Headman considered this, his wizened gaze shifting between Severino, Watt, and Cornelius. He'd been aged in the sort of way that meant he could've been fifty or seventy, his brown skin wrinkled in deep creases around his eyes and mouth, even his nose. When he spoke, Cornelius caught a glimpse of teeth yellowed by time and use, and the uppers were filed to points. The Headman exclaimed a string of words, and this time it was directed at Severino. The two held a fast paced conversation, and Cornelius recognized his and

Watt's names, but no more. The Headman gestured to Antônio, who inhaled sharply but said nothing. Severino shook his head, and it was clear the conversation had devolved into a disagreement.

"What's wrong?" Cornelius asked.

"He believes you are imposters," Severino said, looking between Watt and Cornelius.

Cornelius swallowed. It was the truth, wasn't it?

"What did he say about Antônio?" Watt asked.

Severino flicked a cool look to the young man in question. Antônio was stiff as a board, discomfort evident in every taut muscle. His face though, was blank. "He wants Antônio to travel with us."

"To keep an eye on us," Cornelius clarified.

"Yes," Severino said. "But also, Antônio has shown great promise and they have been trying to send him to university for some time. But he does not want to leave. It is their hope that Antônio may change his mind after working with us."

That surprised Cornelius. He quietly asked, "So ... what? We're to take him on as an unofficial intern and spy?"

"*Cornelius*," Watt muttered.

"I am no spy," Antônio spat in English, and his expression cracked. Cornelius' cheeks heated.

"You are our friend," Watt said. "No one is saying otherwise."

Antônio shook his head and said nothing, but the damage was done. Cornelius rubbed at his temple, nausea and guilt stirring in his gut. He desperately wanted a joint.

"Okay," he said. "Yes. We would be honored if Antônio accompanied us."

This pleased the Headman, and so they ate.

Cornelius' group shared their remaining xarque, condensed milk, and beans with their new friends, who in turn fed them sweet potatoes, yams, squash, peanuts, and fish. Severino would later explain that fish was now considered special in the village, for there was now a lack of fish in the portion of the Paranatinga they lived on. It was a great feast, but each man sat with their backs turned to their companions. To do otherwise would bring about great shame to the person.

Afterwards, they smoked tobacco grown by their hosts. It was unlike anything Cornelius had ever smoked before, making his head spin and body soften like the first time he ever tried the stuff. It was after Watt had been banished from Cornelius' life, and before he had accepted his departure. He'd smoked Papa's pipe, believing he'd gotten away with it until later on that day. Papa chastised him for not only smoking, but not being clever enough to change his clothes to get rid of the smell. Hells, he missed him. The sudden force of his aching struck him like a splitting maul to the heart, and he desperately wanted to be held by his Papa again. But that time had come and gone, and he was alone.

In Portuguese, Severino told a story within a story. Antônio spoke quietly to the Headman, translating the words he didn't understand. "Jacobina, a man who preferred to stay out of arguments and debates whenever possible, was challenged by four friends of his, their own opinions divided cleanly in two. The debate was this; what is the nature of a human soul? He tells them he has a story to prove his theory, that humans have not one soul, but two. One looking from the inside outward, and the other outside in. He told them of a story of when he was a younger man, a freshly appointed ensign with a uniform to match his position. He was treated so differently, addressed no longer in familiar but serious tones. His aunt, enamored with his status, ordered a large looking glass for his room. It was ornate and old, but finely made. His furnishings were modest, but he could not sway her otherwise.

"A transformation took hold, the ensign did away with the man, the external soul shifting as his world did. Three weeks thereafter, his cousin fell ill and he was tasked with managing the farm while his aunt tended to her. The man was left alone, save for servants who spoke little to him, then abandoned him in the night. He thought to leave and tell his aunt, but he could not abandon his responsibilities, so he stayed. His mind unraveled, and he began to ask questions, the kind that pulled at your heart, uprooting thought and reason. He wondered; do I exist if there is no one to perceive me? What is my purpose? He had avoided gazing upon his reflection in the looking glass, but after a week of eating bland food and reciting poems and otherwise, his frayed mind caught distorted features blurred and devoid of color, missing lines. And so, with madness driving him, he put on his uniform and faced the glass straight on before leaving, unable to take the solitude any longer. And then, he found it."

"Que?" Watt asked, eyes kindling with ... Cornelius wasn't sure, but he thought perhaps it was ... hope?

"Himself, the ensign, and the man. For the next six days, no matter what, he would put on his uniform and stand in front of the mirror. He would exist as the way others saw himself, if only for a few minutes a day. But that's all it took to keep the madness away, and his outer soul was satisfied." Severino spread his hands and smiled, his warm eyes around the room, pausing briefly on Cornelius before continuing. "The story, of course, had stirred up Jacobina's friends and upended the debate, but he took advantage of the chaos to slip away."

A chill tracked down Cornelius' spine, and he nearly shivered despite the humid heat trapped within the building.

'*He knows,*' Cornelius thought with a certainty that went down to his very bones.

A Dog

May 19th, 1930

Cornelius was gone.

Watt awoke to an empty spot beside him, and the first thought he had was that Cornelius had left. Turned back. He was gone, for good this time.

He wasn't sure why his mind immediately decided this, but it was enough for his heart to have a fit. He exited the men's house without disturbing Severino, who Watt was convinced wouldn't wake even if a blow horn was raging by his ear. He was equal parts jealous of the man's ability to sleep so soundly, and appalled. How easy it would be to kill him.

Well, that wasn't a pleasant thought. What was wrong with him?

Watt quietly eased out of bed and after only a moment's hesitation, retrieved a small rock from his rucksack. He felt slightly better after escaping outside, into the brisk night which reinvigorated his lungs. The sky made his heart stop and start again, resuming a somewhat steady, if not agitated, rhythm. The moon was a glowing sliver of light accompanied by millions of stars, each one fighting for attention in the great expanse of unpolluted night sky. It was beautiful, a sight that would never exist in the confines of New York City. Or Philadelphia, for that matter.

Watt played with the stone in his pocket and wandered around the building in search of Cornelius, wishing the moon was just a bit brighter. His gaze drifted to a stretch of fencing in the same direction as the river. It shivered beneath a gust of wind, the wire glinting in the night in a painfully familiar way. As did a small red light in the dark, close to the ground and dimmed by shadows. Watt approached slowly, and when he got closer he saw that Cornelius was sitting in a patch of dirt, hugging his knees which were drawn up to his chest. A cigarette hung from his lips, its light dancing in the dark.

When he was within ear shot Watt whispered, "Cornelius."

Cornelius startled anyways, then hissed a curse as the cherry of his cigarette fell. He stashed the butt into his pocket and started to get to his feet, but Watt put his hands out placatingly and sat beside him. "Sorry, I didn't mean to scare you."

Cornelius sighed, tucking himself back into a ball. "What're you doing out here?" He asked, his tone accusatory.

"Looking for you."

Cornelius scoffed. "At least you're honest."

Watt wasn't sure what that meant. "I try to be."

Cornelius hummed, but otherwise didn't comment. Watt accidentally thought out loud when he said, "This is becoming a habit." He gave Cornelius a little smile and added, "Not that I mind, of course."

The corner of Cornelius' mouth lifted, a barely there smile. His gaze traveled over Watt's face, slow and steady as if he were committing Watt to memory. Watt swallowed. What a self indulgent thought that was.

Watt cleared his throat and busied himself with offering Cornelius the smooth stone that had once been in his pocket. "Here. This one reminded me of you."

Cornelius slowly unfurled and took the stone with gentle fingers. He turned it over, rubbing his thumb over the black stone worn smoothed by time. It was mostly round, but had a few curving bits that reminded Watt of a clover. He glanced over at Watt and tried to smile, but it didn't reach his eyes. "Thank you."

Watt opened his mouth, but Cornelius abruptly turned his face away, towards the sky.

He boldly asked, "Do you believe in God?"

Watt had to bite his tongue on his first answer. His second was a highly redacted version. Simple. "Yes."

Cornelius nodded, still fiddling with the stone. "Thought so." He didn't say it with any venom, and yet Watt shifted in place anyway. "I don't hold it against you."

"But you hold it against others."

Cornelius stared at him, then back to the sky. Although the moon was thin, it was marvelous all the same. It had to be two or three in the morning. "A imagem do Cruzeiro resplandece," Cornelius said, lifting his free hand to the stars. His fingers extended, lazily tracing a shape. Watt leaned his head closer, trying to see. Cornelius whispered, "The image of the cross shines."

After a moment, and a little tilting of the head, Watt could see it. Four—five?—stars, arranged in the shape of a cross. There was another star, one that neighbored the left point, but it wasn't as bright as the others. He wasn't certain why it belonged, then he remembered.

"It's the flag," Watt said. "But ... mirrored."

Cornelius smiled, and pride bloomed in Watt's chest. "Yes. And their motto. An entire country bound beneath a cross in the sky." His hand drifted higher, pointing out another constellation. His pointer finger swept across lines that Watt had trouble following, zig-zagging in places. "But why not Centaurus? It's the biggest one up there. One of the biggest constellations in the whole sky, with some of the brightest stars. Or there's Corvus, or Virgo. Back down here, there's Musca."

Cornelius' hand fell to his lap, and he sighed. "I try not to."

"Hmm?"

"Hold it against people. It's just ..." Cornelius shook his head. "I've seen so much done in the name of God that it makes me wonder what kind of bastard he has to be, to want things like that done for him. To allow them to happen. It's—it's—sacrilegious."

"What is?"

Cornelius began turning the stone over in his hands, faster and faster. "This place. All these places."

Watt thought about that. Slowly, he said, "They're offering them education. That's—"

Cornelius shook his head, knocking his glasses askew. "They take far more than they give. It's not fair," he said, voice strained.

Watt hesitated for only a moment before resting a hand between Cornelius' shoulder blades. Cornelius drew his legs up again and rested his forehead against his knees, his chest expanding beneath Watt's hand as he fought for air. Watt didn't know what to say, or what Cornelius was upset about exactly. He wanted to ask, but you only got so many answers from Cornelius. Questions had to be efficient. Careful.

"You probably don't remember," Cornelius said, his voice muffled.

Watt knew he wasn't saying it to be mean, in fact he sounded terribly sad, but it still hurt. Watt couldn't help it.

Cornelius went on quietly, turning his face towards Watt so his voice came out clearer. "But there's a place back home. A school. The Holy Childhood of Jesus Catholic Church and Indian School."

"I remember," Watt said, surprised. He recalled a decent sized church neighboring an enormous set of adjoined buildings, three stories and bedecked with crosses at the tallest points. It reminded Watt of a campus, except it was surrounded by fencing. It was nothing like the fence they sat before now, but ... Watt swallowed. "It's a little ways before the Point, right? It had a bell that rang all hours of the day?"

Cornelius' lip curled. "Yes, that's the one."

They said nothing for a while. Watt could practically feel Cornelius brooding, and his body was warm beneath Watt's hand. He wasn't sure why, but he felt certain that at this moment he was grounding Cornelius, and it was a heady thought. His fingers gently curled and flexed between Cornelius' shoulders.

Cornelius said, "Well, everyone thought they were doing good there, too. Back home it's kill the Indian and save the man, here it's order and progress. But who is all this 'help' actually benefiting? Did these people ask for their names to be erased and their language forbidden? What are you supposed to do when people show up and say, 'accept Jesus, or else' and the or else is pillaging their land, forcing them into servitude, killing children—"

Cornelius inhaled sharply and tucked his face against his knees, cutting himself off. He held his breath, then let it out. In a muffled whisper, he said, "I just don't *understand*, Watt. How can God and Greed exist side by side like this? How did it all go so wrong?" He lifted his head, staring at the fence. His lashes were wet with tears, and Watt's heart clenched.

"They have a cemetery there, you know. Not for the parishioners, but … well, none of those graves are marked and there was no funeral, so I couldn't—I couldn't even say goodbye to him. John wasn't even a boarder, and they got the worst of it. But still, one day he was alive, and the next he wasn't. No one would tell me anything. It was an accident. An *accident*. Mama and Papa said it wasn't our business." Cornelius closed his eyes, and the tears finally cascaded down his cheeks. "But one night, I heard Papa talking about it with Mama. He worked with John's father, you see. He told her that while cutting wood for the clergymen with the rest of the boys, real splendid education there, that there'd been an accident. But he didn't think it was."

He began to cry in earnest and when Watt pulled him close, Cornelius went willingly. Watt stared up at the stars and held Cornelius as the other man wept. He wasn't good with words, but if his arms could offer the other man a semblance of comfort, they would always be open to him. It was the least he could do, especially after having his own breakdown last night.

Watt explored his heart and his own relationship with God, a fragile one tested by war and a family such as his. He'd been raised Presbyterian with the United Free Church of Scotland, which was a world of difference from the Catholics, but he knew they were not exempt from spreading the word of God through missionaries in Africa, India, and other places. Watt didn't think all missionaries could be bad, there had to be a line between spreading the word and converting those who were unwilling. What made people cross it?

Money, of course, and everything that followed. Superiority. Power.

There were many times when Watt questioned God's existence, and sitting here with the wire fencing in view brought all those times back to the forefront of Watt's mind.

Cold. Blood. Mud.

Flames. Grenades. Gas. Bullets.

Metal tags close to his chest, two sets now.

Barbed wire. The snap of a canine's jaw, and flesh giving way beneath teeth.

His left hand ached, convulsing with the memory of flesh that no longer existed. It was a strange thing to lose something like the end of a finger. It wasn't necessary, per say, and by no means inconvenient, not truly. And the pain that sometimes came out of nowhere, temporarily paralyzing muscles and tendons, was tolerable and somewhat quick in its attack. The look of it used to bother him, and that proof of vanity bothered him. Now, he largely ignored that part of his body most of the time, same with the scars on his hands and his chest.

And yet, he'd liked it when Cornelius linked his own finger around that misshapen pinky. Acknowledged him.

This reminded Watt that during all his times of crisis, he'd always come up with the same answer. Of course He existed. How else could you explain the stars and moon that hung above them? The places they'd been, and had yet to see?

The secret love that Watt held in his heart, and the fortitude to have felt it at all? To have survived the war, and the hell that came after?

But he did wonder. Where was God?

Did he condone the actions and words of his followers?

Did he know all the awful ways humans could hurt each other, now?

Did he know all the beautiful ways humans could love each other, now?

Watt became acutely aware of the fact that Cornelius was no longer crying. Cornelius still lay curled against Watt's side, his arms squished between them. One of his hands was trapped too, but the other had a hold of Watt's shirt, right over his sternum. His breathing was shallow, but consistent. For a brief moment, Watt wondered if he should break the silence or offer to move, but ultimately decided to let Cornelius do the breaking. He was content until then.

The thing was, Cornelius was content too. They sat together, watching the stars in comfortable silence. The bodies of dying light moved overhead, too slow to be perceived unless one watched them for hours on end.

———◈———

May 19th, 1930

Cornelius woke with a headache, a sore leg, and a craving for Giovanni's cooking. Or was it Giovanni himself he wanted? Or better yet, was it home he so desperately needed?

The day ahead of them was fully booked, and for once Cornelius wasn't grateful for distractions. He wanted to go back to sleep. No, he wanted to fill his stomach, smoke a joint, and go back to sleep. He couldn't face today. He needed an entire day and night of sleep before he could even think about functioning, or dealing with the emotional vomit he'd dumped onto Watt last night.

And there was the matter of Severino to deal with, but Cornelius didn't know how. He couldn't go asking Severino what he knew based on a significant look given with a seemingly relevant story, he could give himself away. Maybe Severino knew nothing. His heart argued otherwise, but for now he allowed his head to give direction. Best to act aloof. Casual. If Severino had suspicions, Cornelius would wait him out and deal with it then. He just hoped that if the other man did confront him, it would be in private.

Watt, well ... they'd gotten used to treating their late night revelations as simply that, hadn't they? Matters of the night. During the day, they were colleagues. Professional. Friendly. Was he embarrassed to have cried like a baby twice in the man's arms? Yes.

But also, it was the first time he'd let go in so long. He never cried, not with Giovanni or Esther, not even alone. The last time he cried before this trip was … hells, was it when he visited the Institute? Years, then, and now he'd cried on this trip so many times it was ridiculous.

An entire day and night dedicated to sleep was not in the cards, so he rose for the day. After his morning ablutions, his mind cleared and a thought crystallized. Today he would try. The past few weeks had been rough on their group's morale, and that needed to be remedied before continuing on. Perhaps if he pretended hard enough that everything was fine, he could get the others to believe it was true. Besides, it was an auspicious day. Jack Fawcett's birthday.

After readying themselves for the day, Antônio led their group on a tour around the village. The missionaries and agent did not come along as they had their own business to attend to, much to Cornelius' relief. He was also glad he brought his cane as they went beyond the confines of the fence, visiting the gardens near the river and gallery forests. They were by no means trapped in the village, and everyone insisted the fence only kept hostile people out, but it still made Cornelius uneasy. The reservation was over 50,000 hectares, a staggering number that Cornelius couldn't comprehend. Many people lived at the village near the Post, but there were outlying households as well.

Men and women worked in the gardens, each plot nearly an acre in size. Antônio explained they grew manioc and cotton, and that they grew sweet potatoes all year round, with the last harvest in April. Currently they harvested yellow maize, tearing the ears off the stalks and removing the husks.

With the aid of Antônio, Cornelius asked questions of those who stopped their work to speak with them. He asked about the gardens of course, but also if they enjoyed their work. After all, much of what they harvested would go on to the city. Brazil needed laborers, and here they were. He was surprised by the older folk. He expected many of them to be sour about the changes in their community, but he found that most were proud. "Have you visited the buildings yet? Look at all we've done, the clothes we wear and the tools we wield." Surprisingly, there was a common sentiment among them, one that echoed many of the older generations back home. "The young ones, they don't know how to work."

Watt found this bit particularly amusing, but in a dark humor sort of way.

Many of the younger people could speak Portuguese with Cornelius, rudimentary as it was but effective nonetheless. They were more suspicious than their older counterparts, bitter and cynical in a way that reminded Cornelius of himself. One woman in particular gave Cornelius a thorough lecture on the wrongdoings of the karaiwa, the non-indigenous peoples. They brought sickness with them and disturbed the ekuru of their village. Ekuru, Cornelius later learned, was a substance found in all plants and the beings that ate them, and eventually excreted them. It was one of the reasons the Bacairy tended to move often, the buildup of nails, hair, and bodily fluids could bring about bad spirits of sorts, or kadopy.

Cornelius didn't know much about ekuru, but he did know about the sickness that plagued this place. Many places like this, to be frank. Syphilis, and malaria. Malaria was par for the course in the jungle, but syphilis was brought in by all those who colonized, explored, and exploited these lands. Sickness did run rampant through the village here, and the population was straining. Had been straining ever since civilization came knocking. Cornelius tried to focus on the now.

In addition to gardening, the Bacairy were excellent canoemen and fishermen. They learned to paddle around the time they could walk, and despite their numerous migrations over the past couple hundred years it was a skill that always remained. This was common with many of the indigenous people living in the area, but to see them work so smoothly and competently in person was quite different than reading about it. Cornelius and Watt were shown how the bark of a jatuba tree could be transformed into a canoe, a process that Severino had seen many times before but seemed to enjoy nonetheless. There were canoes in various stages, some were still bark upon a tree while others were slabs of bark hung over a smoldering fire. It bode well for Cornelius and Watt, otherwise they'd miss the process as it generally took several days.

To remove the bark, a platform of sorts was built around the tree. Three upright poles surrounded the tree to form a triangle, and cross pieces were lashed between the poles for the workers to stand upon. The outline of the canoe had been drawn upon the bark, and wedges were now nestled between the bark and the wood. The men worked effortlessly as they pried it apart, the task mundane to them but fascinating to Cornelius.

Severino explained that the men fasted until the work was done, and sexual abstinence was required by those involved until the canoe was complete. If a woman in a 'certain state' even walked by, the bark could split. Everything the Bacairy did was with intention, and learning the rituals and aspects of daily life different than his was something that Cornelius always loved.

Another group of men were gathered around an enormous length of bark bent into shape over coals, which had been roasting the inner surface for hours upon hours. An elaborate framework of poles were used to wedge the pliable canoe into place, acting as levers on the sides with cross pieces to keep them from going too far. It was a tedious process, but by the time late afternoon came around a narrow canoe with a slightly flat bottom was brought into existence. With an open bow and slightly raised stern, Cornelius was unsure how well the clay built up on the edges would keep water out.

The foreman led them to the water, stoic against the choking heat and annoying insects that always peaked around this time. Cornelius followed Antônio and Severino, while Watt and Maggie walked beside him. "How do you think those would hold up on Lake Michigan?" Watt asked, nodding to the canoe the Bacairy carried down to the water.

Cornelius chuckled. "On a good day, pretty well I imagine. But the Great Lakes aren't known for their good days."

Watt cleared his throat. "Has there been anything like the Big Blow again?"

Cornelius shook his head. The storm of '13 was one unlike anything the Great Lakes had seen before, a blizzard for the ages. Hundreds of people died, almost twenty ships were lost and about the same were stranded for ages. Ice cold waves raged over thirty feet high, and hurricane force winds wracked destruction for miles across miles. Thankfully his family hadn't suffered any losses or major damage, but Harbor Springs had been a frozen hell for a good while there.

In a roundabout way, it had been one of the best winters of Cornelius' life. The mills, schools, nearly everything had been shut down, and the entire family was stuck at home for days on end. There was nothing to do but hibernate, tend to the woodpile and stove, eat good food, and tell stories. It had been cold despite their best efforts, but Papa's voice was a smooth, warm balm as he told stories and sang to Mama, danced with her. And when Cornelius wanted to know how to lead, Papa showed him with a smile.

"Cornelius."

Cornelius blinked, withdrawing from the tundra of his memories. He was no longer thirteen, but thirty. He was not home with his family, but deep within Brazil with strangers and people that could be called friends. And instead of waiting all winter and spring to see Watt again, he was here, with his hand on Cornelius' shoulder and an inquisitive eyebrow raised.

"Yes? Sorry, I was ..." Cornelius' grip tightened on his cane, and he gestured vaguely with his other hand. "The heat."

Watt squeezed his shoulder, frowning. Cornelius waited for him to ask more questions, but instead Watt tipped his head towards the river. "They want us to try it."

"Oh. Okay." Cornelius gathered his resolve, drawing himself up taller. "Lead the way."

Turns out, the canoe was more than capable of gliding across the water.

⸻◈⸻

Watt had become a dog, helpless to do anything but

follow his master. Cornelius wandered around and took photos of the river, the gardens, the village and government buildings, and so Watt followed.

Cornelius developed all the photos he'd taken since Cuiabá, and so Watt huddled in the makeshift dark room beside him.

Cornelius wrote letters late into the night, and so Watt quietly sketched.

It went on like this for days, not entirely acknowledged save for a few curious looks from Cornelius.

On their last night in the Post, both Severino and Cornelius wrote letters while Watt made the odd shape or two in his journal. They were left alone in the men's house, a rare moment. He sat cross-legged and hunched over the tense curve of a jaw, the stubborn angle of a nose. Eyes wrinkled with concentration, the creases upturned rather than downcast. Maggie huffed from beside him on their bedroll and Watt sighed. He set his pencil down and ran a hand down Maggie's spine, studying the sketches from afar. He glanced at Cornelius, then the paper. He couldn't figure out for the life of him what was off, but something was. Was it the arch of his brow?

"Do you have no letters of your own to write, Watt?" Cornelius asked without looking up from his own paper.

Watt flushed, darting a look towards Severino who was studiously focusing on his own letter, albeit with a tiny smile. Watt closed his journal and said, "Ah, no."

Severino lifted his head. "Surely I need not remind you this will be the last opportunity for correspondence for some time."

A pins and needles sensation began to crawl up Watt's spine, and he said, "You do not. I sent all my letters weeks ago."

"But you have family, do you not? What if—" Severino halted abruptly, as if voicing the worst case scenario might make it true.

Watt opened his mouth to tell Severino it wasn't any of his business, and it was a close thing. Instead, he muttered, "I have said all I need to, Severino." Cornelius' pen paused and it caught Watt's attention. He glared at Cornelius. "Got something to say?"

Cornelius hummed, lifting his pen from the paper. He placed the cap against his lips, contemplating him. The black rubber pressed against the tender flesh there, and the gold of the clip winked in the light of Cornelius' torch propped up on the ground. Watt swallowed, but didn't look away. Finally, Cornelius shook his head, tearing his gaze away from Watt. He tossed Severino a playful smile and asked, "Who are you writing to?"

Severino gave Watt a quick evaluating look before adopting a smile. He shifted his attention to Cornelius. "Isabela, of course, and the children."

"Oh, that reminds me." Cornelius slowly pushed himself to standing. He took a small bundle of photos out of his pack and handed over a portion of them to

Severino. "You might want to send some of these back, or keep them. Either way, they're for you."

Severino flipped through them, his smile widening. "Oh, look. These are fantastic, Cornelius. Ah, you get my good side every time. Thank you."

Cornelius laughed, clapping the man on the shoulder. "Of course, the least I could do."

Cornelius came over to Watt, limping a little, and sat down beside him. Cornelius offered the rest of the photos to Watt, who took them after a pause. "You don't have to—" He started, then trailed off as he looked down at himself.

He stood with Cornelius and Severino on the steamer they'd taken to Cuiabá, smiling like a damn fool. All three of them looked happy. He shuffled the next photo to the front. Watt stared out the window of their hotel room in Rio. His hair was a mess and his eyes were wide, lips parted and slightly curled upwards in delight. The next picture was of Watt again, but sleeping in the hotel in Cuiabá curled in a tight ball around Maggie, who laid in the empty space Cornelius had once occupied. Watt missed that ridiculously small bed.

The next photo was another one Watt didn't know had been taken. Cornelius and Watt stood close together on the banks of the Rio Novo. Cornelius stared up at Watt, glasses slid down his nose and his lips split into a brilliant smile. And Watt ... he was laughing. He'd never seen himself so happy, and he couldn't even remember what had been so damn funny. Of course it had been something Cornelius said, but what?

"Hard to write when all the people that matter are right here," Cornelius whispered, then smiled tentatively at Watt. "Not to toot my own horn."

"You must think awful highly of yourself."

"I do."

Watt chuckled, shaking his head. He straightened the pictures into a neat stack, unable to look Cornelius in the eye. Watt was a rational man and knew he'd been acting petulant. He was nearly forty years old, but in that moment he was a young man again. Jealous that his friends had received letters from back home and had someone to write to. It wasn't just Cornelius that didn't reply to Watt's letters while he was gone, but his family too.

"The thing is," Watt began, glancing furtively between his companions. He cleared his throat and rested a hand on Maggie's side. "Letters don't do me much good. Never have. During the war, the only letter I received was from Cornelius' father. Even now, when I'm away on long periods for trips or anything like that, I generally don't speak to my family until I return. And I don't have friends. The people back at home are ... I am too different. So no, I have no one to write to."

"Besides me, of course," Severino said without missing a beat. "You are more than welcome to send me letters, Watt. And you too, Cornelius. I hope that we all keep in touch after this."

Cornelius smiled. "Me too."

"Yes," Watt said. "I'd like that."

Later that night, long after the lights had gone out and the men had turned in, Watt woke in a cold sweat and the echo of gunfire in his ears. He'd been laying flat on his back with a knee partially pulled up to ease the pressure on his hip, but it was no longer comfortable. He wanted to move, but it was first instinct to wait. Eyes closed, it took him a moment to comprehend what he was hearing, but then it registered. He shouted at his mind to shut off, to stop listening. But he couldn't.

"Ah, you liked that? It is a highly shortened version of O Espelho, a story by Machado de Assis. I read it once in Gazeta de Notícias, it is one of those stories that stay with you, yes? I still have it, if you'd like to read it someday. It is home with Isabela now."

"*Severino*. How long?" Cornelius demanded in a strident whisper.

Severino sighed. "Does it matter?"

"Yes."

The strike of a match, followed by an exhalation. "Before I met you."

"Fuck." Cornelius snarled, his voice low but deadly. "Then why let me come? It is obvious that you have influence over Joaquim."

"What does that mean?"

Cornelius blew out a breath, but said nothing.

There was a pause before Severino replied. Slowly, he said, "For one, I am not one to take gossip as gospel. For two, why not? It was not my business to know in the first place, and it changes nothing. You are a good man, Cornelius. Stupid, perhaps. But good."

Cornelius huffed out a laugh.

After a few moments of quiet, Severino lightly added, "You could stay, you know. Both of you. Joaquim is a good man to work with, and we get along well, do we not? There is plenty of work to do."

Cornelius immediately said, "Thank you, but I made a promise."

"I respect that, but it is dangerous country up there. Not only the land, but the people, they are best left alone. I—I don't want to see either of you lost, or worse, especially for men claimed by the jungle long ago. It is not worth it. Just say that you'll think about it, can you do that? Besides, who is to say the site is not what Fawcett was looking for? Will that not satisfy his family?"

"Severino," Cornelius whispered, and it was said with such surprise and rebuke that Watt nearly rolled over. "I made a promise."

Severino sighed. "Cabeça-dura."

Cornelius hummed. "I can't argue with you there." A few moments later, he said, "I'd like that. The story, I mean."

Severino quietly laughed, and Watt could imagine him fondly shaking his head.

"Do you love her?" Cornelius asked suddenly. The air

was thick with silence for several long moments. Finally, Cornelius said, "I nearly proposed to my colleague. It would have been a matter of convenience for both of us. Protection. But I couldn't imagine being tied to someone I didn't love, so I didn't. Couldn't handle the idea of her rejecting me, either. To be honest."

"I do," Severino murmured after a time. "In the same way she loves me."

Cornelius did not push the matter, but he didn't have to. Even Watt could hear the grey area left behind in that statement. The tent fell quiet, and the smoke gave way to fresher air. Watt didn't fall asleep for a long time, mind gnawing on all the different ways people could love people.

A Hunter

May 26th, 1930

Watt stood on skeletons.

There was nothing remarkable about the area occupying 11° 43' S and 54° 35' W. Long marsh grass covered the ground, and slim trees did their best to survive in small clusters. The birds cried the same as they did anywhere else, and the insects were in peak biting condition. It was late afternoon and the place was as good as any to make camp. But it felt wrong, somehow. Hallowed.

"We can make camp here," Severino said, voice thin. He turned in a slow circle, studying the surrounding patch of land. The last place that Colonel Percy Fawcett was seen alive. The last place they could be seen alive. Severino generally did not take this route to the archaeological site from the Post, it was more of a round about way that took them through marsh land that was currently sparse and barren during the dry season.

Watt exchanged a glance with Cornelius, whose face was drawn and skin ashen. Haunted. Cornelius tried to smile at his attention, but it was tight and looked damn near painful. Was he in pain? Or just tense? He'd been struggling ever since they left the Post, and their mules behind. They would be rendered inefficient in the upcoming terrain, and there was no way to care for them at the site, so they'd been left as gifts. Cornelius looked away, busying himself with withdrawing his camera from its case. As he began to take pictures of the area, Severino approached Watt and the unflappable Antônio.

"Will there be more opportunities, do you think?" Severino asked Antônio. Technically they were still in Bacairy territory, which he was more familiar with.

Antônio nodded, and Watt's shoulders relaxed. "It is grassland for a mile or two, then we meet the basin. That will be good."

"Do we want to try for that then?" Severino asked Watt and Cornelius.

"Yes," Watt said, a hand stroking down Maggie's back. She panted, ears alert but eyes calm.

"Yes," Cornelius echoed, but his attention was on his camera, or more specifically the viewfinder. "Let me take a few pictures first."

Severino ran a hand through his hair and blew out a breath. He muttered, "This place feels strange, no?"

"Wasn't it you who spoke of feeling power in places?"

"Certo."

"Well, there you have it."

A moment passed, during which they watched Cornelius take photos of seemingly nothing important. The trees. The grassy area where a camp could've been made. A bird, some kind of green parrot with a yellow face. Too bad the film wouldn't be able to capture the different shades. Antônio wandered over to Cornelius, his curiosity getting the better of him. At his approach, Cornelius lifted his head and asked if he wanted to try it. Antônio nodded, so Cornelius demonstrated how to do it before handing the camera over. They weren't that far away, so Watt listened as Cornelius explained the specifications of the camera. Watt practically had them memorized, for all the times that Cornelius had recited it. A Kodak Eastman, Autographic. It was an autographic edition because of the little flap that allowed you to write directly on the film. It made him smile, watching them.

"Or ... " Watt began slowly. "Places only hold the power we give them."

Severino considered that. He elbowed Watt and said, "You know, you have more wisdom in you than you let on."

Watt chuckled. "I don't know about that."

Cornelius and Antônio joined them, the camera now tucked away into its case. "Don't know about what?"

"That he's a smart one." Severino jutted a thumb at Watt.

"Of course he is," Cornelius said without missing a beat, brows slightly pinched in confusion.

Watt flushed from his cheeks to the tips of his toes.

He coughed and said, "Let's go."

With Severino leading the way, Cornelius and Watt in the middle, and Antônio in the rear, they continued on. Maggie easily kept pace beside Watt, ears perked and tail curled. Conversation was sparse, allowing the noise of the swelling insects to thicken the air. Watt constantly fended them off, while they hardly seemed to bother Cornelius. The proof lay in the nasty bites along the back of his neck, behind his ears, and somehow there was a real angry one in his armpit. He hadn't told Cornelius about that one, the man was already worried about the ones that were visible.

He wanted to itch at it so badly, and caught himself rubbing his arm against his side in a vain effort to do so. After an hour or so of this, Cornelius called, "Doing alright there Watt?"

"Fine," Watt said, perhaps a bit too quickly.

Cornelius said nothing in response, at least nothing that Watt could hear. The man was notorious for cursing Watt out under his breath. Once his walls were broken, Cornelius was a worrier, especially when it came to Watt. Ever since leaving Cuiabá, he frequently asked each person in the group after their physical condition, whether they had any sores or bites, how they were feeling. He was the one to make sure everyone had eaten and hydrated properly in the mornings before heading out, and in the evenings before turning in.

He didn't ask Watt so much as interrogate and manhandle him, evaluating every inch of exposed skin in search of abnormalities that needed treatment. It was he who treated all of Watt's bites and strictly informed him not to itch. Cornelius was particularly bossy when taking care of Watt, but he couldn't say that he minded it. What he did mind was Cornelius touching his side, fingers to bare skin. The thought of it alone had an anonymous shiver going down Watt's spine. It was simply care, tending to a friend, but there was an aspect to it that Watt could not name, one he was not ready to explore. No, he didn't need Cornelius to do that for him. He could take care of himself. He could.

As the sun retreated, so did the cerrado. The gallery forests expanded until there was hardly any dry grassland between them, the canopies overwhelming and great. By the time dusk arrived, they'd found what Antônio said was the last clearing for some time. Ahead lay a dense treeline and thickening ground vegetation. Watt glanced back the way they'd come. They could still go back. Dead Horse Camp wasn't the place of no return. This was.

The four men quickly put together a camp, stringing hammocks between some outlying trees close to the woodline. There was a small and steady stream nearby, so Severino built a small fire and Cornelius boiled water over it in order to fill their canteens later. Watt walked with Maggie and Antônio in hopes of scaring something out of the low vegetation near the stream. They had plenty of food from the Post, but it would be several weeks before they reached the dig site. Best to live off the land best they could, and supplement only when they needed to.

A few feet ahead of him and Antônio, Maggie made a noise low in her throat, body stiffening. Watt followed her gaze into an area overrun with ferns. Could be anything under there. A snake, an armadillo or tapir, or—

A pack of peccary burst out from the bush, charging at Maggie with canines gnashing and wiry black fur raised high on their backs. Their white faces were streaked with mud, as was the rest of their bodies. Maggie growled, body coiling in preparation to lunge. Watt shouted and fired a shot, taking the wild animal down before it could thrash her. It went down with a great squeal, but Watt hadn't the time to make sure it was dead as another one charged at Antônio.

Antônio had his own gun at the ready, and he shot the animal square between the eyes. It screamed even louder than the first, and the rest of the pack scattered in fear. For a second or two they simply stood there, chests heaving. Finally, Antônio said, "Leave it to the gringo to be scared by a pack of queixada."

Watt laughed, although there wasn't quite enough air in his lungs to do so. "You were too."

"You scared me!" Antônio snapped, but he was grinning.

Guided by Antônio as he worked his own kill, Watt made quick work of butchering the animal. There was a scent gland on the peccary that Antônio insisted they remove before anything else. Situated on the hindquarters, it was hard to miss the area of skin that was not unlike a human breast and generally used to mark trees. Using a wide berth and many reminders from Antônio not to puncture the gland, he cut a large circle through the tough hide and removed it.

Antônio uncapped his canteen of water, instructing Watt to rinse his hands before he did the same. The smell was God awful, and soap would've been greatly appreciated, but after rinsing most of the smell came off their hands. Watt didn't want to know what it would've been like if they had punctured the gland itself. They found a suitable tree to hang their peccary from, using rope secured around the hind legs. Each weighed likely no more than forty pounds, but it was dead weight and Watt was tired. Once they were hung, it was business as usual. While the anatomy was slightly different, gutting an animal was more or less the same. Out with the entrails and anything else that could spoil the meat. He made several incisions around the legs and belly in order to cape the animal. He pulled downwards on the hide until reaching the base of the neck, leaving the flesh beneath exposed. He removed the hide in a single, satisfying piece.

"You are a hunter?" Antônio asked, watching him curiously. His English was intentional and heavily accented. He was a quick study, and had learned enough to ask questions, which he did often. He'd removed the hide from his own animal at this point, and his arms were just as bloody as Watt's, up to the elbows.

Watt stilled, allowing the first thought that came to mind to pass. He said, "When I was small, with my father. Ahh, pai. It is not the same."

"How?"

"It is..." Watt searched for the word staged in Portuguese, but he couldn't find it. "Falso. If you don't shoot anything, it is okay. Here, now, it is important."

"Hmm." Antônio returned, frowning. They went back to work, and all the while, Watt did his best not to think of the thing he'd hunted most in his life.

Other humans.

<hr>

On the one hand, Cornelius was incredibly grateful for the tender white meat roasting over the fire. And on the other hand, well. He wanted nothing more than to swat Watt Johnson over the back of the head.

"You're absolutely covered," Cornelius fumed. He gestured to Antônio. "Look at him. He's got barely a spot on him."

Antônio grinned. He'd changed into clean clothes shortly after turning over the peccary to Cornelius and Severino to prepare. Meanwhile, Watt had sat nearby and helped them in his own way, which was mostly just a lot of sitting and staring. His eyes were glassy, and his skin pale. Maggie had hardly left her post, laying at his feet with her head on his boot. They were covered in mud and probably blood, but she didn't care.

Watt sighed. "It's just blood, it'll dry."

Cornelius' eye twitched. He said, "You're not sleeping in bloody clothes. Get changed, now."

Severino covered his mouth with a hand, stifling laughter. Muffled, he said, "He has spoken, and so it will be done."

Watt's cheeks flushed red, and Cornelius almost felt bad. Almost.

"Fine," Watt muttered, then stalked off to his hammock and pack with Maggie right behind him. None of the men had serious qualms about modesty, but none of them ever went fully nude in the presence of another either. Cornelius was the exception, as he always dressed and bathed in private. There'd been a few times after river crossings that had been close calls, but Cornelius was quicker than most when changing. Nearly as fast as Watt, who Cornelius guessed felt insecure about his scars.

Cornelius watched the fire, glancing at Watt every now and then as he stripped down to his boxer shorts. His boxers weren't much different than Cornelius' own, colorful pinstripes and everything. But Watt filled them out much better than Cornelius did, and the sight of Watt tugging on pants and hopping into them a little had Cornelius instantly regretting his earlier demands. Dear Lord. He'd started to pull his gaze back to the fire when Watt stretched his arms overhead to tug on a shirt, revealing an angry swollen area in his armpit.

Cornelius stood and made it all the way over to Watt before a single thought could occur.

Watt raised a brow at his unsteady approach, but didn't stop tucking his loose shirt into his trousers. Cornelius' fingers skated beneath the fabric, tugging the shirt upwards a fluid motion. Watt's eyes went wide and he inhaled sharply, which resulted in a low whine from Maggie. He started to pull away, but stopped when Cornelius said, "You're hurt."

"It's just a bite," Watt said, indignant. He half-heartedly tried to pull away again, but Cornelius lost his footing and pain lanced up his leg. He shot Watt a withering look. Abashed, he said, "I'm sorry, but I can take care of myself, you know."

Perhaps it had been a bite at one point, but now it was a festering wound. Circular and smaller than the palm of his hand, but hard and highly inflamed. "Clearly not. It's infected, Watt. How long has it been like this?" Cornelius hissed, inspecting the surrounding area.

"D'know," Watt said defensively. "A few days?"

"*Watt*," Cornelius glared at him. "Doesn't it hurt?"

"It's a bug bite, Cornelius. It's infected. I've been keeping it clean, that's all that can be done for it. It's nothing compared to ..." Watt trailed off, and his cheeks flushed. He swallowed, looking away from Cornelius. "It's fine."

Cornelius sighed. According to more than half the stories about the Fawcett group, that's all it took to kill Raleigh, a bug bite gone wrong. True or not, it wouldn't happen to Watt, not on his watch. "Come on over by the fire so I can get a better look at you."

"Cornelius, I—"

"Please?"

Watt stared down at him, his body rigid beneath Cornelius' lingering touch on his side. He barely seemed to be breathing, and Cornelius wondered if he should pull back. Watt's eyes were dark this evening, and his jaw set tight. He searched Cornelius' face for some great epiphany it seemed, but none came. Finally he said, "Okay."

Maggie escorted Watt back to the fire with the others while Cornelius obtained the first aid kit. Watt sat cross-legged opposite the fire from Severino and Antônio. Crackling light flickered across his tanned skin, highlighting the dark blond hair that clouded over his muscled chest, thick stomach, and even a little on his back, where ribs met spine. The hair looked coarser than it was on his arms, and Cornelius wanted to find out for himself if it was. Instead, he knelt beside Watt, and he could feel Severino and Antônio watching as he began to flush the wound with first hot but not boiling water, then iodine. His skin was hot to the touch and flushed red, taut with swelling despite the slight drainage from where he must've been bit. Cornelius bet anything it'd been one of those garapata ticks that had swarmed them. Hells, that had been ages ago. Was the head still embedded?

It was quiet for some time, in a sense. There was

the neighboring forest and the soft whisper of grass tousled by the crisp night air, the occasional pop in the cinders or sizzle of grease upon fire. Cornelius leaned back and considered the wound once it was cleaned, debating whether to pack it or not. He could fit the tip of his finger in there, and it probably wouldn't hurt to put some gauze in. But he hadn't found the head of the tick, and that worried him. Had it gone deeper, or fallen off?

Watt's eyes flicked to his, his crow's feet were pinched with pain.

"Sorry," Cornelius muttered. "Almost done."

"It's fine." Watt smiled tightly. "Good thing your first aid skills are still impeccable."

Cornelius chuckled. "Growing up with a litter of brothers will do that to you."

"What is your story?" Severino asked, gesturing between them. Antônio was checking the meat, but it was clear he was listening as well.

Watt glanced over his shoulder at Cornelius, waiting for him to give a version of their story that fit best. But in that moment Cornelius was very tired of stories, and he wanted nothing more than to deal in truths.

He decided not to pack the wound, but he did cover the area with gauze and a bandage. He distracted himself from the feel of Watt's tanned skin beneath his fingertips by dredging up old memories. In English, allowing Severino to translate his story for Antônio, he said, "When we were children, his family visited the place I lived during the summer, when it is most beautiful. We met at the local ice cream shop, and I tagged along when my brothers offered to give him a tour of town. I was always following Jimmy around, even if I wasn't supposed to be, and it only got worse when this one showed up."

Watt smiled. "We never minded."

"This is true."

"Why not?" Antônio asked in Portuguese. "Why not follow your brother around?"

Loathe to do so, Cornelius bid Watt to put his shirt back on. He ached to light up, but he didn't. He sat down beside Watt so he was facing Antônio and Severino properly. Cornelius told his story in English, his brain unable to come up with Portuguese words for most of what he wanted to say. "It wasn't the done thing, girls playing with boys, running around town and getting into trouble. Papa could convince Mama to turn the other cheek most of the time, but when the ritzy types came into town it always put her into a mood."

Cornelius finished a little breathlessly. Although Severino already knew, it was still terrifying. And he didn't know how Antônio would react, who Cornelius respected greatly. Watt's elbow brushed against Cornelius', but he didn't mind. In fact, he wanted to lean against Watt's arm and stay there awhile.

Brows furrowed, Antônio said in English, "You are not a girl."

"My body is. Not my heart."

"Oh." Antônio's face creased with concentration as he mulled it over. Severino glanced between Antônio and Cornelius, looking slightly bemused. It must've been nice to feel so lighthearted, and not like your gut was in your throat. Maybe he shouldn't have said anything. Maybe this was a mistake. Watt pressed his knee against Cornelius', and in response he flashed Watt a quick, nervous grimace.

"What happened next?" Antônio asked.

A sigh of relief escaped Cornelius, and so did the rest of the story. They had been friends, meeting up every summer when the Johnsons came to town. They'd taught Watt how to be a kid, that much he was sure of. But during the tail end of that last summer, Watt fell ill.

Cornelius had kept him company, and when it looked like he might not pull through, he changed his body to match his heart, and went to tell Watt the truth. It had started to storm, but Cornelius didn't care. Watt had to know who he was before he died. He came in through the same window he always did, and told a delirious Watt everything.

But Callum Johnson had been on the other side of Watt's door, listening to everything. Waiting for the perfect moment to strike, Cornelius had thought. He'd taken Cornelius by the arm and dragged him away from his friend, from shelter. When he threw Cornelius outside, he dislocated his shoulder. Cornelius screamed, but it had been nothing compared to Callum's furious roar, banishing him from his property, from Watt, from everything that mattered. Then he'd shut the door in Cornelius' face, locking him out in the rain. He'd made it home hours later, drenched and shivering, both from the pain and the cold. He hadn't even seen his parents or siblings yet dressed as he was, hair sheared, but they didn't care.

The confrontation between Callum and Papa was one that occurred while he'd been sleeping, but Jimmy had described it to him in great detail. After a heated exchange, Papa had knocked Callum to the ground with a single hit, sending blood spraying everywhere. He came home, told Cornelius he was banned from the Johnsons' property, and that was the last Cornelius had heard of the Johnsons for ages. Anything he heard about them was gossip or news he sought out. The loss of contact continued until early this year. Severino did not know this part, or if he did Cornelius had not told him. Cornelius did not tell them about the lost letters between them, or the feelings he harbored for Watt. He had a sense Severino knew the way he cared for Watt went beyond the care of a friend, but then again Severino often smiled like he knew all the secrets of the world.

After it was all said and done, Cornelius' chest hurt from the bombardment of cigarettes and truth, and his head was light from the release in pressure. He couldn't get a clear read on Antônio, the man was as serious as a stone. Eventually, he asked in Portuguese, "So what you are. That is not normal." Antônio shook his head. "No. Accepted."

Cornelius exhaled shakily. In kind, he said, "Not generally, no."

"Then why tell me?"

"You asked. And I wanted you to know that I—we—think of you as kagõro."

A stricken look crossed Antônio's face, fleeting and sudden but there all the same. "You said I was a spy."

Cornelius shook his head. "I was wrong to say that, and I want you to know I do trust you. And I'm glad you came with us. We both are." Cornelius glanced at Watt, who nodded. Antônio studied them both for a long moment, then swallowed and looked away. He pushed himself up to standing, and excused himself in favor of hiding away in his hammock.

Cornelius looked at Severino, who simply waved a dismissive hand. He whispered, "Give him time to think. He will come back for food."

Cornelius' gut clenched. Sometimes, there wasn't enough time. Sometimes, certain things couldn't wait. And the thing was, he'd said what he needed to Antônio, something he should've said long before this. But at this point, it felt futile. He wasn't sure why he craved Antônio's respect so much, but he did.

Watt sighed, long and explosive. He was smoking from his pipe, staring up at the sky with a rough pebble rolling between the fingers of his free hand. Unbidden,

Cornelius' hand drifted to rest over the stone in his own pocket.

"We don't have much time left," Watt said, and Cornelius wondered at how the man could read his mind.

June

Pretty Snake

June 6th, 1930

The days were long, and tempers shortened as each one passed. One moment everything would be fine, and the next someone was at someone else's throat. Even Watt had that urge beneath his skin now, begging him to do something brash. Scream at the sky, or claw at the dirt with his hands. Throw Cornelius down for a good fight, or something like that.

After they'd traded cerrado for jungle, the vegetation thickened and trails thinned. Trails that after a couple of days only Severino recognized, for even Antônio was in unfamiliar land now. Severino kept getting too far ahead, and he apologized each time for leaving them behind, but he was clearly getting frustrated. It was subtle, hiding in the pinched lines around his mouth every time he looked back. The closer they got, the more anxious he became. What was he so hard pressed to reach? The site wasn't going anywhere, and they were making good time, all things considered.

Cornelius' own frustration was not as subtle. He

cursed Severino out, never to his face but none too quietly either as they attempted to keep pace with their guide. He picked fights with Antônio every time the young man offered his help, which was often as Cornelius struggled with the terrain. Every once in a while, however, Cornelius relented with a mighty grumble. He never accepted Watt's offers for help or to take a break, which resulted in Watt snapping back at him a few times. Cornelius never argued otherwise when Watt called him a stubborn jackass, though. Watt wanted to know Antônio's secrets, but was ultimately glad that Cornelius accepted help from someone. Even if that person wasn't him.

Two weeks after they left Dead Horse Camp, Watt got his chance to satisfy that urge of his calling for trouble.

"It is not safe," Severino said, slicing a hand through the air. "We are in—"

"I am well aware where we are, Severino, and if I wanted to go trekking a few leagues into Morcegos country I'd agree with you. But I'm only going right over there. I'll be fine," Cornelius said, using that placid tone of his which sharpened even the nicest of words into daggers. He had a sack of clothes under his arm, his cane at hand, and a very noticeable .38 tucked into his trousers. That poor cane had been to hell and back, but still held strong.

"I will keep watch," Antônio offered.

Cornelius shot him a look. "Absolutely not."

Watt choked on the smoke curling in his lungs, and he wasn't even the recipient of that glare. His lungs had been protesting for weeks now, all the cigarettes and pipe tobacco was taking its toll on his damaged lungs. His frayed nerves needed something, though. Cornelius hadn't smoked any cannabis for weeks, maybe it was gone for all Watt knew, and he and his companions were dry. A feature that most adventuring parties didn't share and Watt hadn't cared much about it 'till now. He could go for a drink, or two.

Antônio didn't choke, but he did wither, shoulders curving inwards ever so slightly. He readjusted his hat and walked away, grumbling as he did so.

Severino swelled, a finger raised in Cornelius' direction. "You are—"

Cornelius did not give Severino the satisfaction of finishing his sentence. He stalked off, disappearing between the nearby trees. Watt blinked when he saw Maggie close at the man's heels. Cornelius frowned down at her, then glanced back at Watt. He hesitated, then continued onwards. They'd settled into a sort of clearing surrounded by hills, vegetation had to be cleared away to make room for their hammocks and gear. It all felt claustrophobic, and Watt fretted for several moments before turning away and joining Antônio near their hammocks. There was no fire tonight, and the evening was especially cold. To reach the site they had to pass between multiple hostile tribes, the same ones theorized to have taken Fawcett captive. Needless to say Severino and Antônio were on edge, likely Cornelius too.

Severino came up behind them, running a hand through his dark hair that had grown lengthy with time. He shook his head. "He doesn't make things easy, does he?"

Watt turned on his heel, hands balled into fists and feet settling into the proper stance.

Severino put up his hands.

Neither of them spoke, but an entire conversation took place across the small distance between them. It was spoken with shifting weight, tightening fingers, creasing wrinkles.

'Leave it alone, Severino.'

'You know I'm right, Watt. He's got a death wish, and you know it. He's going to get us all hurt because of it.'

Watt took a step closer. He didn't want to hear it.

"Who's taking the first watch?" Cornelius asked. He stood a little ways behind Severino with Maggie by his side, his chin thrust defiantly into the air. As if somehow he'd heard the entire thing, and dared them to question his sanity aloud.

Severino turned, and the genuine relief that overcame his shoulders soothed the anger flaring in Watt's chest. Cornelius noticed the way Severino sagged, and the fight seemed to go out of him too. Cornelius rubbed a hand over his face, dislodging his glasses. He said, "Look, I'm sorry. I just needed to ..." Cornelius' face reddened, and Watt wondered if it was from the way he rubbed at his face, or something else. What had Cornelius been doing in the few minutes he had alone if not changing or relieving himself?

The knuckles of Cornelius' right hand whitened, his nails digging into the sack of clothes tucked against his side. Watt's heart leapt to his throat, and when he spoke his voice was thick. "Let's all just start over, okay?"

Cornelius looked at him strangely, but Severino was already nodding. "Okay," he said, then patted Cornelius gently on the shoulder. "Okay."

They ate a cold dinner of dried out peccary and beans, and Watt gave Maggie the last can of Ken-L ration he had. From now on, they'd be sharing meals. Cornelius took the first watch, same as he usually did. Watt readied himself for the night, distracted by the sound of Cornelius rinsing his hands using his canteen. He fought a strange urge to turn around and watch the blood clinging to the man's fingertips rinse into the dirt and grass. It stirred a part of him he didn't understand, and as with most things of that nature, he locked that curiosity deep within his heart, and threw away the key.

The next morning, Watt woke with a gentle nudge to the ribs. He flinched awake, reaching for his knife. A hand settled on his hammock to keep him from flipping, and Cornelius muttered, "Oh, fuck off," which settled Watt.

"What's wrong?" Watt asked blearily, rubbing at his

eyes.

A small weight fell onto Watt's stomach and he immediately sat upwards, eyes flashing open. Cornelius held fast to his hammock so he didn't tip, fully dressed in a less dirty change of clothes, his combed hair damp and slightly tame. He stood over Watt and gave him a quick, tight smile. "Happy Birthday. Don't take too long, o patrão wants to get going."

A laugh disguised as protest emerged from somewhere behind Cornelius, and then Severino poked his head around Cornelius. "Do I get no credit for letting him sleep in for twenty minutes?" Severino grinned at Watt, bright eyed despite the fact the sun was barely above the horizon. "Feliz Aniversário, Watt." He stepped around Cornelius and dropped a stone with a thin middle which smoothly tapered to thick edges, the shape impossible. He tugged at Watt's ear, then went on his way to wake Antônio before Watt could say thank you.

Cornelius rolled his eyes, but gave Watt another smile that was less tense this time.

"Thank you," Watt said, his voice hoarse from sleep and emotion. He placed a hand over the gift, holding it against his sternum. "You didn't have to give me anything."

Cornelius contemplated him, then quietly said, "I know." He turned away to start packing his things, leaving Watt with the mysterious package on his chest. He rubbed at the grit, or more likely bugs, irritating his eyes. Maggie stretched on the ground beside him, sniffing upwards curiously.

"Hey, girl. No, this is for me, not you," Watt murmured, reaching down to give her good morning pets. Maggie licked his face, and he chuckled. Watt meticulously untied a length of twine which secured roughly folded paper flaps, wondering when Cornelius had the time to do this. His pulse pounded in his throat, and he willed it to calm down. He was thirty three years old now, too old to be excited over something like a present.

It wasn't often someone remembered his birthday, let alone gave him a gift. The last time anyone had made a big deal about it was in the barracks, and most of those men were gone now. It had been an exhilarating feeling, to be celebrated. To be known. And at that age, he knew himself too, or thought he did. But he wouldn't want to be twenty one again. He'd rather be thirty one, as bad as those years were, sweating and aching and finding out who he truly was, what he truly believed in.

Watt's breath caught when he found nestled within the thick brown paper a few vague rectangular shapes wrapped in thin and delicate golden yellow tissue paper. Shoestring leather was tied around the belly of each object to keep the tissue paper in place, and a small blank white card was tucked beneath the brown cord of the largest object. Watt withdrew the card and flipped it over, revealing Cornelius' handwriting.

'Happy Birthday, Watt. I hope we find what you're looking for, and this will help you capture

the full beauty of it all.'

Watt swallowed against the lump building in his throat and glanced up, but Cornelius was not in immediate sight. He treated the beautiful yellow paper with as much care as he did the brown paper, and after a minute or so he was presented with three items. First was a sketchpad, spiral bound with a black covering Watt guessed was cotton, but the raised texture threw him off. There were no distinguishable markings, no branding. It was plain, but well made and durable. Small enough to fit in his pocket, but only just. Watt ran his thumb over the edges of medium weight paper, noting the off white color. Enough to last him a good while, if he was careful. The sketchbook he had now was painfully full, there were only two pages left which he'd been saving for the site.

The second item was a hefty box of pencils. Regular pencils, not mechanical ones or something designed especially for artists. They were just like the ones Watt had, yellow with a square lead. They were all he cared to use, and had said so in passing one day when Cornelius asked about it. When had the been ... São Paulo? Watt smiled, and set them aside with the sketchpad.

Last was a black lacquered tin, a bit larger than a pencil case. There were some scratches along the bottom, and the corners of the tin were worn as well. The lid had four equally sized square domes. Watt opened the lid, revealing a metal plate on a hinge. A paper sticker on the plate proclaimed the object to be Windsor & Newton, made in England. He folded the plate back, revealing a palette of watercolors in the bottom of the tin. Three rows, two of which were entirely full while the middle was only half full. Twenty six colors in all, with a small area set aside for brushes. There were two, one with a fine tip and another that was slightly thicker. Watt touched the hairs of the fine brush, then his fingers wandered to the small squares that beheld dry pools of color.

He sat there, staring down at the gifts in his lap. Long enough to blink away the tears pricking his eyes, and swallow the hot emotion congesting his throat.

When Watt finally prepared for the day and joined the others for breakfast, he found himself unable to stop smiling. Severino had a breakfast of condensed milk, papaya, and oats, waiting for him. He took one look at Watt, then grinned. He elbowed Cornelius, then nodded to Watt. "Hey, what'd you give him?"

Cornelius frowned at Severino, then looked hesitantly at Watt. Upon seeing his face, he scowled at Watt. "Are you ready to go?"

Watt closed the short distance between them and hugged Cornelius. He stiffened, but when Watt started to pull away Cornelius hugged him back with great force. Watt had to bend down to rest his chin on Cornelius' shoulder, but the ache in his spine was worth it. He whispered, "Thank you."

Cornelius squeezed Watt once, then pulled back and dusted himself off. He flicked a quick look at Severino and Antônio who were eating together, then gave Watt a gentle shove. "Hurry up and eat so we can get going."

At first Cornelius and Severino took the lead, but eventually Severino fell back with Antônio and Watt to check out his new gifts. Antônio was especially enamored with the watercolors, and Watt made a mental note to test them out with him later. Maggie trotted alongside Cornelius, and Watt was just starting to regain control of his smile when Cornelius looked back at him. Cornelius shook his head, which did nothing to hide his own escaped smile, and continued leading the way.

———◈———

June 12th, 1930

Cornelius knew that when taking the word of an archaeologist, you had to accept it with a grain of salt for they were some of the most optimistic people around. Thankfully, Joaquim and Severino had not been exaggerating regarding the scale of their project.

Blisters plagued Cornelius' feet, and his hip screamed in solidarity with his knee. Walking was a generous term for what he'd been doing, and his brain was ablaze with frustration and exhaustion. He took a guilty sort of comfort in the fact that he was not alone in his struggles. Watt's birthday had bought them a temporary reprieve from the foul mood they'd all been stewing in, but it was only that. Temporary.

Watt was exhausted. Completely, and utterly, exhausted. His eyes were bruised and swollen, and he was covered in bites. The bugs wouldn't leave him alone no matter what precautions they took, and their insistence was taking their toll on his sanity. The infected bite under his arm was healing, but there were dozens of others vying to be next for infection. He hardly spoke, and when he did it was to the point. Yes, no. Maybe. Fuck off. That last one he'd said to Cornelius in the dead of night, when insomnia had brought them together and made Cornelius say ridiculous things which made Watt laugh even if he hadn't wanted to. Severino and Antônio were in better shape than either Watt or Cornelius, but they were exhausted and plagued by insects too.

They came upon the site at noon, drenched in sweat and flies. The unmistakable noise of humans preceded the sight, for there was an enormous hill to crest. Regardless of this last obstacle, Severino laughed hoarsely. "We've made it."

Cornelius could have wept with relief, and he tried not to think too far ahead in fear of his body giving up its remaining adrenaline in anticipation of rest. Maggie panted heavily, and Cornelius' own breath sawed in and out of him. Severino got a little ahead of them, while Antônio kept Cornelius and Watt company as they grappled with the incline. Antônio was constantly looking out for Cornelius, and it was becoming more difficult to be angry with him about it considering the number of times he kept Cornelius from falling. He'd even stopped telling Watt off, allowing his companions to fortify him. Without them, he surely would have curled up and died somewhere along the way.

The hill was steep, embedded with rocks and decorated with thick vegetation. There was a vague trail where the underbrush had been thinned, the path Severino had carved on the way out. Despite this, Severino still had to work at some new growth with his machete. By the time they reached the peak, Cornelius was about ready to fall backwards. Severino was already halfway down the other side, which was far more bare than what they'd climbed so far. It wasn't quite a cliff, but sheer enough it would've been easy to lose your footing and crash all the way to the bottom.

Watt, Cornelius, and Antônio stood together, chests heaving as they watched Severino sprint ahead. It wasn't just simple relief from finding camp after so long in the wild. To Severino, this was a homecoming. This was where he belonged, deep in the jungle with other like minded people. With Joaquim, who Cornelius strongly suspected was a kindred spirit.

Cornelius smiled, and to Watt he said, "You know, I don't think I've thanked you yet."

"For what?" Watt asked, bewildered.

Cornelius chuckled, leaning against his side. "Inviting me."

Watt laughed, a wholehearted sound that shook his

body and in turn, Cornelius'. "Don't thank me yet, aventurier."

Cornelius grinned. He looked over at Antônio and asked, "Are you ready for this?"

Antônio shook his head, looking unusually apprehensive. Watt reached around Cornelius and took a hold of Antônio's shoulder, squeezing gently. "Come on."

They made it down the hill together, taking it slow and steady. Cornelius felt twelve years old all over again, giddy and on the precipice of something new. Besides the pain wracking his body, of course. The trees weren't as thick down here, but it was still rocky and overgrown with grass and ferns. They followed Maggie, whose sense of direction hadn't led Cornelius into any holes yet. Ahead, a clearing littered with crumbling stone construction awaited them. Great stone arches and avenues with great walls were among the visible architecture, along with circular raised areas that reminded him of how the huts were situated in Colombia, in areas of high runoff. Cornelius looked back over his shoulder, tracing the small mounds and valleys they'd already passed without a thought. Would they find more bones of buildings beneath the soil?

"Oh," Watt said, his voice thin.

"Yes," Cornelius whispered.

It was hard to say what was natural and what was not, for each mound and valley would have to be investigated, but even the central area seemed large enough to host a small village, once upon a time. The real question was, how old was this place? Decades? Centuries?

After passing through most of the ruins, they found the present day encampment settled on what appeared to be the far end of the site. Severino stood in the midst of a large group of people, embracing a man much shorter than himself. They patted each other on the back, cheeks flushed and smiles wide. Heads turned their way as they approached, mostly curious and friendly if not indifferent. Cornelius recognized the Carmines, and Anderson. He felt unsure about the former, and irritated by the latter. He'd somehow forgotten about Andrea in the past few weeks, but now his temper flared with renewed vigor.

Severino pulled away from the other man and extended a welcoming hand in their direction. "Welcome to our humble cidade." He gestured to the man at his side. "May I introduce our site manager, Joaquim de Silva."

Joaquim extended a hand to Cornelius first. Also in English, he said, "It is a pleasure to meet you, thank you for coming all this way."

Joaquim's handshake was warm, and his grip strong. He was a whip thin man, the same height as Cornelius and surprisingly close in age. From the way Severino talked about him, he expected an older and wiser man. He had a statuesque nose, dark sun-wrought skin, and slicked back dark hair that curled around his ears. He hadn't shaved in a couple days, which only amplified his handsome ruggedness. He wore trousers and shirtsleeves, both of which had been worn already a few times, and his scuffed knee high leather boots fascinated Cornelius. He carried himself in a way that suggested he knew how handsome he was, but didn't give two shits about it.

"It's an honor, Senhor de Silva," Cornelius said, a little dazed.

"Please, call me Joaquim. And you are?"

"Cornelius. Thank you."

"Of course, of course." Joaquim nodded, shaking Watt's hand next. "You will find we are an unconventional bunch here."

"Sounds like we're in the right place, then. Watt, if you please," Watt said, shaking Joaquim's hand with that genial, good ol' boy smile Cornelius hadn't seen in some time.

Joaquim smiled, revealing crooked teeth and genuine feeling. He shook Antônio's hand next. "And Antônio, is it? Welcome, we could always use an extra hand. Lots to do."

"Thank you for having me," Antônio said, his voice low.

"Come, let's introduce you all to the rest of the herd."

Dr. Charles Rowland was exceptionally fit for an older gentleman, a botanist of Irish origins with the shocking red hair and beard to prove it, albeit touched with white. He hailed from NYU, same as most of the other foreign scientists, while Joaquim and his team were from São Paulo University.

Thomas Anderson had changed since Cornelius saw him last. His fair skin was flush with sun, creased by age and years in the field, and his hair was thin wisps of blond. He wore glasses now, something Cornelius had always pestered him to do. Nearly twenty years his senior, Thomas hadn't worked as many digs as Cornelius had, but he'd put in the years at the sites he had worked. He'd been stuck at Ur for the past eight years, and Cornelius thought his presence being drawn to a new project was a good sign of things to come. He was, in Cornelius' opinion, one of the good ones.

Anderson pulled Cornelius in for a hug, which surprised him. Their previous relationship had been pleasant, but nothing extraordinary. The last time they'd seen each other, Thomas had just learned one of Cornelius' greatest secrets, thanks to Andrea Carmine. And now they were all together once again. Cornelius thought he'd been prepared, but nothing could've prepared him for this. The air had been tense and awkward before, but now it resonated with pleasant warmth. Anderson pulled back and said, "It's good to see you, old boy."

Cornelius readjusted his glasses, cheeks flushed. "It's good to see you too, Dr. Anderson."

Anderson grinned, arms wide with feeling. "Please, you heard the man. First name basis around here."

Cornelius smiled, unsure where it came from or how to stop. "It's good to see you, Thomas. I'd like you to meet my colleagues, Watt and Antônio."

Greetings were exchanged, and Watt was as warm and genuine with Thomas as the older man was him. Watt's smile was tired but easy, and his shoulders were temporarily loose with relief. It soothed a part of Cornelius that he couldn't describe, seeing them together. Bridging the good parts of his life, perhaps.

The interns were next, all archaeology students from São Paulo. Benedito, a slight man with a nervous smile, was outnumbered by three women. Terezinna, Ana, and Nair. Cornelius took an immediate liking to Terezinna, she walked with swagger and shook hands easily but with a sure grip. Her soft brown eyes were bright with interest, and Cornelius didn't miss the way they flicked sideways to a breathtaking woman that could only be Francesca Carmine.

Cornelius hadn't ever met Francesca, but her resemblance to Andrea was striking. They shared dusky brown skin and jet black hair that shone in the sunlight, although hers was cut into a blunt bob which complimented the strong curve of her jaw. The geologist wore high-waisted trousers which complimented her thick curves, and they were tucked into knee high leather boots. Cornelius got the sense the shirtsleeves she wore were her brother's, he was a big man but it fit her near perfect. When she shook Cornelius' hand with a tight grip and stared deep into his eyes, he knew that she knew everything. He couldn't say how, but certainty settled into his gut like curdled steel.

"Dr. Sawyer," Francesca said, her Italian accent smokier than the cigarette pinched between her painted lips. Her makeup was minimal, thin black eyeliner that flicked at the corners and brick red lipstick, but it was more than enough to knock anyone dead. "I've heard so much about you."

"And I'd love to learn half as much about you," Cornelius replied. "I have a feeling you're the more interesting Carmine of the two."

Francesca raised a thin brow, and her lips curved around the cigarette. Her brother cut in, thrusting his hand in Cornelius' direction. Begrudgingly, Cornelius shook the all encompassing hand he used to know oh so intimately. As the younger of the two, Andrea's accent was far more American than his sister's, but the Italian side still slipped out every now and again. Like now, when he was attempting to be coy. "Ah, Cornelius. How good it is to see you again."

Their eyes clashed, and Cornelius' fingers tightened around Andrea's. Cornelius had sworn that the next time he saw this man he'd knock him out cold, not shake his hand. He'd thought he was ready for this, but evidently not. The only thing that held at him at bay was his mission, and his respect for his companions. Cornelius smiled, baring his teeth. "Dr. Carmine."

Andrea's maple brown eyes creased at the edges, and the smile that overtook him was wolfish in nature. Andrea was a big man, with a thick chest and thighs for days. His face was all angles though, hard and beautiful in the way marble was. He was clean shaven, and the well defined muscles in his throat were taut with tension. Cornelius had once thought him one of the most beautiful men alive, second only to Watt. But now the sight of him only made him nauseous.

Like a pretty snake.

Watt made a noise, almost like a cough. It was enough to break the moment, and when Andrea saw Watt he practically beamed. He tossed Cornelius' hand aside, brushing past him to reach Watt. "Ah, Walter, I'm so glad to see you!" He shook Watt's hand, then pulled him in for a hug and slapped him on the back in the way old friends did. Andrea was fluid in the motion, while Watt was rigid in returning the embrace.

"Andrea. It's good to see you," Watt said, each word more stilted than the last.

"It's been far too long, we must catch up. I want to hear everything," Andrea said, and the damn bastard seemed like he meant it.

But he'd seemed pretty genuine when he promised not to tell anyone Cornelius' secret, either. They'd have a talk before the night was out, that was for damn sure.

Something New

June 12th, 1930

The tents were the grandest thing Watt had seen in weeks.

A small commune of field tents were set up on the rear of the site, where the ground was relatively flat and free from any potential ruins. They were all built in a similar manner, enormous cotton canvas stretched over tall poles driven into the ground, with pallets for a floor. Two of them were much larger than the rest, and centrally located between the smaller ones. The equivalent of a societal hall for eating and gathering, and the main tent for working. He hadn't been inside either yet, but Severino had pointed them out before dumping Cornelius and Watt off at their tent.

Watt could smell grilled meat wafting from one of them, and he tried to imagine all the equipment and artifacts that could be in the other. Water sloshed in the deep basin he'd been given by Joaquim for washing, and he tried to steady his pace. The closest water source was half a day's trip, and all stored water was used sparingly. Work and food was all well and good, but the moment Watt had laid eyes on an empty cot his heart shuddered with relief. There were two, and since each one was pushed up against a wall of canvas, Watt hadn't felt bad picking one first. He'd chosen the cot closest to the flap, and Cornelius had wordlessly slung his pack onto the other one. A solid crate with a removable lid was situated beside each cot, offering a storage space and table all in one.

Watt set down the basin of water he'd been given onto the crate, then dug out the bar of soap he'd tucked into his pocket and put it beside the basin. An unlit lamp hung between the crates from a metal stake, which was driven into the ground via a crack between two pallets. Watt frowned at the crack, imagining Cornelius' cane sinking into it and snapping at the tip. It was well made, but all things had a breaking point.

"What's wrong?" Cornelius asked, sitting down beside his pack on the cot. His fingers trembled in his lap, and when Watt nodded towards them he gripped the edges of his cot. "I'm beat. That's all."

Watt sat down, moving his pack to the floor at his feet. He nodded at the crack. "I don't like the looks of that. Your cane could get caught."

Cornelius huffed, running a hand through his sweaty hair. "If that's the least of our problems here, I think we'll be okay."

"Is it?"

"What?"

"The least of our problems. You and Andrea seemed ..." Watt trailed off, threatened by the storm building in Cornelius' eyes.

"What?"

Watt inhaled, long and deep. Quietly, he said, "I'm on your side, you know. No matter the reason. Just say the word, and I'll lay 'em out."

Cornelius blinked, startled. Then he grinned. "Lay 'em out? What are you, my personal bodyguard?"

Watt flushed. "All I'm saying is, we're a team, right? And teams work best when everyone is on the same page."

Cornelius' smile disappeared. He turned away, fidgeting with his bag. "I hear you, and thank you. But I—I've got it handled. Andrea won't be a problem." He glanced back up at Watt. "Besides, I wouldn't want to turn you against such a good friend."

Watt immediately shook his head. "We're acquaintances at most. I haven't seen him since Egypt."

"A travesty, to be sure," Cornelius said. Watt opened his mouth, but Cornelius added, "We should get ready for dinner. I, for one, am starving."

Watt closed his mouth, trapping all his questions and protestations between his teeth. It was clear Cornelius was hiding something, and Watt thought they were past all of that now. It stung, and Watt told himself it was only the aches and pains of the long journey that had Cornelius all clammed up.

He dug out a relatively fresh change of clothes, his

second pair of boots, and a comb. He glanced at the flap, then over his shoulder at Cornelius, who had his back to Watt.

He cleared his throat and said, "Do you mind if I go first?" Cornelius visibly stiffened as if struck by lightning. Watt hurriedly added, "I can go—"

"No," Cornelius said, his voice high. He coughed, and a bit more casually said, "No, it's fine. We've shared a room before, nothing new there. Just let me know when you're done."

True, they had shared a room before, and changed clothes in the same space. But Watt felt ...

"Okay. I'll try to be quick."

Cornelius chuckled lightly, but said nothing else.

Watt made quick work of it, dunking a scratchy washcloth into the water and scrubbing his face with it before soaping up and moving onto key areas. The cool water more than made up for the texture, and he sighed. He washed and dried his upper half first, then slid his shirt on before moving onto the bottom half. His cheeks flamed the entire time, and he forced himself not to look over his shoulder.

He couldn't feel Cornelius stealing glances at him, and if he was, well ... there was no harm in looking at the human form. Watt finished washing without further delay. He pulled on his socks, boxers, and trousers in a rush. He laced up his boots, then hurried out of the tent with stammering promises to bring back fresh water for Cornelius. When he returned, the man's shirt was off.

Watt walked right into one of the center support poles, damn near spilling water all over and taking the tent out in one go. "Shit!"

Slightly alarmed, Cornelius glanced over his shoulder at him, brows raised. "Alright there?"

Watt blinked, stricken by the flush in Cornelius' cheeks. "I—uh—yes. Water. I have water. Fresh water."

"Just set it down there. Thank you." Cornelius nodded to the crate beside his cot. His shoulders were rigid with tension, and his arms were crossed tight over his chest. A thick band of red surrounded his ribs, where a brasserie might have once been. Watt had never seen a brasserie in use, but he didn't think they were supposed to be worn so tight.

"Watt?"

Watt blinked, then forced himself into motion. He set the basin down where Cornelius had instructed, then retreated to his side of the tent. He busied himself with unpacking, withdrawing everyday items he'd want later. His notebook, sketchbook, the rocks he'd collected yesterday, and his pipe to name a few. This last one he loosely stuffed with tobacco, doing his best to ignore the sounds Cornelius was making. Clips coming undone with a fine snap. Fabric rustling to the floor, or perhaps sweeping over Cornelius' skin. He closed his eyes, trying to banish the image of Cornelius' body into the darkness of his mind.

But there was no forgetting the soft rolls around

Cornelius' middle, the flesh spilling pleasantly over his waistband. The breadth of his wide and well endowed shoulders, which were far more muscular than Watt had anticipated. The small mole neighboring his spine, which matched the one alongside his ear near perfectly. Watt had a sudden desire to press his thumb over it. To feel if it was smooth, or an artifact to be caressed over again and again.

"I'm done," Cornelius said, sounding a little breathless.

"I'm going for a walk," Watt said in a rush, unable to turn around. "Lay of the land. Getting the lay. Of the land, I mean. I'll be back."

He fled the tent, embarking on a very long walk.

June 12th, 1930

Cornelius had made a mistake.

He did his best to smile, even if he wanted to cry. Eat, even if he couldn't taste the food. Talk, even if he wanted to scream.

What had he been *thinking*?

Well, he knew the answer to that. He'd thought there had been a moment between them, perfect for revealing naked truths. Not that he'd have shown Watt anything else but his back, but still. It had been a truth that he offered to few other people. And what had Watt done with it? Run away as soon as possible, refusing to look Cornelius in the eye. Even now, seated directly across from Cornelius at a table with over a dozen other people, Watt would not, or could not, bring himself to look at Cornelius. It was—

It was fine.

Cornelius had forgotten the line between them, and Watt had firmly twanged upon it, reminding Cornelius of its heavy existence. They were colleagues. Partners in their expedition, and friends of a sort, but nothing more. The trip had brought them closer, but in the end Cornelius was who he was, and Watt was who he was. They were never destined to be partners. There would never be a future for them, in Brazil or outside of it. Not that Cornelius had been searching for a future between them, thinking beyond today and into tomorrow. Of what could be, if they stuck together after this was all said and done. If there was an after, anyways.

Truly, Cornelius should've been thanking Watt, he'd sorely needed that reality check.

Conversation flowed around him in the canteen, niceties were exchanged and tidbits of gossip shared in hushed tones. Cornelius and Antônio sat opposite Watt and Andrea on handmade picnic benches, and Joaquim's crew sat around them. Severino and Joaquim had taken dinner to Joaquim's tent, a fact that no one seemed to think much about since Joaquim apparently always ate in his tent. The curious side of Cornelius desperately wanted to know if his suspicions were correct, but it wasn't his business. Terezinna asked Watt about their trip while the rest of the interns listened, enthralled by Watt's quiet and frankly boring answers. Yes, the trip went well. No, they hadn't encountered any trouble. Yes, it had been long. No, Watt hadn't been to South America before.

No one engaged with Cornelius, no doubt due to the frown he couldn't get rid of, which only deepened his foul mood. He watched as Watt deftly offered Antônio control of the discussion, which had shifted to Bacairy Post. Watt seemed lost in all the attention given to him, and was glad to be rid of it if only for a moment. For a brief moment their eyes met, and Watt's expression wasn't unlike that of a spooked owl. Antônio began to come out of his shell and explain the shift away from fishing and into agriculture when Andrea opened his mouth, stealing the spotlight away from him.

Andrea threw an arm around Watt's shoulder and said, "You know, we were in The Valley of the Kings together, Walter and I. The excavation was enormous, and it took us years to find anything. And then along came Walt—"

"Watt," Cornelius said. Andrea's brows pinched in confusion, and Cornelius added, "His name's Watt."

Andrea laughed awkwardly, glancing sideways at the tense Watt who had discreetly shrugged off his arm. "Much changes over the years, names and nicknames included. But I don't need to tell you that, do I?" Andrea said this last bit in a low, conspiratorial tone that mocked a whisper, clearly heard by everyone gathered. He might as well have slapped Cornelius. It was a clear statement as any. Andrea was going to do the same thing here as he did in Ur.

It was Charles Rowland who diverted the conversation into safer waters. The Irishmen set his fork down and said, "Let's hear something new, Andrea, we've heard all your stories before. Cornelius, Thomas here tells me you've worked with Mason. Tell me, is it true he's a hound for plants?"

Cornelius exhaled slowly and nodded, plastering a genial smile on. "Yes, we worked together in Ur, and in Colombia as well. I regret to inform you the rumors are true, he's got the greenest thumb I've ever seen."

Charles smiled, and lines crinkled his eyes. "And do you?"

"Oh, not at all, but he still tries to convince me otherwise. Although there is a fern that has survived my incompetence so far."

"Is that so? And who is tending to her for you?"

And just like that, Cornelius was the heart of conversation. Everyone listened as he talked about Esther, from her origins in archaeology as a mere intern to her current position as Curator.

"She sounds fantastic," Ana remarked, and a dreamy expression softened her dark and rugged features. She was the tallest woman in the group, although she constantly hunched her shoulders in an effort to be anything else. Her black hair was shaved close to her head, a surprise to Cornelius but not to anyone else, it seemed. The cut contrasted with her feminine style, she seemed to prefer dresses to Terezinna and Nair's trousers. Those two had fairly long hair, but dressed the same as Francesca did. In trousers and men's shirts. Cornelius was hit with a sense of Parisan déjà vu.

The big round lenses of Ana's glasses were smudged, and Cornelius wanted to wipe them clean. Instead, he fidgeted with the stone Watt had given him. He wasn't sure when it had made it out of his pocket and into his fingers, but he was glad for the distraction.

"She is," Watt said, then cleared his throat. "We met briefly a few months ago, when Cornelius and I became acquainted. I was very impressed."

If buttering up Cornelius was Watt's idea of making things right, he had another coming. Because nothing was wrong. He was the one being awkward and dodgy. Not Cornelius. Everything was *fine*.

Queer Sort

June 13th, 1930

Watt could not think straight.

He sat beside Cornelius and Severino in Joaquim's tent, and it took everything in his power to focus on the site leader's report. The mention of a tumuli in the southern quadrant piqued Cornelius' interest, and when he spoke Watt had to redouble his efforts. Focus on the words, not his voice. Maggie had been confused by his distress all morning, but remained by his side despite all the new people.

"You've found a burial mound?" Cornelius asked. "Is this the first?"

"We believe so, but there is still much work to be done before we can be sure," Joaquim said, conducting their report in English. His accent was thick, but he spoke in a slow and thoughtful way.

"There are no ruins there." Severino leaned forward in his seat. "What makes you think it is for burial use?"

Joaquim offered Severino an apologetic smile. "We found the cemetery, in this case an urn field, nearby.

We found it a few days after you left."

Severino was undeterred. He'd shaved and washed up last night as well, and the morning light had him practically glowing. "This is wonderful news! I am sorry to have missed it, but this is good, Joaquim."

Joaquim relaxed. He wasn't as polished as Severino this morning, but Watt could appreciate that he was fine to look at, dusty clothes and all. "It is good, and more work. We are grateful for your help, both of you, even if it is only for a short time. Severino tells me you are dedicated to your mission, so I will not pry you from it. But know that you are always welcome here."

Cornelius nodded. "Thank you, we appreciate that." He glanced sideways at Watt, his smile tight. "Just point us in the right direction and we'll get to work."

"Yes, thank you," Watt said, a hollow addendum. He'd found it impossible to forget that this was only temporary, save for last night. Sheer exhaustion and relief had softened his mind. It had felt good to sit with other people and talk, to eat and be unhurried. To lay down in a relatively soft place in the middle of nowhere and wake under the same canvas roof as the man he'd come to call a friend, and prepare for a day of work in the dirt. Watt glanced at Cornelius, trying to make the word fit around him. But it wasn't enough. Regardless, it was a cycle Watt could've repeated for a long time. For the first time, he briefly entertained the idea of taking Joaquim and Severino up on their offer, and staying for longer than intended.

Joaquim chuckled. "I like your enthusiasm. Breakfast first, then we work."

—◈—

Later that evening, they made their way back to their shared tent with Maggie in tow. Cornelius frowned at the beaten down path ahead of them, his mask had dropped the moment they'd gotten away from the others. He relied heavily on his cane, and Watt hoped that he would take it easy tomorrow. It had been a long day full of information and dirt, and had the opportunity to go on for longer. The others were meeting up around the fire pit, and had invited them. He wasn't sure if he could do it. It didn't sound like Severino and Joaquim would be there, and he didn't mind the crew thus far. But Andrea had been ... quietly obnoxious today. Lurking, smirking. Watt didn't know what had happened between him and Cornelius, but it was more of a problem than he'd realized it would be.

Watt could only handle a moment of silence between him and Cornelius. He said, "What do you think?"

Cornelius cut a look at him, his expression unreadable in the shadows of dusk. After a moment he asked, "... about?"

Watt floundered. "The camp. Joaquim. All of it."

Cornelius turned his attention back to their path. He was quiet for a few moments, then, "It's only another stop in the journey."

Watt hadn't expected that. "Right ..." he trailed off, unsure what to say. Cornelius was especially quiet, and Watt knew the weird air that existed between them since last night was all his fault. He just didn't know what to say, or how to fix it.

When they got back to their tent, Maggie immediately jumped onto Watt's cot and laid down with a huff. Cornelius went over to his own cot and stared down at it. Watt watched him, and he startled when Cornelius' head suddenly jerked up. "I'm going to the fire," he said, and began to storm past Watt.

Watt took a hold of his upper arm. "Can I come with you?"

Cornelius stopped, staring up at Watt in surprise. Lips pressed thin, he searched Watt's eyes. Watt stared back, hoping Cornelius found what he wanted. He'd give the man anything if it made everything go back to normal between them.

"Of course," Cornelius whispered, then shrugged Watt off. Watt's hand fell to his side, and he flexed his fingers. Neither man moved for the flap leading to the outside world. Hesitantly, Cornelius said, "I didn't mean to make you uncomfortable. Yesterday. I—I was just—"

"Doing the exact same thing I had done. There's nothing to apologize for. In fact, I'm the one that needs to apologize. I was just surprised. I didn't—" Watt cleared his throat, and when he spoke again it was low and a bit strained. "I didn't know you trusted me like that."

Cornelius' chest rose and fell with great effort. His hand twitched in an aborted movement towards Watt's face and ended up settling on his shoulder. He whispered, "Me either."

Watt's eyes burned. He opened his mouth, but he couldn't speak. Cornelius' smile was unsure, and perhaps a little pitying, but it undid Watt all the same. Like a finishing blow, Cornelius stepped forward and wrapped his arms around Watt.

Watt was being hugged. Held. It was as overwhelming as it had been back in that abandoned village, when he'd revealed his greatest secrets. Cornelius had held Watt beneath the moon and stars, comforting him. It thickened the searing emotion building in Watt's throat, and so he encircled Cornelius in his arms, holding him tight in an effort to make it all go away. For a moment, it worked. There was nothing but them, and everything unspoken between them but palpable all the same.

Until Andrea Carmine lazily called from outside, "Watt, Cornelius! Are you going to join us?"

Both men startled, jumping away from each other like they'd been caught necking. Maggie grumbled at the same time Cornelius ran a hand over his hair and hissed, "That damn man."

"I can hear you!" Andrea teased from right outside their tent, his voice too close for comfort. "Don't keep us waiting."

His footsteps trailed away from their tent, and Watt sighed. "Still want to go?"

Cornelius straightened to his full height and snatched a cigarette from his case. It was bent and badly damaged, but lit up with a fierce and angry glow. "Of course, can't let him win."

"Win?" Watt shook his head, fondness driving the movement. "I'm still waiting for you to tell me how to play the game."

"Trust me, you don't want to," Cornelius said, leading the way out of the tent. Maggie followed them out, panting heavily. The area beheld a different quality at night, thick with possibility. Too many possibilities, all watching from the darkness. Waiting to pounce.

Watt kept close to Cornelius, separated only by Maggie trotting between them. As they approached the bonfire and its curious guests, Watt imagined how the three of them looked. Cornelius' cigarette dangled from his lips, his hands occupied by his cane and a trouser pocket. He had such a confident air about him, it seemed impossible that a man like this could break.

Watt knew how he felt, but he didn't know if that translated into the way he looked. Tired, sore, nerves flayed open and heart mildly irritated. He pulled his shoulders back and rolled his neck, hoping it would be enough to make him look as at ease as Cornelius did. Maggie, meanwhile, seemed to be pleased and interested in equal measure. Her ears were perked, and her tongue peeked in and out of the side of her mouth. It'd be hard like this to tell she was exhausted as well.

"Ah, there you are!" Anderson called, pushing out of his folding chair. He clapped Cornelius on the shoulder, and offered Watt a big smile.

"I must confess, I nearly went right to sleep. It's been an adventure," Cornelius said, laughing quietly.

"We'd love to hear it, if you feel up to it that is," Rowland said from his seat beside Anderson's abandoned chair. "I'm not as young as I used to be, but one's never too old to hear stories beside the fire, and ours have gotten rather stale as of late."

"I can imagine. You've been here for how long, a year?" Cornelius took up one of the empty chairs nearby Anderson and Rowland, and so Watt followed suit. Anderson sat too, reaching down to pet Maggie when she sniffed his leg. Watt didn't know these fellas well, but he preferred their immediate company to the others.

"Give or take," Rowland said. He nodded to Andrea and Francesca, who sat across the fire in the same folding chairs as everyone else did. "Although I believe those two, and Thomas here, were the first Americans to have boots on the ground. I didn't come until a few months later."

"And if my ears don't deceive me, you could've been here at the beginning too, isn't that right, Watt?" Andrea asked.

Watt tilted his head, lifting a shoulder. "The timing was off, but I'm glad to be here now."

"And how long do you two plan on staying?" Francesca asked, her eyes intent on Watt. Terezinna and Nair who sat beside her seemed equally interested in his answer. Nair was observant, tight brown curls hung over big dark eyes that took in everything.

Watt cleared his throat. "About a month, we're simply passing through."

"Really? Where else could you go beyond here?" Nair asked, glancing around the fire. "We are it for a while, yes?"

"Say, where is Antônio?" Cornelius asked suddenly, adjusting his glasses as he looked around.

"Oh, he's with Benedito and Ana," Terezinna said, smiling a little. "They were discussing the habits of the local jaguars last I heard."

"Jaguars?" Watt asked, his skin prickling.

"Oh yes, there's a prowl of them to the north. But don't worry, they don't come into camp." Nair waved a dismissive hand, missing the glance shared between Watt and Cornelius.

Good to know they'd be entering jaguar country, but then again they'd been passing in and out of jaguar territory for months and hadn't encountered one yet.

"Did you encounter any jaguars on your way in? Or any other creatures?" Rowland asked.

And so Cornelius began to tell the story of where they'd been. Only then did Watt realize the man had smoothly avoided the earlier question regarding their future. He listened as Cornelius spoke of the wondrous

French architecture of Rio, the industrious São Paulo, the venomous Butantan Institute, and the growing Cuiabá. He did not mention their encounter with Senhor Galvão, and Cornelius was subdued but informative when telling them about their stay with the Bacairy. By the time it was all said and done, the group was fully enamored with him.

All except Andrea, of course. "And tell me dear Cornelius, were you able to broaden your horizons during your journey? Adopt a love for something new besides ... oh, what was it you read all the time back at Ur? Oh yes, that *children's* novel, the Wonderful Wizard of Oz."

"Oh, I love that story!" Terezinna exclaimed, which brought a hesitant smile to Cornelius' lips.

Nair looked between him and Terezinna. "I'm afraid I haven't. But a ... wizard? That sounds interesting."

Cornelius lazily inclined his head. "I find there's nothing wrong with old favorites, and adults can find much to learn from children's stories. *Some* of us may have missed the lessons the first time."

Andrea grinned. He shifted his attention to Watt, which pricked every one of his nerves. "Are you a friend of Dorothy, too?" Andrea asked, eyes tracking up and down Watt's frame. "I never pinned you for one, but ..." His eyes drifted to Cornelius, then back again. Cornelius' face reddened, and he opened his mouth. Heat flushed over Watt's body not dissimilar to the uncomfortable way he'd felt back in Maxine's.

Anderson grumbled and said, "All right, that's enough."

Francesca shook her head, hiding what could've been a smile. Cornelius shot her a look, then pinned Andrea with a seconds-long glare. He stood, movements jerky and stiff, his hands balled into fists. "I think I'll turn in for the night." He nodded to the others, saving Watt for last. He said, "Good evening," and fled like a man with a demon on his heels. Watt glanced between his retreating back and Andrea, unsure what just happened. He'd never seen Cornelius turn away from conflict before.

Anderson stared at the fire, his mouth set in a firm, disapproving line. Without looking at Andrea he said, "I thought you would have developed some tact by now Andrea, and respect for others. Clearly, I was wrong." He glanced at Watt once, his gaze slightly curious. He looked close to asking a question, and Watt's stomach dropped. Without Cornelius by his side, he felt out of his depth surrounded by these people.

Instead, Anderson only stretched his arms overhead, then stood and said farewell for the evening. Rowland did the same, offering Watt a downcast smile before leaving. Watt followed suit, not wanting any further part in Andrea's games. He'd never minded Francesca when they worked together, but something in the way she'd smiled after Andrea's question had made him uneasy. Watt watched the older men as they walked ahead of him, their steps in sync and arms brushing. He was startled when Anderson glanced back at him, offering a quick smile before disappearing into the tent he evidently shared with Rowland. Made sense, they were of the same age and same easy going demeanor.

When Watt returned with Maggie to their tent, Cornelius was laid out on his cot, eyes closed and hands tucked behind his head. If it weren't for the rapid rise and fall of his chest, Watt would've thought him asleep. He cracked an eye at Watt, then closed it and asked, "Everything alright?"

Watt just about collapsed onto his own cot, landing face first onto the pillow. He groaned. It wasn't a mattress, or even halfway comfortable, but right then it felt like the best thing in the world. Anything but the ground. Maggie laid down on the pallet beside his cot with a groan. Muffled, Watt said, "I feel like I should be asking you that."

Cornelius scoffed. "He just gets under my skin."

"I couldn't tell."

"Asshole."

Watt laughed into his pillow, then turned his face towards Cornelius. He'd rolled onto his side and was staring back at Watt with a tender expression. There was about four feet between their cots, but it felt like nothing due to the way Cornelius was smiling at him. It was soft, but so real.

That smile faded, and Cornelius said, "They didn't ... say anything to you?"

Watt tried to shake his head, but the pillow caught most of the movement and his hair ended up doing most of the shaking. He felt so heavy, like a great weight was pushing down upon him. Or maybe it was coming off, now that they'd finally settled in after such a long day, a long journey. God, he was tired.

Cornelius made a soft noise of assent.

"Cornelius … what'd he mean? What was he asking me?"

Cornelius didn't answer.

Watt opened his eyes. Ah, that was difficult. When had they closed? With great effort, he mumbled, "Cornelius."

Cornelius sighed. In a whisper, he said, "It's a … euphemism. For people of our sort. Oz is a queer sort of place, you know."

"Men who like men?" Watt asked, surprise coloring his groggy voice.

Cornelius coughed. "Hells, you are terrible at this. Yes, but not only. Women and … you know. Other women."

"Andrea likes—"

"Watt, for hell's sake, keep it down."

Watt fell silent, his mind tripping over itself. Andrea had been asking if Watt was a friend of Dorothy. No, he'd said, '*are you a friend of Dorothy, too?*'

That implied a kinship between him and Cornelius, and by the knowing look in Francesca's eye, maybe her too. And Anderson had recognized the phrase, was he …?

Watt felt his world shift, just a little bit.

June 30th, 1930

Two and a half weeks.

They'd been there for two and a half weeks, and Cornelius had successfully avoided being alone with Andrea for the entirety of it. Watt, if possible, had clung to Cornelius even more so than he had in Bacairy Post. Whereas before he thought it peculiar, now he was simply grateful. Watt's constant presence made the experience actually enjoyable, and for a short time Cornelius forgot their true purpose.

He got on incredibly well with Joaquim, and he admired how the man efficiently managed his site and the people within it. He was obviously a leader people turned to, but it never seemed like he was superior to the rest of the team, for he did the dirty work in addition to the rest. There were two active dig sites in the area, the tumuli and its surrounding urn field, and the village itself. They found the village and its numerous constructions last year, and so they were further along there. The urn field was another matter, however.

This is where Joaquim placed Watt and Cornelius, working beside Thomas, Benedito, Antônio, and Francesca. She examined the layers that Cornelius and the others gently unearthed, and despite that first night Cornelius found that he didn't mind Francesca. She was professional and pleasant enough, much unlike her brother. Or unlike how he usually was. Andrea hadn't insulted, bothered, or even so much as looked at Cornelius funny since that first night. He was genial, respectful, and confusing. He was acting like the man that Cornelius had first met, and cared for. Cornelius tried not to look into the act too closely, waiting for Andrea to show his true colors once again.

The performance was broken on a night like any other. After working since six in the morning, the group called it a day at six in the evening, abandoning work in favor of washing up and regrouping for dinner. Usually most of the crew went out to the bonfire after filling their bellies, but Antônio and Benedito stayed behind in the canteen to socialize, and so Watt and Cornelius often did too. Sometimes Charles and Thomas stayed behind, the ladies too, but tonight they all attended the fire. Out there instruments were played and stories told, the types of which varied greatly. Cornelius found himself going out there more despite Andrea's presence, devouring the high energy from the others.

But tonight he was craving the quiet company of Benedito's group. The intern still seemed baffled by his sudden flock of companions, but took it in stride. Tonight, Benedito, Antônio, and Watt discussed the implications of something or other, while Cornelius pretended to listen. His mind was elsewhere, in places it shouldn't have been.

Cornelius had never worked such an efficiently run excavation, nor one which such a pleasant team. That wasn't to say everyone got along all the time, but issues were communicated and dealt with immediately instead of leaving to fester and deteriorate morale. Despite having been here for over a year, Joaquim's team was just beginning to understand what lay beneath their feet. Deep within Cornelius' heart, he believed it was the place Fawcett had been looking for. That to go any further looking for it, or him, was folly, because the man was dead and the city he was looking for was *right* here.

There was another part of Cornelius that liked the way Watt was here. Relaxed, and happy. Cornelius still found it hard to decipher how the man was truly feeling for he was more excellent at putting on masks than Cornelius was, but he thought it was true. Watt was happy here. He had a routine again, a daily purpose and people who wanted to listen to what he had to say. Would that happiness last though, if they gave up on their quest? Watt beheld a certain type of honor and pride, and begrudgingly Cornelius did too. A man did not go back on his word, and if they did, it could haunt them for the rest of their lives.

"Cornelius?"

Cornelius blinked. Benedito and Antônio were exchanging a look. Watt stared at him, worry creasing his brows. Cornelius shook his head a little. "Sorry, I—I'm a bit tired. I think I'll turn in for the night." He pushed away from the table, standing a little uneasily. He hadn't been using his cane for a few days now, and acutely wished he had it.

"I'll come with you," Watt said.

"No, stay. It's early yet." Cornelius gave Watt a reassuring smile, effectively stopping the man in his efforts to get up as well.

"If you're sure." Watt relented.

Cornelius patted his shoulder, then nodded to Antônio and Benedito. "Night fellas. See you in the morning."

Cornelius left the canteen behind, wandering down the path back to their tent. The night was crisp, and the stars bright. The moon was just beginning to rise over the broken canopy, a waxing crescent that shone with all its might. Cornelius swatted at a vague insect, grumbling as he dove inside the tent for shelter. The grumbling soon transformed into a curse.

Andrea was sitting on his cot, hands clasped between his knees and head bowed. Upon seeing Cornelius he stood, looking a bit sheepish. "There you are," he said quietly, then took a step towards Cornelius.

Cornelius didn't budge from his place just inside the tent flap. "What do you want, Andrea?"

Andrea ran a hand over the back of his neck and tried on a smile. "Easy, I only want to talk."

Cornelius fought the urge to cross his arms. He kept his stance easy, but his feet were planted.

Andrea stood before him now, his shoulders hunched

and dark eyes big and shining in the dim light.

"We have nothing to talk about. There is nothing you could say that I want to hear, and nothing I—"

"I'm sorry, Cornelius," Andrea whispered.

Cornelius laughed.

The man who had once been his lover, his friend, had the audacity to look affronted. "I am," he insisted.

"Do you even know what those words mean?"

Andrea flushed. He reached for Cornelius' hand, but the warning look in Cornelius' eye stopped him. His fingers curled into a fist, which fell to his side. "You don't have to believe me for it to be true. What I did, it's unforgivable. The behavior of a man spurned and threatened."

"Threatened?" Cornelius laughed again. He hadn't drank in over a month now, but he felt drunk with fury and delirium. "When did I ever threaten you? When did I ever do anything but support you and care—" Cornelius jerked his gaze away from Andrea's pleading stare. He whispered, "I trusted you, Andrea. And you betrayed me in a way that no one ever has."

Andrea ran a hand through his hair. "I know."

Cornelius glared at him. "Is that why you're here? Are you going to warn me this time?"

"Yes, actually. But not—I wouldn't do that to you, Cornelius. Not again. I'm here to apologize for then, and how I acted when you arrived, and to ask you to stay."

Cornelius blinked, uncomprehending. "And why in

the hell would I do a thing like that? Why would *you*?"

Andrea smiled tentatively.

Cornelius scoffed in disgust. "Do you really think I'd take you back?"

Andrea quickly looked away, brows pinching in concentration. Cornelius tracked his line of sight, but it appeared the man was simply lost in thought, staring at the canvas of the tent. Quietly, and without looking at him, Andrea said, "No. But I thought maybe you'd have some common sense. You like it here, I can see it. And this quest you're on, it's pointless. You know it, and I know it. We all do. Things may be ... broken, between us, and I admit my part in that. But that doesn't mean I want to see you search after certain death. It is dangerous country, and for what? Skeletons?"

Cornelius sighed. "Something you wouldn't understand."

"Try me."

"I made a promise, Andrea. And I *always* keep my promises."

Andrea swallowed. He finally met Cornelius' gaze and said, "I'll leave. If that's what it takes to get you to stay, I'll do it."

And this. This gave Cornelius pause. He searched the other man's eyes, and found nothing but honest truth. He believed that if he asked Andrea right then to leave, he would. Unfortunately, this meant that Andrea had somehow changed. While he was still Andrea, there was a facet to him that had emerged in their time apart.

He also knew that he wasn't obligated to forgive him.

"Not everything is about you, Andrea. It's like I said. I made a promise."

Andrea flexed his hands open at his sides, then nodded jerkily. He exhaled and said, "As stubborn as ever, Cornelius Sawyer." He extended a hand to Cornelius, as if to shake. "I'm glad to have known you."

Cornelius pulled back the flap of the tent. "Goodnight, Andrea."

Andrea left, giving Cornelius a sidelong glance as he passed. Once he was gone, the tent was oppressive. Too quiet. His lungs itched for a cigarette, but he'd finally gotten the darts back down to a sane number. He paced the small area between his and Watt's cots, running his hands through his hair and the conversation through his mind over and over again.

How dare he.

How dare Andrea come in and tell Cornelius exactly what he'd wanted to hear for years upon years, when it no longer had any effect at all? The part of his heart that used to be saturated with anger and grief now felt empty, an endless wasteland colder than Lake Michigan. It was disorienting, like he'd been carrying a great weight only to realize he hadn't really been carrying anything at all and was now off kilter without its burden.

After ten minutes of pacing and fretting, Cornelius realized he was waiting for Watt. This infuriated him. He'd put his heart into another man's hands, again.

And what was worse, this time he *knew* the outcome would result in his heart being broken, and welcomed it. He knew that Watt didn't love him back, and yet he wanted him anyway. He wanted his quiet presence, his reassuring wisdom and endless friendship.

After twenty minutes, Cornelius couldn't take solitude any longer. He escaped the confines of the tent and lit up a cigarette, doing his best to forget about his troubles for a little while.

July

Long Haul

July 1st, 1930

There was noise behind him.

Watt froze, fingers tightening around the straps of his pack. His heart raced, and the crisp morning air wasn't so cold anymore. It was still dark out, and everyone was usually asleep at this hour. There was another sound, ground cracking beneath a careful foot. One of those jaguars, perhaps. He wasn't far off from camp, but far enough to be easy pickings for any big predators. Watt reached for the revolver tucked into his waistband, slowly turning around to search for the source of the noise.

Cornelius came up behind him, and Watt's hand fell to his side. He was fully dressed with his gear upon his back, sweat dampening his brow already. He gripped his cane in one hand, the other was fisted at his side. He raised his hand and opened it, palm up, to reveal the piece of quartz Watt had left behind for him. He glared at Watt who stared back at him, unsure what to say. Cornelius' stubborn frown was illuminated by the fading moonlight, and Watt wanted to reach out and smooth it into a smile.

"I'm coming with you," Cornelius whispered, barely there but firm all the same. His hand fell to his side, and his furious eyes beheld all sorts of accusations.

"You don't have to," Watt said, and tried very hard to mean it. He kept hearing Andrea's words over and over again, followed by Severino's distant plea from weeks ago. He hadn't meant to eavesdrop either time, but last night had been the final nail in Watt's heart. "They're doing good work here, real work. I can go on alone. This isn't—I won't drag you into madness, Cornelius."

Cornelius closed the small distance between them, slow enough to give Watt time to back away. He did not.

Cornelius gazed up at Watt, their chests inches apart. His steely eyes seemed to glitter in the dark, like Lake Michigan under full moonlight. "I made a promise, and I intend to keep it."

"Aventurier," Watt whispered, overcome with an intense desire to bend down, and kiss Cornelius.

He—he wanted to kiss Cornelius.

He wanted Cornelius.

Cornelius' eyes flared and he lifted his chin a fraction of an inch, lips parting. *Oh*, and he was wanted in return. He was wanted by, and wanted, a man. Not just any man, but his—his Cornelius. He wanted to. It could've been easy, should've been easy. But no matter how much he wanted to, Watt could not break through that wall. It would shatter everything, demolishing the foundations of everything they had built in the last few months. And he couldn't—he wasn't—

Cornelius' lips curled into a small, sad smile. Like he knew. And he probably did, because who else knew Watt better than this man? His best friend. Because yes, that was what Cornelius was to him, now and always.

Hoarsely, Watt said, "Cornelius, I ..."

Cornelius waited, and when it was clear Watt had no more words to explain himself, he took a step back and half turned away. He firmly, but not unkindly, said, "Come on, we better get going."

If Cornelius was disappointed, he did a fine job of not showing it. Meanwhile, Watt felt every one of his emotions was written on his face. Shame, disappointment, anger and frustration. If he could not accept himself, lose himself in the most wild of places, how would he ever?

Their course was due northwest, into territory that was only a vague area on their map, the edges of which and specific landmarks unknown. It had been unknown when Fawcett tried to go this way, breaking through dense jungle on his round about way back to the coast. Watt had left a letter addressed to Severino and Joaquim on his cot, which he was sure that Cornelius had seen, filled with his intentions and projected route, leaving them with the same sentiment that Fawcett had given to his last point of contact.

'If I don't come back, don't come looking.'

He'd left Cornelius a note too, right by his bedside. It had been short, messy, and apologetic. *'I have to find out what happened to him. You deserve to be safe, and happy. Please forgive me. Yours, Watt.'*

He'd been so sure the man was asleep, but now Watt wondered. Maybe he'd been awake, wondering if Watt was really going to leave him behind again. It wasn't because he'd wanted to, and he was selfishly so grateful that Cornelius had followed after him. Watt loved Maggie, but her company could only go so far to keep him sane.

The way was relatively clear for a short while, sparse trees and generous mounds and ditches continued for about a mile. Cornelius set the pace, not slow but not rushing either. Watt followed him while Maggie scouted the area ahead of both of them. For a while he didn't mind, he could still see her at this distance. But as they went on, the ground smoothed out and the vegetation thickened, the trees growing larger and ferns closer together. As the sun rose, the bugs multiplied exponentially, and so did the opportunities for predators to be waiting in the brush. Watt called Maggie back to his side, and Cornelius looked over his shoulder at him.

"Alright?" Cornelius asked.

Watt nodded. "Just want her to stay close."

Cornelius studied him a moment, then tilted his head and shrugged. "I'll admit, I'm about due for a breather."

Watt agreed and they took a break to drink, assaulted by those damn black flies the entire time. Had they been this bad back at camp? Before taking a sip for himself, Watt withdrew the small metal bowl from his pack and poured some water into it. Maggie drank gratefully, and Watt did the same from his canteen. When Watt lowered it from his lips, he found Cornelius was giving Maggie some of his own water.

Watt's hand twitched, and he quickly secured the top back onto his canteen. "You don't have to do that, she's my responsibility," Watt said, then winced at his short tone.

Cornelius lifted a brow, putting away his own canteen now. He took his cane in hand, withdrawing it from where it'd been tucked between his arm and side. "I know," he said, mildly bemused. He reached down, stroking a hand between Maggie's ears.

Watt opened his mouth to ... well, not protest, but *something*. Cornelius turned away, and Maggie turned her gaze to Watt, panting heavily. Watt sighed, shaking his head. "He will be the death of me," he muttered, taking care of Maggie's bowl before following after Cornelius.

The day unfurled much better than Watt had anticipated laying in his cot late last night, when he'd imagined doing this alone. A low level tension and awkwardness had overshadowed their morning, and threatened to bloom over lunch time. Watt had packed enough supplies for both of them, out of habit, and neither of them commented on it, besides for Cornelius ordering

Watt to share the weight between them. As they ate, Cornelius sparked conversation. At first it was little and relative things, like the birds that flew overhead and the sound of rushing water just barely tickling the ears. They complained about the bugs, which they both agreed hadn't been as bad back at camp.

"I wonder what Antônio is doing," Cornelius murmured, staring off into the trees.

"I miss him already." Watt admitted, fidgeting with the sweaty cuffs of his sleeves. He felt like he should say something about Cornelius' missed opportunity, but he didn't know what. Guilt twisted his gut, and he thought about confessing to eavesdropping last night. He hadn't meant to, but it felt wrong to intrude on Cornelius and Andrea's conversation. And sure, he could have walked away. But Watt couldn't have even if he wanted to. Cornelius had sounded distressed, and Watt wanted to be ready if he needed him.

After lunch they descended further into the tightening jungle, and Watt took the lead this time with a machete at hand. He followed Maggie and moved slowly, careful of everything he touched. After Watt looked over his shoulder for the fifth time in ten minutes, Cornelius wryly said, "I'm not going anywhere."

Watt exhaled, his soul finally settling.

And so they went. Deeper into Brazil.

July 2nd, 1930

That first night had seemed so hopeful, so full of possibility. So much in fact, that it had Cornelius acting incredibly stupid. Or rather, more stupid than he'd already been.

When twilight came the next day, they settled in a copse of trees alongside the edge of a small expanse of grassland, utilizing the illusion of safety and a place to hang their hammocks. While there had been no sign of indigenous peoples yet, they weren't far from Kalapalo and Nafaqua territory. Each had blamed the other for Fawcett's death, and the repercussions of the whole affair had left a lasting impact on the area. Great distrust festered, especially in the hearts of the Kalapalo people.

Cornelius ate his beans, studying Watt as he did the same. He wasn't even really looking at Watt, more so seeing through him as his mind worked. Watt caught him staring and paused, spoon lowering. "What?"

Cornelius pulled forth the first thing that came to his mind. "Why do you think everyone's gone the opposite way that Galvão told them to?"

Watt considered him. "Pride, I always thought. Or maybe distrust."

Cornelius hummed in vague agreement. He thought for another moment, then slowly asked, "Do you think we were ever in real danger from him?"

"Why?" Watt asked, looking at him curiously.

Cornelius lifted a shoulder. "I don't know. Just thinking about it."

Watt fed Maggie from his spoon, frowning as he did so. He had no more rations for her besides his own food, and while she had lost some weight she was still healthy. "Maybe not. I think we'd have heard from him by now. Or maybe he'll wait to strike after we've left the camp. Or maybe he is too preoccupied with cattle."

Determination set between Watt's thick brows, and Cornelius tensed. He only had a split second to prepare for whatever was coming his way, and it wasn't close to enough. "I would like to know the story between you and Andrea," Watt said.

Cornelius sighed, setting his bowl down in his lap. He didn't want to talk about Andrea. He wanted to put Andrea and everything else behind them. But he owed this to Watt, the truth. Watt had been nothing but unflinchingly honest when it came to divulging the parts of his life that he didn't care to revisit. He did wonder about the sudden interest, but then again Watt had asked before, hadn't he?

Cornelius pushed the few remaining beans around his bowl. "There's not much to tell. We worked in Ur together, and we were ... *together*." His face was already aflame, but he went on anyway. "He wanted to settle down, I didn't. He went his way, and I went mine. That was it."

Watt waited for a moment, then said, "And?"

"And ... what?"

"And why can't you forgive him?"

The question lay between them like a dropped snake, coiled and ready to strike. Cornelius' head jerked up. "What?"

"Um ..." Watt's cheeks flushed a deep scarlet. He set his bowl down, allowing Maggie to finish it off. Tentatively, he looked up at Cornelius. "I came back to check on you the other night, when you went back alone after dinner? But I could hear you two talking, and I didn't want to interrupt. I wasn't trying to—I just—I—I wanted to make sure you were going to be alright, that he wasn't going to hurt you."

Cornelius shook his head. He was annoyed Watt had been eavesdropping, Andrea would never hurt him physically. But there was an ember of gratitude inside him that kept Cornelius from overheating. He set his bowl down for Maggie too, and she dutifully licked away what remained. He pulled the little case out of his pocket and lit up a joint. He'd been doing his best to slow down and savor them, and had been doing well, all things considered. But all things came to an end. After it was lit, Cornelius puffed heavily on it.

"Last one," Cornelius murmured and offered it to Watt, who hesitated for a moment before his fingers nudging against Cornelius', taking the joint carefully. Watt began to inhale, and Cornelius declared in a plume of smoke, "He'd seen me naked."

Exhaling, Watt immediately coughed, thrusting the joint back towards him. Cornelius took secret pleasure in throwing the man off kilter. Served him right for eavesdropping. He could picture Watt standing outside the tent, his gentleman and protector sides warring within.

Cornelius took the dart and went on, less dramatic this time. "He knew what I was, or rather what I wasn't. He'd seen all of me with his eyes, touched all of me with his hands. He was the first person I'd fully and completely trusted. I didn't love him, but I cared for him. I thought we could've been ... I don't know. Friends that traveled and played together, but free to go our separate ways. I don't know how to explain it, other than when I looked to the end of my life, it wasn't him beside me. I wouldn't—*couldn't*—make the promises he wanted from me. Andrea needed security, not—"

Cornelius waved a hand, unable to grasp the proper word. "He needed more, and he couldn't understand why *I* didn't want more. I think that's what hurt him the most. He was so upset, and if I'd known he was going to ... well." Cornelius sniffed. He'd done the hypothetical game regarding Andrea too many times to count, and he didn't care to do it again.

Watt had gone completely still, his features pinched with concern and something darker. Cornelius closed his eyes and took a long hit of the joint. His eyelashes were wet, but no tears escaped. He wasn't sure where the sudden rush of emotion had come from, but it shook him to his core. Eyes closed, he released trembling smoke and brittle truth. "He told everyone. He comprised my safety, my dignity. My identity. Told it 'round the campfire like a fucking ghost story, like it wasn't my life on the line. I'd never been so angry in all my life. And then that first night we were here, it was all the same. Taunting me by the fire, in front of the others, and you."

Watt said nothing. Cornelius opened his eyes, which burned something fierce. Watt's eyes were wet too, and lit with a fury that Cornelius had never seen the likes of before. Not in him. A bit choked, Watt said, "Why didn't you tell me? I could've—we didn't have to—"

Cornelius smiled. He didn't know where it came from, but allowed it to stay. "It's alright, Watt."

"No, it's not alright. That's—that's—" Watt puffed with anger and emotion, and Maggie rubbed against his hand. He didn't seem to notice though.

"I know. I've spent a good part of my life being angry at that man, trying to clean up the mess he made and understand what it was all for. But I ..." Cornelius' head was soft with the cannabis, and he struggled to find words again. He shook his head and settled on, "I'm done with that, now. It doesn't mean I've forgiven him, I don't think I ever will. But I'm done tearing myself up over it."

Cornelius stood. He paced over to Watt and knelt between his spread legs with a barely withheld groan of protest. He took Watt's hands in both of his, squeezing tight. He stared up at Watt, who gazed down at Cornelius with eyes that had darkened to molasses. He held onto Cornelius with a trembling but sure grip. "You can stop doubting me, Watt Johnson. I made a promise to you. To Nina." He smiled over at Maggie, who was watching them with her tongue lolled out to the side. "To Maggie. I'm in it for the long haul."

Watt's mouth parted in surprise, and he swiped his tongue over his bottom lip. He blinked and looked over at Maggie, then Cornelius. He squeezed Cornelius' fingers and whispered, "And what did you promise her? Dog bowls made of gold?"

Cornelius laughed. He laughed so damn hard that it startled both Watt and Maggie. It was deep, strumming the threads tangled within his heart. He said, "I promised I'd keep you out of trouble, Watt Johnson. And that's just what I'm going to do, no matter how many times you try to leave me behind."

"Oh," Watt said, and he laughed quietly. "Funny thing, that. Aren't you full of trouble?"

Cornelius laughed again, he felt so goddamn light that he might float away.

Watt pulled Cornelius up until their foreheads were touching. Cornelius' breath caught, but it wasn't a kiss Watt wanted. He repeated that over and over again as Watt stared deep into his eyes. Watt whispered, "I didn't want to. Leave you behind."

Breathless, he said, "I know."

They separated, too soon for Cornelius' liking,

and resumed their trek into the unknown. Cornelius thought, *'Not a bad start to the next step in their trip, not bad at all.'*

Always Would

July 29th, 1930

They had been lost for an eternity.

Watt squinted down at the map stretched out in his hands, despite the fact the paper had previously been soaked through with sweat and rain, and they had no way to know which way was up or down. Cornelius knew without looking at the map that any remaining ink was sparse, the whole damn thing rendered pointless. They'd have better luck with their navigational instruments, if those hadn't been swallowed by the marsh.

It hadn't taken long for their endeavor to nosedive, for it seemed the land was against their every step.

A few days after they left Joaquim's site, the weather had shifted into perpetual thunderstorms that lasted for three days straight. The sound was unlike anything Cornelius had ever heard, each thunder crack shook the ground with the full force of their rage. The rain fell in heavy sheets, pinning the trio into a makeshift shelter for days upon end. It was a close fit, and would have been intimate and awkward if not for the insects burrowing into every nook and cranny available. They ate very little, since a fire and hunting for any supplemental protein was impossible.

When the rain had cleared and travel was possible again, they were faced with mud, flooding, and surprise marshes. With the jungle as thick as it was, it reminded Cornelius of what he'd read the everglades to be like. Thick with trees, predators, muck, and water. Serious flooding had occurred and it took days for all that rainwater to seep back into the ground, which had been hardened by drought. One wrong step introduced the first surprise marsh, which had sucked Cornelius in up to his waist. Watt had gotten the worst of it trying to pull him out, and their gear had been caked with mud. What wasn't claimed by the swamp, anyway. The landscape changed little in terms of landmarks, and it gave the illusion of traveling in circles. Hell, for all they knew that was true. Cornelius had fallen more in the past month than he had in all his life, even more than on their way to the site. He hurt everywhere, he was exhausted, and he was annoyed.

"I think ..." Watt looked up, frowned at the surrounding jungle, then back down at the map again.

That was it. Cornelius splintered apart.

"For hell's sake Watt, for once in your life just admit that you failed!" Cornelius shouted, and birds took flight overhead. He hadn't even realized the words were coming until they'd been thrown into the air between them.

Watt jerked back, stunned. His mouth opened and closed, then he methodically folded the map. He clutched it in his hand and said, "What are you talking about?" He shook his head and laughed, the sound rang hollow. "All I do is fail."

Cornelius jabbed a finger in his direction. "Oh, don't you *dare*."

"No." Watt straightened, his body going rigid. "My life may look like a string of successes to you, but it is not. I am lonely and odd and queer in a way that has nothing to do with my ... habits!" He threaded a viciously shaking hand through his hair, knocking his hat into the grass. Maggie whined, a shrill noise Cornelius had never heard before. But he'd also never seen Watt like this before. His eyes were wild, and he sucked in air like his life depended on it.

Suddenly, Cornelius felt very small as he watched the other man come undone. This was his fault. He did this. Maggie whined again from her place at Watt's feet, but she wasn't looking up at him. Cornelius' attention was redirected when Watt's previous near shout drained to a whisper. "I could give two shits about recognition and wealth and everything else. That sounds ungrateful and I'm sure it is, but what I want is to be *happy*. In that, I have failed for nearly every day of my life. Except ..."

Watt stared at Cornelius, his hand tore out strands as it dropped to his side. "Except for the past few months

... with you." He said this last piece like a revelation, and the words sank into Cornelius' bones deeper than any prayer ever would.

Cornelius said, "Watt, I—"

Maggie yelped, her cry high and sharp. She jumped and spun in place, her cry transforming into a vicious growl.

"Maggie?" Watt startled, hands reaching down to steady her. "It's alright girl, I'm alright."

Watt's hat falling into the grass. The shrill cry Cornelius assumed came from Maggie.

Time slowed, and the next few moments unfolded in fractured bits and pieces, pieces that would never come back together, no matter how much time passed for Cornelius. At that moment, all he could foresee was Watt bitten.

Watt dying.

Watt gone.

He didn't remember putting his knife to hand, but his fingers closed around the familiar handle all the same.

Cornelius lunged before Watt could run his hands further down Maggie's body.

Cornelius yelled, "Snake!"

He hit his knees and grabbed the snake by its tail, stretching it taut with all the strength and bravery he could muster.

"Cornelius!" Watt cried in alarm.

Maggie yelped and turned 'round in an effort to bite

him, but Watt caught her by the snout just in time.

Cornelius brought the knife down, striking behind the snake's head. Bone and flesh were severed in one clean motion.

The headless body twitched and writhed in Cornelius' hand, wracked with death defying nerves. Warm blood splattered across his hand, his arm, his clothes. A fleck landed near his eye. Cornelius nearly threw the corpse but had enough sense of mind to simply drop it. The fangs, and head still attached to them, were embedded into Maggie's back leg, the upper thigh. The eyes rolled in the snake's head, and Cornelius thought he could still hear it hissing. Or maybe that was the air rushing in and out of his own lungs. He couldn't tell how much was post-mortem movement and how much was Maggie moving around. She was crying, quivering in pain and drooling all over Watt's thigh.

Watt stood doubled over and held her head against him, whispering frantically to her. "Maggie, oh Maggie. It's alright, girl. Shh, it's alright." His wide, terrified eyes flicked to Cornelius, as if he could stop Watt's heart from breaking. Tears streamed down Watt's flushed face, cutting through the dirt on his cheeks.

Cornelius cleared his throat, which did nothing to shake off his nerves. He said, "I—I'm going to try and pull it out now."

Watt nodded furiously. "Okay. I've got her."

Cornelius reached for the snake's head, fingers trembling.

"Be careful," Watt added.

Cornelius said nothing, because despite all the blood and its lack of a body, he was quite sure the thing was going to turn 'round and bite him. His fingers brushed against the snake's scales and he shivered, revulsion coursing through him. But the snake did not move, at least not to bite him. Those eyes still rolled, furious and indignant.

Keeping in mind the way the snake masters had milked snakes, he pulled the upper jaw in an upwards and back motion in an effort to unhinge the fangs. Maggie protested against the pull on her flesh, and Watt soothed her with a string of soft praise. With great care, Cornelius removed the whole affair from her leg. He gingerly tossed the head onto the path back the way they'd come, then stood and located his bag. He must've shucked it in the place he'd been standing before.

"What're you doing?" Watt asked, his voice strident.

"See if you can get her to lay down," Cornelius said, rifling through his supplies. "We need to treat it." It only took him a moment to locate the first aid kit he'd made, complete with the antivenin. By the time he returned, Watt was sat down in the dirt with Maggie pulled into the space between his legs, her head tucked against his ribs. She was twitching.

'*Fuck*,' Cornelius thought.

"Do you think—wait, is that—Cornelius?"

"It's a bushmaster," Cornelius said and knelt in the

space between Watt's spread legs, laying out the antivenin kit and necessary cleaning supplies. He wiped off the blade of his knife with the corner of his shirt, then squinted at Watt. "Can you hold her still? I'll need to shave the fur in order to get a good look at the bite, then douse it in the iodine and administer the antivenin."

"But that's for—"

"Do you want me to save her or not?" Cornelius barked.

"Yes," Watt croaked, arms tightening around Maggie. "Yes."

Cornelius took a deep breath. "Then hold her."

He worked as quickly as he could without making mistakes. He wasn't able to shave her as close as he would've liked, but it would do for now. The punctures were deep, and the holes jagged. He poured iodine perhaps far too liberally than he should've, but alas. Maggie whimpered, and Cornelius did his best to ignore her. To ignore everything in this situation that wasn't the wound itself.

He prepared the second to last bothropic ampule they had, then the enormous needle. His stomach rolled and he inhaled slowly, doing his best to steady his trembling fingers. Finally, Cornelius locked eyes with Watt. "Are you ready?"

"Yes. Do it."

Cornelius steadied Maggie's shaking leg and injected her with the antivenin. He prayed to the universe, to Watt's God, to anyone who was listening, that it worked. She whimpered beneath his ministrations, but not once did she try to bite him again or pull against Watt's hold. She gasped for air, and by the time Cornelius withdrew the needle from her flesh, he was too.

He secured the used ampule and needle into a separate case, then sat back on his heels and wiped his forehead with the back of his hand. Watt had his face buried in the scruff of Maggie's neck, his spine bent at a painful angle. Cornelius felt like the moment was too big to break with words, so he set to work once more in silence.

He placed a clean gauze pad over the puncture wounds, then wrapped the bandage around her leg. He did so in an X-shaped motion, covering probably far more than he needed to of her thigh. Even if the antivenin worked, they would still have to contend with infection in a place where it festered so easily. The humidity and the mud, the bugs and travel. The best course of action would be to go back to the site. They'd have a better chance of finding their way back rather than the unknown. Their supplies were low, Maggie was hurt, and the idea that they might find Fawcett in this place had long since withered and died.

And when did that happen, exactly?

"She bit me," Watt said, muffled by Maggie's fur. He lifted his head, eyes swollen and mouth twisted downwards. Cornelius had never seen him look so miserable, but he didn't see a bite.

"Where?" Cornelius asked, a bit dazed.

Watt's eyes were a bit glazed too, like he was somewhere else. "The fence. I was bleeding, find home, find a way home. Stuck in a fence, scared. She didn't mean to, she was just scared. She's scared." He began panting, breathing in short bursts. "It hurt. I screamed. But she didn't eat it. Took me home instead."

Cornelius swallowed against the hysteria rising in his throat. He went to rest a hand on Watt's shoulder, then faltered upon seeing the blood all over his fingers. "Watt," he whispered. "I'm right here."

Watt blinked rapidly, coming back to himself. "We have to go back," he croaked.

He opened his mouth to say, '*I know*,' but stopped. Goosebumps swarmed his skin, and he shivered beneath the distinct weight of an unknown presence watching them. His gaze wandered over the small, barely cleared out portion of the jungle, their slice of their world. He felt sure they were alone, that it was only them here. Them, and the wild. He listened, sure he heard someone speaking. No, it was ... *it* was calling them.

The voice of wild places sung to Cornelius, and Watt. He looked around too, eyes wide with fear and perhaps a little bit of awe.

It was the bright and hopeful tenor of the birds, and the solid bass of life pulsing in the ground beneath their feet. The gentle swish of foliage surrounding their little company, and the rustle of the thick canopy overhead. And even fainter than that, but present all the same, the sound of water. They were at the heart of the world, and she was singing to them.

The birds cried, *'not yet.'*

The mud groaned, *'just a little bit farther.'*

The leaves whispered, *'there are secrets here.'*

The water promised, *'life, the secret of life.'*

It was all beckoning them to try once more. They weren't truly lost, not if going home was an option. And what was waiting for them at home?

"Do you—" Watt whispered, reaching for Cornelius' hand.

Cornelius took it, squeezing tight.

And like a cloud passing over the sun, the presence faded and the voice receded, back into the depths of the unknown.

Cornelius shivered. He whispered, "It's too late in the day to go anywhere. Let's make camp here for the day, and see what tomorrow brings."

"Cornelius, what *was* that?" Watt's knuckles were white from how hard he gripped Cornelius' aching fingers.

Cornelius shook his head. "I ... don't know. I think we're both just tired."

Watt barked out a short, delirious and giddy laugh. Cornelius startled, then he started laughing, too. Harsh and wet, full of frustration and relief and something like hope. Because all was not lost, not yet. Not while they were still holding hands, bodies coming together until their foreheads met. Watt's forehead was sweaty, and his hair was rough where it stuck to his skin. Cornelius didn't care, he was probably just as disheveled. Their laughter died a slow death, lingering in the space between their lips. Their hands were still clasped between them, and they stayed like that for a little while longer. Existing in the other's space, the air between them thick with love. Discounting Cornelius' own feelings, it was a different sort of love. One that was forged through hardship and kinship, trust and the knowledge that this person beside you, they were in it for as long as you were. Neither time, distance, or meddling from others could sever a connection like that.

Oh, Cornelius was done for.

He loved Watt. He *loved* him. Always had, always would.

Watt lay with Maggie in his arms and listened to Cornelius as he moved around camp. He'd done everything, from taking the lead during the event to setting up an acceptable area to make camp in less than ideal conditions. Watt had watched as Cornelius cleared brush and vegetation from a small area between the trees, checking for critters and otherwise. He'd hung up their hammocks between a few sturdy but small trees, and instructed Watt to rest with Maggie.

"A calm patient is a healing patient," Cornelius had said, but Watt knew it was because of him, too. Watt was ... well. Cornelius had said it, didn't he? Watt was a failure. He'd failed to keep their direction, to keep Maggie safe, or to act quickly in an emergency. He'd frozen.

Besides his time in France, bleeding out and trapped in the woods like an animal, freezing beside the long dead body of the man he'd cared for, he'd never felt so much despair before. He'd locked up, costing Maggie precious seconds. He'd never hesitated in a time of crisis before, not in wartime or otherwise. But God, this was *Maggie*. He hadn't been able to leave her behind, and now his cowardice could be the death of her. Cornelius had tried to warn him, and did Watt listen?

And again, if he'd listened to Cornelius even a day sooner and turned back for camp, Maggie wouldn't have been bitten. Well, now the fever dream of ambition had been broken, and Watt could see every mistake he'd made clearer than ever before. How could he ever repair them all? He was a man built of fractures, and was falling apart at the seams.

He closed his eyes and thought, *'that's what you get for running through bramble and jungle, those thorns will get you. That's what you get for taking the word of a widow clinging to something intangible like magic and faith.'*

But ... was magic and faith so ridiculous? He thought

about the voice they'd heard, for by the look on Cornelius' face in that moment it was clear he'd heard it too. The sensation of the world opening her eyes and perceiving you, and henceforth judging you worthy enough to hear her siren song. It was a sound you heard with your heart more than your ears, and wasn't that intangible, too?

His fingers glided through Maggie's coat. She lay entirely on top of him and her heart beat against his, fast and unrelenting. She wasn't asleep, only resting through the pain.

"Watt," Cornelius whispered, and his fingers skimmed over the curve of Watt's shoulder. "Food's ready."

Watt opened his eyes. Cornelius stood over him, his hand coming to rest on Watt's collarbone. His brow was furrowed, and his face was dirty. There was a scratch above his eyebrow, fresh and weeping blood. Watt reached out and wiped it away before it trickled down into Cornelius' eye.

Cornelius took him by the wrist with his other hand, raising that same brow. "I'm fine, just a branch got me."

"You're bleeding."

"I've been through worse."

"Me too."

Watt tugged against the slight grip, reaching upwards for Cornelius' neck. His fingers curled against the side of Cornelius' throat, and his fingers tightened around Watt's wrist.

Watt pulled Cornelius down, and kissed him.

It was not at all what he thought it would be like. It was gentle and chaste, almost disbelieving in nature. Cracked lips met dry lips. Cornelius stiffened, nose brushing against his own as he pulled back enough to catch Watt's eye.

"Watt," he whispered. "Are you sure?"

"Aventurier. Please," Watt whispered back. "Embrasse-moi, si tu veux."

Cornelius exhaled, and the air was caught between them as he bent down for another kiss. He released Watt's wrist, trailing his fingers up Watt's arm before tangling them in the sweat damp hair curling at the base of his neck. His other hand tightened in the fabric over Watt's collarbone.

In turn, Watt cupped the back of Cornelius' head, tugging him down insistently. Watt yielded his mouth to Cornelius who slid his tongue in, exploring with a slow sort of desperation. A need to feel every inch of Watt's mouth, inside and out.

A little moan escaped Watt, barely a whimper even, but Cornelius' grip in his hair tightened all the same. That drew another sound out of Watt, and Cornelius hummed in response. *This* was what he imagined kissing Cornelius to be like. Intentional and deep, all consuming and full of care.

For a minute, the world was simple. He was kissing Cornelius, his friend. His confidant. His person. More than that, it was as if his soul was being embraced, comforted, and seen. His entire body lit up with the sensation and attention, and after a little while he had to draw his knee up in an effort to hide his arousal, shifting Maggie off to the side. She huffed in protest, then grumbled at their antics.

Cornelius didn't straighten to his full height, but he did pull back enough to leave Watt with a gentle parting kiss on the lips, then the side of his mouth. His fingers loosened their hold, and both his hands slid down to rest on Watt's chest. He studied Watt, lips curved into a soft smile and eyebrows pinched in confusion. Like Watt was the most curious and wonderful thing he'd ever seen.

"I didn't know you felt that way," Cornelius finally said.

Watt inclined his head, cheeks hot. "I told you how I felt."

"About men, but not ... me." He lifted a shoulder, gaze drifting elsewhere. "Not all men who enjoy men want men like *me*, if you get my meaning. And that's fine, people like what they like."

Watt guided Cornelius' attention back to him with a gentle palm to the cheek. Cornelius' eyes were wet, and his lips were pressed into a harsh line. "I like *you*, Cornelius."

Cornelius looked like he was fit to argue, but in the end he sighed, leaning into Watt's touch. "God help you then." He closed his eyes and admitted in a whisper, "I'm fond of you too, Watt. You have no idea."

Watt looked forward to finding out.

For Now

July 30th, 1930

Cornelius slept fitfully and was awake for the day long before Watt was. Long before the sun, even. Hypotheticals, irrational fantasies, and worst case scenarios loomed in his mind. And none of those had anything to do with Watt, who brought along an entirely different stream of thoughts. Hells, they'd *kissed*.

He'd been kissed by, and kissed in return, Watt Johnson. It was wonderful, heartwarming, and everything Cornelius had ever wanted. It was a kiss to end all others, because surely nothing could be better than that. Except for perhaps ... a second kiss.

No. He couldn't think like that. Watt had been emotional last night, vulnerable and not in his right mind. He'd wanted comfort, and Cornelius had given it to him. He should've known better, been the responsible one for both their sakes. But Cornelius hadn't been in his right mind, either. He never was, but especially not when it came to Watt.

What would Watt desire in the light of a new day,

faced with all the difficulties ahead of them?

Surely not Cornelius, not irritable and arrogant and weak Cornelius.

And if all he wanted was comfort in this difficult time, could Cornelius do it? Could he hide his heart and give Watt what he needed?

He wanted to say yes.

But deep down, he knew he couldn't.

He couldn't be with Watt ... like that, not without being able to express his love. And if he couldn't be selfless for the person he loved, because he did love Watt, what right did he have to love him in the first place?

Typical, selfish Cornelius.

It all made his head hurt, but his heart ached worst of all.

The sun had not quite risen when Cornelius climbed out of his hammock, but some bruised light had begun to make way for dawn. It was just enough to see by, but he slipped a torch into his pocket just in case. He checked his pistol for moisture or dirt, same as he always did when rising for the day. He withdrew a small canvas bag that held his secondary outfit and boxer shorts from his pack, then glanced back at Watt. He was still asleep, his arms wrapped around Maggie's middle. Did the man ever move in his sleep?

Maggie was awake, sleepily watching Cornelius. He tried not to feel too hopeful about that, he needed to be the realistic one. And yet, he couldn't imagine her dying. He believed if he gave the thought any credence, surely it would come true. Like a cruel prophecy. And he couldn't do that to her, or to Watt.

He gave Maggie a half smile, then walked a little ways from camp and relieved himself behind a tree. Thankfully there was still some paper left, for he didn't recognize any of the plants around him. Wiping with an unfamiliar bit of greenery was a gamble to say the least. The canopy was thicker here, and it blocked out most of the sky. There was more underbrush here too, mostly ferns and struggling saplings. He thought he could hear water running, and debated investigating the source. He was already on edge though, and decided to wait for Watt. He kept an ear out and his gun within reach, and quickly began to change his clothes.

He was grateful that his shorts weren't too soiled, and that this painful cycle was tapering off to an end. It was always short, but brutal, and there was no comfort to be found in the middle of nowhere. In fact, the humidity and heat made it all so much worse. The pain, the mess, the sweat and everything else inconvenient and infuriating that came with being born with a body like his.

Cornelius had brought two pairs of modified shorts into the wild, not wanting to deal with disposing of cheap pads that were uncomfortable to begin with. And somehow those made him feel like less than a man, bulky and easier to get hyper fixated on. The boxers were better, more natural. They were the new sort with rubber in the waistband and bold stripes of color, the fabric a comfortable cotton which was easier for Cornelius to alter than silk. He'd added more layers of fabric in the crotch area, and cinched the hem around the thighs a little. It was natural packing, and practical for when unexpected accidents happened. He'd yet to bleed through them, even during this punishing journey.

He finished changing, rolling his old clothes into a tight ball which he shoved into the canvas bag with a grunt. The trousers and shirt he wore now had been worn a few times already, and all of his clothes could do with a wash. Perhaps he and Watt could search for that water, Watt could carry Maggie if he needed to. Maybe there was a better area to camp nearby. Of course, staying by the river could attract unwanted attention, so they'd have to stay in the treeline if possible.

Ah, but they were going back.

Right?

When Cornelius returned to camp the sun had risen, and so had Watt. He'd laid out what remained of his good shirt on the ground and Maggie lay upon it, drinking from water from her dish. *'Queen of the Amazon,'* Cornelius thought. Watt was stroking a hand down her back and when he saw Cornelius coming, he tentatively smiled. He smiled with those lips that had felt so wonderful against his. Lips that had said he cared. That he wanted Cornelius.

"Morning. She's drinking," Watt said, gesturing to

Maggie with great pride.

Cornelius swallowed, his throat tight. He gave Watt a little smile and knelt down beside him so he could pet her. "That's good. How you doing, girl?"

Maggie lifted her head, water dripping from her muzzle as she licked his hand. Cornelius chuckled softly, stroking beneath her chin. He glanced at the bandage, noting that no blood or otherwise had leaked through to the outside. That was a good sign, but he couldn't be sure which direction her wound was turning without looking at it.

Watt glanced between Cornelius and Maggie. "What's wrong?"

Cornelius blinked, coming back to himself. He shook his head. "Nothing."

Watt studied him, working his bottom lip between his teeth. That was new, and treacherous. "Somehow, I don't believe you." Watt reached out, his palm settling against Cornelius' jaw. Watt's thumb rubbed under his eye, and Cornelius inhaled shakily at the unrestrained contact. "Didn't sleep well, did you?"

"Listen." Cornelius took Watt's hand and gently pried it away from his face. Watt's fingers immediately slid between his. He'd meant to let go, but their joined hands settled between them. "We need to—" Cornelius cleared his throat, but the damn tension wouldn't let up. "We should probably come up with a plan."

'*Damn coward*,' Cornelius cursed himself inwardly. He couldn't talk about them, not right now. Not while

Watt was looking at him like that.

Watt nodded seriously. He shifted his gaze to Maggie, and concern knitted his brows together. He was quiet for so long that Cornelius thought he wasn't going to speak at all. Make Cornelius lead the conversation. He opened his mouth, but as soon as he spoke, Watt did too.

"You were right—"

"We should keep—"

"Sorry, you go first," Watt said quickly, blushing.

Cornelius blinked, transfixed by the rising color in Watt's cheeks, then his words. "Wait. You want to go back?"

Watt shrugged, and the color deepened. He ran his free hand through his hair. "No. I don't *want* to go back. But my stubbornness has ..." He glanced over at Maggie, fingers tightening around Cornelius'. "If I'd listened to you, even a minute sooner, she wouldn't have gotten hurt. We're low on food, and there's not much game here. Even if we took anything down, starting a fire could draw attention. And Maggie, she needs to rest."

Cornelius hesitated, breathing shallowly. "Do you think we can find our way back?"

Watt studied him for a moment. Then he said, "You don't want to go back, either."

"No, but I agree. It's the logical thing to do."

Watt's molten eyes flicked back and forth, tracking every minute expression crossing Cornelius' face.

His gaze was fierce and without rebuke, and Cornelius wondered how much Watt had been restraining himself before. Did he always look at Cornelius like this? Or did the kiss change his perspective, and he stared with less abandon now?

"What changed?" Watt asked.

Unbidden, Cornelius' eyes drifted down to Watt's lips. He swallowed on reflex, immediately cursing himself. He glanced over at Maggie, then back to Watt, doing his best to focus on the man's eyes. Eyes creased with humor and age. Damn him.

Cornelius cleared his throat and said, "Maggie's hurt. And I think ... I think if we were looking for the lost city, then we should've stayed right where we were, with Severino and the others."

"But?"

Cornelius sighed, pushing his glasses back up his nose.

"What?"

Cornelius tried to glare at him, but there was no heat in it. He said, "I heard water. When I," he gestured to his clothes, "went for a walk, I heard water running. And I wondered. That's all."

"You wondered." Watt looked over at Maggie. "You hear that, girl?"

Cornelius rolled his eyes. "Are you trying to be difficult this morning, Watt Johnson?"

Watt grinned, effectively disarming Cornelius. "Can't let you have all the fun, can I?"

Cornelius laughed. "What's gotten into you?"

"Nothing." Watt's smile broadened, and he shook his head a little. "But I'm wondering now, too."

Cornelius decided that perhaps he could be Watt's comfort, if it meant more smiles like these. He could be whatever the man wanted, or needed, and when it was all said and done, well.

He'd be happy, for now.

July 30th, 1930

Watt was composed of contradictions.

He was happy, and not just on a surface level, but all the way down to his bones. His best friend was hurt.

He was awake for the first time in what felt like years. He was lost in the heart of the world.

He wanted to keep going. He wanted to go back.

He wanted. God, did he want.

But it was clear by the look in Cornelius' eyes and the rigid way he held himself that last night had not been as enlightening for him as it had been for Watt. Or maybe it had been, but instead of discovering happiness in their kiss, Cornelius had discovered that he didn't want Watt. Not like that.

He stared at Cornelius' back as the man led the way, slowly making a path through the vegetation as it thickened impossibly further. He cut through choking plants and vines, his cane strapped to his pack. Watt held Maggie close to his chest, readjusting her in his arms every now and then. He cradled her lower body, careful of her bad leg, and she rested her head and front legs on his shoulder. She didn't care for it, and Cornelius thought it might be alright if she walked for a little while, but for now Watt carried her. Less opportunities for the bandage, and therefore her leg, to get infected.

The ferns were enormous through here, and so were the trees. They were only five minutes from the place they'd camped last night, and yet it felt like a world away. Cornelius paused, then glanced over his shoulder and said, "Do you hear it?"

Watt paused. Maggie's ear twitched. He said, "Water."

Cornelius nodded. A hesitant expression crossed his face, and he crossed the short distance back to Watt. He stroked Maggie's fur and studied her eyes. He looked back up to Watt, his face carefully blank. "What do you want to do, Watt Johnson?"

'Kiss you,' Watt thought. *'I want to kiss you again.'*

"I'm following you, aventurier."

Cornelius' cheeks flushed, and he tried not to smile. With as much sternness as he could muster, Cornelius said, "I'm serious, Watt. Are you sure this is what you want to do? I don't—I can't have you regretting this, or resenting me for it." Watt felt like he'd been doused in ice water, and his fingers tightened in Maggie's fur. Something must have shown on his face, because Cornelius added in quick staccato bursts, "I'm talking about going forward. With the search. We can go back to the camp. If you want."

Watt said, "We're long past the point of going back, Cornelius."

He hoped that Cornelius heard the words for what they were. A promise.

Cornelius ducked his head a little and pushed up his glasses. "Okay." He looked up at Watt, unable to fight his grin any longer. "Okay. Let's go before your arms fall off."

Watt said, "Lead the way."

Unsurprisingly, the water was not as close as it seemed.

The ferns and trees grew exponentially as they'd traveled, and Watt wished that he'd listened to Rowland's lectures more often. Were these plants some of the new species he'd discovered, or something entirely different? The landscape had become treacherous, each step unsteadier than the last. Cornelius pushed on until the late evening, and only stopped after the third time Watt suggested they stop for camp. The moon was a thin shred, and it did not offer as much light as Watt would've liked when setting up. The sky existed only in small pinpricks through the suffocating canopy. They'd found no water, not even a marsh, only more jungle.

It was clear Cornelius didn't want to stop, and it was

also clear he was frustrated. "It's playing with us," he muttered.

Watt looked up from the knot he'd been securing. "What?"

Cornelius grumbled from the other end of the hammock, then loudly said, "Nothing. Never mind."

Watt didn't push it. Besides, he agreed with what Cornelius didn't say. Ever since they'd left Cuiabá their journey had been arduous, tough, and exhausting. But it had completely changed tone and difficulty since parting ways with the others, like the land had been against them every step of the way. Save for that moment after Maggie had been bit, when they'd first discussed going back. The ... not quite a voice, or a song maybe, had convinced them to keep going.

Distantly, he wondered if a siren song was a perfect adjective for that moment. A song intended to entrap, and doom, all those who heard it.

After the hammock was up and Maggie was safely tucked within it, they consumed porridge in relative silence. God, if Watt never had to look at porridge again. When the last bite hit Watt's stomach, Cornelius abruptly said, "I want to check her leg. It's been a little over twenty four hours, enough time to start turning one way or another."

Watt's stomach churned, and he nodded. "Okay."

They settled down in an area that Cornelius had cleared, the ground mostly dirt and trampled grass. He said, "We better be quick, before the bugs get us."

Watt settled Maggie between his legs in the same fashion he'd done before, and she groaned in protest against his side. "Now now, none of that. It'll be over before you know it." Watt murmured, running a hand down her back.

Cornelius chuckled, offering Watt his torch. "Glad to see she's well enough to complain."

"I think she'll be okay," Watt admitted, shining the light on Maggie's leg as Cornelius began to unwrap the bandage.

"I do too." Cornelius hesitated for only a moment before continuing his work. "But let's not get too ahead of ourselves, okay?"

Watt swallowed the lead in his throat and said nothing.

Once the bandage was removed, all that was left was the gauze, where dark blood had seeped through. The light began to tremble, and Watt steadied his hand. Cornelius gently lifted the gauze, pulling hair as he did so. Maggie whined, and Watt ran his free hand through her fur once more.

"Sorry, girl," Cornelius said, glancing between the gauze and her leg. He murmured, "I wish we had alcohol, or more iodine." Tentatively, he discarded the gauze and inspected the wound with careful fingers.

He was quiet for so long that it had Watt feeling uneasy. "Well? How's it look?"

"Hmm. It's too early to tell. There's some drainage, and it's warmer than I'd like."

Watt's heart sank.

Cornelius glanced up at him, then back down to the wound. He delicately cleaned it with a shred of fabric dampened with water from his own canteen, which was dangerously low. "That just means we have to take it easy, that's all. She's still drinking, and eating. And there's no necrosis, which we'd already see if the tissue was affected by the venom. No bleeding from the eyes, no seizures. We have a little iodine left, but I think we better save that for water, for now."

Watt just kept on nodding along to Cornelius' words, doing his best to keep calm. He didn't want to stress Maggie out, and had nothing to say that wasn't choked worry. Cornelius finished treating Maggie's wound, using less bandage wrapping than he had before. He ran a hand over Maggie's belly, scratching gently. "There you go, sweetheart."

Maggie pulled out of Watt's embrace and turned to lick Cornelius' fingers. Cornelius chuckled, allowing her to do so.

"Thank you," Watt whispered, and Cornelius looked over at him.

"Of course," he said, then tentatively shifted closer and pressed a kiss to the corner of Watt's mouth. Watt immediately turned his head, transforming the kiss into something more. Cornelius' lips upturned against his own, and he chuckled.

Maggie groaned dramatically, wiggling from where Watt still held her. "Ah, sorry Mags," Watt said, opening his arms. Maggie pushed to her feet and yawned, then ambled away to investigate their surroundings. She wouldn't bear weight on that leg, keeping her foot tucked up off the ground. Watt wanted to put her back in the hammock, but she seemed to be content stretching out her other legs. "Don't go far."

"She'll be alright, it's good for her to get moving." Cornelius remarked, watching her closely. "Well, better get off the ground." He patted Watt's thigh once, then stood and offered Watt his hand.

Watt took it.

It was a good night, despite everything. They'd started rationing about a week after leaving the dig site, and it was starting to take its toll on Watt. He was perpetually hungry, and felt weaker than he had in his entire life. None of the plants Antônio, Severino, or Charles had told them were safe to eat were available. This, despite the implications, heartened Watt. It meant they were somewhere new.

Watt offered Cornelius some of his water since he'd sacrificed some to clean Maggie's wound. They were both running low, and that scared Watt more than the dwindling food supply. If they didn't find water soon, they'd be in a world of trouble. The distant sound of it coursing through the earth teased him, and Watt resolved to find it tomorrow. He *would*, by God.

Cornelius busied himself with tidying up the first aid kit before turning in, utilizing his own hammock as a precarious table of sorts. Watt wanted to assist, but

Cornelius waved him away. "Go on, you and Maggie get tucked in."

Watt hesitated at Cornelius' side. Cornelius looked over at him, a brow raised. Watt whispered, "Could we ... say good night? Is that okay?"

Cornelius' confusion melted into fondness. He closed the first aid kit, then turned to face Watt straight on. "Yes, of course."

Watt froze, suddenly feeling unsure. It felt as if they were standing on the precipice of a great waterfall, or perhaps it was simply a line they could never turn back from. He didn't know why, for they'd kissed now, and more than once at that. But something as simple and tender as saying good night, as something more than friends, was frighteningly intimate.

Cornelius took the next step.

His stomach pressed against Watt's, and their legs collided awkwardly. His hands slid against Watt's own before moving up his forearms and beyond. Nimble fingers crested Watt's shoulders and danced over the column of his throat. Blunt nails scratched against his ragged beard, and fingertips settled along the thinning muscles of Watt's cheeks. Despite the fact Watt was the taller of the two, he'd never felt so small.

But it wasn't ... it wasn't the small he felt when his father talked down to him, or the small he felt being associated with grave robbers, or living when so many of his comrades had died.

He was small, like a child receiving praise and comfort from a loved one.

Like a young man receiving a medal, not because so many had died and he had lived, but because true courage had been shown.

Like an older man given a second chance to make things right.

Small, like a human in the universe, on a perpetually spinning rock that would see more ages than he ever would, with the one person he longed to be with more than anyone else in the world.

He opened his mouth to tell Cornelius all of it. To tell him how he felt, because he was sure that Cornelius didn't know, not the whole of it at least.

Cornelius' lips filled the space where an opportunity once dwelled, and his tongue swept it away for good measure. He came onto Watt with a determination that strengthened his tongue and drove a leg between Watt's thighs.

Watt gasped and Cornelius inhaled acutely, stealing the air for himself. Caught off guard, Watt stumbled backwards a little, hands hanging uselessly at his sides, and Cornelius followed. Watt's spine connected with the tree securing Cornelius' hammock, and he grunted. Cornelius rutted against him, his kiss growing sloppy and insistent. Watt's arousal was painful and sudden, and it was all too much. He finally remembered how to use his hands, and he took a hold of Cornelius' hips. He pushed the man back, who panted like he'd run a mile.

"What's wrong?" Cornelius asked, his steely eyes

beacons in the darkness. "Is this not what you had in mind?"

Watt tried to speak, but he couldn't. He couldn't organize the thoughts in his head, let alone enough to pour them into the space between them. A great heat had spread over his body, eliciting goosebumps in its wake. His head was a fog, and all he could focus on clearly was Cornelius' spit slicked lips.

Cornelius' gaze flicked down to Watt's arousal, then back up. He waited, and when Watt did nothing, Cornelius adopted that apologetic and sad smile he'd used the first time Watt had wanted to kiss him, and didn't. He began to retreat. "I understand."

His hands slid away from Watt's face.

"No." Watt snatched them back. Cornelius stared, bewildered. Watt brought their hands close to his chest, which heaved with great effort. His voice was thin when he sputtered, "I desire you more than anyone else I've ever laid eyes on. But I—that's—I'm—"

Cornelius caught on, and saved Watt from his floundering. He kissed the corner of Watt's mouth, silencing him. Against his skin, he whispered, "You've never ...?"

"No," Watt admitted, the word no more than a rasp.

"With anyone?"

Watt shook his head a fraction, and his beard scratched against Cornelius. "Never."

Cornelius stilled. "And ... kissing?"

Watt swallowed. "No."

Cornelius retreated a bit and gave Watt a little smile.

Thank God, there was no pity in it. Understanding, yes. But never pity, and Watt was a fool for ever thinking there would be. He said, "Ah. Then perhaps tonight we'll say good night the old fashioned way."

"It's not that I don't want to, Cornelius," Watt said, quick and quiet.

Cornelius' cheek dimpled as his smile turned sly, gaze flitting downwards for just a moment. He kissed Watt again, gentler this time. In the fractional space between their lips, he murmured, "You deserve more than a tree to the back for your first time, Watt." His brows pinched, and a strange expression fluttered across his face before disappearing. "And I'm not in a hurry. It's just that—I thought that I was—I thought that's what you ..."

Watt pulled Cornelius flush against him, wrapping his arms around him as tight as he could without hurting him. He rested his chin in Cornelius' hair lank with sweat and dirt and closed his eyes, breathing him in. Belatedly, Cornelius' arms encircled his waist, and he held fast. His face rubbed back and forth across Watt's chest for a moment, then Cornelius let out a long exhale.

Watt nearly told him then, and he wasn't sure what held him back. Instead, he said, "I would follow you anywhere, no matter the reason."

If the resulting squeeze from Cornelius was anything to go by, it was enough. For now.

Of Use

July 31st, 1930

Cornelius did not understand.

He tossed. And turned. Fretted and fussed.

He had never misread a situation before, and to do so with Watt, innocent and inexperienced Watt, had him feeling about two inches tall. He must've terrified the poor man, if the expression on his face was anything to go by. How could a man like him have never been with someone before? Hells, he hadn't even kissed anyone before. It was unfathomable. And yet, the truth had been in Watt's trembling fingers and his wide eyes. Cornelius had been Watt's first kiss, and damn if that didn't inflate his pride, and his anxiety. He'd never been in this situation before, what good was he if it wasn't his body that was needed? He'd refused Andrea when the man had asked for more than his body, and truly hadn't that been the same reason he and Giovanni didn't work?

The eternal question kept him up for most of the night, and when morning became a real threat he beat the sun to the punch once again. When was the last time he'd slept through the night? No matter. He was alight with a fire that demanded only one thing. Be of use.

Because why else was he here, if not to be of use?

He descended from his hammock in a fluid motion, and readied himself without making much noise. Maggie awoke, and she lifted her head from Watt's belly. Cornelius silently pleaded with her to be still and not wake the man beneath her. It was too early, she and Watt needed all the rest they could get. And water, but that was Cornelius' job. His throat was dry, and his tongue was sandpaper. He could only imagine how Watt felt, given that he not only shared his food but his water with Maggie.

Cornelius ensured his knife was in one pocket, and the other was packed with scraps of fabric that had once been his good dress shirt. He opened the bag of meager provisions they'd rationed out, then closed it. He could do without food for now. Hopefully he'd come across something along the way. He checked his gun and tucked it into the waistband of his trousers, then gathered the empty canteens. He thought about bringing his camera along, but this wasn't the time for that. In fact, he decided the best course of action was to think as little as possible. To let his mind wander, and the jungle lead him to where he needed to go.

Cornelius left camp, following the sound of water and his own heart pounding wildly in his chest.

July 31st, 1930

Watt was alone.

He wasn't surprised when he woke and Cornelius' hammock was empty, and was only mildly confused to find Maggie gone as well. Cornelius had been making a habit of waking earlier and earlier, but Maggie hardly left Watt's side anymore, especially after her injury. He blinked away the gritty remains of sleep, and rubbed at his eyes for good measure. Everything was so bright, unbearably hot.

Watt sat up with a start, nearly flipping the hammock. He managed to stand upright, then promptly swatted at an insect biting at his ear. He staggered against the unexpected force, and groaned. He fought the urge to rub at the bite, and looked around camp. Their packs hung suspended from a moss covered limb the same as they had the night before. There were fresh tracks in the mud, composed of boots, paws, and the distinct tip of a cane. Something was decidedly off, but he couldn't put his finger on what. A chill settled over Watt's skin, despite the harsh sunlight doing its damnedest to break through the thick canopy. It had to be mid-morning.

Watt took a deep breath. He shook his head a little, trying to clear the fog from his mind. Cornelius must've left the camp. He either took Maggie with him, or she followed afterwards. But why? Why not wait to explore together?

Watt's lips cracked, and he grimaced at the flash of pain. He stalked over to their packs and procured the small tin of Vaseline from the first aid kit. He swiped some over his lips, then put the tin and kit away. He rifled around for his pocket watch, and his heart lurched upon seeing the time. It was half past noon. He stuffed his watch into his pocket, then studied the immediate area surrounding their packs. Upon closer inspection, he realized what was missing. Their canteens.

Cornelius had gone looking for water. Alone. He didn't want to believe it, but there could be no other reason.

"Oh, that damn man," Watt growled. His fingers twitched and he dropped his watch. He managed to catch it before it hit the ground, and was rewarded with a massive head rush. He braced his hands on his knees and breathed for a moment, then slowly straightened. Watt stared at the deserted camp, weighing his options.

He could search for his companions and possibly not find his way back, or Cornelius and Maggie. He wasn't confident in his ability to keep his way, given their current situation. Namely, the fact he couldn't think straight.

He could stay right where he was, waiting for their return. Trusting that they would come back, that neither of them were hurt or lost. He didn't know if he'd be able to take that. Waiting.

"Damn it," Watt hissed. He ran a hand through his hair, which was thick with sweat and God knew what else. "One thing at a time."

The camp was already fairly sparse, so he set to work taking the hammocks down. If Cornelius came back soon, it'd be nothing to set them back up. If not, it would make leaving that much easier. After the hammocks, he searched for trash or any paraphernalia that belonged to them, but there was nothing. Cornelius had already picked up last night.

Watt set up on a crooked, mossy limb that hovered above the ground and began sharpening his machete. He'd burn a little more time, wait a little bit longer. With his thoughts enraptured by the methodical sound of blade scraping against sharpening stone, he was left with the sounds of the jungle and his work. A few minutes later, he stopped. Lifted his head.

The distant sound of rushing water was louder than it had been yesterday. His brain stuttered over the how, and he temporarily blamed the roaring in his ears on his own failing body. But this wasn't the usual tinnitus that plagued him. It was distinctly water ... falling. Crashing.

'*It's playing with us,*' Cornelius had said.

Watt forced himself to sit still, and think. Had the water called to Cornelius, too? Is that why he left without Watt? Did it manipulate him into a wandering stupor?

Would that same fate befall him, if he followed the sound too?

He was being ridiculous. At the beginning of this venture he'd decried the Fawcett's superstitions, and now here he was wondering if water was a malicious taunting thing, or a friend to be followed. Regardless of whether the hypothetical water was trying to tell him things, it was late afternoon by now and Cornelius had not returned. Watt could not wait any longer, not without his conscience eating him alive any more than it already had.

He checked his gun, his knife, and the machete before taking up the burden of Cornelius' pack and his own. He did his best to straighten to his full height beneath the weight, but he was too broken. His slightly hunched posture would have to be enough.

Watt followed the tracks out of camp. Well defined mud gave way to trampled grass, debris, and snapped sticks. He kept alert, scanning his surroundings with keen, if not tired, eyes. The water continued to roar in his ears at the same volume, as if he were walking alongside a raging river, not between mossy trees and towering ferns. A fluttering on the trail ahead caught his attention. At first he thought it was a butterfly, but as he got closer he realized it was a shred of fabric. He removed it from the branch it'd been caught on, then rubbed it between his fingers. It was Cornelius' shirt, the one he'd cut up to bandage Maggie's leg.

But why?

Watt looked back the way he came, then the trail still ahead of him. It was becoming fainter, the vegetation ahead was unwieldy and easily swallowed any signs of passage. As much as he loathed to do it, Watt tied the fabric around the branch once more. He had a feeling Cornelius had put it there for a reason. Perhaps there was a nearby area of interest. About ten minutes later, the reason solidified when Watt found another scrap of fabric.

"Of course," he whispered, touching the fabric tied around a thin sapling. "To keep from getting lost."

He shook his head, cursing himself for not thinking of such a brilliant idea. How much time had he wasted worrying about getting lost, when there was an easy solution like this?

Hope bloomed in Watt's heart for the first hour. Without the fabric, he'd have lost their trail ages ago. He focused on one step after another, one marker after another. But after walking for twenty minutes without finding a sixth scrap of fabric, despair began to take root. He slowed his step, searching every area he passed through for signs of a struggle, of Cornelius passed out on the ground, or Maggie's tail swishing through the air. But there was nothing. No evidence of where they'd gone next, and the water—

A harsh glint of light teased Watt through the trees, as if reflecting off the surface of water. It was there and gone again, its source veiled by crowded plants and distance. Without much else to rely on, Watt headed in that direction. He walked for about five minutes before stopping. He rummaged through his pack for his own spare shirt, then sliced it into pieces. The fabric parting beneath his blade was oddly cathartic, and his mind drifted.

Where had the shirt been made? Where had the splitting threads come from, or the buttons that popped and flew? Did it ever expect to be torn to pieces in the middle of a jungle?

Watt shook his head. It was a shirt. A piece of fabric. Nothing more.

He tied a piece around a low hanging, spindly branch, then pushed on. He wondered, afterwards, why he'd bothered. So they could find their way back to a camp that was now abandoned? To find their way back to the place they'd been lost at before? It was human nature, he supposed, to have the illusion of control. To know what one was doing, even if they truly didn't.

Watt's head throbbed with a passion, and his legs were so damn heavy. He walked for what seemed like hours, but the sky, or what he could see of it, never seemed to change. The light refused to dim into the evening, and no clouds passed over the sun. Watt came upon a quartz that looked suspiciously like the one he'd given Cornelius, but he refused to believe it. He began to stop more often, not to place markers, but to catch his breath. The water was all encompassing, maddening, suffocating. Water, everywhere and nowhere. He was drowning in solid earth and liquid worry. If he lost

Maggie, he lost a part of his heart as well. But if he lost Cornelius, he lost the entire damn thing.

With shaking fingers, he pawed through his options for food. Four cans, two of beans and two of condensed milk. A cloth satchel filled with an odd mix of dried fruits. His stomach was in knots to begin with, and the thought of eating anything nauseated him. Despite the fact they'd been shitting in the jungle all along, the idea of doing so without the meager protection of a nearby camp and companion to warn him of trouble was unnerving. He thought perhaps he could manage the condensed milk, but not the entire can. They were supposed to be sharing them, anyway. He'd wait to eat together.

Watt stood, then stumbled beneath the weight of their packs. He gritted his teeth, righted himself, and kept going.

Human Nature

Dusk arrived, to Watt's surprise, and so did a permanent chill that settled deep into his bones. Thought ceased to exist eons ago, save for those that required the body to put one foot after another. To gasp for air, and push through the pain.

His fabric ties had long since been devoured by the jungle, and the shirt he wore now was saturated with sweat, blood, thorns, and the smeared remains of insects and plant material. His burden was lighter, he'd combined their belongings into his pack, leaving Cornelius' bag with everything they could bear to leave behind buried beneath his last fabric tie. They didn't need Cornelius' camera, film, or his notebooks, but Watt couldn't bring himself to bury them. It was like burying a part of Cornelius himself. Despite carrying less, Watt was as downtrodden and fatigued as ever. He heard nothing but water, and saw nothing but moss covered trees. He'd entered an endless monotony of step after step, tree after tree, breath after breath.

And later, Watt would mark this as the moment that saved him. Devoid of thought, overwhelmed with the sensation of living in the moment, existing as a mere thread in life's tapestry. In short, he'd let everything go from his mind, making room for the truth to take hold and unfurl.

It started, as life so often did, with a light.

Watt stumbled over a rock, and as he steadied himself on hands and knees a flash of color danced on the edge of his periphery. He shook his head, sure it was another trick of the eye. But when he focused again, there it remained. A pulsing dim light that wasn't entirely green, but not entirely yellow either. It reminded Watt of fireflies in the height of summer, flickering between the blades of grass and grain.

His heart seized, and reality shuddered. No. It couldn't be.

Watt groaned as he pushed himself to his feet. He set his course, direction unknown, and made his way towards the light. The moment he stepped off the unmarked path he'd been blindly following, pebbles crunched beneath his boots. Watt didn't want to take his eyes off the light again, but he had to. There'd been no rocks before, only dirt and grass and moss and—

And tiny bones and stones populating the riverbanks, bleached by the sun and eroded by time. The origin of the river lay dead ahead, breathtaking and heartbreaking all at once. Water crashed from a great height, hundreds of feet above his level, if not more. Great slabs of stone cradled the mouth of the waterfall in a bowl like fashion, all red rock, withered vines, and scorched plants. Skeleton-like, bone white trees sprouted from the riverbanks, their roots clawed out of the packed red dirt, desperate for water and stifling air. The swelling tide threatened to overtake the banks, water churning in a fierce torrent that rendered it a foamy and disturbing brown. Steam rose from the river, as did a great boiling stench that reeked of dead fish, rotten plants, and pollution.

Watt blinked, and the vision faded. The stones and water remained, as they always would in one fashion or another, but the smell, steam, pollution and bones, that all disappeared. The waterfall's surrounding flora was no longer dead and aged, but thriving and taking root in every red crevice it could. Fish dove in and out of the water, which was still foamy, but it churned with the debris of a healthy riverbed instead of rot and death. It was breathtaking, unreal and heavenly.

And of course, high above Watt and out of reach, was a stone tower full of light. Pulsing. Waiting. Beckoning him to try his luck, and climb to the top of the waterfall.

If Watt had undertaken this trip alone, he would've gone right for it. Exhaustion and injuries be damned, he would have found a way to scale the sheer cliff faces and see once and for all what that damn light was. If there was evidence that Fawcett had found it too, and left his mark in one way or another. But he had not undertaken this trip alone. Watt was swiftly reminded of that fact by the persistent barking that cut through the waterfall's raucous noise. He staggered, heart pounding as he searched the area for Maggie. She was close, but out of sight.

Birds, monkeys, and other small animals occupied the area, unafraid of his presence. They watched him from a distance, curious and on high alert. Maggie's barking didn't bother them, which led Watt to believe she'd been doing it for some time. As he got closer to the base of the waterfall, her barking was dulled by its roar. Watt stared at the powerful curtain of water, his hands curling into fists. Darkness had started to fall in earnest, and there was no moonlight yet. It was difficult to see what was behind the falling water, whether it was a cavern or more sheer rock. Or perhaps a small, shallow area. Shallow, but deep enough for a man to fall down and drown in.

A cold, heavy feeling settled in Watt's gut. He called, "Maggie?"

Maggie stopped barking. A second passed. Then she redoubled her efforts, both in volume and ferocity. Watt realized the sound was not coming from the waterfall, but above it. Watt craned his neck back, trying to catch sight of her. The peak of the waterfall was nearly impossible to see from here, and it was clear he wouldn't be able to climb the rock face even if he wanted to. If he wanted to reach it he'd have to go around, approach it from the side. He backed up, trying to get a better look.

There, right the precipice of the cliff before it gave way to water, stood Maggie. Upon seeing her, Watt's heart cracked. Upon seeing him, Maggie went wild.

"I'm coming!"

Adrenaline erased all of his pains and aches, his dehydration and exhaustion. He searched for the best way up the bluff, having to backtrack a little to do so. Eventually he found a traversable portion and climbed, fingers scraping red rock and feet slipping every so often. The incline was steep enough to torture his thighs, but not enough to deter him. Maggie danced in an awkward circle which sent pebbles skittering down his way, she'd moved closer but refused to leave the peak entirely.

Watt made it to the top, aided by Maggie shoving against him to make the final push. His chest heaved, and he only had seconds to recover as his surroundings registered. The river was much wider up here, and a small island split the stream into two before the water spilled over the edge. Island was a generous term, but it was large enough to house debris from the river such as vegetation and tree limbs, the stone tower thrashing light across the land like a lighthouse, and Cornelius.

Cornelius was half slumped against the tower, and upon seeing Watt he tried to stand. Bioluminescent light flashed across his face, illuminating his wide eyes full of pain and fear. He crumpled to the ground, his cry drowned out by the water's demanding babble. Watt started forward, eyes darting from the raging river to the light source hidden in the top of the tower. It was brighter than fireflies but flickered like them, and the color sharper than anything he'd seen before.

The river was impassable here. The current raged, and to try and cross it on foot would be suicide. How had Cornelius gotten to the island in the first place? Upon meeting the water Watt cast his gaze down the shoreline, noting the area they were in. An enormous basin trimmed with mountains that towered higher and higher as they stretched away from where he stood. The waterfall was at the lowest point, and beneath the moonlight the river shone like a mercurial road as it stretched across cerrado and fields, its origin shrouded by distant jungle that crowded the far edge of the basin. The only vegetation available immediately were scrawny trees and thorny bushes, more like the stuff he'd been tearing through.

Watt tore his gaze away from the unexplored. There were no hostiles in the immediate area, which was all that mattered. His hands flexed at his sides as he refocused on Cornelius who, with great difficulty, pushed himself upright. He didn't have his cane, and agony was written in every harsh line of his body. He yelled to Watt, and his voice cracked as it crossed the distance. "Go back! I ..." The remainder of what he said was swallowed by the waterfall, but the defeated look on his face told Watt everything.

Watt shook his head. This would not be a promise he kept. He cupped his hands and called back, "No! I'll find a way."

Cornelius shuddered, and he wiped angrily at his

eyes. He opened his mouth, but the following words were lost to the water.

Watt's heart twisted with indecision, until finally he held up his hands again and shouted, "Wait for me."

Cornelius' face flooded with panic. Watt stared at him, trying to channel every bit of comfort he could. He didn't turn away until Cornelius nodded, and even then he struggled to look away. It wasn't like he could go anywhere, but Watt keenly felt he was about to disappear any moment.

Watt dropped their pack to the ground, and his head buzzed when he bent down to quickly check Maggie's wound. The bandage had come off her leg, and his heart paused beating as he searched for what would surely be a dirt packed injury. After a moment, he realized that he was combing through fur.

Thick fur, not the shave job that Cornelius had given the area when dressing the wound. A wound that was, now, nothing more than a set of raised pink lines, the edges of which were puckered by rough treatment during the healing period. Watt rested a hand beneath Maggie's muzzle, gently turning her face towards him.

"What happened to you two?"

Dawn was on the horizon when Watt attempted something incredibly stupid, and Cornelius was unable to do anything but watch. He'd dozed on and off throughout the night, watching Watt as he worked. They'd tried formulating a plan together, but it was near impossible to hear each other without breaking their vocal cords.

Regardless, it became clear what Watt planned to do as he prepared vines throughout the night, transforming them into a makeshift rope. A large rock sat off to the side of his work area, dutifully protected by Maggie until Watt was ready to tie the rope around it.

It was a terrible idea.

The tower was a cool weight at Cornelius' back, and besides Watt's presence the stone was the only thing keeping him grounded. Despite the fact that they were separated by the river, seeing Watt again was a constant relief to his soul that would not ebb.

How many days had passed since he'd heard Watt's laugh?

How many nights had he spent cursing himself for not telling Watt the truth?

He'd lost count. He'd lost everything, including himself.

And now Watt was here, working through the night to execute a rescue mission without an ounce of sleep. Once upon a time, Cornelius might've wondered why Watt had kept looking for him after all this time. Why the man hadn't turned back and left Cornelius for dead, like he'd promised he would all those months ago. But now, he knew.

Cornelius' head throbbed in time with his pulse, as did his leg. He was fairly certain something vital had torn in his knee and ankle, it was a different sort of pain than what normally wreaked havoc on his leg. Hot and sharp, growing furiously when put under weight or through movement. A concussion was likely as well, but he wasn't sure. His mind had been playing tricks on him long before the river had swept him away.

Watt was preparing to sling the monstrosity of vine and stone directly at Cornelius, so he pushed himself to his feet, shifting most of his weight to his good leg. He braced himself to dodge as best he could, and was temporarily distracted by how Watt looked. Two images collided in his mind, that of a rancher lassoing cattle and a Scot winding up for the hammer toss. Watt hurtled the rock towards him, startling Cornelius into action.

It made it a third of the way across the stream before *thunking* into the water. Watt frowned, and reeled it in.

He threw it again, and again. Cornelius deflated after a half dozen attempts, his chill giving way to heat beneath the rising sun. Eventually, Watt lost the rock to the current and was forced to give up. Cornelius shouted, "Take a break!"

Watt's face twisted with frustration, and he shook his head with such violence Cornelius thought he'd break his own neck. A ragged shout clawed out of Watt, the force of which broke through the water and fractured Cornelius' heart. Watt dropped to his knees and dug his fists into the ground, bowing his head.

Cornelius' stomach, already tormented by hunger, filled with bile. He'd previously accepted his fate, marooned on this island and lost to anyone who might've cared to find him. But Watt had brought hope with him, reigniting the base desire all creatures had.

'I must live.'

Cornelius straightened as best he could, testing his limbs. Under normal circumstances he was an excellent swimmer, but malnutrition, dehydration, and exposure were all against him. But if neither of them could make it across without being sucked into the current and tossed over the falls, then there was only one option. This thought was sealed by the appearance of an odd visitor, or rather a hundred or so odd visitors.

A kaleidoscope of blue morphos fluttered down the river, bringing with them a light breeze that smelled distinctly of moss. Cornelius was stunned by the sight, they had not encountered a single butterfly yet during this trip and now there was a whole rabble of them. Their muddy undersides made their iridescent sky blue wings shine all the brighter, especially beneath the rising sun's brilliant rays.

The head of the flutter continued right past the crest of the falls, unbothered by the loss of their watery path, and into the sun.

Cornelius caught a glimpse of Watt's expression through the cloud of fluttering wings, eyes swollen from crying and lips parted with no small bit of wonder. If this moment wasn't a sign, Cornelius wasn't sure what was. He had to get to Watt.

The stone tower resided at the tip of the island, leaving only a small rocky shelf all around it. Cornelius was disappointed he couldn't find a way inside the mysterious construction, the stone was smooth all the way around with no door, only arch shaped windows too high up for him to reach. Maybe on a day he'd better use of his body, and a ladder. He was too focused on surviving to think much more about it. The island's tip overhung the falls, making it the perfect launching point. Cornelius limped towards the point, and his movements went unnoticed until he slipped and nearly fell into the rapids before he was ready. Maggie barked in response, and was followed by a shout of protest.

Cornelius looked over his shoulder to see Watt frantically waving his arms and shouting Cornelius' name, his figure partially blocked by the tail end of the kaleidoscope. The exact syllables were lost to the wind, but the shape of his name was hard to miss on Watt's lips. Cornelius forced a bold smile he didn't quite feel, and shouted, "I'll see you down there!"

He turned back to the task at hand, focusing on the rock at his feet. He shimmied around the tower, clutching at the rough stone with his stinging fingertips for dear life before making it to the shelf that faced the falls. His heart pounded in his ears, and exhilaration lightened the pressure in his lungs. The view was astonishing. Tons upon tons of water rushed on either side of him, crashing to the river below which stretched on for miles upon miles. Jungle, marshes, galley forests, fields, and eventual cerrado unfurled before him. He took a moment to soak it all in. Brazil, and all her beauty. All the things she had already given Cornelius. Friends. Adventure. Peace. But most importantly, himself. If he died, drowned or otherwise, at least his heart was whole again and his soul was at ease.

There wasn't much room for a running start, so without much ado Cornelius shoved off the pillar, launching himself into the falls.

His dive was by no means graceful, but no bones broke when he made an impact with the water.

He crashed through the surface like a damned sturgeon, sinking deep beneath the tumultuous curtain.

There was nothing but water in every direction, the unexpected depth bode well for his landing but not for kicking off bottom.

Pain rocketed through his entire body as he kicked, pedaling an imaginary bicycle that would not lift him no matter how hard he pulled and pushed at the river with his hands. Every time the surface was within reach, the waterfall's curtain shoved him back under. He couldn't get away from it, stuck in place as if forced there by a magnet. In fact, his efforts were so futile that he couldn't maintain a vertical position. He began to sink.

The light from above dimmed, and Cornelius' lungs ached with the sudden urge to cough. Panic exploded in his heart, and a sensation flashed over his body like the worst cold chill he'd ever felt, but with all the heat of the sun. His limbs weakened, refusing to cooperate with his will. His body began to convulse with the need to expel his lungs. This was it. He was going to drown. He—

A familiar hand slapped against his knuckles. Then his fingertips. Cornelius forced all his remaining energy into reaching. They slipped and searched for each other, and a sob crashed through Cornelius' defenses protecting his lungs. He began to choke, and his muscles spasmed with the intrusion.

Arms interlocked, fingers digging into flesh with a bruising surety. A second of relief overwhelmed everything else, even the water overfilling his lungs.

His arm was promptly yanked out of its socket, the pain sudden and fierce but secondary to his lungs, leg, and head. To everything, really.

By the time they broke the surface, Cornelius' vision had given way to darkness, and consciousness was only a thread of an idea. What he did remember, later, was the vague impression of hard ground, and Watt sobbing.

He did not remember powerful thrusting of hands upon breastbone and the way his sternum creaked, or how Watt briefly paused before releasing a string of curses followed by, "I'm sorry. I'm so sorry."

He was not aware of Watt slicing his shirt and bandeau down the middle, or the tears crashing onto his bare chest. When hands met breastbone again, they pumped with an efficiency that broke bones in an effort to reach Cornelius' heart. After a pause, air was forced down his throat in two long bursts. Water escaped his lungs and chased after the reviving lips, bubbling out of Cornelius like a spring. He coughed, hacking until there was nothing left to do but retch.

Finally, and with great difficulty, Cornelius breathed. It hurt like hell, and the pain was enough to bring him back under. He took hold of consciousness by the throat, stealing a look at his savior before passing out.

Watt stared down at him, soaking wet and glistening beneath the morning sun. He was tauter than a bow-string, his thick brows furrowed together and his eyes pinched by harsh lines. A lush canopy framed one side of him, and a cloudless sky accentuated the other. It was more colors more than anything else, out of focus compared to the sheer detail and familiar landmarks in Watt's face.

"You're beautiful." Cornelius tried.

While it was long and mostly incoherent, Watt seemed to get the gist of it.

He relaxed, if only a fraction. "And you're impossible, Cornelius Sawyer. Damned impossible." He bent down awkwardly, pressing a kiss to Cornelius' forehead. "Thank God you're alright. I—oh, your shirt. I—I had to—here."

Watt took off his shirt and draped it over Cornelius' chest, only to find he'd already fallen asleep.

August

?

Damn Impressive

August, 1930

Over the years, it became increasingly difficult for Cornelius to blackout. When he did, he usually took his time coming back to himself the next day. But this time, the moment he teased the edges of wakefulness, consciousness electrified him. Literally, his whole body jolted with the sudden realization it was awake. *Alive.*

Cornelius released a shaky exhale, and his body greeted him with waves of pain. He opened his eyes, first taking in the nearly full moon peeking around the edge of a canopy ... no, well not just canopy. There was a thick roof over his head, constructed of palms and makeshift beams. The walls around him were secure, and he lay upon something familiar. Canvas, maybe. He shifted his head to better see Watt sitting beside him, cross-legged with his chin tucked against his chest. He occupied the single open side of the shelter, the entrance big enough for them to pass through but no more. Moonlight reflected off the coursing river and wet stones that were a short distance beyond Watt, and illuminated him with an unnatural brightness.

The watercolor set that Cornelius had gifted him was in his lap. Blue paint was smudged all over his fingers, which still clutched at his work and brush despite his ragged snores. Cornelius' heart skipped a beat, which reminded him of how it had struggled alongside his lungs. Of how for a moment there, it felt like it had stopped beating. His body was heavy, but his chest especially. Each breath was laborious, like he was dredging air from mud. Instead of reaching for Watt like he wanted to, he cataloged the ways his friend had changed since the last time he saw him.

His hair had been bleached to a light gold during his time in the sun, as had the lengthy beard which was thin and patchy in places, no longer dark. Watt's hair was damp and uncombed, which had the knotted ends curling against his shoulders. His complexion had darkened greatly, and numerous sunspots and freckles decorated his hollow face and flushed neck. He was thin and flecked with injuries, scratches and welts and bites and even a nasty slice through his right brow that had been left to heal the hard way, leaving the scar angry and rough. If Cornelius had to guess, Watt was lucky he hadn't lost the eye.

Ultimately, Watt looked like Cornelius felt. He hadn't realized how much of a physical toll the trip had taken on them until abruptly removed from that gradual transformation. He was the thinnest he'd ever been in his life, with still some fat around his stomach, but he felt weak and unhealthy, his energy drawn from a shallow well. He wasn't sure how long he'd been out for. His injuries had a fresh sort of twang, but were well tended to as was the rest of his body, dressed in fresh dry clothes. Watt had built a shelter, which could've been done on the second day or so, but he had no idea. It had been daytime when he dove into the water, right?

Regardless, he'd been asleep long enough.

He needed to piss, which was an amazing sensation after being dehydrated for so long, but the thought of moving was a daunting one. He laid there in denial for another minute or two, idly petting Maggie laying beside him. She slept hard, her weight heavy and leaden against Cornelius' side. He didn't mind. She could sleep on top of him for the rest of her life, if she wanted. Without Maggie looking out for him, Cornelius would've been lost to madness and worse. Why she had abandoned Watt in favor of looking for Cornelius he would never know, but he would also be forever grateful. He'd tried to shoo her back to camp, but she had insisted on following him on his stupid quest for water. What should've been a few hours trip at most, had become a nightmare.

He was stiff and sore in muscles and bones he didn't even know existed until he tried to use them. And fuck, his chest hurt. His bad leg protested in an aggravated fashion different from its usual gnawing ache, and his shoulder screamed from the confines of the sling put upon him. If he didn't intentionally flex his bandage wrapped ankle, it was a mid-level pain that simply existed. With as much stealth as he could, he sat up and tested it once, just a little, and hissed out a curse.

"Cornelius?" Watt startled awake, sending his work to the ground as he lunged for the place Cornelius had once been.

"Easy there," Cornelius said through gritted teeth and a stomachful of bile. "I'm right here."

Watt blinked, processing that Cornelius was sitting up of his own volition. He shifted and promptly took Cornelius' hands in his, then bent down and brought them to his forehead. "Oh, thank God."

The nausea building in Cornelius' gut subsided a little, replaced by relief. Staring at Watt while he slept was nothing compared to holding him, being held by him. If Cornelius were a God fearing man, he might've thanked Her too. Instead, he pulled a small, hoarse laugh from deep within his tired heart, just for Watt. He whispered, "It's alright, my love. We're okay. We're together again."

Watt's head lifted. His lips, still peeling but recently moisturized, parted. He stared at Cornelius, throat working as he tried on a few different words. Cornelius gently tugged a hand out of Watt's grip and cupped his cheek, running his thumb over the smooth planes of his face.

"That's right. You're the love of my life. You, Watt Johnson, are my love." Tears built in Watt's bloodshot eyes, and they burned in Cornelius' own. "Always have been."

"You know, that explains a lot." Watt laughed wetly and shook his head.

"Does it?" Cornelius laughed a little too. It hurt like hell, but he couldn't have stopped it if he tried. He winced, then asked, "Like what?"

Watt frowned, then rose up a little bit more on a knee. He carefully pressed his lips to Cornelius'. Cornelius opened to him immediately, but Watt kept it easy and slow. He pulled back and whispered, "Explains why I nearly died on that beach with you. I—I didn't think I could bring you back. You ..." Watt's voice cracked, and he took a moment to steady his breathing.

Cornelius' skin went cold in a sudden flash that reminded him of the sensation of sinking, of alarm bells ringing through his body.

"You scared me. You scared me to the point that even while I was breathing air into you, I was planning how to join you if you didn't make it. And that's ... I have survived everything else in my life, but I could not—cannot—survive a world without you in it. And I've been tearing myself apart, because what kind of person thinks that? But it makes sense. I've always loved you, Cornelius. But ... I *love* you. It's like you said, you're the love of my life. You're it for me."

"Oh, Watt." Cornelius kissed Watt. "I'm right here. Come, come lay with me."

Watt obeyed without argument. He laid on his side facing Cornelius, who settled slowly but surely on his back. Watt pulled a thin and worn blanket over them, then hid his face against Cornelius' good shoulder. Cornelius sighed, and it still hurt but the air came easier this time. He closed his eyes, memorizing the feeling of Watt beside him once more. He never wanted to be without him again.

They spent a long time in silence, and Cornelius was nearly asleep when Watt whispered, "I didn't believe her. I thought she was a grieving widow, grasping for straws. I doubted her, just like everyone else had. I was going to tell her no, and then she said he'd asked for me specifically. I think she could tell I thought that was a mighty convenient load of bullshit, because she said, 'Not to fret, you aren't who we need. But the Herald of Dawn needs him, and he needs you. He's the One,' and this she said with capital importance, 'he's the One who will find my family and bring them home.'"

Watt laughed softly, then sniffed. "It all sounds so outlandish, and I thought so at the time. But ... when she said it was you that we needed, Cornelius Sawyer, the archaeologist I had been longing to meet, I just ... couldn't say no. And even though I've been telling myself there's no way that Fawcett's message to her could've been real, I think a part of me wanted to believe it. I should've told you. I meant to, especially after the deal with Galvão, but I couldn't find the words." Watt exhaled hard against Cornelius' shoulder. "I guess it doesn't matter, does it? It was never real. It was all for nothing. Her son was never a Herald of anything, and we were never meant to find them."

Cornelius laughed, and it hurt like hell.

Watt startled, pulling back to look at Cornelius who gasped and laughed and gasped some more. Watt had never looked so confused, and maybe a bit hurt. Cornelius reached over and tugged at Watt's arm with his good hand, urging him to come closer. Despite his confusion, Watt went willingly. Cornelius stared up into his eyes and whispered, "You're such an idiot." He gave Watt's cheek a little shake. "We found each other again. That's gotta count for something."

A watery smile crept over Watt's face, and he laughed. "Yeah?"

"Yes." Cornelius pulled Watt down for a gentle kiss.

Watt returned the kiss with a bit more hunger than Cornelius expected. He returned it eagerly, but the passion only lasted a moment before he flinched in pain. Watt pulled away, and Cornelius groaned. "Hellfire, I can't believe you let me jump off a waterfall. Everything hurts."

Watt rolled his eyes, unable to hide his amusement. "You twit. Like I can stop you from doing anything." He sighed, feigning defeat. "As much as it scared me, I have to admit ... it was pretty damn impressive."

They exchanged a much gentler kiss before settling in for the night. They didn't speak, but it was a comfortable silence. Cornelius watched the night stretch on, and when he finally drifted off it was only after Watt began snoring once more.

Aqui! Aqui!

August, 1930

Watt hadn't drank coffee in weeks, possibly months at this point, and yet it was if caffeine was rampant in his nervous system. Cornelius was in a mood after they woke for the day, but that was to be expected. He was in pain, needed help, and was without his two greatest aids, his glasses and cane. Both had been lost before Watt found him, and he hadn't asked what had happened to them. There would be time, when Cornelius wasn't so keenly feeling their absence.

To kill two birds with one stone, Watt carried Cornelius to the river's edge where he could wash and relieve himself. Cornelius wore only a pair of boxers, and the poor excuse of a sling Watt had made. Cornelius wanted to save the shirt he'd been wearing for later. It was relatively clean, Watt's, and the only one they had left that was easy to put his arm through. It had been a nightmare to put the shirt on in the first place, thankfully Cornelius hadn't been awake for the horrifying scenario that was Watt putting Cornelius' shoulder back in place, then threading his body through the fabric. He'd felt like he was animating a marionette doll with half the strings cut. It had been much easier to slip it off, with Cornelius being awake and able to help.

He was unnaturally quiet, so Watt filled the silence with assurances there were no dangerous fish, or parasites (that he'd found). Watt lowered Cornelius onto his ass in the shallows, where there was a slight current but nothing strong. The waterfall was quieter than before, and calmer too. They were a good half mile downstream from it, which had to help. The tower was visible from here, but as dark as ever. It appeared so ordinary, nothing like the flashing lighthouse he'd imagined before.

"Are you good?" Watt asked, handing over the meager bar of soap he'd tucked into his pocket. It had seen better days, but the fact it existed at all was a miracle.

Cornelius stared down at the soap now clutched in his hand, along with the handle of his coffee mug, before thrusting both at Watt. "No, actually. Could you give me a moment, then help me? I'm just so tired."

"Of course," Watt said, and took the soap back before wandering upstream a little ways from Cornelius. After Cornelius cleared his throat meaningfully, Watt turned around. He was briefly struck by how familiar this was to the moment in the tent. When he'd run away from the sight of Cornelius' bare back. He hadn't really looked at Cornelius when carrying him over, but now he could do nothing else. His boots sank into the surprisingly soft riverbed as he approached, and the water was cool as it splashed against his legs and soaked through his trousers. He squatted behind Cornelius. "Ready?"

Cornelius glanced over his shoulder and gave Watt a hesitant smile. "Go easy on me."

Watt flushed from his toes to his ears. He splashed water up Cornelius' back, his arms, his chest. He filled the mug and had Cornelius tip his head back, then poured water through his hair. Cornelius closed his eyes, falling into a quiet sort of stillness and submission that only made things worse for Watt. The mug wasn't very big, so it took some time to wash and rinse the soap Watt scrubbed into Cornelius' hair. Next, he passed the soap bar over the tanned skin of his back. Cornelius was riddled with bruises and insect bites, but nothing too serious.

"Do you want me to uh ..." Watt coughed. "Wash your front?"

"Yes," Cornelius said and closed his eyes, his breathing quickening beneath Watt's ministrations. He didn't curl in on himself or try to hide his breasts, like all that time ago at the dig site. His posture was proud, and whereas before he possessed an *'I dare you to comment'* look in his eyes, now he was simply at peace. Relaxed. What a foolish man Watt had been, to have run off like he did.

Cornelius gasped and Watt was startled back into himself, to what he'd just done. Cornelius' eyes were still closed, but his lips were parted in response to

Watt's fingers and the soap brushing over his hard nipple. "Sorry, I—I think you're good now. I'm just going to ah—rinse. Just rinsing is left. Sorry."

Watt did his best to rinse Cornelius quickly, thoroughly, and platonically. It was an awkward and arousing event, but Cornelius gave Watt a shy, flushed smile and a quiet thank you after being dried off and draped in Watt's shirt again. He opted to put his trousers on later, after his boxers had dried.

Watt carried Cornelius back to the shelter and gently sat him down on a bed made of their hammocks and bedrolls. Hesitantly, he showed Cornelius the band of fabric he'd destroyed, taking a knee beside him. "I had to cut it off when I ... it was in the way. But I can mend it. I meant to, while you were sleeping, but I ..."

Cornelius took the torn fabric in his hand and stared at it, then shook his head and gave it back to Watt. "No, thank you." He lifted his chin and gave Watt a measuring look, and Watt could practically see the walls building in his eyes. "Well? What's going through your head?"

"I was just wondering. Are you ... that is ... do you mind that I look? That I ... touch you? Or is that something you don't like? I—I didn't mean to just now, but in the future, so I know. If I need to know, that is."

"Oh." Cornelius' eyes widened in surprise, then he looked away and wiped at his face. "I don't know. I like being touched, and looked at, more often than not. I like being wanted, but sometimes when I'm feeling ...

off, I can't stand it. But I'll tell you, don't worry. So, tell me honestly. Did you like what you saw?"

Watt took hold of Cornelius' chin and did his best to sound confident. Assertive.

"Please," Watt whispered, voice cracking. "Please don't make me say how much I want you. How much I need you. Because I—I swear to God, Cornelius, I need you to get better, and do what you promised."

A trickster's grin spread across Cornelius' lips, washing away those walls of doubt in his mischievous eyes. "What did I promise? I'm a bit foggy."

"Heal." Watt kissed Cornelius, then knocked their foreheads together. "Get better."

"Fine," Cornelius grumbled, but he seemed more at ease than before. He stole another kiss and whispered, "You know, it's not fair you've seen far more of me than I've seen of you."

Watt sucked in a breath. "*Cornelius.*"

Cornelius sighed. "Fine."

Watt prepared them breakfast, which was a glorious sight. Juicy jabuticaba, banana, and pacu that Watt had speared and smoked the previous day while Cornelius slept. The area was surprisingly plentiful, the vegetation lush and well nurtured, the river higher than he'd originally thought and well populated with fish. All this combined with the early morning heat and unusually thick humidity, Watt had a hard time believing they were at the tail end of the dry season.

Cornelius sat with Maggie, and his tired frown distracted Watt from his observations. Maggie had hardly left Cornelius' side today, which in Watt's experience meant there was great inner turmoil. If Cornelius minded her closeness, he didn't comment on it. Watt couldn't help but smile when he offered Cornelius his plate, which earned him an inquisitive glance. Watt quietly admitted, "I was just thinking about that day on the Prince, when you warned me against bringing her along. Now look at you."

Cornelius took what Watt offered, smiling a bit. "And where would I be now if you'd listened?" After a pause, he sedately added, "I don't know how long it was for you, but I was gone for a long time, Watt. Just before everything went ... vague, she found me and stuck by my side. I lost track of the time, but I just kept going. I figured if anyone could find their way back to you, it'd be her."

Guilt stirred in Watt's gut, and when he sat beside his companions he kept his gaze down. "I didn't know what to do. I woke up and you were gone, and so was she. I didn't know if you took her with you or if she followed, or if you were taken. I didn't know whether to stay behind and wait in case you came back, or go after you in case you needed help. I waited a little while, but then I couldn't do it anymore and set off to find you. If I hadn't spent so much time being decisive, I would've found you sooner. I'm sorry. Not like I was much help to begin with, but at least you wouldn't have had to spend the night alone. I just—I don't understand why you left.

Why—"

Watt lifted his head, only to find a horrified look on Cornelius' face. He immediately scanned their surroundings, but there was nothing, no one. Cornelius' hands were shaking, so Watt took his plate and set it aside, then captured Cornelius' fingers between his own. "What's wrong?"

Cornelius closed his eyes and slowly shook his head. "Watt, what are you talking about? We were gone for—a week—two at least, I don't know." He opened his eyes, which widened upon seeing Watt. "Hey," he said, fingers breaking free of Watt's grip to hold his face. "Oh, no, please."

"What? No." Watt's eyes stung, and his throat was unbearably hot. "No, it wasn't—"

Memories flashed through the edges of his awareness, beginning with finding Maggie, her wound healed and fur grown in. Further back, the haunting vision of the river and his initial ordeal finding it, all those hours (days?) spent wandering, searching. Disappearing.

"I—" Watt tried, but air caught in his throat, his lungs. He'd known, rationally, that his malnourished, beaten, and dehydrated body had endured an ordeal far greater than could occur in one day, two even. But two weeks? He would've surely died. He blinked, overcome with visions of him curled up in a ball, sleeping in the mud. Him, swiping blood away from his swollen and injured eye. "No ..." He reached up with a shaking hand and scratched at the still healing wound, expecting to find hot blood trickling down his cheek.

Cornelius pulled Watt close, and Watt was so far gone that he didn't notice the way the other man was wrought with pain, both in his ribs and heart. They spent a long time like that, but Watt didn't forget a minute of it. He had no idea what to say, how to explain what had happened, whether it was his own mind or as Cornelius had once said, the land was playing tricks on them, or something else entirely. It terrified him to think he had lost so much time, let alone try to process it. And so, he cried.

He should've been ashamed of how much he'd cried during this trip, but Cornelius never made him feel bad for it, which allowed the tears to pass quicker than they would've otherwise. No longer restrained or repressed to escape later when pressurized, but welcomed and washed away with comfort and kindness in due time. Eventually, Watt pulled himself back together. He would have plenty of late nights ahead of him, ample opportunity to explore the dark places of his mind where time should be.

Without lifting his head from Cornelius' thigh, for he had curled around it while Cornelius played with his hair, he asked, "Why did you leave?"

Cornelius sighed, tugging gently on the ends of Watt's knotted curls. It hadn't been this long since he was a kid. As Cornelius began to speak, Watt wondered what on earth he looked like. When was the last time he'd checked?

"I will be the first to admit what I did was stupid, especially now. But ... I wanted to help, to find water. You were so exhausted, we were all thirsty, and it was the only way I could think of to help."

"But we could have done that together," Watt said, and a little of his buried frustration on the matter bled through. He'd already suspected that was why Cornelius had left, but he hadn't wanted to believe Cornelius was that reckless. "We're partners."

"We're not equal partners," Cornelius muttered, avoiding Watt's eye.

"You're not serious," Watt said. "Cornelius, you are one of the most competent men I know, and I respect you greatly. You have proven yourself over time and time again, and I love you as are. Even when you're being a bull headed prick."

Cornelius glared at him, but said nothing. Then his eyes widened, and his lips parted. "What'd you say?"

"That you're a bullheaded prick?"

"That you love me."

Watt's heart skipped. "Well yes, I suppose I did. I ... I thought it was rather obvious."

"Oh." Cornelius lifted his chin, and Watt obliged him with a tender, soft kiss.

Abruptly, he was struck by an idea and abandoned Cornelius and searched out his pack. Cornelius watched, confused until Watt settled back down beside him, closer this time. "I've been meaning to show you this." He turned his sketchpad round to show off what he'd been working on. Light pencil sketch work laid down the foundation of their endeavor at the top of the waterfall. The perspective was of the sun, and the light work made the waterfall sparkle and their faces nearly too bright to see. The island was stark with massive breadths of water on either side of it, spilling over the edge and down, down.

Not into the river Cornelius had dove into, but a cloud of murky water that spilled down onto the corner and the next page. Cornelius reached to turn the page, then hesitated to capture the rest of the details, his finger hovering over where his eyes tracked. Namely, Watt's vague figure on the side of the river with arms reaching, a blur of black and brown color that was Maggie careening down the cliff side, and the kaleidoscope of blue morphos with Cornelius at their center. His expression was hard to read, but the posture of his body was calm, the dive perfect and confident like a kingfisher.

Cornelius was quiet for so long that Watt glanced at the painting, at him, then shut the sketchpad with an abashed expression. He'd meant to show Cornelius how much that moment had meant to him, how breathtaking and brave Cornelius was. Cornelius blinked a few times to clear his eyes and said, "It's beautiful, Watt. I—I've never seen myself like that before. Do you think I could have it?"

Watt nodded quickly. "Yes, of course. I made it for you."

"Oh, Watt." Cornelius rubbed a hand over his face. "What's a fella to do when you're being so sweet?"

Watt grinned, and maybe puffed out his chest a little bit. "Heal. Get better."

Cornelius laughed, but sobered only a few moments later. God, Watt hated that his smiles kept dissolving into worry. Cornelius said, "You need to get better too. We both do."

"Yeah." Watt swallowed, casting a look around outside their shelter. "There doesn't seem to be anyone nearby, if there are locals they've been leaving us alone. Between the fish and the fruit, I think we can stay here for a little while. Try to regain our strength, build up our supplies, your bones can heal. Then what?"

Cornelius shrugged. Watt stared.

"What?" Cornelius asked, nonplussed.

"I—you—well. You're the plans man. I figured you had a plan."

Cornelius laughed. He said, "Haven't you learned yet, Watt? Make plans and the Amazon laughs, God laughs, if you will. Let's just focus on making it through the next few days."

"It's going to be at least a couple of weeks before you're up for heavy travel." Watt hedged.

Cornelius sighed. "Let's eat, this is too much on an empty stomach."

Watt's own stomach growled in agreement. Cornelius insisted he could walk over to the fire pit on his own, and he did with Watt's help to stand and take the weight of his bad leg. Cornelius lowered himself to the ground with a grunt, and Watt fretted the entire time. He arranged their breakfast, and pride warmed his chest when Cornelius began to eat. Watt sat beside him and did the same, albeit at a slower pace. After a short time, Cornelius lifted a shoulder and took a bite of a particularly large jabuticaba globe. "Alright, couple of weeks then."

He chewed slowly, and juice dribbled out of the corner of his lip. He studied the inner white flesh, turning the purple skinned fruit this way and that. A distant rumble caught both their attention, and introduced a nasty grey sky in the distance. "You know," Cornelius began dramatically. "I'm willing to bet we're in the rainy season now. So don't feel bad, I thought my adventure had only taken a couple weeks, not entire months."

Watt gave him a long suffering look. "There's no way we lost that much time. We'd be dead."

Cornelius waved a hand carelessly. "Maybe we are."

"That's not funny."

"Well something funny is happening!" Cornelius announced grandly, then popped the rest of the fruit into his mouth. "Might as well enjoy it." He moved on from the fruit to the fish, and a pleased noise escaped him. Cornelius ate his breakfast with a renewed vigor, and Watt just stared at him.

Cornelius grinned. "What?"

"Maybe you still have a concussion."

Cornelius laughed. "Or maybe I'm done trying to fight my destiny."

Watt flushed. "You're going to milk that, aren't you?"

"I can—never mind. Dear, this pacu is amazing." Cornelius teased. "Come on, eat. Enjoy the outside while you can, I have a feeling we're going to be grounded for awhile."

Watt sighed, and allowed himself to fall into the lie. Everything would be fine, as long as they pretended.

Cornelius might have been losing his mind. But for once, he didn't mind. Funny, that.

The rest of the day, and night, was absolutely miserable. After eating they had picked up, with Watt doing most of the work, and retreated to the lean-to. It was well built considering the time and resources that Watt had available to him, but the storm that moved in on them was of biblical proportions. The fronds could only divert so much water, and the framework of the limbs shuddered beneath the howling gusts of wind.

Watt lay closest to the entrance, which he had barricaded from the inside with brush and more fronds. He took the brunt of the elements that penetrated every weak point of their shelter, and Cornelius lay between him and Maggie. She faced the wall, her back against Cornelius' side. Nearly every position hurt, and while laying on his back hurt the least, it was hard to see

Watt's face.

Watt lay curled beside him, careful as can be. While they were so close, there was also a great distance between them. Watt was so afraid of hurting Cornelius, that he had hardly touched him at all. It was irritating, the only true injuries Cornelius had were his possibly broken ankle and ribs. And his recently dislocated shoulder was back in place, it just hurt like hell. The concussion had to be long gone by now too, the headache he fought was likely from his weakened state.

Between the weather, his pain and anxieties, Cornelius slept fitfully on and off throughout the night. He couldn't even soothe himself by stone, as it had been lost to the river and he didn't have the heart to tell Watt or find a new one himself. By the time the storm cleared off, he was exhausted. He didn't want to get up, and wouldn't have it wasn't for Watt's insistence. Watt offered to carry Cornelius to the river to wash and relieve himself like he'd done yesterday. Unlike yesterday, the water was a raging beast. It had climbed the pebbled shoreline, and was not far off from their camp.

"I can piss on my own, thank you," Cornelius said, pushing Watt's offered hand away. Watt gave him a look, and Cornelius scowled. "Been dealing with a bum leg for most of my life, I'll be fine."

Watt rolled his eyes. And not in a subtle way, either. Cornelius opened his mouth, but Watt held up a finger.

"Fine. But hold on one minute."

Cornelius was too shocked to do anything else. Watt usually did as Cornelius said, and his attitude was ... disconcerting. Cornelius leaned heavily on the tree Watt had built their shelter against, listening to his companion blunder through the jungle. Everything still hurt, but being upright gave the mind a certain boost. Maggie's back arched as she stretched at Cornelius' side, tongue lolling as her jaw widened. When Watt returned, her tail began to wag and she rubbed against his leg. Oh, to be as easily pleased as a dog.

Watt held a branch in his hands, about the same length as his cane but much wider around. The bark had been freshly peeled, exposing the creamy green flesh beneath. One end was narrower than the other, but substantial enough it wouldn't snap off. Watt offered it to Cornelius and said, "It's not quite right, but it'll give you something to lean on."

Cornelius swallowed, wrapping his fingers around the makeshift cane. It was cool to the touch. For a moment they both held it, staring at the other. Cornelius pulled hard, yanking Watt down to his level, then darted forward to lay a deep kiss on his lips. Watt still wasn't close enough, so Cornelius bit Watt's bottom lip and pulled. Watt made a noise in the back of his throat, the echo of a whimper, and came willingly.

"Encontrei-os! Aqui! Aqui!"

Cornelius startled out of the kiss, flipping his grip on the cane in preparation to wield it like a bat. Watt stepped in front of Cornelius, reaching for the gun tucked into his waistband. Maggie barked twice, then took off for the shoreline at a dead run. Cornelius squinted, trying to make sense of the distant pebbled shoreline, rushing water, trees, and a ... a man?

"Is that ..." Cornelius began, glancing at Watt for confirmation.

No longer reaching for his gun, Watt raised his hand high in the air and waved, his smile clear as day. "Antônio!"

Cornelius sagged with relief, lowering his cane into the mud so he could lean upon it. Tears immediately welled in his eyes, and he choked on a laugh when Maggie took off running to meet their new companion. "I can't believe it."

Watt slung his arm around Cornelius, who slumped against his side. Watt kissed the top of his head and whispered, "We're going to be okay."

It took Antônio no time at all to reach them, weaving through the washed up debris along the riverside with ease. Not only was his easy movement magical to Cornelius, so was his presence. Where the hell had he even come from?

When Maggie caught up to Antônio, he acknowledged her but didn't stop running. He didn't really stop running when he caught up to them, either. Watt held them steady when Antônio collided with them, throwing his arms around Cornelius and Watt. He was hot and sweaty and real, and the familiarity of him had not only Cornelius choked up, but Watt too. Maggie whined, pacing around the three in dizzying circles.

Antônio said, "I knew it. I knew it." He lifted his head, looking to Watt first, then Cornelius. "You idiots."

Cornelius laughed, shaking his head a little. "What're you doing here? How'd you find us?"

"We couldn't go back without knowing you were okay. After Severino found your belongings, we thought you had to be upstream." Antônio patted Cornelius on the back, which jarred his injuries unpleasantly, but he didn't care. "This is northeast from camp, twenty miles now. I think."

Cornelius exhaled as if gut punched, and Watt's fingers twitched against his skin. Twenty miles was nothing compared to how long they'd been traveling, searching, lost.

"Joaquim did not know this was here." Antônio added, as if that would help anything. He stepped back, keeping his friends within arm's reach. His chest heaved, and he ran a hand through his hair. It was a few inches longer than before, and damp with sweat. He appraised them, an uncharacteristic nervousness to his features. "Are you alright?"

Cornelius nodded in a numb and automatic sort of way, but Watt said, "He's hurt, and in poor condition. But otherwise, yes." He craned his head around Antônio, trying to get a look downstream. He glanced back at Antônio uncertainly. "What day is it?"

"October 3rd," Antônio said. While this did not shock Cornelius as much as their limited distance had, it did seem to rattle Watt. He hadn't lost, or gained time rather, like Cornelius had during their separation.

Cornelius scowled, breaking out of his melancholic confusion in order to prevent Watt from falling into the same trap. "You're in poor condition too. I've never seen so many of your ribs before." He eyed Antônio. "Wait, where did you find our equipment? We lost it in the swamp, not the river."

"We found signs of a camp, and rags tied to trees. We followed to the river, and found—" Antônio held up a hand, while the other dug into the pocket of his trousers. "No equipment, your broken cane, and these." He withdrew his hand, unfurling his fingers to reveal Cornelius' glasses. The left arm was bent and the right one was missing entirely, no doubt from where he'd cracked his head on that rock. Miraculously both lens were intact, but fractured beyond use or repair.

Cornelius straightened, shifting his weight to his cane instead of his partner. With trembling fingers, he gingerly took the glasses from Antônio. He whispered, "Thank you, Antônio." He met Antônio's eyes and gave him a grateful smile. "Thank you for coming for us."

Antônio smiled. "Kagõro. Yes?"

Watt rested a hand on Antônio's shoulder, and echoed Cornelius' sentiment. "Kagõro."

A man's shout rolled in from the distance, and they all turned to see Severino stumbling out of the treeline and onto the beach. Joaquim was not far behind him, ready with a steadying hand. Severino grasped it, and didn't let go when he regained his balance. Upon seeing them, Severino began dragging Joaquim their way.

Antônio glanced at Watt and Cornelius, then said, "Stay here." He dashed away, leaving them alone for quite possibly the last time for a long time. Cornelius watched him run for a moment, then slowly turned his gaze on the area they'd been staying. The waterfall, the pebbled beach, and the little niche of jungle they'd settled into.

"Cornelius?" Watt whispered, fingertips grazing his elbow.

"Yes?" Cornelius looked at his companion, his friend, the man who had saved his life time and time again. He knew what was coming, but let Watt speak his peace. There had been too many unsaid things between them, and this didn't need to be one of them. Not again.

"No matter what happens, we stay together, right?"

Cornelius slid his hand against Watt's, entangling their fingers. Surely, he had to have lost his mind. To have this person making promises to him like this, to be rediscovered by friends that cared for them, and to have experienced such a beautiful and vibrant world. Real or not, well deserved or not, Cornelius would enjoy it all.

"I'm yours as long as you'll have me, Watt Johnson. I just hope you know what you've signed up for."

Watt smiled, and it was brighter than the Brazilian sun. "Careful, Mr. Sawyer. That almost sounded like a vow."

"You did make me a promise, you know." Cornelius teased, although his words did ring with decades old truth.

"Where would we go?" Watt revived the question he'd posed back when all this truly began, his thumb rubbing over the back of Cornelius' hand as if he were the man's own personal soothing stone.

Cornelius lifted his chin and Watt obliged his quiet request for a kiss, despite their incoming company. It didn't matter, they all knew, and still cared for them. Still deemed them worth saving. Watt's lips were soft and yielding beneath his own, which for a moment was all that mattered. One day soon, he'd find all the other soft places of Watt, and reveal his own as well. He withdrew enough to speak, and grinned against Watt's own blooming smile.

Cornelius whispered, "Where wouldn't we?"

Historical Sources

The Voice of Wild Places is a book that was three years in the making, and required research that spanned books, websites, articles, video footage, and other paraphernalia. You can find a full list of links available at neshamapublishing.com

These are the books I read while researching, and highly recommend for further information on exploration during the late 19th century and early 20th century.

- The Lost City of Z: A Tale of Deadly Obsession in the Amazon by David Grann.

- Exploration Fawcett by Percy Harrison Fawcett.

- Into the Amazon: The Life of Cândido Rondon, Trailblazing Explorer, Scientist, Statesman, and Conservationist by Larry Rohter.

- The story Severino tells is a highly redacted version from The Looking-Glass: Essential Stories by Machado de Assis.

The effects of the residential schools Indigenous peoples were forced into in Canada and America are still prevalent today, and I highly recommend educating yourself on the history of these schools. The following reads are a good start.

- Education for Extinction: American Indians and the Boarding School Experience, 1875-1928 by David Wallace Adams.

- Unsettling Truths: The Ongoing, Dehumanizing Legacy of the Doctrine of Discovery by Mark Charles & Soong-Chan Rah.

- Stealing Little Moon: The Legacy of the American Indian Boarding Schools by Dan Sasuweh Jones.

- Medicine River: A Story of Survival and the Legacy of Indian Boarding Schools by Mary Annette Pember.

Acknowledgements

What was supposed to be a short and fun romp through history became a wild adventure through time and space, and it wouldn't have been possible without the support of my friends, family, and dedicated readers.

I want to especially thank Henni and Kat for reading this story in its early stages, and championing me through to the end.

Benedetta has not only brought my characters to life in her many beautiful artworks, but also read this story early on and kept me going. Other talented artists I have worked with for character art include Just Miss Art, and Léa Charbonnier. I greatly appreciate Thistle Artworks for the beautiful cover art of the paperback, and working with me to give these characters the illustration they deserve. I also want to thank Crossroad Art for their hard work on the hardback edition, and all the projects we've worked on together.

The Right Here Write Queer crew, my beloved fellow indie authors, were instrumental in helping me with this book, from researching to marketing and everything in between. Historical projects require a party, after all, and I am forever grateful for them. Also, without Luna Daye this book would not exist, for it was the gay along the way Tumblr post that she sent me which started it all.

Punki, your interest and admiration will always fuel me to write more stories, and I can't wait to read yours someday. Andrew, thank you for letting me wrangle you into yet another project, at least we got to talk about old knives this time.

I would also like to thank my Patreon members, Amy, Emily, and Ivan, for supporting me. Your contributions have helped bridge the gap for me and made writing this possible. A huge thank you also goes to the Kickstarter backers who supported the pre-release campaign.

And thank you, dear reader, for reading Cornelius and Watt's story.

About the Author

Noah Hawthorne craves inclusive stories with wild adventure, flawed characters, queer love, and found family. Noah originally began publishing under the Aelina Isaacs pen name, and after some self-discovery adopted the new pen name Noah Hawthorne, which is dedicated to writing books with trans leads.

Adventures in Levena is a cozy urban fantasy series by Aelina Isaacs, and follows a group of friends as they find love later in life.

The Rebel Foxes by Noah Hawthorne is a standalone dystopian fiction with mutant shapeshifters overthrowing society.